I0571510

THE FALL

BOOK 3 IN THE LAZARUS STRAIN CHRONICLES

SEAN DEVILLE

SEVERED PRESS
HOBART TASMANIA

THE FALL

Copyright © 2019 Sean Deville
Copyright © 2019 by Severed Press

WWW.SEVEREDPRESS.COM

ISBN: 978-1-922323-46-0

Warning

Please do not feed the zombies

- Graffiti sprayed on Lincoln's memorial

Characters

MI13
Colonel Nick Carter
Jeff Brazier
Natasha Sloane

UK Civilians
Andy
Florence
Jessica Dunn
Judy Dunn
Tom Dunn
Brian Metcalf
Susan Metcalf
Reginald Clay
Viktor

UK Military
Captain Beckington
Captain Stephen Haggard - SAS
Colonel Wilson Smith
Corporal Christopher Whittaker

Gaia
Azrael
Brother
Father
Gabriel
Mother
Uncle

US Government/Military
David Campbell - DIA
Jacqueline Fairchild - US President
Dr Jee Lee - US CDC
Major Carson USMC
Captain John Fairclough

US Civilians
Clarice Reece
Jessy Whitethorn
Elizabeth Wood

TOP SECRET

THIS IS A COVER SHEET

FOR CLASSIFIED INFORMATION

ALL INDIVIDUALS HANDLING THIS INFORMATION ARE REQUIRED TO PROTECT IT FROM UNAUTHORISED DISCLOSURE IN THE INTEREST OF NATIONAL SECURITY OF THE UNITED STATES.

HANDLING, STORAGE, REPRODUCTION AND DISPOSITION OF THE ATTACHED DOCUMENT WILL BE IN ACCORDANCE WITH APPLICABLE EXECUTIVE ORDER(S), STATUTE(S) AND AGENCY IMPLEMENTING REGULATIONS.

UNLAWFUL VIEWING, REPRODUCTION OR TRANSPORT IS A FEDERAL OFFENCE UNDER 18 U.S. Code § 798 AND PRESIDENTIAL EXECUTIVE ORDER AND CARRIES A TERM OF A MINIMUM OF DEATH BY FIRING SQUAD

(This cover sheet is unclassified)

TOP SECRET

703-101
NSN 75690-01-21207903

FEMA
Federal Emergency Management Agency

Department of Homeland Security

From: The Office of the President of the United States

Re: Implementation and expansion of Executive Order 13295

By the authority vested in me as President by the Constitution and the laws of the United States of America, including section 264(b) of title 42, United States Code, it is hereby ordered that:

1) Anyone found to be or suspected to be infected with the Lazarus virus (designation H4N2G7) to be transported to the designated city and state FEMA quarantine facilities.

2) Due to the threat imposed upon the nation, the need for Martial Law is justified. All military and law enforcement personnel are hereby compelled to aid the Federal Emergency Management Agency and the Centers for Disease Control in helping isolate those infected with the Lazarus virus.

3) Anyone interfering or refusing to comply with the execution of quarantine activities by military and law enforcement officers should be remanded to indefinite detention until such time as a military tribunal can be convened to hold a hearing on the charge of treason against the nation to those involved.

4) The use of lethal force is justified in response to those who try and act against the greater good of this great nation.

5) Due to the work of the British scientists Dr Moneel Patel and Colonel Wilson Smith, an XV1 antiserum has been developed which has been deemed effective in treating those infected with the virus. Until such time as the antiserum can be synthesised, all efforts should be made to identify and isolate individuals immune to H4N2G7. They are to be transported to USAMRIID under military escort. At the time of writing, only 2 individuals have been designated immune within the confines of the continental United States.

6) Antiserum obtained from immune individuals will be limited to those in command and control positions.

By Order

Jacqueline Fairchild, President of the United States of America.

THE FALL

23.08.19
Preston, UK

Another man dead under his command. Would this shit never end?

Even one life was too many, and yet his job demanded he accept the risks that came with it. There was no need to ask how many people had died following his orders because Nick knew the number like it was etched onto the insides of his eyeballs. Despite that death toll now well into double figures, Colonel Nick Carter would forever remember the faces of every one of them until his dying breath.

Nick knelt by the lifeless body of Brodie and knew that there would be plenty more corpses to follow and that there was nothing that he, or anyone else, could do to stop that. Lazarus wasn't like anything he had previously encountered, and with the military in full retreat on all fronts, it was only a matter of time before the country fell.

And then where would they all be?

Likely there wouldn't even be time to bury Brodie's body. To honour one man's sacrifice when millions were now at risk might also feel perverse considering the scale of the death that had been unleashed across the country. Nick looked at the people around him, noticed the resigned faces on some of those involved in what was most likely now an unwinnable war. Jessica, Azrael and Whittaker were the only hope they had, but Nick's ability to utilise that hope had been seriously curtailed by the attack of the undead on the Preston army barracks. The blood of the immune may have held the answer to Lazarus, but without access to a medical laboratory and the scientists to run it, the cure might just as well be an old wives' tale.

They needed scientists as well, and as far as Nick was aware, there wasn't anyone near him who fitted the bill.

"Where do we go?" Jeff asked. He still wore his gas mask, so his face showed none of the pain associated with losing one of his own, but Nick knew he was suffering. Besides, men like Jeff rarely let the inner turmoil break through to the surface, but it would still be grinding him up inside. Nick had seen too many broken bodies and broken minds in his time to deny the vulnerability of the human psyche. Jeff would keep it together just as Nick would. They had to, but the pain of their loss would follow them relentlessly.

"I'll get onto army central command, see if they know of anywhere that's secure," Natasha insisted. The hierarchy of the UK military were holed up at NATO Allied Maritime Command in Northwood, but how long was that facility going to hold the line against the zombie hordes that were, even now, pouring out of London? It would be a last stand, a frantic defence to try and keep some kind of order on the British isle.

"I know where we can go," Jessica stated quietly but with a determination that cut a scythe through the air. Nick turned to her and noticed the resolve on her face. This woman, who had seemed so vulnerable when he had first encountered her in that hospital emergency ward several days ago continued to surprise him with her strength.

"Go on." Even the most outrageous idea was sometimes worth considering when you were at the end.

"My brother's farm. It's isolated, secluded and easily defended by natural barriers."

"I don't really think…" Jeff started, only for Nick to silence him with a gesture. Jeff was the man he trusted above all others, but a leader had to know when to make his own decisions.

"Where is this farm?" Nick asked. He had witnessed what happened when the zombies got together in large groups, seen how they could just wash over defendend positions. As powerful as the country's military were, perhaps a different tactic was required.

"It's about two hours' drive into the Peak District," Jessica insisted. "I even know the way." She had been abducted, quarantined, prodded and probed only for the promised protection offered to her to be seen as impotent. Even with their best intentions, she knew that the men and women who were tasked to defend her would ultimately fail in their mission if things didn't change. If she was going to survive, Jessica was well aware that now was the time for her to take matters into her own hands.

"Might be worth checking out," Nick agreed. "I think the further we get away from population centres, the better it will be for us. At least for the time being." He looked around at the people who were now looking to him for answers and saw no further voices of protest.

The farm it would be. Really, what did they have to lose?

23.08.19
Tristan da Cunha island, Atlantic

The world never learnt about the three men who destroyed the world. Even if the average person on the street learnt of their identities, it wouldn't have done anyone any good.

In their planning, the rulers of Gaia had built an underground facility to secure themselves against all conceivable eventualities. They called it the *Ark*, a facility able to house a thousand souls. Mothballed and almost forgotten by the now dead inhabitants of the sleepy island on which it was constructed, it sat there unused, waiting for the day when humanity would make their ultimate mistake.

When Lazarus came, everything changed.

A thousand people could have been saved, and yet when the exterior doors were finally shut, there were less than fifty people inside to experience the safety promised by the concrete walls and the filtrated air. Lazarus had escaped without warning and before any of them were ready, so the exodus to Gaia's last refuge had been rushed and chaotic. Only those who had received the imperfect vaccine were allowed into the safety of the vast concrete bunker built into the side of the island's volcano. By the time the bunker was sealed off, anyone not already inside was doomed to face the apocalypse with the rest of humanity.

The only exception to that rule would have been for Mother, but she had no interest in such salvation.

The escape of Lazarus was not how The Three had intended the virus to be used. There was no control over it, no order… only a random devastation that reeked of chaos and the end of all things. Lazarus was a weapon of last resort. It was supposed to have been used to show the dangers of mankind's medical practice, to turn him away from the science he craved… back towards a natural balance between man and nature. Nobody had ever planned for this kind of carnage.

There needed to be a certain degree of honesty here in that perhaps Mother had been right all along in her rejection of the creation of Lazarus. Nobody could deny that Mother was usually right about most things. The only error she had ever really made was in inviting The Three into the fold of the organisation she had constructed from the ashes of the old Soviet Illegals programme. Of The Three, Father had been predominantly responsible for the present impending downfall of man. The birth of Lazarus had been his plan after all, although Brother and Uncle shared a degree of responsibility. Come the time of their judgement, they would all be viewed equally.

Why they still insisted on using their code words rather than their real names was something known only to the secretive heads of Gaia. Even amongst themselves, they used their strange titles, as if doing otherwise would somehow reveal their secrets to the world. Was it that they were still wrapped up in their own hubris to accept the idiocy those titles represented?

The Three had planned to change the world, to make it a better place for their offspring. What kind of world would their children grow up in now?

A simple fire at their secret Thailand research facility had changed everything. Initially, they thought they had contained the threat, only for it to escape into the surrounding countryside in the carcass of a reanimated cat. That cat passed it onto an unsuspecting peasant who then brought the virus back to his own village. Worse than that, though, he then transported it to a city of over eight million people. From there it spread unchecked and unnoticed around the world via Bangkok's busy and structurally impressive international airport.

It had spread around the globe before anyone even knew it existed.

None of that could be corrected now. All the hierarchy of Gaia could do was to hope Lazarus did its job before mankind's ultimate weapons of war could be turned upon the zombie hordes. Zombies didn't care about the fallout from atomic fire, but the beautiful creatures of nature did. China had already used its nuclear weapons against its own people, those who ordered the destruction now likely dead due to a revolt from within the Chinese military. Many of those who commanded the world's largest army had family in Beijing, and they learnt too late of the nuclear fire that was unleashed on the country's capital. Outright revolution against those who authorised the attack was really the only logical response to the intolerable slaughter of those you held dearest.

To The Three though, China didn't matter when there were other countries with nuclear weapons that threatened the very stability of the planet's biosphere. Britain, Russia, France, the USA, Israel, India and Pakistan all had the potential to end the dream that Gaia had been created to propagate. The paradise they desired risked becoming a radioactive wasteland. Of all the nuclear powers, The Three deemed Russia the next most likely to use atomic fire in its own self-defence, and it was ironically the country that Gaia had been able to infiltrate the least. The Three would be shown to be wrong in that regard also for it was to be the liberal democracies of the West that would irradiate the land.

Lazarus had been the greatest of mistakes, and the three leaders of Gaia had inexcusably compounded that mistake by deliberately ordering the further release of the weaponised version of the virus. Brother, the weakest of The Three, now realised the egregious error they had committed, but he knew the other two would never admit that error out loud. He thus kept his own counsel, safe in the knowledge that he would at least survive.

Their plan hadn't been to make the human race extinct, just to reduce its burdensome numbers that were rapidly destroying the planet and its ecosystem. Perversely though, in the great scope of things, perhaps this was all for the best. The Earth would most certainly be a better place without humanity on it. No matter what was done to the world, there was always the comfort to know that, millions of years from now, the biosphere would correct itself and adorn the planet's surface with a myriad of new and beautiful creatures.

Could the actions of The Three be the forerunner to a new Eden?

The Earth would prevail, even if humanity ultimately perished. How long before the footprint of its civilisation was removed from existence? How long before the scars healed and the cities and roads were eroded so that there was no longer a trace of man?

23.08.19
Washington DC, USA

Jessy woke to the sound of sustained gunfire. She had not been asleep long enough for the nightmare to hit her again, but it would come. There was no escaping the nocturnal realm that the immune were inexplicably linked to. The dream would manifest again and again, and everyone in that realm would suffer the torment. Everyone but the horsemen, the ones who chased with their promise of damnation.

She sat nervously, waiting for the voice that would call to her, trying to ignore the throbbing from her hand. The flesh there was red and inflamed, but there were none of the black tendrils that she had seen on the skin of the others who had become infected. What also surprised her was how quickly the wound seemed to be healing. The holes made by the zombie's teeth had already stopped weeping. At this rate, there was a chance she might even escape without scarring. Still, Jessy re-covered it with the bandage she had grabbed from the room's med kit. It would need proper medical attention, a human bite not known for its sterile nature.

Obviously, the zombie's bite hadn't been as bad as she had originally feared. Perhaps that was why the symptoms of the virus didn't seem to be taking hold as she had expected. She had no way of knowing she had already been exposed to Lazarus and had in fact been the primary vector for its transmission throughout the people who had fled to the Whitehouse Bunker. Even though she was blessed with an immunity to the virus, such knowledge might well have broken Jessy.

There was more gunfire outside. Had these rescuers gone out of their way just to save her? Everyone else was either dead or reanimated, she was sure of that. It didn't make sense for them to risk coming just for her, unless... of course, the nuclear football. While it wasn't essential for the launch of the nation's Nuclear Weapons, the special briefcase was a powerful symbol as well as a tool for doomsday. And with the Attorney General now the President, Jessy could see why that would be important to her.

To Jacqueline Fairchild, the symbols of power were as important as the power itself.

"Hello, Ms Whitethorn, can you hear me?" The male voice from the other side of the metal door was like all her Christmases come at once.

"Yes, I'm here," Jessy shouted, not sure how soundproofed the thick metal door was. The Presidential bunker below the Whitehouse had a safe room inside it, and that was where Jessy had locked herself away as the last of humanity had fallen to the infection.

"Jessy, my name is John. Please open up so we can get you out of here."

Jessy stood and approached the door. She held the pistol that she had found in here, not overly sure she knew how to use it. She should have been relieved that rescue had come, but with everything that had happened, there was a part of her that was wary of her would-be rescuers. What if she was, indeed, infected? What if they decided she was too much of a risk to leave alive? Would they just shoot her? Would they then pile her lifeless corpse up onto one of the many pyres that were undoubtedly burning across the city and the nation?

How many corpses would be torched before all this was over?

"Ma'am," John insisted, and Jessy did the only thing she could do. She opened the door before someone took it into their head to blow it. A single marine soldier stood there in clothing designed to protect against biological contagion, gun held ready and aimed right at her. Jessy almost panicked. "Ma'am...Jessy, I'm going to need you to put down the gun." Jessy did as she was ordered, bending her knees so she could place it carefully on the ground. John's voice sounded ominous, distorted as it was by the respirator. Still, she could kind of tell it wasn't his intention to hurt her.

"Thanks for coming for me." John nodded.

"Ma'am, I know you're scared, and I will need you to follow my instructions. That way we can get you out of here and get you safe. Can you do that for me?"

"Yes. I think so."

Two other soldiers appeared, both dressed the same. One carried the Nuclear Briefcase that surprisingly Jessy had only seen once before. Jessy suddenly had visions of it being plucked from the dead hand of the Secret Service Agent she had last seen carrying it.

"Alpha team to Overwatch, Football acquired," John said. Jessy knew he was obviously speaking to someone off-site.

"Is there anyone else alive?" Jessy almost pleaded. She felt somewhat guilty about locking herself away behind cold hard steel. What if someone else had survived? Could she have somehow helped them? But nobody else had come begging for entry, and if there had been anyone else down here, really, what could she have realistically done? Trained soldiers and Secret Service agents had been overwhelmed by the events that had unfolded. She wouldn't have stood a chance. Hiding as she had done was the only reasonable option that had been available to her.

"No Jessy. We didn't find anyone else. Now, please step out of the door. I'm going to ask you not to make any sudden movements, and please keep your distance from us unless instructed otherwise." Jessy complied with John's orders, the fear of getting shot competing with the joy of being rescued.

Further off in the bunker more gunshots rang out, making Jessy jump. The undead were still here. Were these men enough to keep her safe?

"We need to get the assets out of here. We only have a short window before that horde reaches our location," the soldier next to John said. *Assets?* Thought Jessy. John didn't ignore his fellow soldier, but his concentration was on Jessy.

"Jessy," John said, "are you injured?"

"I've been bitten," she said, the words drying in her mouth. She choked up and fought back sobs. Had she just signed her own death sentence? Would her saviour raise his gun and shoot her between her now tear-filled eyes?

"Let me have a look," John ordered, Jessy raising the aching limb for his inspection. "I need to do a blood test of you, keep your hand held up." Jessy did as requested, and was surprised when John pressed a finger pricker against her thumb.

"Ow," she said, more out of surprise than pain. John gently held her hand and pressed the welling blood against something that very much reminded her of a pregnancy test. Jessy suddenly remembered the time, several years ago, where she had waited with bated breath as the test she had taken showed her she wasn't actually pregnant. The wrong result with this test, she suspected, would likely be much more severe than to be told she was carrying an unwanted baby. A baby would have curtailed her career. A wrong result here might see her brains be splattered all over the wall.

"Sorry," John said, releasing her hand. He placed the test strip device into a self-sealing plastic tube, and Jessy watched it disappear into one of his pockets.

"Can you move quickly?" the other soldier asked her.

"I think so," she said.

"Good." John actually sounded relieved. "We are going to move to the surface where a helicopter is waiting for us. When we get outside, it's going to be noisy. The army is trying to regain control of this part of the city. I want you to focus on the helicopter and know that I will be right behind you."

"Okay," Jessy said, getting control of her breathing.

"Alpha team to Overwatch, extracting the assets now."

***

She heard it even before she had reached the ground floor of the Whitehouse, the sound of thunderous battle. The ten-man squad that had rescued her propelled her and the Football up several flights of stairs, and then through the bullet-ridden and body-strewn corridors of the building that the British had once burnt to the ground. Some of the bodies she saw were clearly several days old. While she had been down below, carnage must have raged here. She tried not to look at the dead as she passed them, but several of the corpses gazed up at her with eyes blacker than pitch. There had been a battle for the White House whilst she had been in the bunker, and humanity had lost.

Everything was a blur, panic threatening to grip hold of her in its loving and reassuring embrace. Jessy kept it together, mainly helped by the calmness that John had displayed in her initial rescue. If only she had been able to see his face, but only a maniac would have entered a biological hazard like the White House without proper protection.

If she was immune, what did it mean for her?

She was surprised by how well these men knew their way through the corridors, never taking a wrong move, walking her swiftly to the front of the building and out onto the White House lawn where the reason for John's warning became clear. The day around her was filled with smoke, fire and mayhem, the noise of the helicopter struggling to compete. Its rotors were running, ready to whisk her off to safety.

Jessy felt a gentle hand in her back to defy her brief hesitation and then she was whisked across the White House lawn, the open door to the helicopter the only thing she concentrated on. She didn't look at the zombies being blown apart outside the White House perimeter fence, nor did she see the men there sacrificing their lives to help get her out of there.

John stopped her from entering, withdrawing the blood test device. He held it up before his face, his head nodding when he saw that the result met his expectations.

"Good to go," John said with satisfaction.

Her foot hit the first step, and then she was inside, men bundling in with her. The door shut, and the helicopter began to rise. Jessy had always hated helicopters, but not at that moment. To her, it might as well have been sent down from the heavens by a host of angels.

"Thank you John," she said, relief finally flooding her, her whole body relaxing into the seat. She nearly fainted, and clumsy hands helped her get strapped in. Sat in the middle between two huge men, she wasn't able to see properly out of the windows to either side. She couldn't see the way Washington DC burned.

"Overwatch, contact Major Carson," Jessy heard John say. "Tell him the intel was correct and that we likely have another immune individual for him." Jessy listened to the words, the hope that she could escape the virus through her own immunity suddenly punctured by the sharpness that was thrust into the side of her neck. She felt the warmth injected into her as the plunger on the syringe was depressed, her arms suddenly pinned against her sides.

"Sorry Ma'am, orders" were the last words John said to her before she drifted off into the realm of chemical oblivion. Jessy thought they had come to save her, but she would soon find that the rescue wasn't for her benefit. Captain John Fairclough felt bad about sedating the woman in this fashion, but orders were orders.

23.08.19
Glasgow, UK

Nicholas Connery didn't believe a word if it. The news channels told him that there was a virus ravaging parts of the country, but there was no way the dead were rising up from the ground, that was just simply impossible. Surely if that were the case, the streets outside his flat would be flooded by the zombie hordes.

All he saw out there were police and the army.

This was clearly something more sinister, something he knew had been coming for decades. This was the damned New World Order making their power play. The stock market crash and martial law had nothing to do with the "undead". That was just a ruse to get everyone scared for their lives whilst rich families increased their already immense fortunes.

Frightened people did what they were told. They were compliant, malleable. And Connery wasn't going to fall for it.

He had known this day would come. The one bookshelf in his pitiful flat was filled with books that told him the *truth* about the world. As he told people loudly, and often, he didn't believe in conspiracy theory, he believed in conspiracy fact. The forces of darkness would come, and they would seize ultimate power using deception and the threat of an enemy that would bring the populace into line. That was exactly what was happening now, he was sure of it.

Connery gave them their due of course. He never would have thought they would have used a zombie apocalypse. The way they had done it was also impressive, the doctored images given to the masses over the TV and the internet exceptionally well done. Even he had almost fallen for it. Almost. They weren't going to play him for a fool.

The nighttime curfew didn't have anything to do with his safety. It was just to keep the streets clear so that the *"powers that be"* could erect their checkpoints and their containment camps. He knew that was coming, and he didn't fear the very real prospect that he was on a list somewhere. As he often said to his friend who shared his somewhat bizarre ideas about the world, he had already reserved himself a bunk in the re-education centre.

As a self-confessed conspiracy nut, he had taken preparations for this day, without actually thinking about the long term implications of what such a world-changing event would mean. He had cupboards full of food and bottled water, so he didn't need to venture outside his flat for sustenance. He had books to read and candles for when the power went out, which would all be part of the softening up process. Of course, the next step would be for law and order to seemingly break down, so using the candles at night would have to be limited. He didn't want those desperate for food to have a beacon they could follow. Just as with the rest of the UK, the rioting would eventually hit Glasgow, and the people would cower and beg for salvation from their omnipotent overlords.

The food and the books would only last so long, however. There was also a more pressing problem that he hadn't really accounted for. Already he was feeling it, the cabin fever that was creeping into his mind. Connery wasn't the kind of person who could spend long periods alone. He needed social interaction, which was the big flaw in his survival plan. Cooped up here, with nobody to talk to now the internet and the phone networks were down…it was sending him bloody doolally. It had only been a couple of days, and already he was feeling lost and afraid.

Connery realised now that he should have worked better to create a support network. Most of his mates didn't share his controversial opinions, but they tolerated them because he often used humour to express his unconventional beliefs. He liked nothing better than to be down the pub, a cool pint in hand, indoctrinating those who had eyes but who could not see. Pubs, there was another example of how the oppression had been building over the years. Pubs were one of the last safe places people could meet and discuss ideas, and they had been closing down in their thousands over the years. All part of some non-existent master plan that was now being unveiled to the world.

In desperation, he had even been outside in the times allowed by the quarantine. Connery had found the streets deserted, except for the puppets of the New World Order, and he hadn't dared approach them. He knew the types they recruited into the police and the military these days, even though he had never met any of them. The YouTube videos, all self-selecting and biased, had shown him everything he needed to know about the uniformed jackals that would prey on the weak. So he had kept to the shadows and tried to find anything that was open. Everything was shuttered tight, and without access to a car, he couldn't go far. Even with a vehicle, he would have just encountered roadblocks and demands for his identification.

"Citizen, your papers please." The four words he probably dreaded more than any other.

Before he knew it, they would be forcing everyone to take the tracking microchip for *their safety*. It was always about safety, wasn't it? Give up your liberty for the promise of security, and remember to think about the welfare of the children.

You could, therefore, understand Connery's surprise when he discovered that zombies were in fact real. The crushing silence and the boredom of his apartment had dragged him back out onto the street. Strangely there were no police or military this time, and he could almost taste it in the air that something was wrong. There were distant sounds that he couldn't quite place that should have sent him scurrying back to safety. Foolishly, he didn't listen to the voice in his head that told him to get the hell off the streets. Instead, he took it upon himself to discover what was causing those sounds. There was something familiar about them, and yet they were totally alien to the surrounding environment.

At the end of his street, he turned left, pulling the hood of his coat up as a light rain began to fall. The air smelled of smoke, although he couldn't tell where it was originating from. Something else for him to worry about because, in martial law such as this, there would unlikely be any emergency services to deal with the raging fires. A conflagration could take and spread unchecked through the terraced houses and the apartment buildings that made up this part of the city. Without civil order and emergency services, the cities would become death traps. Perhaps they had been designed like that, to suck in as many people as possible to aide in the great purge that was planned.

He knew there was to be a purge because the "experts" he listened to and read religiously said there would be. Seven billion down to five hundred thousand was the ultimate plan, the survivors all trapped in compact cities overseen by a political and economic elite that believed in transhumanism and eugenics. Connery had to wonder if he even wanted to survive in such a world. It never once occurred to him that if this elite were so all-powerful, why was it that they had allowed the population to grow so out of control in the first place. It was never good to let logic invade an awakened mind.

The noise got louder, and from the corner of his eye, he saw curtains twitch. Most of the people who lived in the city would have followed the instructions given to them by the media, at least at first. When you learnt that all the major arteries out of the city had either been sealed off or cut, there really was little point trying to flee. Connery himself knew he should have left Glasgow, but he didn't for the simple reason he didn't have anywhere to go. He had spent all his free time researching about the coming dystopian future instead of actually acquiring skills to survive when the shit finally hit the fan. What was he going to do, fill a backpack with food and go and camp in the woods? Firstly, he didn't have a backpack, and secondly, he hadn't the slightest idea of how to survive without civilised warmth and shelter.

Connery realised too late that he was in no way prepared for the world he had been secretly longing for. And wasn't that the truth of it? He had fallen into the whole conspiracy web because, on some level, he actually wanted to see it all come crashing down. Secretly, in the darkest rooms of his heart, he knew that he had been a failure by conventional standards, and he hated the world around him for highlighting his own inadequacies. His corrupted ego and arrogance told him he would be one of the survivors, but when a light was shone on his plans, they were seen to be nothing but mist and mirrors.

When Connery found out what the noise actually was, it was already too late for him.

A single zombie was walking down the centre of the street, its left wrist handcuffed to a car door it was dragging along with it. How on earth that had come about, Connery didn't know. But when he saw the way the creature moved, the blood that covered its face and the blackness in its eyes, Connery knew instantly that he had been wrong. This wasn't some plot to cow the population. The zombie menace was, in fact, real, and he had willingly walked away from the illusionary safety of his flat.

Part of him froze for several seconds before he had the sense to turn and run. The zombie came after him, but it was hindered by the door. The noise it made wasn't though, it was like an alarm to anything in the surrounding area.

Unfortunately for Connery, he had another issue. The other thing he had been neglecting was his own fitness: beer, pizza and marijuana his staple diet. Secondary school was most likely the last time he had actually done any intentional exercise. Running for the bus was the only test he put on his legs, so despite the terror in him, Connery found that he quickly tired. It wouldn't have been so bad if it was just the one hampered zombie. But as he fled, the streets that bled onto the one where he wheezed seemed to fill with jackals regurgitated from hell itself.

Whereas he had walked the streets alone, now the undead surrounded him. While not all of their number came for him personally, there were enough of them running at him full pelt for Connery to realise he didn't stand a chance of getting back to his home. Putting on a last desperate burst of speed that sent fire coursing through his lungs, Connery actually stumbled, his muscles and joints not used to such abuse. He didn't fall, but his foot landed at an odd angle, sending pain shooting into his ankle.

Connery found he couldn't run anymore, and the monsters were closing on him rapidly as if he was the last human left on the planet. The only thing left for him was to seek some kind of refuge, a futile plan at best. The closest home was to his right, and he navigated the rusty gate that led to a pathetically unkempt front garden. The PVC door shook as he desperately slammed his fists on it.

"Please," he begged, "let me in." The door remained firmly closed of course, the only sign of life inside a dark shadow that he briefly saw move thanks to the door's privacy glass. The person in there clearly wasn't in any hurry to be a good Samaritan.

"Please," he begged again, the word almost choking him. Connery heard something impact the gate behind him, and he frantically looked behind to see four zombies stood on the pavement. Their black eyes seemed to stare at him as if Connery was the most amazing thing in the world. For a moment, they just seemed to stand there, gazing in awe at some unique exhibit put on the world for their endless amusement. Then they came at him as one, two more running up from behind, the remaining mass of them surely only moments away.

The gate and the low wall that marked the boundary of the property gave him a brief respite. Some of the zombies climbed, another simply tumbled over the wall. The gate itself lasted mere seconds before it was ripped from its housing by the enhanced strength of the undead attacking it.

Connery turned fully around to face his end, his back against the cold door. Any second he hoped that the door would open allowing him to fall back into safety, but such fantasy never happened. They were on him quickly, their fists punching into his face and gut. A hand grabbed him roughly by the neck, and Connery felt himself lifted off the floor, his feet drumming madly. He couldn't breathe and the hand squeezed tighter, praying that he would black out in time because he had watched enough Hollywood movies to know what was coming. As if sensing his thoughts, the grip on his neck weakened slightly, just enough to stop peaceful oblivion from taking him.

A zombie punched him in the gut again, only this time the skin ripped, the decaying hand forcing its way into the abdominal cavity. Surprisingly the lack of pain lied to him about the damage being done, until the zombie gripped and pulled, yanking his guts out through the wound, another zombie gripping and pulling at the hole, tearing it wider. With the muscles of his abdomen decimated, his small intestine billowed out like a grotesque, slime-coated slinky.

A third zombie tried to scoop them up, forcing the tubing into its mouth. Around Connery's neck, the hand suddenly released itself, and Connery crumpled to the floor, the zombies climbing on top of him, almost fighting each other to get their turn. He felt something bite hard into his thigh, and then the worst of it came. A slick hand pressed against his forehead, pinning his skull to the floor whilst another hand came at his left eye, ripping the organ from its socket with fingers that were caked with the blood of a thousand victims. Connery's scream filled the air, the only human sound amongst the undead mob, and it sent them into a further frenzy. He was methodically and ruthlessly ripped apart. For whatever reason, this was one human that wouldn't be joining the zombie ranks.

The undead feasted, and they got their fill even though not a single one of them was satiated by the meal they tried to devour. Glasgow became just another city lost to the horde.

23.08.19
Florida, USA

When Ryan's phone had unleashed the Presidential alert telling him the world he knew was ending, he did the only thing that made sense to him. He phoned his wife and told her to get the fuck back home. This was while he was in the cab of his truck driving frantically to the school where his two young daughters were.

Ryan hadn't been the only parent to drive up frantically outside those school gates, the pavement clogged with the vehicles of desperate people.

When the first of the parents had turned up demanding their children be released, the staff at the school had been more than happy to unload their charges. The more parents to arrive, the less the burden on the teachers became. By the time Ryan turned up, it had been decided that it was best to send all the children home and close the school for the next couple of days. This decision was based partly on common sense, but also on the instructions of the Florida Department of Education. Apparently, the schools were supposed to have been warned before the Presidential alert was sent out, but somebody somewhere didn't get the message. The result was understandable chaos.

Most of the teachers stayed until the last child either left or was collected. Some didn't, their desire for self-preservation put into overdrive by the risks Lazarus represented. Children were one of the prime ways pathogens such as Lazarus spread throughout the population. Just ask how contagious kids can be when the flu or norovirus is going around. Some would be critical of those teachers who abandoned their sacred duty, but most people would understand. Really, when it came down to it, even if it was your job to look after others, a significant number of people really only cared for their own offspring and themselves.

It took Ryan all of five minutes to park up, collect his girls, and leave the school for the last time. By the time he got home through the chaotic traffic, his wife was already there, and he watched with relief as his two treasures ran to the woman he had grown distant from over the last six months. They still lived together, but her work as a county prosecutor was driving a wedge between them. The arguments that had become more frequent had always been in hushed tones in an attempt to hide from the two nine-year-olds the gulf that was increasing every day.

Sometimes adults needed to realise that it was all but impossible to hide the truth.

With the tension that had existed between them, Ryan was surprised when his wife instantly agreed with his plan to escape the contagion. He had expected resistance, a desire on his wife's part to shoot his notion down in flames. The opposite happened, and the hug she gave him had taken him totally by surprise. Even the worst of times could be filled with moments that make your heart sing. It was just a shame those moments were so fleeting.

The plan was simple. Drive to the harbour with all the food they could pack in the car and venture out into the Gulf of Mexico on Ryan's fishing boat. It was a good plan, the best that most people could come up with, but life never was and never had been fair. Lazarus was not going to allow Ryan and his family the satisfaction of survival.

That had been two days ago, and already the boat felt more like a cage than a refuge. The kids were restless, despite their mother's soothing voice that tried to reassure them. The children knew that things were bad, despite their limited experience at the game of life. Just the drive to the marina had shown them enough insanity to give them a clue as to the truth about human nature, the smoke from the shore now speaking volumes about the violence that they had escaped.

Their supplies were sufficient for perhaps a week, and water wasn't an issue due to the desalination system on board the boat. Technically the boat wasn't solely Ryan's, he half owned it with his brother. But his brother was in

Vegas, and with the way the phones had been playing up, he hadn't yet been able to have more than a five-minute conversation with him.

Ryan's brother used to be a marine, he could handle himself. He also wasn't saddled with two kids and a wife that had slowly learnt to despise him.

The initial problem that followed was boredom. In their panic, they had concentrated on the essentials which hadn't included anything except an iPad and the phones they had on them. So the kids were agitated, and now that the immediate emergency was over, the tension between him and his wife was resurfacing. It was obvious from the boat's radio and what they could see from their offshore position that returning to land was a bad idea right now. How long would they be able to keep it together in the rather cramped conditions the boat presented though?

They also weren't the only people to have made this choice. Other boats were dotted around them, the occasional ride past by the Coastguard reassuring many that some sort of order was still in effect. Nobody bothered them, which was a blessing, lulling them into the false belief that they had done enough to keep themselves safe.

It was his wife who spotted the bird first. A seagull, it landed on the stern of the boat, its movement strange. Looking at something he'd seen thousands of times before, Ryan knew there was something very wrong with the creature. It looked sick, but his brain didn't connect it to what had been happening on land, so to blame him for what happened next would be a bit harsh. Having never seen a zombie in the flesh, it would be unfair of anyone to expect him to recognise a zombified bird. Still, his inner voice was shouting something at him, the bloody footprints that the bird was leaving on the pristine whiteness of his boat perhaps all the warning he really needed.

Ryan chose to try and shoo the bird away instead of locking himself and his family in the boat's galley. When the bird came at him, and when it took his eye before flying off in its erratic fashion, he really wasn't to know that the virus had been passed to him. When his wife tried to stem the bleeding by ripping open the med kit and holding the dressing against his face, Ryan wasn't to know that he passed the virus onto her. And with children who needed comfort to soothe them from the vision of their father being half blinded, the mother then passed the virus onto them.

Ryan wasn't even the first to turn. The children were. And with his one remaining eye, he got to witness them tearing his wife apart while he sobbed helplessly, unable to hurt the darlings that had quickly turned into demons. Instead, he threw himself into the mercy of the ocean and let the cold water take him. It took three days for the current to send Ryan(Z) back to shore.

23.08.19
Preston, UK

The last of the defenders at Fulwood Barracks had been overwhelmed, the sound of gunfire now eerily absent. It had been hours since the attack on the barracks, and yet there were still dozens of zombies present in the parade grounds and in the surrounding buildings. They all pretty much ignored Smith without him even having to order them. For some reason, Smith now held no interest for their kind. All they cared about was feeding off the living and the propagation and enlargement of the ever-growing zombie battalions. Smith just didn't factor into that.

When Smith had fled the firefight, he had retreated to the apparent safety of his room, staying there for several hours while his mind battled with what to do next. Through the turmoil of his own bubbling insanity and the constant interruptions by The Voice, Smith was finally able to settle on a course of action, although it was vague and likely to change. He didn't realise it, but everything that made him the man he had become was slipping away.

In a brief moment of concern, Smith realised he couldn't remember the face of his own mother.

Wandering back to the medical block, he stood witness to the carnage that had occurred there. For the most part, the undead had fared far worse than their human counterparts. The SAS soldiers guarding Jessica had been formidable foes, less than half a dozen of them lying dead around him. Still, the soldiers had lost the battle, the undead now able to feast on the bounty that was presented to them. Not all those who were killed came back from the dead. Whereas most zombies were forced by circumstance and the demands of the virus to take a bite of flesh here and a morsel there, a select few occasionally took the opportunity to gorge themselves on what was the sweetest of meat.

The undead lost in the battle could replace themselves easily from the surrounding general population within less than an hour. There was no need for a zombie boot camp, unlike the soldiers who required months of training to make them effective killing machines. With the only human defenders now defeated, the undead would ransack the neighbouring houses and take everyone they encountered. Doors and windows were merely an inconvenience. It was not surprising then that humanity was unlikely to win this war.

The enemy to man could create warriors easily and at a much faster pace.

The APC's were long gone, carrying the immune and the bastards that had dared to defy Smith. The Voice inside Smith's head had wanted Jessica dead and had planned for Renfield to kill her in some insane plan that, in hindsight, was doomed from the start. Colonel Carter had stopped that happening, and now even the maniac Renfield was dead. More importantly, with his demise, Renfield was no longer a threat to Smith and had taken Smith's secret to the grave with him. Renfield had never been an ally, just an insane and unpredictable means to an end.

Why Renfield had opened fire like that, Smith would never understand. If he hadn't, Smith would likely be on-board one of the APC's now. Instead, he was alone, surrounded by the undead.

Because Renfield and the SAS soldiers had mostly died before the virus took hold, their bodies were prime pickings for the zombie legions. Meat was actually quite rare due to the way the virus worked, so when it was offered up, it was never ignored. What was left of the bodies now lay scattered outside the medical facility, limbs ripped from the torsos in the unstoppable feeding frenzy at the end of the short battle. The remnants of an arm lay at Smith's feet, and he nudged it with the tip of his boot. Remnants was a more than adequate description because pretty much all that was left was bone and the tough cartilage that held the bones together.

Some of the carrion he saw had been stripped to the skeleton.

With specific regards to the corpse of Renfield, two persistent zombies seemed relentless in their attempts to get the last of the flesh from within the dead man's rib cage. One zombie even had its head wedged right where the lungs used to be. Smith watched their actions, fascinated by the craving that so effectively owned the undead. A third zombie was trying to shred the skin off the chest with its teeth, the clothing long having been ripped away. The death of Renfield was no great loss.

Stepping closer, it became apparent that one of the zombie's attempts to eat the lung tissue it clutched in its claw-like hands was futile, the mouth already full of matter that could never be swallowed.

And still it fed. Still, it tried to force the tissue into the blocked cavity.

"*This is no good*," The Voice suddenly said to him. At first, Smith didn't answer, but he felt The Voice pressing into his conscious thoughts. It demanded his attention.

"*I said, this is no good.*"

"Yes, I heard you."

"*What are we going to do about this?*"

"We?" Smith was incredulous. "There is no 'we'. You are just a figment of my imagination." Perhaps even a side effect of the cure Smith had developed. In truth, the trauma the virus and his cure had waged on Smith's mind had created a split personality, as well as eradicating any remnants of empathy or guilt from Smith's brain.

"*No*," The Voice insisted, "*I am so much more than that. More than you could possibly understand.*"

"I'm stood here talking to my own imagination." Smith was reassured that he could find the humour in it.

"*You still haven't answered me.*"

"What exactly is it you want me to say?" Smith said the words out loud. As before, to speak to himself in his own mind would somehow blur the reality and the boundaries of where he finished and where The Voice started. Smith was by far the stronger of the two, but how long could that continue? Would there come a time when The Voice simply drifted away? Or, frighteningly, would it be Smith who disappeared, only to be replaced by the psychotic alter ego? Smith had freely given The Voice control of his body once before…he wouldn't be doing that again.

"*We can't let Jessica live. And Whittaker. None of the immune can be allowed to persist. They are a threat. If we can't kill them in this world, we must do so in the other place.*" The other place? What did that even mean?

"They aren't a threat to me. I owe Jessica my life. Without her blood, I…we would have been one of these things." Smith pointed to the nearest zombie, who seemed to sense the gesture. It turned its head towards Smith, foul juice drooling from its bloodied maw. Smith stepped away, no longer wanting to look at the desecration of the corpses around him. "And what other place?"

"*You will see. It is where I go when you deny me what is mine by right.*"

"The only place you need to go is to hell, and you can fuck off while you are doing so," Smith said the words as menacingly as he could, but The Voice just seemed to laugh in response.

To his left, the relatively untouched body of a dead soldier sat up. Clearly, the undead knew who carried the virus and who didn't. Did they always leave their own kind alone? Smith believed they did, at least most of the time.

"*I have a good idea,*" The Voice said. It sounded pleased.

"What good idea?"

"*The quarantine barracks. That's where we should go next.*" The zombie soldier stood up, the bite mark on its neck undoubtedly what had killed it. *Why did resurrection occur over such a wide timescale?* Smith asked himself. Some came back in minutes. For others, it took hours. Wavering for a second, the zombie wandered off in search of sustenance, almost falling as it tripped over the legs of one of its kind that lay destroyed on the ground.

"*Never mind all that,*" The Voice demanded. "*We need to go to the Quarantine barracks.*"

"Why would I want to do that?" Smith asked, although he was already coming around to the wisdom of the action. For some reason he couldn't yet explain, it felt like the right thing to do.

"*Would you rather be alone for the rest of your days with only me to talk to?*"

Smith wasn't listening. He had suddenly become fascinated by one of the broken zombies on the ground. It flapped helplessly, and Smith wandered over to have a closer look. He might as well, it was the direction he intended to head in anyway.

***

Stephanie(Z) lay on its back, the left leg that had allowed it to walk no longer attached to its body. The other leg left the hip at an odd angle, a result of the grenade blast that had destroyed its status as a bipedal entity. The severed leg lay just over a metre away, twitching uselessly.

It found it difficult to turn over, the grenade having also crushed some of the spinal vertebrae as well as obliterating most of its left hand. None of this mattered to Stephanie(Z) mind you. Its primary concern was the delectable flesh that lay within crawling distance, saliva pouring from its mouth at the prospect of satisfying the yearning that twisted its innards with a sensation that might once have been described as pain.

Something walked close to it. Not one of its kind, but also not the prey it hunted. Stephanie(Z) felt itself lifted and turned over. As this was done, it got to smell Smith and found him totally unappealing. When he had first recovered from taking XZ1, Smith had still been considered a tasty morsel by the undead, but the changes in his body that were still ongoing meant that was no longer the case. Smith could walk through a horde of thousands and emerge completely unscathed.

"There you go," Smith said. Now on its front, the damaged Stephanie(Z) began to crawl, no thought of even thanking its benefactor.

"Stop," Smith shouted; Stephanie(Z) finding itself compelled to follow the orders, the words of which it didn't even understand except on some primal level. Despite the fire within, Stephanie(Z) could not resist the instructions that had been given to her. A hand patted its fetid head, and further words entered what was left of its brain, releasing it from whatever spell held it captive.

"Very good, carry on."

The feral need took over once again, and Stephanie(Z) dragged itself over to the nearest corpse, a zombie already feeding there freely moving over to make room. There was plenty to share here. There was no need to be greedy.

23.08.19
Rising Bridge, UK

Nick's convoy stopped in the abandoned petrol station forecourt, which likely hadn't been open for several days. The shop that would normally sell travellers an array of cariogenic and cholesterol inducing snacks had clearly been ransacked, the windows shattered. That didn't matter, the occupants of the APC's had no need for such nutritionally devoid consumables. They had brought their own supplies, which was probably for the best because the shop had been stripped barren of anything that could be eaten.

From two of the APC's, armed SAS poured, spreading out to create a defensive cordon. If there were people about, they were clearly cowering in their own homes, the only threat here coming from whatever Lazarus could throw at them. The zombies that had chased them from the Preston Barracks had long been left behind. Nobody was willing to take any chances though, not with a foe that had become so unpredictable and so utterly ruthless. There was no Geneva Convention when you fought the undead, no prisoners, no mercy and no real way of knowing just what they were going to do next.

The stop had been Captain Beckington's idea. Despite their escape, they had still brought Lazarus with them, the blood that coated the exterior of the APC's as deadly as the air exhaled by infected individuals. They had needed to crush several of the undead in their escape meaning the very tracks that sped them on would have the plague in the treads. Blood also painted two of the APC's, evidence of where the vehicles had crashed into a mini-horde that had foolishly tried to stop the two-tonne beasts.

"We need to do what we can to clean the gore off these APC's."

Two SAS appeared from the shattered station shop after several minutes of search. One carried bottles of bleach that had been left on the shelves, the anti-viral properties of their bounty seemingly of little interest to the previous looters. The other had as many spray bottles as he could carry, again containing kitchen cleaning solution. While they had no kitchen surfaces that needed to be purged of 99.9% of all known germs, the hypochlorite they contained would work miracles on any particles of Lazarus that their NBC suits would be assaulted by. Now they had the means to clean their vehicles and themselves.

They had also switched the station's electricity back on and acquired the code to run the jet wash.

"Try the fast food joint as well," Beckington suggested, referring to the burger joint that lived next to the petrol station. Despite being a captain, he was well aware that the SAS had their own way of doing things, so he resisted the temptation to sound like he was giving them orders. Not even their own commanding officer treated them like that. "There will be bleach and cleaning products there." Two soldiers nodded their agreement and ran off to raid the place that had once tried its best to destroy the arteries of the local population.

The country had for decades been paranoid about Salmonella, E.coli and Listeria. Now all that was forgotten. Only Lazarus mattered now.

Beckington was well aware that the situation was far from an ideal stopping point. What they needed was a proper decontamination set up. But such equipment had been left behind in a place that was now too dangerous to venture. The plan was thus to use the petrol station jet wash to clean the detritus from the undercarriage of the APC's, which naturally risked turning any virus there into an aerosol, the fine mist weaponising something that was already incredibly deadly. Such efficiency could only be risked because of the protective clothing the soldiers were still wearing. The Bulldog APC's were not just designed to protect those inside from bullets and shrapnel, but also from nuclear, biological and chemical agents. Once the exteriors were clean, the soldiers would have little to worry about. For now, at least.

Beckington stood by the jet wash as the first APC was driven over. He had suggested this particular petrol station because it was on the way and was relatively devoid of human population buildings around it. The only other human structure within fifty metres was across the road, the sturdy stone structure clearly visible. There would be no sanctuary in that church, but Beckington suddenly found himself concerned by its presence. A soldier made ready to use the jet wash, but Beckington told him to wait.

"Hold up. I just want to check that church."

There was no sound escaping the building, its main door open, but that didn't mean there wasn't anyone inside. The last thing he wanted was for them to create a deadly mist that would float across the road and infect unsuspecting worshippers. He was here to try and prevent this shit from spreading. Gun in hand, he ran across the road, mindful that danger could be anywhere in this day and age.

Outside the front door, a body lay motionless, its skull caved in, the shovel used discarded by the side of the body. Beckington nudged the corpse with his gun, exhaling with relief when there was no movement. He sensed someone behind him.

"Can't have you walking off on your own, Doc," Jeff said with genuine concern. Beckington nodded, he was still a soldier at the end of the day, but also the only doctor.

The concern for danger was well founded. Stepping through the reinforced oak door, Beckington's gasmask spared him the oppressive odour, but Beckington was still warned about what was inside. A bloody smear led from the entrance towards the pews, a body clearly having been dragged. He took a step forward, mindful to keep out of the blood as much as he could. Inch by inch, the interior of the church came into view, the chaos there evident for anyone with eyes to see.

Some of the pews had been pushed over, others forced out of their normal regimented order. Two bodies lay ruined to his left, another in pieces scattered along the aisle. By the alter, there was movement. The vicar was easily identifiable by his crimson-stained white robes. Beckington had no doubt that the vicar was undead because the creature was presently knelt by the altar eating a corpse's face.

The Doctor backed up. There was no telling what the level of infestation would be here, the hidden rooms of the church a mystery for what they enclosed. Better to just leave the dead be, and on his departure, Beckington pulled the huge door closed as silently as he could. He wasn't surprised to find one of the SAS soldiers waiting outside for him with Jeff. Was he now really that important?

"Undead inside," Beckington said, and the three men marched back to the APC's. They would need to be on even higher alert now. Hopefully, the sound of the vehicles hadn't roused anything in the vicinity, but best not to tempt fate by firing off shots.

Beckington gave the all clear for the men to start cleaning the APC's. Then they would disinfect the exteriors of their own suits before once again boarding their rides.

23.08.19
Houston, USA

"I met your husband," Reece said. She was no longer wearing her deputy's uniform which had started to stink. The infected weren't allowed the luxury of showering due to the risk of spreading the virus, so a sponge bath from a bucket was all she could manage. She had been given standard military fatigues with one of the sleeves cut away to allow ready access to the monitor on her arm. The belt with her gun and holster was still around her waist though. They hadn't taken that off her yet. Her badge was also pinned to the left breast pocket just so everybody knew who she was.

For the moment, she was still an officer of the law.

"So I hear," Doreen Clayton replied. Even with the mask the middle-aged woman was wearing, Reece could see she was smiling. The mask wasn't for Doreen's protection, because she was already infected with Lazarus, but she wore it more out of habit than anything else. "He's a stubborn son of a bitch, but that's kind of what I love the most about him." Doreen grabbed Reece's arm gently. "Thanks for stopping him getting his damned head blown off."

"Hey, it's what I do."

Like Reece, Doreen had been allowed relatively free rein to wander throughout the Astrodome. She may also have been infected, but she was a highly experienced trauma nurse, and thus her services were invaluable to the none infected staff of the hastily constructed facility.

There was a gnawing tiredness in Doreen's eyes, but also a determination and a strength that was lacking in many of those who had been brought to this facility. She still had some fight in her, despite the way her symptoms were steadily worsening. Not everybody was as durable, in fact, most of those who were brought just gave up and resigned themselves to their fate. Reece had witnessed it, people just surrendering, seeming to die even before Lazarus had hit its peak within their bodies. She had even heard reports of a massive increase in suicides in the city's population, those sent out to bring the infected to the quarantine zone sometimes bringing back a corpse instead of a live human. Slowly and methodically, Lazarus was taking its toll.

Suicide, when you were infected, was also inherently selfish when you thought about it. Unless you killed yourself by eating a shotgun round, you just ended up leaving a ravenous zombie for somebody else to deal with.

During her brief time in the Astrodome, Reece had seen the best and the worst of what made people human. She suspected though, that as the days progressed, any good here would be swallowed up by the growing desperation about what was happening out on the city's streets.

Many of those here had been brought under armed guard, some turned in by their own friends and relatives. Fear of the virus was, for many, a greater motivator than the tattered fibres of human loyalty. The fact people were here showed they had surrendered to the forces sent out to get them, and thus were invariably the least likely to present any kind of resistance. The "sheep" and the law-abiding were easy to deal with. Those with a more belligerent stance to the orders enacted by the state Governor generally ended up on the wrong end of superior firepower.

Some had been brought here in chains. The criminals and those who resisted attempts to put them into quarantine were dumped into the temporary prison facility where rights and privileges were non-existent.

The police and the army didn't have the resources to fight the zombies and mess about with defiance from the local population, so a zero-tolerance policy was implemented. Those who tried to fight back were generally just obliterated by overwhelming force. If you were *lucky* enough to be arrested, you were dragged away in shackles and forcibly microchipped. Reece had seen that done first hand. She didn't agree with it, but she understood the functionality of the procedure. The existing prisons weren't being used because Lazarus was already ripping its way through them, the confined culture almost the perfect environment for the virus to spread. The Harris County Jail, for example, had seen an explosion in infections, the army having to move in to deal with inmates that passed to the other side. Correction officers couldn't be expected to kill inmates on demand, although some did.

So far, they had left the dead bodies in the cells. You could imagine how bad that was starting to smell.

America had always been harsh on its lawbreakers. But under martial law, the criminals found the usual way of doing things null and void. There were no lawyers, no courts and no judges. All that was suspended. There was just cold hard steel and the unforgiving stares of soldiers that would shoot you for the slightest infraction. Those who fell to the whims of *justice* were separated away from the main Astrodome and NRG stadium over in the Houston Methodist Training Centre. The rumours of the atrocities allegedly going on there were hard to hide or ignore.

Reece wondered how long it would be before those committing crimes were just shot on sight. She hoped that particular scenario would never happen, but she wasn't naïve enough to rule it out. And if it happened, it would only take one shift in thinking for that policy to be turned towards those found to be infected. Human rights were rapidly disappearing as a factor for consideration. Now it was all about survival, not of the individual but of the nation. How long though before that sent the population of Texas against the military, a population that was heavily armed and suspicious of the federal government at the best of times? Or would they just accept what had to be done? Reece knew the answer to that.

Being infected as she thought she was, Reece felt it was unlikely that she would live to see such a descent into tyranny happen. You had to be thankful for small mercies.

The two women sat across from each at a metal table bolted to the concrete floor. They were in a rest area which had been set up for infected individuals who had volunteered to help. They both wore the arm mounted monitor that was locked on and which kept a constant check on the status of their health. Reece had kind of gotten used to it, but in the rare instances she slept, she had the irritation of having to lie on her wrong side. That aspect hadn't occurred to her when Doctor Lee had asked her which arm would be best for the device. It was a minor inconvenience that didn't come close to the trauma of being infected with Lazarus.

"I worry about him though," Doreen added. "He will be the first to admit he has a temper. I can keep it under check because he adores the very ground I walk on. With me not there though, I just know he's going to get into trouble. He's always been bullheaded."

"Don't you mean *if* you're not there," Reece admonished. "It's not over till it's over. Look at me, I'm feeling better with every passing hour."

"Honey," Doreen said with a knowing smile, "I'm not dumb enough to blow smoke up my own ass." A cough struck her suddenly, causing Doreen to double over slightly, pain racking through her body. "You see, this virus is some end of days shit. If there's a cure, it won't find its way into my veins." Doreen didn't let on that she figured her ability to help would end in hours rather than days. Her limbs had started aching now, which made movement difficult, and the cough was an indication her lungs were on their last legs. Within twelve hours, it was likely she would be bedridden. Doreen would do what she could to help others until that time came. There was no other way for her to be.

"I hear you. But there's always hope."

Doreen shook her head sagely. She had twenty years of life experience on Reece. The younger woman still had a lot to learn about the true nature of the human condition.

"Have you got a man in your life?"

"I did, once," Reece said sadly. She looked blankly across at the other people sitting around, saw the resignation and dejection that filled the room. "He died though, in the line of duty." Doreen leaned over the table to grab Reece's hand with both of hers. For some reason, Doreen was the first person she felt she could open up to about her lover's death. Why was that? She'd known the nurse less than a day, and yet Reece felt she would tell her everything if asked. A person like Doreen didn't deserve this, but Reece was glad she was here. Selfish certainly, but that was the way it was.

"This life we have been given can be a curse more than it can be a blessing. But it's all we have, and for me, that's enough."

"I learnt that early on," Reece admitted. She could see it in the eyes that Doreen had not had the easiest of lives. Reece was about to say something more, to share the ache that had burned into her soul only for the moment to pass. That was when Dr Lee entered the rest area as if drawn by Reece's need for secrecy and psychological isolation.

Jee spotted Reece instantly and came over to her. The Doctor looked distracted, as if she had a secret that she desperately needed to tell.

"Ladies," Jee said as she grabbed a spare chair and sat down with them. She didn't wait for an invite. The protective suit she wore was burdensome, and it felt strange for her to be the only person in the room wearing it. She would have preferred to wear the full level A biohazard suit, but that just wasn't practical. Instead, she wore one designed to protect against Ebola. Designed at John Hopkins Hospital, it had a large clear face screen which gave her more visibility as well as being less threatening in appearance than a gas mask. There was also an easily changeable exterior oxygen supply hanging from the back of her waist, which was what was causing the difficulty in sitting. It also had a built-in cooling system which was a blessing, even with the air-conditioned air of the Astrodome. All the medical staff were similarly kitted out. It was still cumbersome and time-consuming to take on and off, but it gave them the protection they needed to get the job done while allowing them to monitor the patients that needed monitoring.

As for the army, well they wore their own shit which was as intimidating as hell.

"When was the last time you got some sleep, Doctor?" Doreen asked. Reece smiled at this.

"I asked her the same thing several hours ago. I'm assuming the answer is still little to none."

"I can sleep when this is all over," Jee replied. She seemed more serious than normal, her usual jovial nature cut short. Despite her own predicament, Reece felt herself worrying about the Doctor. She wondered whether Jee was taking the mounting deaths under her watch hard, perhaps bearing every one as a personal failure. There was a chance that Jee was too empathic for the job she was being asked to do.

"I spoke to your husband like you asked," Jee informed Doreen. "I told him you were still okay." Doreen nodded her thanks. She had given Jee the number of her husband's satellite phone previously. It was one of the perks of volunteering to help, getting word out to loved ones where possible.

"What's wrong?" Reece asked. She saw the trouble on Jee's face.

"Well, lots of things. But for you Clarice, I actually kind of have some good news. You're getting out of here."

"What do you mean?" As if in answer, Jee produced a small key, and she waved it at Reece, beckoning for the arm. Dumbfounded, Reece offered the limb up, and Jee unlocked the monitor from her. Finally, Jee smiled, although it was forced.

"You are immune, Clarice."

***

Ever since the altercation with Clayton's Militia that had almost ended in a firefight, the guards on the main entrance to the Astrodome had been wary of trouble. The city around them was on fire, the National Guard and Law Enforcement just about able to hold it all together. Things were getting precarious though, the violence escalating as people started to resort to desperation. The constant flow of buses was filling up the quarantine facilities rapidly, the makeshift prison that had been set up also beginning to creak with the weight of humanity that was being pushed into it. And out on the street, the number of undead was rapidly growing while those battling the infection only seemed to be getting weaker.

Zombies didn't need to sleep, and although they craved it, they didn't need to feed to function. They were relentless and spreading. So bad was it becoming that some of the soldiers were beginning to *joke* that they perhaps didn't have enough bullets for the task at hand. There was also the psychological toll that was being paid by the men and women battling Lazarus. People were already starting to break under the strain.

The last thing the soldiers on the front gate expected to see then were helicopters descending from the heavens. Nobody had warned them of any such arrival, so when one of them landed on the road directly in front of their guard post, a tingle of concern was raised. They were definitely military, US Marine markings all over them, but some notice of their appearance should have been forthcoming. The helicopter stayed on the ground long enough to unload five men, before it rose back up into the smoke-filled sky where it hovered menacingly.

As with every soldier that was engaged in operations, the newcomers all wore the uncomfortable and laborious NBC suits that would hopefully protect them from the ravages of Lazarus. Although less than ideal to be wearing in the Houston sun, such outfits were the only thing guaranteed to keep a person virus-free. The first man to step off the helicopter walked with authority and radiated a presence that told everyone he was an officer, someone who was supposed to be here. Someone in charge that you didn't want to get on the wrong side of. It was obvious to any casual observer that he was the man in command, and this leader of men marched forward, his entourage in step behind him. He presented himself to the guards on the gate.

"Major Carson, United States Marine Corps. I am here to take charge of a patient for transfer." Before the Corporal on the gate could say anything, the Major thrust the mandatory plastic wrapped request documents at him. Looking over the paperwork, the Corporal found he didn't know what to do. A week ago he had been changing the oil and stripping out busted spark plugs in the cars brought to his brother's auto shop. Now he was sweating his balls off making sure only those who were authorised to enter the infection treatment zone did so.

"Sir, I will need to check this with my commanding officer."

"You do that son," Carson said in an almost mocking tone. "But be quick about it. This heat is a killer, and I have places to be."

Within two minutes, Carson and his team were in a jeep being ferried to the Astrodome. The guards on the gate might not have been warned, but their commanding officer was well aware of Carson's arrival. Carson's reputation had preceded him, so it was the commanding officer's opinion that the sooner he and his men were gone, the better it would be for everyone concerned.

***

"Immune? Does that mean I can get out of here for good?"

"In a sense, yes, but not in the way you're thinking."

"I'm thinking a bottle of red, a long bath and to be able to sleep in my own bed again." Would that even be on the cards though? From what she had seen from the numbers of people being brought in, half the city would probably be in ruins. Her apartment might not even be there anymore. Likely she would just end up back on the streets doing the only thing she knew how to do.

"No, that's not the way this plays out," Lee said with definite sadness. There was regret all over her face. She liked Reece, and she knew that what was going to happen next was going to be difficult for her to understand. When you spent your entire working life upholding the law, seeing how it could be so abused was going to really hit Reece hard, despite the good news she had been given. Personal freedoms and liberties, the things that had made America the country it was…well, they were now pretty much a thing of the past.

"What are you trying to tell me, Jee?"

"Firstly you need to understand that I had no say in this. If it were up to me, I would let you stay here. We need all the help we can get. But it's your blood."

"What about my blood?"

"You're immune Clarice," Doreen interjected. "That means your blood might hold the key to curing Lazarus."

"Okay, so take what you need," Reece insisted. "I want to help, I really do."

"It's not as simple as that."

"I don't like the sound of this," Reece warned. She could see the troubled look on Jee's face.

"It would make more sense for Clarice to stay here. We have the facilities to work on the cure," Doreen insisted. There was the threat of anger in her voice.

"Don't you think I know that?" Jee almost shouted with exasperation. "Look, sorry, I don't mean to take it out on either of you."

"I know dear," Doreen said. She knew not to attack the messenger despite the unpleasantness of the message.

"Will someone please tell me what's going on?"

"Clarice," Jee said, "the military is in charge of the fight against the virus now. They are moving all immune individuals to a single facility."

"Moved? Where?" Jee paused before spitting it out.

"Fort Detrick...Maryland."

"But that.... that's on the other side of the country."

"I know," said Jee. "And apparently I'm going with you. Neither of us seems to have a choice in this." For Jee, it didn't seem like such a bad move. She was going to be helping the team at the heart of finding the answer to Lazarus. It wasn't like she even lived in Texas, she had just been sent here to help coordinate the Governor's emergency plan, as well as acting as the CDC liaison. This could very well be described as a step up for her.

"When do I leave?"

"Sometime today."

"Who's taking over from you when you go?" Doreen asked, shocked. Jee gave her an embarrassed look. "Oh God, not Dereck?" Dereck was Doctor Lee's number two.

"He's more than capable of running things here," Jee said defensively.

"Bullshit," Doreen said, rejecting her false praise. "The man's an incompetent, egotistical idiot."

"My hands are tied," Jee said. "Things are bad out there. The CDC is having to abandon its headquarters in Atlanta." Lazarus had struck hard and fast, gouging out the very heart of the agency that would be tasked with fighting it.

There was a commotion at the entrance to the rest area. Several soldiers entered, one pointing towards Reece and the two people with her. Carson stood there for several seconds, appraising the women.

Stopping off at Houston had been no great chore for him, and it tempered the failure of the operation he had been running in Nevada. He and his team had been dispatched to fetch a suspected immune individual from Las Vegas. That had been a waste of his time, the individual in question taking their own life when faced with the unfolding apocalypse. The woman's body was already halfway to the research team at Fort Detrick with the hope that some good could be salvaged from the cadaver.

Carson folded his arms and Reece witnessed him whisper to one of the soldiers with him. That soldier scurried off somewhere. Carson stepped over, two of his men coming with him like loyal lapdogs. The fourth one guarded the room's only exit.

"Ladies. Deputy Reece, I am Major Carson, United States Marine corps." One of the things Reece hated the most about this place was her inability to see any of the faces of the soldiers guarding the infected due to the respirators they all wore. It made them seem impersonal, even oppressive.

"That's nice for you, honey, but the girls are having a chat here." She quickly saw any attempt at charm wouldn't work on this man. His body language just shouted hostility.

"By order of the President, I am to transport you to a secure facility at Fort Detrick. If you could come with me please." When Reece didn't instantly move, Carson added the word "Now," with exaggerated insistence.

Jee stood up from her seat, turning around so Carson could see her face, a photo of which had been attached to the briefing documents Carson had been given before his arrival here. "Ah, Doctor Lee. Excellent. You will be coming too, I believe." Jee seemed to nod sheepishly. She found herself wondering how the Major knew what any of them looked like.

"And what if I decline your generous offer?" Reece insisted. She had taken an almost instant dislike to Carson.

"You don't have a say in the matter," Carson advised. "I would rather you came willingly though. It's too hot out there to be dragging you out kicking and screaming."

"I don't think there is any need to take that tone, Major," Jee admonished. Carson gave Jee a withering glance before turning his attention back to Reece.

"The hell you say," Reece protested. "I still have rights."

"No, you really don't. And I will need you to surrender your firearm, deputy." Reece surged up from her uncomfortable seat, her anger bubbling. The soldiers with Carson spread out slightly in response, ready for what might follow. Several of the people using the rest area vacated it, not wanting to get caught up in what was likely to be impending violence. With all the deaths occurring, people were developing a sense for when trouble was about to occur.

"I'm still on duty here," Reece insisted.

"Not any more. You are relieved for the foreseeable future. Houston doesn't need you anymore, but your Nation does."

"I work for the Sherriff's Department, you don't have any jurisdiction over me."

"Deputy, words are coming out of your mouth when you really just need to stay silent and accept this." Carson sounded pissed off now.

"There's no real urgency is there? I will need to get my research before I go, so that gives Reece a chance to say goodbye to people at least," Jee said. Carson turned his attention to her once again. His eyes seemed to blaze with malevolence behind the glass portals in his mask.

"I regret there will be no goodbyes. And you should be ready to leave already. You were informed of our arrival. What do you think this is, some kind of game I'm playing?"

"Hey, I'm not in your goddamn army. I've got a facility to run here. And besides, nobody actually told me *when* you would be arriving so you will need to give me fifteen minutes at least. My research is important, or would you rather I go without it?" Jee tried to move past him but found Carson blocking her exit. "The sooner you let me go, the sooner I can be ready. It's your clock that's ticking." Carson seemed to stare at her for several seconds before eventually moving to one side. Jee scurried off before the Major changed his mind, her heart pumping from the stress of the brief confrontation.

Carson turned his full attention on Reece once again.

"Gun, now." To emphasise the point, the two men with him aimed their own weapons at Reece.

"You've got to be bullshitting me. And you know you're not going to shoot me," Reece countered. "It's clear how important I am if you've come all the way across the country to fetch me."

"I don't have to shoot you," Carson said menacingly. He raised a finger in the air and the two guns being aimed at Reece were suddenly aimed at Doreen. Jee saw this all unfold before she left the rest area. As mad as it was, she chose not to intervene because she knew she had no power to stop any of this from happening.

"Get those guns the fuck out of my face," Doreen demanded. She was too appalled to show any kind of fear, the anger bringing on another coughing fit. "I'll rip that mask off you and make sure you end your days here." The threat was ignored by Carson.

"Deputy. It doesn't have to go down like this. All I require is your compliance," Carson insisted. With everything covering his face, Reece couldn't tell if he was enjoying his use of power. Most likely he was. She had met people like him before in both the criminal and law enforcement setting. Carefully, she pulled the gun from her holster and placed it on the table. She suddenly felt vulnerable without it, but she really had no choice.

"See, isn't that easier? Corporal, take Deputy Reece into protective custody. We need to make sure nothing bad happens to her. As she so rightly said, she's important." Carson didn't even try to hide the sarcasm in his voice. Reece realised she was probably in a hell of a lot of trouble here.

23.08.19
Manchester, UK

Viktor knocked lightly on Susan's door, even though he felt he didn't owe her any kind of courtesy. The sooner she accepted her fate, the better it would be for everyone involved. Clay was weak, and Viktor knew exactly how to exploit that weakness. Before the virus had been unleashed upon the world, Viktor had been happy to work for Clay, receiving a generous financial sum every month as well as other perks. He was also happy to supply Clay with the women needed to feed his depraved habit, knowing that eventually, it would result in the downfall of the crime boss. No matter how careful Viktor was at disposing of the bodies, the British police were not stupid. It was a certainty that Clay's secret would be uncovered eventually.

Clay's influence through bribery and blackmail was limited because this was no longer the 1970's. There would always be people looking into Clay's activities, and Viktor had prepared for the day when they came for his boss. When that eventuality happened, Viktor had planned to just move on as he had done so many times before. He didn't have that luxury anymore, nowhere in the world would be safe, not even for a man like Viktor. To survive in the growing apocalypse, you needed others around you, people competent and capable at surviving. Even better if you were the leader of such hard and ruthless men.

Viktor was essentially an opportunist by nature. It was the way he had stayed alive.

In the last day or two, Viktor had noticed a definite decline in the mental state of his employer. Clay seemed more paranoid than normal, more jittery, despite the menacing façade he wore. Where once they had been rare, he was now becoming prone to violent outbursts. Clay still held the loyalty of his men and was making the right moves to maintain that loyalty. But he had already had one of his top men killed as a result of a supposed power play against him. There had been no real betrayal, of course, just subtle whispers from Viktor's duplicitous lips. It was so easy to sow the seeds of doubt, so easy to remove the support structure that propped up Clay's organisation without having to actually act directly against the man himself. All Viktor had to do was subtly imply disloyalty and let Clay's own inherent fear of betrayal work its magic. It helped when the alleged disloyalty was nurtured with a grain of truth.

Then, when the time was right, Viktor would deal with Clay and step into his shoes. There weren't many obstacles to stop that now, but Viktor needed Clay to lose the plot a bit more to create distrust in the men under him. The problem with ruling by fear and intimidation was that there was always a willingness to choose something better if it ever came along. Viktor felt he was that something and there was no need for him to rush or take foolish actions. Time was his friend here, and Clay would do most of the work to bring himself down.

It was still a dangerous path to follow for Viktor. He had to be mindful that Clay didn't even trust him fully. For example, Clay had not informed Viktor about his plan to acquire the antiserum from the military couriers until the XV1 was safely locked away in the large safe in Clay's ridiculously opulent bedroom. For sure, Viktor knew of the plans to ambush the soldiers, but only Clay and the informant at the hospital where the antiserum had been made were aware of the contents of the package one of the soldiers was carrying. Viktor, however, had easily been able to deduce that Brian had been sent out to get something of ultimate importance, the men's chattering about the midnight raid on the couriers full of meaning to him.

Only after it was acquired did Clay inform Viktor of the great gift they had been able to steal.

The antiserum was thus essential to Viktor's long term plans, but he had no way of accessing the safe where it was most probably stored. It was a combination lock, and Viktor was not known for his safe-cracking skills. While he could ultimately blow the thing, that wasn't something he could do silently or without Clay's knowledge. There was also a question mark about the safety of the antiserum, and that was, above all things, what Viktor was waiting to have confirmed.

He wanted Clay to prove that the antiserum was safe and that it worked. If Viktor were in Clay's shoes, he would first pick a test subject, inject them and then put said subject in harm's way, that was assuming there was more than one dose. With proof that the XV1 worked, Clay could then inject himself and become one of the few individuals on the planet immune to the virus. What was then to be done with any remaining vials of antiserum if any existed? Viktor had no guarantee that Clay would choose him to be the recipient. There were too many variables for Viktor to just sit back and accept whatever was offered. That wasn't the kind of man he was. So Viktor plotted and schemed behind Clay's back, creating his own secret agenda.

Ultimately though there was a flaw in Viktor's plan. He wasn't a doctor or a scientist, and he wasn't to know that XV1 wasn't a cure per se. It was a short term measure, the immunity to the virus that it gave likely to wear off after several months at best, quicker with the viral mutations that were already occurring. So Viktor was intent on killing his boss for a cure that wouldn't keep him safe for very long.

Viktor knocked again, and when he got no response, he opened the door and looked in. Susan was asleep on the bed, as he had expected her to be. There was a discarded bottle of vodka on the floor by where she slept, and the clothes she had been asked to wear the previous day were discarded across the room. That was no way to treat a Versace, especially as there weren't going to be any more of them ever made.

Viktor sighed with disgust, picking up the dress and almost reverently placed it over his arm. He would return it to its plastic covering and bring something more suitable for Susan to wear.

She wouldn't like what he brought.

Viktor decided to let her keep the dressing gown for now, but only because Susan was presently asleep in it. Clay had decided to give her a day to come to her own conclusion about what was best for her future, and those minutes were ticking down. It was all part of the game Clay liked to play. Whatever path she chose wouldn't matter, because her life was as good as over. As broken inside and as dependent on alcohol as she was, Viktor reckoned she wouldn't even last a week before Clay tired of her. And that was if she chose the better of her two options. If she foolishly rejected Clay's generous offer...well, that wasn't even worth thinking about. Many of the men who worked under Clay had a less than chivalrous attitude when it came to women.

It wasn't just the dress Viktor had come to fetch though. More important was what was left of the alcohol. They had let Susan have her fill, but there wouldn't be any more of that free for all supply. Any drink she was allowed from this point forward would be doled out strategically, under the control of Clay himself. Viktor picked up the three bottles of liquor that were still unopened. He had stocked the room up prior to Susan's arrival, so he knew that the empty bottle lying on the floor represented the last Susan would ever have unless she behaved herself. A scary prospect for an alcoholic. Normally a person with Susan's dependence would need medical supervision to break their addiction due to the dangerous symptoms that sometimes came with withdrawal. But alcohol would only be prohibited if Susan declined Clay's most munificent offer. And if she did that, Clay wouldn't care what happened to the woman.

It was all part of the plan. Viktor felt he knew what was in the mind of Susan, and when the nausea and the tremors started in earnest, Susan would be banging on Clay's door, begging him to do whatever he wanted to her if only she could have just one drink. Viktor had abused and manipulated the broken and the lost for years now. They were as predictable to him as they were abhorrent. It was quite possible that Viktor didn't even know what the word *pity* meant.

The last thing he did was lock the door to Susan's room. They would give her a few hours to stew in there, let the torment of her own body really work on her. Then Clay would ask her what her decision was, which would hopefully break Brian's allegiance to him if only a fraction. Brian made a lot of noise that he wasn't concerned about what happened to Susan, but Viktor reckoned that was more bluff than truth. Viktor had seen men like Brian before and knew that they were often more dangerous than they first appeared. He was either excruciatingly loyal which meant he would never accept Viktor as his leader, or he was playing a duplicitous game, perhaps vying for his own push for the big time. Either way, Brian was a clear threat.

If Viktor were eventually to take over from Clay and run this operation, Brian would definitely have to go. Any move on Brian had to be done carefully though. He was well respected by the men, a man who had proven his worth to Clay and his organisation. Viktor was not going to make the mistake of underestimating him. The one thing he had learnt early on was to always respect the abilities of those you ultimately intended to kill.

23.08.19
Houston, USA

"What's all this, Clarice?"

Reece wasn't the only law enforcement officer here, seven others had been diagnosed with carrying the infection, four still able to function. One of them, a State Trooper called Calvin stood in her path now, blocking Carson and his men from marching Reece through the wire maze of cages to the exit they needed. Calvin and Reece knew each other in passing and had gotten to talking on occasion now that they were both stuck here. The badge and the uniform gave you an instant connection whenever you saw it, often resulting in a desire to protect your own.

Calvin and Reece had both seen the disturbing trend amongst the soldiers stationed at the Astrodome. As the death toll amongst those infected rose, the easier it seemed to be for the soldiers to step in and desecrate the bodies before they reanimated. If Reece had to give her opinion on the matter, the men doing what should have been an unpleasant and soul destroying job seemed to be rapidly becoming desensitised to it. And while black humour would always be a requirement to psychologically handle such traumas, some of the banter she heard between the soldiers went beyond what she considered acceptable.

It wouldn't be long before people started to be shot before they died. Reece could smell that in the air, just as she would have been able to smell the alcohol on the soldier's breaths if they weren't all wearing respirators. The commanding officers knew full well that the men here needed something to help take the edge off the horrors they were being asked to do. That was a lesson from history. Most people, even soldiers, weren't capable of wanton slaughter without some sort of chemical cosh to blur the edges of the horrors that could be committed.

"Out of our way, Trooper," Carson ordered dismissively. Calvin had his hand casually placed on the flap of his holster, the thumb there ready to flip the strap off so he could draw.

"I'm all right, Calvin. You don't want to get involved with this." Reece knew that if Calvin persisted, this would only end one way. Carson and his men were of a breed where they wouldn't think twice about killing anyone that got in their way. And there wasn't anyone here who would lift a finger in response. The soldiers who patrolled and guarded the infected wouldn't care because they had their one shit to worry about. They themselves were seeing and dispatching the recently deceased on an hourly basis. The execution of a living breathing individual probably wouldn't amount to anything more than raised eyebrows.

The rules had changed, and many of the laws Reece had spent her working life trying to enforce had pretty much been abandoned.

"The deputy is being escorted to another healthcare facility. That's all you need to know Trooper. Now move aside. I won't tell you again." One of the things that Reece had noticed was how Carson did all the talking. None of the men with him ever uttered a sound. She was also sure that they would perform every order he gave to them, no matter how abhorrent it might seem.

Calvin looked at Reece suspiciously.

"You're sure, Clarice? You only have to say the word."

"I'm sure Calvin. Best you not interfere." Reluctantly, Calvin stepped aside, and with a gentle nudge from behind, Reece was told to continue. If Reece had been in handcuffs, things might have gone down differently, so she was thankful that Carson hadn't ordered that. Calvin, for his part, looked impotent now, the illness clearly advancing in him. He had stepped in because he felt it was the right thing to do, but he also wasn't a fool. Even if the other armed officers were here, any standoff or firefight would have ended with people just getting shot. There was already enough of that going on in the world. While Reece appreciated the support from her fellow officer, she was relieved that he made the right move and stood down.

"So tell me something, Major," Reece inquired over her shoulder, "what happens to me when we get where we are going?"

"Rest assured you will be treated with dignity and respect," Carson said. The words sounded like a recording as if Carson had said them a thousand times before.

"You mean like I am now?" Carson didn't answer that.

As a small group, they moved through the last of the cages, the people trapped inside rarely giving them a second glance. The plight of one Sherriff's Deputy was of no concern to the condemned and the dying. Occasionally someone would beg her for help as she passed, but Reece could only ignore them. Maybe leaving here wasn't such a bad thing after all. In the last few hours, Reece had noticed a slight shift in the way things were being run. Any humanity that was being displayed seemed to be evaporating, replaced by cold, hard killing efficiency.

There was no doubt that the Astrodome and the related structures had been converted into a place where people were brought to die. The smell in the place was definitely getting worse as well. Not such a problem to those wearing respirators, but certainly an issue for everyone else, like those faced with the indignity of being trapped in one of the hundreds of cages. She wondered if this was what Hell smelt like? Vomit, faeces, piss all mixed with the pungent tang of disinfectant.

Reece had even overheard two of the CDC doctors talking about the possible need to start euthanising people. They could only house so many people in here and the NRG stadium next door. When those facilities reached capacity, they wouldn't have the luxury of stopping the busses from arriving, because the number of citywide infected was growing despite the attempts to contain the problem. This would also be made worse by the new field test for the virus that was soon to go into mass production. This wasn't what Reece wanted her state and her country to become, an efficient production line for death.

Desperate situations called for an even more desperate response, though. Reece didn't think she wanted to be around to witness any of that. It didn't matter so much when she believed she had days, maybe even hours to live. But that death sentence had been removed from her, allowing Reece to turn her mind to the predicament of people other than herself. If she stayed here, she just knew she would be forced to say or do something, and that was unlikely to be in her best interests despite the apparent respect some of the soldiers had for her.

All that was mute now because she was being removed to God knows where and that changed the game altogether. It might have been selfish, but with the Astrodome behind her, she would only have her own worries to focus on.

The main exit was in sight now. Reece felt better knowing that Doctor Lee was coming with her and she hoped that any rapport she had built up with the doctor could help offset the militaries' fondness for being such utter dickwads. Carson worried her. She hoped he was just the errand boy sent to fetch her, but Reece had a feeling he was more than that. Heaven help her if he was somehow running the show. Men like him always seemed to rise to the top of the shit heap, shovelling whatever they could down onto the people below on their climb.

Three soldiers ran past, a sense of urgency palpable in their actions. Carson grabbed one of them and asked a question that Reece couldn't hear.

"We have trouble in the kid's section," came the response before Carson let the soldier continue on his way. Reece looked behind at her escort.

"Problems?"

"Just keep walking." Reece resisted the temptation to salute sarcastically. It was true that she resented the way she was being treated. Her immunity meant she was important, and she was more than willing to do what she could to help cure this virus. She just wanted to have a say in what was done to her, and there was a growing fear that she would be nothing more than a glorified lab rat.

Carson received several salutes as they made it through the security checkpoint that led to the outside world. He returned only one of those salutes to a marine reservist. The others he just seemed to ignore. That told Reece even more about the man. It told him he made judgements about people without even knowing their skills or their character, that his ego was powerful enough to make him think he was somehow important in the great scheme of things. He was a dangerous man with a mission and a purpose. Reece had met him less than twenty minutes ago, and she already despised him.

Outside the heat hit her, but that didn't bother her though; she'd had a lifetime of it. The place she was being taken was a different matter entirely, that would be cold, something Reece had never been able to tolerate. You would never find Reece hurtling down a snowy slope or trekking through a mountain trail in winter.

The Sikorsky Stallion helicopter was waiting for them in a part of the carpark that wasn't covered in an array of tents and portacabins. The engine was turned off, the immense bulk of the helicopter seemed ominous with its black paint job.

"Your ride awaits, Deputy," Carson said from behind, and Reece reluctantly walked forward. Within thirty steps, she reached the helicopter where the side door was already open, allowing her reluctant access. She doubted this would be the vehicle for her full trip. More likely it would transport her to another destination, and from there she would take a military jet.

Reece could sense that the man behind the fifty calibre door mounted machine gun wasn't even looking at her. His attention was purely on the threats that might be inbound. Did he know something she didn't? Reece climbed up into the helicopter reluctantly.

***

"I shouldn't be telling you this," Jee said into the satellite phone. "I'm worried that you will get people hurt...but I fear what's going to happen here when I'm gone."

"Thank you for telling me," Rupert Clayton said on the other end. He was fuming but knew to keep the anger under check. Doctor Lee may have been a representative of the detestable Federal Government, but she was freely telling him about the way Carson had treated the woman he adored. She was not the enemy here, but an ally volunteering him information.

"I thought you had a right to know. This Major Carson won't be here to threaten your wife but...but I think you need to keep an eye on what's going on in here."

"I have men inside," Clayton advised her. "They will tell me when I need to act." Jee noticed that he didn't say *IF*. Jee broke the connection with him, the phone going into her bag. This wasn't the sort of thing she should be doing, but she felt somehow responsible for the thousands of lives that were being ended in the Astrodome, lives that she was leaving behind.

Yes, she really wasn't sure she should have done that. It was one of those decisions you made and then agonised over for weeks in case it was the wrong path to take. Men like Carson were likely an aberration in the US military, so she doubted most of the soldiers guarding the infected were as dangerous as him. Things could go bad though, despite the good intentions that were behind the quarantine of those whose lives were forever ruined by contracting Lazarus.

Jee had once read a book called *Ordinary Men* about how average, mainly family men were converted into killers who helped purge 1940's Poland of the Jews. She was well aware what terrors so-called decent people could be forced and manipulated into perpetrating. The USA was heading towards a time where civility and human kindness would be considered a weakness rather than a strength.

Despite the fact they were infected, the people in here deserved to be treated in the best way possible, and Jee knew that with her absent, there was a risk that things could get dark pretty damn quickly. Dereck was a competent doctor, but his skills as an administrator and a team leader were seriously lacking. He was a classic example of someone rising to a level too far above their ability. Any effective influence the CDC had in how the quarantine was run would end with the departure of Jee. She even wondered if that was part of the reason why she was being shipped out. Several times she had needed to butt heads with the military commander here, and it was clear he was getting tired of her interference. The military might well have been put in charge of fighting Lazarus, but surely they still needed to be held accountable via civilian oversite.

This place needed someone to keep it in line, to keep the military in check for as long as possible. And Dereck wasn't the person to do it. Jee suspected that was why she had felt compelled to ring Doreen's husband and tell him what she had witnessed here. Carson's actions were the first step down the totalitarian nightmare that was threatening to engulf the country. As a lifelong Democrat, Jee had detested many of the decisions made by the then Attorney General Jacqueline Fairchild. The woman was far too religious for the good of the country, and now the damned woman had been made President. How does that even happen?

In Jee's opinion, nothing good could come of that.

Jee wasn't surprised to learn that Rupert Clayton had contacts in here. He was a well-known militia leader. It was only natural that there would be men and women in the military who would be linked to him. Many of the soldiers here were National Guard, ripped from their normal lives to help fight the plague sweeping across the country. Jee just prayed he didn't do something stupid.

With her ready bag and laptop, Jee gave one last look at the office she had briefly owned. She wouldn't be coming back here, something she wasn't too disappointed about despite her sense of duty. The research facility she was going to would hopefully allow her more opportunity to do what she did best, as well as allowing her the freedom to spend most of her time without the confining hazmat suit enveloping her. Working in the field was necessary, but she had always been best in the sterile environment of the laboratory.

Closing the door behind her, Jee made her way towards the exit.

"Doctor," someone said behind her. It was Doreen, and Jee stopped long enough for the woman to catch up to her.

"Doreen, I can't stop."

"How can you allow them to do this to Clarice?" Doreen insisted.

"I don't have any say in this."

"Bullshit. The CDC is supposed to be in charge here."

"Supposed to be, but the army is really calling the shots. What I have to say about anything won't matter for much longer anyway." There it was again, the concern she had about Dereck being the lead CDC operative. He didn't have the guts or the skills to stand up to the army if they got it into their head to change the strategy. Even if Jee was staying though, would things be any different?

"You can't leave that man in charge. He's not up to it." Doreen actually sounded scared now, something that Jee had never witnessed in her before. She looked so frail and weak as well, the strength of her character likely the only thing still keeping her upright. Jee looked around the corridor they were in, noticing that there was nobody else around and that there was a lack of surveillance cameras. Reaching into her bag, she took out the satellite phone.

"Here. Keep this hidden and keep it safe. I've spoken to your husband, and he says he has people in here. If things get really bad, use it to ring him." Doreen seemed to hesitate as if the phone was red hot. "Keep it switched off at all other times though. You won't be able to recharge the battery, and if anyone sees you with it…well you know the rules." Patients of the facility weren't allowed phones. The normal cell phones were useless anyway because the networks had been shut off. But the military had insisted on tight control over the flow of information in and out of the Astrodome. Doreen finally grabbed it and placed it in the medical kit she carried slung over her shoulder.

"Thank you," Doreen said.

"I'll do what I can to look after Clarice," Jee said. "But this virus is going to bring the worst out of us. So remember if you call your husband, do so only for the direst of reasons. By ringing him, you will put his and your own life in danger."

"I know that, but the silly old goat will risk himself for me no matter what I say. I've convinced him to hold off once, I doubt I can do it again."

"You'll do what's right for him," Jee answered. "I have to go now."

"I know. I'm sorry if I sounded angry with you." Jee nodded and walked off, holding back the emotion that was threatening to burst out of her throat.

***

Outside, the helicopter was waiting for her. Jee reckoned that Carson would have been happier to leave without her, but even he had to follow orders. The door to the helicopter was still open, and she climbed on board, the soldiers who had come with Carson completely ignoring her. Carson, for his part, seemed to be trying to stare her down.

"I still say you shouldn't be keeping us waiting like this," Carson scolded.

"And you already have my answer to that." The seats next to Reece either side were filled by two of Carson's men, so Jee took the seat along from them, placing her bag on the ground by her feet. Reece was sandwiched between the two soldiers, Carson and the remaining two facing opposite. For the first time, Jee noticed that one of the soldiers sat next to Carson had Sergeant's stripes.

"Fine." Carson's tone clearly indicated that it wasn't fine.

"You okay?" Jee asked Reece. Reece just nodded tiredly. From the corner of her eye, Jee saw that the Sergeant opposite was fiddling with a medical bag. Unzipping it, he took out a loaded syringe.

"What the hell is that for?" Jee insisted.

"Oh hell no," Reece insisted, only for the two men either side of her to grab her arms. The fact that she was already strapped into her seat made it easier for them.

"Sergeant," Carson ordered.

"What the fuck are you doing?" Jee demanded. Nobody answered her. Instead, the Sergeant lifted himself from his seat and menacingly moved over to Reece whose head was now being held to one side. Reece was struggling valiantly, but it was no use, the soldiers too strong for her.

"Keep her still," the Sergeant demanded, "I'd rather not break the needle off in her neck."

"Stop this," Jee begged.

"Fuckers," Reece roared. She kicked at the Sergeant, getting a good shot onto his shin, but he barely seemed to flinch. The Sergeant moved closer, and Reece found her legs were no longer a weapon, the needle quickly descended into her neck. The fluid was warm, not unpleasant, and the drug took mere seconds to take effect. The Sergeant sat back down.

"Damn you," Reece slurred. Already she felt her consciousness slipping away, the words difficult to formulate. The men held her until it was clear their captive was no longer able to struggle.

"Why?" Jee asked.

"She has a mouth on her," Carson said. "I'd rather not be disrespected all the way back to Maryland. Also, we had an incident where an immune individual went berserk injuring one of my men before killing themselves." Carson didn't clarify how that suicide occurred.

"How can you do this?" Jee insisted. This was America, shit like this wasn't supposed to happen.

"Be thankful you aren't getting the same treatment," Carson threatened. Jee sat back into her seat, suddenly terrified of the world she now lived in. There would be nobody Jee could complain to about this. She knew it, knew it with certainty. The clarity of the situation finally hit her. Jee was merely along for the ride.

Lazarus had changed everything. Even if they found a cure and stripped the planet of the viral threat, there was a strong chance the nature of the country would be changed and damaged irreparably. This would soon no longer be a place for those who were unable to follow orders. The USA had become a land where authority and the word of law were now paramount. Individual liberty, one of the core principles it was founded on…well that didn't even get a look in any more.

23.08.19
Preston, UK

The entrance to the quarantine block was under assault by half a dozen zombies, and Smith sent them scampering off with a single word.

"Leave."

There seemed to be a moment's hesitation, and then the zombies took off at pace, leaving the way free for what Smith knew he had to do. In his right hand, he carried the case with the three vials of XV1. In his left, he carried a holdall which clunked metallically as he hefted it. Having acquired the key to the door, Smith unlocked it and stepped through. Around his waist, the automatic pistol felt heavy in its holster.

The building that had been used for the quarantine area was long and well protected from escape. The windows had all been reinforced with bars, the main door formidable enough to withstand the zombies attacking it. They were strong, but even the undead had limits. Before entering, Smith stood outside for a moment, still able to smell the evidence of the battle that humanity had lost. Those who had been able to had fled, the rest were either being consumed, had resurrected, or were locked in the building he was about to enter. There might be other survivors scattered throughout the surrounding buildings, but Smith didn't care about them.

Smith stepped through into what was effectively a primitive type of airlock. As the door closed behind him, he stepped over to a second door that led to where the quarantined soldiers were being held. He could hear the men, even with the door firmly closed.

There were forty-seven of them in total, and Smith gazed through the reinforced glass of the door to see some of them staring back at him. Each infected soldier had been given a bed and a bucket, those not looking at him lying down in their own misery. It was likely that several were on the brink of death and resurrection, the two dead bodies that he could see lying close to the door a testament of that. As horrific as it was, Smith could fool himself that what he was about to do was basically a mercy. He wasn't aware that for many, the last moments of life represented a moment of utter ecstasy, and Smith's actions were about to rob these men of that. Just another crime to add to the many he was accumulating on his karmic ledger.

Placing both the case and the holdall on the floor, he unlocked the door and stepped carefully through with gun in hand.

"Hello," Smith said. Most of the men in the room had never seen the Colonel before, but his rank was clear for them all to see. None of them stood to attention.

"What happened out there, sir?" one of the men asked. The soldier stepped forward as he spoke, but the gun pointed at his chest made him reconsider that.

"You men are here because you are all infected," Smith stated. There was a fold up chair propped against the wall to his left, and Smith grabbed it so he would have something to sit on. Suspicious eyes watched him warily.

"The good news is I have a cure for some of you." The men murmured to each other excitedly. Some looked at their fellow soldiers, others kept their attention squarely on Smith. Several of the men saw right through Smith and witnessed the malevolence that now resided in the Colonel's corrupted soul. As he looked over them, Smith reckoned at least a third of the men were too far gone to be of any use here.

"*This will certainly be interesting,*" The Voice said. Smith couldn't find anything in that statement to argue with, although there was no real excitement for him here. He just knew this had to be done. There was a very compelling argument that it was better to let these men self-select and have a chance at life than to all die horrible deaths. It would make the process of selection a whole lot easier for Smith who knew very little about these men. Why though? Why did he feel the need to cure three of these men? Was it purely about proving the effectiveness of his experiment? If so, who exactly was he proving it to?

No, it was something more than that.

"*Surely it's obvious,*" The Voice said, goading him. Smith could almost taste the answer, but every time he came close to discovering it, it flittered away out of his reach. The why would have to wait for now.

"When do we get the cure?" a soldier shouted out urgently.

"Now hold your horses, I haven't told you the bad news yet." A grin spread across Smith's face, and of the men who were standing, several took a step back. Smith wasn't sure if it was himself smiling or whether this was the alter ego forcing its will onto him. He wasn't even sure he cared anymore.

At the far end of the room, one of the soldiers lying down began to thrash. "Can someone deal with that, please. It's a tad distracting."

As with the quarantine facility where Corporal Whittaker had been held, these men had also been issued with a single knife to dispatch any of them who died. Here it was a Sergeant who had taken command of that weapon, wielding it expertly. Without any noticeable hesitation, the Sergeant made his way over to the dying man. They had all seen how the virus killed, this was nothing new to them.

"*Do you think he might be one of them?*" The Voice asked. Smith didn't answer himself. Instead, he watched the efficiency with which the group came together to destroy the dangers in the dying man's brain. Knife in at the base of the skill, slip it through the bone and move it around in a rough circular motion. Cleaner and more reliable than using a bullet.

Smith wondered how these men felt about killing one of their own. Did the guilt and the dismay rip them up inside? Or was it seen as a necessary act of self-preservation? Whatever it was, every man here knew the fate awaiting him, and Smith had every intention to play on that knowledge. With every mounting death, the psychological pressure and the symptoms within their own bodies would build. There would also be the very pressing realisation that they had all been abandoned here to their own fate. Abandoned by an army that no longer cared.

The unfairness would be a fire that Smith could feed for his own ends.

"The bad news is that I only have three doses of the cure. No where near enough for all of you. And, while I have taken it myself, I can tell you it is a far from pleasant experience to undergo. There is a very real chance that some of you here won't even survive the procedure." Smith stood up and momentarily stepped outside the room. He returned carrying the holdall.

"You should all back up a bit there," Smith ordered, using the gun to emphasise what he was saying. Those who could followed his orders. Stepping forwards, Smith emptied the contents of the holdall onto the floor: knives, wrenches and several hammers falling out. There wasn't a single person who wasn't looking at him with anger and disbelief. There was only one reason for all this.

"*Survival of the fittest,*" The Voice rejoiced.

"Only the strongest of you would survive the cure, and I really don't have time to work out who the best candidates are." Smith paused to let his words sink into the men's minds. "You will have to do that for me. Remember, I can only save three of you." With that, Smith left the room and locked the quarantine room door behind him. Best not to give those present any notions that they could somehow use their weapons against him.

He watched what happened through the door, those held captive in the room momentarily hesitant, the bonds to their fellow soldiers still strong. Smith knew how it would go, though. One of the men would eventually snap, either his nerve would break, or his desire to live would override years of training. Then there would be a mad scramble for weapons, fists and feet used until something more lethal could be acquired.

Smith wasn't wrong, but he was surprised that it was the armed Sergeant that broke first. The Sergeant had already stabbed two men before the rest of the group reacted. Chaos ensued, and The Voice made known its approval at the entertainment. For himself, Smith felt nothing. He got no pleasure watching his subordinates kill each other, nor did he feel any kind of remorse.

Numbness was all he had, which, when you thought about it, should really have been a concern for him.

Emotionally, he was rapidly dying inside.

23.08.19
Manchester, UK

Susan woke up with a humdinger of a hangover. This wasn't just a headache, the whole structure of her body seemed to be in open revolt. For a moment, a sudden fear that she had contracted Lazarus struck her, but clearly, it was an excess of booze that had brought this on. With her escalating drinking over the past few years, hangovers actually rarely visited her. She'd settled into a level of consumption that subdued the demons without bringing on full oblivion.

Last night though, she had really gone for it. For several minutes she just lay there, not even wanting to open her eyelids. The thing was, with her eyes closed, the nausea seemed to build, and she knew there was no way she was going to keep the contents of her stomach where they belonged. Dragging herself from the bed which she barely noticed was stained with her own urine, Susan staggered to the bathroom where she stayed for the next thirty minutes.

Even with her tolerance, she had borderline alcohol poisoning.

When Susan finally stopped calling Jesus on the porcelain telephone, there was only one desire holding a central place in her thoughts. More alcohol. She was suffering, and she hoped that a few shots would calm things right down, all assuming she didn't just regurgitate it all backup. Obliterating herself seemed like the only viable option to the predicament she found herself in. It was better to retreat from the reality that was pounding her in the face than stand up to the truth of the situation. Clay had asked the unthinkable of her and had threatened the unimaginable.

So determined was she to destroy what was left of her brain cells, she didn't even bother to shower despite the stench that was coming off her skin and soiled bathrobe. Stumbling now, desperation taking over, the horrors in her mind demanded quenching. That was when she realised the new problem that now faced her. There was no alcohol.

She was sure there had been bottles left on the side, Susan was certain of it. Ripping open the doors to the drinks cabinet, she frantically searched for something, anything. There was nothing, the desperation building within her. The only thing she would be able to drink was water, and while it would keep her alive, it would do nothing to help her deal with this living nightmare. Checking the same cupboards several times, even painfully checking under the bed, Susan came to the burning conclusion that there was nothing in the room that could help her with her pressing need. That was also when she found that the door to her room was locked.

Pulling on the handle, it didn't even pretend to budge. There was no movement at all, external locks engaged in three points on the door. If she had been Brian, she might have considered ramming it with her shoulders, but all that would do was bruise her flesh and add to the discomfort she was already suffering. The door felt solid, more than what you would expect from an average internal door. Although she had pulled that door closed several times, its sturdiness never really occurred to her. Susan had no way of knowing it was wood over a steel frame, so she was disappointed when the chair she wielded did nothing to break her out of her difficulty.

The chair instead broke, to Viktor's great amusement. He watched her via the hidden cameras, the surveillance room next to hers. There was a risk now that Susan would try and do something stupid, and if she did, Viktor would be forced to intervene. He didn't think she was the type to attempt suicide, though. Admittedly her constant drinking was a form of self-destruction, but it was a slow, lingering death without the act of that final definitive plunge.

Susan collapsed on the floor by the door and began to sob, the fight stripped from her. This was a stage Viktor had seen so many times, the denial of the situation finally beginning to flood out of the victim into pain and definite guilt. She would blame herself for this before the anger set in. That was the stage that Viktor needed to work her through so he could get her into the depression that Clay enjoyed so much. Clay so relished the opportunity to hear them weep.

Susan didn't know how she was going to cope with this. Even with the torment of her hangover, she could feel the pull of the addiction calling to her. That pull would become stronger until it became a torment in its own right. The physiological responses of her body would only be made worse by the ever increasing psychic need that demanded she pickle the cells of her liver and brain. She had no idea what Viktor had in store for her over the next twenty-four hours. When she reached the height of her despair several hours in, Viktor would appear and give her the liquid she so craved…but just enough to start the process all over again only for it to once again be denied.

He didn't want to break her, that was Clay's greatest enjoyment. Viktor would, however, soften her up, just how Clay liked them to be. Together, Viktor and Clay would take her to the very brink of what she thought possible to endure, and then they would take her further than she would ever think possible.

Viktor had no idea that Clay actually had a different plan in mind.

23.08.19
Leeds, UK

Part of him knew that this had to be a dream, but the burning of his skin felt real enough. How could such agony be in one's imagination? He was one of hundreds, perhaps thousands, marching relentlessly to a destination without end. It was difficult to see, the wind whipping the razor-sharp sand into his bleeding eyes. It was only his first time here, and yet it felt like he had endured this for a millennium, time seeming to have no purpose in this land that humanity could never hope to survive in. Somehow he knew that the body he rode in wasn't really his own, more like something he had just slipped into. That didn't make the experience any less real, anguish for every second of every minute in what felt like forever. Time itself might not even exist in this place.

Such torment should have stripped him of his sanity, and yet Andy knew that aspect of him would remain permanently intact. He wouldn't be allowed to escape that easily.

He also knew he would continue to survive, despite the weakness in his limbs, despite the agony that plagued every fibre of his being and the relentless damage and slaughter being performed on his flesh. That wasn't the worst of it though, the fear that seemed to constantly grow, urging him on despite the torment every step caused in his now shattered and ruined feet.

A thousand scars upon a thousand scars.

As had happened so many times, he stumbled to a knee, daggers of ice and terror lancing through his flesh there. Only this time he felt hands gently take hold of him, pulling him back up to continue with the flight afresh.

"Let me help you, brother."

The words weren't spoken, for the violence of the wind would have made any words inaudible. Instead, the voice whispered calmly in Andy's mind, and with what sight he had left, Andy saw what was most likely a man, ruined far in excess of how Andy's body now looked. Was that the fate this place had in store for him? To be turned into a charred and pitted creature, to have the facial features flayed and the cock between his legs singed away.

"I know you," Andy found himself saying, even though there was no doubt that this was a complete stranger.

"We are all known here, brother," the voice said. All around, Andy could feel the figures moving closer to them, moving as one mass as if to gain some kind of protection in numbers. Andy found himself stepping forward once again for there was nothing else for him to do.

"I can't go on," Andy pleaded.

"You must, and you can. There is no other way."

"But how, in this? How am I supposed to withstand the pain?"

"The same way you have withstood everything else in your life. One step after the other."

Even over the wind, he heard the howl from far behind. Andy did not look back, did not dare for fear of what he might see there. But the stranger looked, as he had done countless times before.

"Never stop," the stranger ordered, "no matter how hopeless it seems. This is nothing to what will happen if they catch you."

"Who?" Andy almost begged, already somehow knowing the answer.

"The horsemen," came the reply. "They have been ghosts for so long, but now I fear they will soon be upon us." Together they got back into an endless rhythm, the stranger who was known releasing Andy and drifting off to help another. Before he left, Andy felt the need to ask one more question.

"Who are you?"

"I am known by several names, but you can call me Azrael."

Andy woke to his own great surprise, the memories of the desert quickly evaporating into confusion. How was it he was still alive? His skin felt damp from the sweat that had been drawn by the dream, and perhaps from his own body's ability to fight off the virus that had been in Iain's infected blood. Lying there for a moment, Andy found it difficult to even separate the dream from the real world.

What if this was the dream? What if this was an escape from the harshness of that life?

He sat up, recalling the events of this morning, recalling the horror of having to kill what was already dead. The zombie Iain had come at him, the shotgun Andy had been armed with ending the threat posed…but not before Andy had been showered with fluid that had poured from the zombie's mouth. There was no doubt in Andy's mind that whatever infection had created Iain(Z) had been transferred to his own flesh. And yet he seemed fine.

"Am I alright?" He felt he had to say the words out loud, to somehow break the hold the failing light and the desert had on him. The glow of his watch told him he'd been asleep for over seven hours.

"I'm okay, I must be." The TV had told him the infection took hold within an hour of exposure to bodily fluids, even quicker if he had been bitten, but here he was well past that deadline. He had frantically showered after fighting off his zombie neighbour, but there was no illusion of safety in that action. Running water and a handful of shower gel were not enough to eradicate the most lethal plague ever to hit mankind.

Sitting up in bed, he turned to the bedside cabinet and turned the light on. Only he would have if there was any electricity. A spark of fresh panic formed then. Andy had always known that the power would fail eventually, but he hadn't considered that it would occur so soon. Perhaps it was just the bulb, the faint sliver of hope stringing him along.

Any residual tiredness was gone now, and he leapt from the safety of his mattress to turn on the room's main light via the light switch by the door. Nothing happened.

"Shit."

Normally there would have been a small pile of clothes at the end of the bed for him to step into, but those had been bagged and discarded before his emergency shower. They were easily replaced by clothes from one of the room's wardrobes. With everything that was happening, he felt it bizarre that he was bothered about losing a shirt and a pair of fucking trousers but bothered he was. He had always been a minimalist when it came to clothing, limiting the amount he held based on sheer necessity.

How was he to replace his wardrobe now should he need to discard more of his attire? Even worse, how was he to wash what he had left? Without electricity, every advantage of civilisation was gone. The fears that should not have been a concern for modern man began to flood into him. There was so much he had taken for granted, all now stripped from him. Unless…

Moving with purpose, Andy went into his ensuite bathroom and found to his relief that fresh water still came out of the tap. But it was definitely diminished, and it wouldn't be long before the pressure in the system failed completely. While it was possible that the power was just out here, he believed the failures would spread rapidly with nobody to control and maintain the flow of energy to the city. He still had the bath full in the other bathroom, as well as the plastic containers. But now the clock was ticking.

Anything he did from now on would be for nothing if he ran out of water. Water was life, and with the piped supply failing, he only had about two months stored. It wasn't just his own hydration, but basic cleanliness that was threatened. Returning to his bedroom, he picked up the shotgun and ammo belt from the floor and ventured downstairs. The gun felt reassuring in his hands, an edge to survival that most in the country would not have. He was in a better position than most, and yet he still felt uniquely exposed to the world that would now be filled with a danger the majority of mankind wouldn't be able to survive. By embracing technology and civilisation, Homo Sapiens had left themselves vulnerable to the arrival of the new Dark Age.

The key to the front door was in the lock, and he turned it to allow access to the fresh air outside. The simple pleasures such as a gentle breeze would now become the only thing to keep him sane, even if it was tainted by the faint whiff of burning.

Andy had expected it to be quiet outside, but it wasn't. Something else had happened while he'd been asleep, a shift in the nature of the community around him. It took him a moment to realise that there was a new threat to face, and this time, it wasn't the undead. Someone was shouting, and the words loudly announced the new menace that had been unleashed.

Zombies weren't the only hazard people now faced.

"Ladies and gentlemen, may I have your attention?" The voice was coming from the bottom of the cul-de-sac, and Andy ventured down the steps at the front of his property, walking over to the gate at the end of the drive. As quietly as he could, Andy removed the lock. He could just see a group of seven people down the road a bit, and they all held some kind of implement as an obvious melee weapon. There was thus no mistaking their intentions. Andy doubted that any of them had noticed him, and as the sun continued to sink on the horizon, it seemed to get darker with each progressive minute. Without street lights, the cul-de-sac would get dark very quickly.

One of the group, a big burly lad, was handed a jerry can and, removing the lid, he started to walk up towards Andy, pouring the contents in the centre of the road. As he got closer, the lad noticed Andy and gave him a sneer. It was supposed to be intimidating but had no effect. Andy felt nothing but derision for what was being done here. When you have already faced your worst demons, a young punk like this was nothing to be afraid of.

Andy made sure to make the shotgun he brandished very noticeable. That stopped the guy in his tracks and, dropping the can, he scurried back to the safety of the group. Heads turned to where Andy was positioned, and he stood firm, refusing to retreat from this latest example of intimidation. The leader of the group met Andy's gaze and held it for several seconds, before carrying on with his speech.

"There are no police near here anymore. The local cop shop has been abandoned, which means you are all on your own. So here's what's going to happen." The only female in the group bent down to the ground and started playing with her lighter. Almost instantly, a wall of flame spread up the road. One in the group whooped with delight.

Gasoline. *Such a waste,* thought Andy.

"We are reasonable people, and we don't ask for much. But you have two choices. You can hide behind your doors in the hopes that we will go away." There was a strange laugh from one of the group members at that. "That might work for you," the leader continued, "or you might find someone pouring petrol through your letterbox in the dead of night. Who can say what the future holds? There are, after all, bad people about."

The girl who set the fire couldn't have been more than fifteen, and while her leader had been speaking, she wandered over to one of the neighbouring gardens and picked up a stone that just fit in the palm of her hand.

"Or," continued the leader, "you might find your windows being put through." With a nod to the girl, the rock was thrown through one of the house's downstairs windows. It wasn't something Andy was concerned about himself because he had security shutters pulled down on the ground floor. If not for having to kill zombie Iain, he would have worked on boarding up the upper floor today as well. His house was a fortress compared to the others in the close. Ironically, that might make it more of a target as the days progressed. His was likely to be the only home that wasn't about to be stripped bare.

The group though, they bothered Andy. They were the threat he knew would emerge from such an emergency, the thing he had hoped he would never have to deal with in his lifetime. It was something he was willing to face, though, just as he had faced Iain.

"So, to stop this dreadful eventuality, we will require you all to pay a tax for our...protection." On the horizon, Andy saw smoke rising into the air. Likely this wasn't the only group at work. Were they working together across this estate? The last of the daylight was minutes away from disappearing.

"We'll be back in twenty minutes," the leader stated. "Please leave your offerings outside your front door. If you want to make it through the night, you had better ensure I am impressed with your generosity. Jewellery is good, food is even better." There was an unusual level of charisma in the man speaking, the guy probably loving every second of his new found power. Likely a drug-addled loser in normal life, the apocalypse had revealed his true colours and his true potential. "And alcohol, well that goes without saying."

The leader met Andy's gaze again, only this time he wandered over, mindful of the flames that were already dying down.

"Good evening," the leader said to Andy, stopping about eight metres away. Andy reckoned he was about twenty years old, wiry but far from weak. The clothes he wore were more than he should have been able to afford, which suggested to Andy an individual not averse to breaking the law. Andy broke open the gun and put two fresh cartridges into the chambers. At this range, they would be very effective.

"Nice gun."

"Thank you. Best you move along now lad. You'll get nothing from me."
Andy wondered if any of the neighbours were listening to the conversation. Of
course they were, and not a one of them would emerge to help him.

"Now that's not very neighbourly. Don't you want us to be friends?"

"Pal, I don't even know your name."

"My friends call me GT," he said with a smirk. "You can call me Mr
Thorpe."

"I'll call you cunt and laugh while I'm doing it." The smirk disappeared
from GT's face.

"I think we'll be taking everything you have for that."

"Really?" Andy said, snapping the gun closed. "You've got a pair on you,
I'll give you that much."

"Really," GT insisted, pulling his jacket up to reveal a pistol stuck in the
belt of his jeans.

"Do you even know how to use that thing?" Andy asked.

"Oh yes. So we'll be taking the shotgun as well." GT didn't flinch when
Andy rested the barrel on the top of his gate and aimed it at GT's chest.
Surprising courage, but perhaps helped by the previous intake of illegal
substances.

"I can give you the contents of it now, as kind of a down payment." Even
with the failing light, Andy could see that GT's pupils were heavily dilated.
The guy was definitely high as fuck.

"You don't have the guts," GT blustered, but Andy finally saw the
hesitation there.

"You won't be the first person I've killed," Andy said forcefully. Looking
at the rest of GT's group who were now witnessing the altercation with wide-
eyed fascination, Andy expanded on the threat. "And I doubt you will be the
last. Think you can pull that piece before I blow a hole in you?"

"Bullshit, I doubt you've ever even shot it."

Since dealing with Iain, something had changed in Andy's head. It was as
if a gene for violence had been switched on. In his thoughts, Andy went over
the pros and cons of what he had to do here in a rapid calculation. This was the
new world, where the only order was that which you made yourself. On the one
side, he could use threats and the promise of violence to get his message across.
On the other...

"Fuck it." Andy pulled the trigger. The first round of buckshot left the
gun and hit GT straight in the abdomen, taking the man off his feet. At this
range, Andy couldn't miss, and Andy watched as his victim fell, the girl in the
group shrieking, breaking away to run to her felled hero. Andy watched her
from the corner of his eyes and fired the second shell into the fallen figure.

The old order was gone. Survival now demanded a new way of thinking
and acting.

"No!" the girl screamed, close enough to see the gruesome damage done to
GT's body. With well-practised motion, Andy broke open the gun to replace

the cartridges. He took his time, knowing the chances of anyone else having a gun to be slim.

GT lay moaning on the ground, still alive. That wouldn't last for long though. If there weren't perforated organs, there was the chance of him bleeding out. If by chance he survived that, there was then the inherent risk of infection. Even if this group of reprobates got GT to a working hospital, death was almost guaranteed. Andy slipped through the gate.

The girl didn't come any closer and keeping the shotgun trained on GT, Andy walked over to the second man he had shot in less than a day. GT tried to go for his gun, despite the pain he was in, but it didn't take much for Andy to wrestle the weapon from him.

"Mine I think," Andy said, stuffing the pistol into his own waistband. He had almost surprised himself when he had pulled the trigger, but looking around him, Andy knew it had been the right and only thing to do. The pistol would definitely be useful, assuming it was actually capable of firing. You couldn't expect a thug like this to maintain his weapon properly.

"You bastard," the girl screamed at him, and Andy pointed the shotgun at her.

"Your mates seem to be leaving you," Andy said. The girl looked behind herself to witness the truth of the other five gang members running off. With their leader down, their bravado evaporated to show the cowards they truly were. GT reached for Andy's leg, but that just invited Andy to stamp down on the hand, creating a fresh howl from GT who Andy saw was likely on the brink.

The girl looked back at Andy, down at GT, and then her resolve finally left her. She too turned and fled.

"If you come back, I'll kill you all," Andy screamed after her, somewhat fearful of the anger he heard in his own voice. Was that how quickly a man like him could become a cold-blooded killer? He felt no remorse about killing Iain, and he knew it would be the same for what he had done to GT. There would be no sleepless nights agonising over what he had done here today…which might actually be a bad thing if the nightmare persisted, as he suspected it would.

Before returning to the sanctuary of his own home, he glanced around to see the faces of his neighbours looking back at him behind their curtained windows. There was no gratitude in any of those features despite the fact Andy had likely saved them all. The only emotion he saw was fear. To fear the mob was understandable, but to fear the man who had saved you from the mob? He knew, right then and there, that none of his neighbours would survive what was coming.

They didn't deserve to.

23.08.19
Sydney, Australia

For some unknown reason, hundreds of zombies had wandered onto Bondi Beach, which gave Bruce the perfect view for his target practice. Lying on the fourth-floor roof of the apartment he lived in, Bruce lined up another head in the scope of his hunting rifle. Steadying his breathing, he slowly squeezed the trigger and watched with satisfaction as the zombie jerked. That was the twenty-seventh he had killed so far today, and he was determined to do his part to end the zombie menace.

Bruce had a thousand rounds of ammunition, and he intended to expend every one of them. After that, he wasn't entirely sure what he was going to do, but he knew it would involve alcohol and the man he had tied up on his bed. His captive was a neighbour who had been mistaken by Bruce's good historic behaviour. Bruce had always been so charming, so courteous, he had surely been the ideal person to help now that they were all trapped in this building.

Downstairs on the ground floor, a group of zombies had been trying to break into the building, so far with little success. Their presence, however, meant that anyone left in the building was trapped. Bruce would have shot them, but he just didn't have the correct angle to get at them from his present position.

His neighbour had come to him expecting a fellow survivor only to find himself the recipient of a rear naked choke from a merciless predator. Bruce's fun with his neighbour would come, but first, Bruce would kill as many of these dead fuckers as he could. His dad had introduced him to hunting whilst Bruce was still young, and it was something that had crept into his blood to become almost an obsession. There wasn't a month that didn't go by where he didn't pack up his Yute and venture into the outback.

For once, the excitement had come to his door.

The sun beat down hard on him, but his tanned beach body could weather that assault without difficulty. The cap shaded his eyes, and the six-pack of beer that was half consumed kept his body suitably hydrated. When nature called, it was no great hassle for him to piss over the side. Bruce would stay here until the light fell, and then he would go and engage in his other passion. Forced sodomy.

Chambering another round, he shot another zombie, disappointed in his aim. The bullet sliced through the zombie's neck, causing the head to tip awkwardly to the side.

"Bloody useless mate," he said, scolding himself. It shouldn't take more than a single bullet to kill one of these fuckers, and he corrected his aim and made amends for his tardiness. The zombie was a former police officer which made the prize even juicier, and it fell to the sand.

With a black sharpie, Bruce ticked off another line on the low wall that marked the edge of the roof.

"Twenty-eight," he said with a sense of satisfaction.

There was an increased noise from the ground floor, and momentarily abandoning his weapon, Bruce squirmed to the edge of the roof so he could look down. The building's main entrance was protected by a concrete veranda which protected the zombies whilst they tried their best to gain entry. More were running over now, the sounds of his shots definitely inviting more undead to the party. He hadn't realised that his shooting was what was drawing so many of them to this location.

There was the sound of something giving way, what he could see of the zombies below seeming to surge. How long before the door failed? It was sturdy, as were the reinforced windows, but it was surely only a matter of time. Even if they did penetrate through, Bruce reckoned he was safe up here on the roof. Might it be better to put off the slaughter for the fucking though?

No, Bruce needed the light to shoot. The bitch downstairs could wait. He cracked open another beer, relishing the fact this was the most fun he'd ever had in his entire life. It might be the apocalypse, but Bruce was going to be one of the few people to actually enjoy it.

At least for a time.

23.08.19
Preston, UK

After the first few minutes, the slaughter had become tedious. He'd seen enough death the last few days, he didn't need to see any more. Despite the vocal objections of The Voice, Smith had left his vigil and had ventured outside into the fresh air. The atmosphere inside the quarantine room had been tainted by death and despair which, while not distressing, had left Smith feeling jaded. Someone had tried to mask the aroma with copious amounts of bleach, but that had only made the stench worse. In the past, the cooling breeze outside would have felt refreshing to him, but today it was just something to fill his lungs with.

The simple things held no enjoyment for him now.

Smith figured half an hour would be enough for the men to self-select themselves. The hope was that he would return to find three able candidates strong enough to accept the antiserum. He really didn't want to waste a dose on someone who would die during the process. Their battle would be further complicated by the fact that anyone killed would need to be dealt with in the now traditional fashion. Killing each other was bad enough without having to fight off zombies with the meagre melee weapons Smith had left them with.

Thirty minutes was plenty of time to think, and his mind pondered how he had ended up here, The Voice now quiet. Where did The Voice go when it wasn't ranting in his head? Smith thought. Was it like tuning into a radio station, the sound always there but only noticeable when he turned his head a certain way perhaps. Smith actually experimented with that idea, turning his skull this way and that to try and illicit a random utterance. The Voice stayed strangely silent now that it had been denied witnessing the violence it craved.

The time slipped by and, looking at his watch, Smith was astonished to see that the required time had passed. From where he sat outside, no zombies were now visible, the last of them having likely drifted off in search of fresh humanity. There was plenty of that in the streets and houses around the barracks. The sense of despair of the average person must have been almost unbearable. There they were, living close to an army barracks that had at one point housed hundreds of men. Had the surrounding civilians considered themselves safer than most, only for their very defenders to be slaughtered and overwhelmed?

Everything around him was peaceful, almost serene which really didn't fit with the butchery he had just orchestrated. Would this stillness be the world once humanity had left it? An empty husk bequeathed by civilisation, slowly decaying to dust so that nature could reclaim the planet for its own. As resilient as the undead were, it was clear to Smith that the ravages of time and decay would return them all to the ground eventually. Nothing lasted forever, and when the last of them fell, the virus would fall with them.

Enough of such whimsical notions. It was time to get this show on the road.

When he returned to the quarantine room, three bloodied figures were staring at each other in a nervous standoff. They had finished methodically ending any chance of the bodies around them resurrecting, having survived Smith's Battle Royale. They all had injuries of one sort or another, which was something Smith hadn't properly considered. Hopefully, none of the victors had received life-threatening insults to their bodies because that might hamper the results of the upcoming experiment. Smith didn't think so looking at them and was surprised to see that the Sergeant with the knife was not one of the survivors. Such a man should have come through this on top, but Smith was willing to take whatever the fates gave him.

All three of those who remained were Privates, although ranks were a pointless concept now when you thought about it. Across the country, if the army weren't being defeated, it would be disintegrating, fragmenting into smaller units as those who wore the uniform realised there really was no point fighting for a country that no longer existed.

"So you are my champions," Smith stated. "Impressive. The temptation for you now will be to kill me. Just know that I am the only person who can administer the cure to you. I'm also the only one with a gun," Smith said, waving the firearm he held at them. "Finally know that if it weren't for me, you would all be dead a day from now anyway. I know you will reject the concept now, but in truth, you all owe me your lives. That is a debt I expect you all to repay with interest, but if you choose to reject my offer, you are free to stay here and rot with the bodies around you." Standing in the doorway, Smith picked up the case containing XV1 and backed up so his champions could leave the room. They all did, and, keeping a safe distance from them, Smith led the way for the three men to follow.

Smith knew he was right in what he said, but it didn't stop the utter contempt he felt oozing off the three soldiers. They could think what they liked for they would probably hate him even more after they experienced the side effects of XV1. He hoped that, with time, they would see the wisdom of why he had done things this way, but Smith suspected that much of that would be dependent on how his little experiment was going to play out.

Smith hadn't told the three everything that he had planned for them. It was important that they retained a modicum of hope as well as a good helping of ignorance. He still wasn't totally sure himself why he was even doing any of this.

The first survivor was called Dawson. He was nineteen and a bull of a man. The only fight Dawson ever remembered losing was to Lazarus, most men not even close to his equal. Dawson had no idea how he had acquired the virus, the symptoms appearing just over a day ago, passed onto him from a fellow soldier. During the fight for dominance, he had broken several bones in both his hands as he had fought those struggling to get one of the weapons left for them. Even with the damage, Dawson had continued to rain down devastating punches that few could withstand. In all, he had killed ten men, one who he had even considered a friend. It was a price he had been willing to pay for his own life, friendship an overrated concept in his mind.

Dawson was not well liked amongst the majority of his fellow soldiers. He was overbearing, prone to use his size to get his way. A bully for want of a better word, but one who knew when to toe the line and show the officers the reverence they expected. For some reason, he was also not in possession of anything resembling a sense of humour, rarely saying anything of any worth. Deep down, he was someone who would always put his own welfare above that of the men around him. Not a soldier you wanted covering your back when you were in the thick of it. He was feared and tolerated, but not trusted.

The second man was called Shah. As a Hindu, he had initially experienced a degree of bigotry from his fellow squaddies, but he had soon dealt with that with his cutting sense of humour and his ability to match anyone he met pint for pint. Right now, with the blood still dripping off the hammer he held, he felt delirious from the effects of the killing rage he had devolved into. At Smith's insistence, he dropped the hammer before leaving the confinement of the quarantine room. Such weapons weren't needed now.

If Shah was honest, for a time there, he had lost himself to a barbarity he didn't even know he was capable of. Had he displayed such against an enemy on the battlefield, it probably would have rewarded him with a medal for gallantry. Here, it gave him a chance to be a part of Smith's ongoing and somewhat depraved experiment. In his heart, there was no shame at what he had done, relief the dominant emotion felt having defied the odds. For some reason, he found himself wondering if his father would have been proud of him which depressed his spirits somewhat for he feared that the answer to that question would have been no. Shah's father had been a peaceful man, who had escaped seeing his son join the military via the heart attack that took him when Shah was only fifteen.

Cartwright was the third person to survive, although he had lost an ear in the process. Whereas the other two had relied on sheer brute force, Cartwright had retreated in the initial stages of the fight. Being at the edge of the group, he had slunk away and hid so that most of the work was done for him. Only towards the end did he re-join the battle, extracting a knife from the throat of a Corporal he hated. He made short work of those closest to him.

Like Dawson, he was of poor character and lacked any kind of morals. Why he had even joined the military was a mystery to himself and those who had schooled him, the latter glad that he was off the streets and under the thumb of an organisation that might be able to teach him the concept of respect.

Unlike Dawson he wasn't actively disliked, but nor was he a favourite with his fellow soldiers. If you had asked the Sergeant of his troop to select the man most likely to engage in criminality, Cartwright would have been picked.

His army career wasn't exactly going to plan mind. At the start of the outbreak, he had been locked in a barrack's prison cell for drugs possession. If not for Lazarus, he would likely have been tried and convicted and sent to the Glasshouse for several years. The apocalypse saved him that, every able-bodied man deemed essential for the fight that had quickly become unwinnable. It was just unfortunate for him that he contracted the virus from sharing a cigarette with a fellow soldier.

"I suppose we had better get on with this then," Smith ordered. Really, there wasn't any need to wait around.

23.08.19
Manchester, UK

Brian had been sent out on another errand. The first warehouse he had ransacked yesterday still had stuff that needed to be shipped to Clay's mansion compound. The soldiers that were guarding it were no longer there, the sandbag emplacement they left by the main gate the only real evidence that they had even been guarding it. In a way that was both good and bad. Good because Brian wouldn't have to bother with any more negotiations to get the stuff he needed for Clay. The bad was why the soldiers had left. If they weren't here, it meant that the situation in Manchester had deteriorated rapidly. The army had seized all the main stockpiles of food so that it could be controlled and distributed to the population. The challenge was that if the army now felt the food supplies weren't worth defending, then what did that say about the future of the country? More reason to get this job done so he could retreat back behind the high, thick walls of Clay's mansion.

With the engine idling, Bulldog slipped out of the passenger seat of the van and used bolt cutters on the chain holding the gate closed. The soldiers had at least locked the place up tight before abandoning their posts, the intact chain also indicating that no other crews had come to claim the contents of this particular warehouse. Brian had been surprised in that he'd expected to see more activity by the competing gangs that worked the streets of Manchester. Mind you, only the Crane Close Crew had anything close to the organisational structure that Clay's organisation possessed, and they had been slaughtered on the night of the seventeenth. The Russians and the Ukrainians might become an issue as the days progressed, but somehow, Brian didn't think so. The way it was looking, for Manchester at least, Clay was going to be the last man standing. Clay was the only one who had been given any kind of advanced warning.

Bulldog opened the gates and motioned for the three vans to pass through, another man joining him. Both men were armed with AK47's, an intimidating looking and sounding weapon. They would stand guard whilst the rest of Brian's crew loaded up whatever they could. Ideally, they needed an articulated lorry to move the stuff from the warehouse, but the roads were perilous enough without trying to navigate one of those beasts around. Vans would have to do.

On the way here, Brian had seen his first zombie. It had wandered into the deserted road they were travelling along, Brian driving the lead vehicle. At first, he had slowed, thinking it was just a pedestrian, someone perhaps who was injured and required help, something that would never be offered by Brian and his team. But then the zombie had turned face on, and Brian had seen the eyes, his foot going to the accelerator. Running at the van full-on, the zombie had been smashed by the bumper, going under the van, the wheels crushing parts of it. That was not something Brian would want to make a habit of for the van could only take so much punishment of that kind.

Someone was also going to have to clean the van down, which was a task Brian would be more than happy to delegate. Top dogs like him didn't do such menial work.

The three vans pulled up outside one of the main loading bays of the distribution warehouse. Inside would be food to keep hundreds of people going for weeks, as well as an array of other goods like toiletries and pharmaceuticals. There was also of course alcohol, which Clay was allowing his men to take for themselves so long as they controlled their intake. Word was if Clay found any man too drunk to function, he would personally make that man eat the bottle the alcohol came in, piece by shattered piece. Nobody considered that warning to be an exaggeration and so nobody had so far broken that sacred covenant. It would happen, mistakes like that always did when you were dealing with men who lived for so long on the edge of violence. They often had a tendency to let their base desires overwhelm them, self-destructing in spectacular fashion. Britain's prisons had been filled with such.

Brian stepped out of his van, issuing orders. The soldiers had locked the building up tight as well, so it took several moments for Brian's crew to force entry through the security doors. The Yale lock didn't last more than thirty seconds before it was picked, the men streaming inside. Brian watched them enter, some of them visibly excited as if they were kids at Christmas. While most of the country were fighting for their lives, those in Clay's gang had so far pretty much been a law unto themselves, escaping the hordes and the violence that had swept the nation. It had been no surprise to Brian that most of them had easily abandoned any ties they had in the outside world. Most of the men who Clay employed were dispossessed, fractured from any family they might have. Those that weren't were still men of violence who cared only for themselves. The few who had expressed their primary allegiance to loved ones hadn't been invited to hide behind Clay's walls.

Yesterday they had also raided a tobacconist, and Brian extracted one of the cigars he had acquired for himself from his top pocket. This was just the moment to indulge, and he walked away from the vans to stand in the car park where he could be alone with his thoughts. There was a lot for him to think about because his future was now on a truly uncertain path.

There was virtually no sound around him, so what better time to get that cigar lit. These little luxuries would become few and far between over the next few months, the whole industry of man shutting down, especially in this country. What was Clay's plan long term? If it was to hide out in his mansion until the virus burnt itself out, what came after? Would there be any people left? Sooner or later, alcohol and card games weren't going to be enough for these men. A lot of them were young, full of testosterone and sexual needs. Without women, those needs weren't going to be close to being fulfilled, which was a problem every army throughout history had needed to deal with.

You couldn't rape the women of your enemy in this battle, not unless you wanted your cock bitten off and eaten. And even those apparently alive and not infected could be riddled with the early stages of Lazarus. Like no time in history, just having sex could be a death sentence.

It was one of the reasons Brian had used his initiative. Before hitting this warehouse, they had stopped off at an out of town sex shop. Pornography would keep the men going for the time being, as would keeping them busy with tasks that wore them out. Eventually though, boredom and frustration would set in, and that was the true enemy of what Clay was trying to create. Being alive just wouldn't be enough for them. Brian wondered if Clay realised that? The walls of Clay's estate would hopefully keep the undead out, but most empires in history had crumbled from within.

And that all put Susan in a very dangerous predicament. How would the men under Clay's command react when they saw him enjoying the attentions of an attractive woman while they were all left with their hands? They certainly weren't the kind of men to resort to, or even accept, homosexuality. These weren't liberal-minded Guardian readers we were talking about here. Clay's men were hardened thugs, and if any of them played for the other team, they kept that knowledge a secret from the majority.

Would Clay play it smart, or would he flaunt Susan under their noses? Brian knew that Susan would choose Clay over the other choice given to her. To do otherwise would be suicidal. While part of Brian regretted bringing Susan to Clay's mansion, he had to factor in the truth that at least she was still alive. There was no way Brian would have agreed to abandon Clay to protect Susan on the outside, his annoying sense of obligation to her didn't go that far. If she had refused Clay's offer, how long before the undead had her throat ripped out? How long before another gang of feral youths took her for themselves?

As horrific as Susan's prospects were, staying at Clay's was still the best chance she had to survive as far as Brian could see. All she had to do was keep Clay happy between the sheets. Surely that wasn't so difficult. If only Brian knew exactly what that would entail. If he had known about Clay's perversions, about the dozens of shallow graves in the nearby forest and if he had been able to look inside the mind of Viktor, things might have been different.

The fate of humanity might have taken a very different path because Brian would never have allowed Susan to fall into Clay's clutches.

***

Clay sat in his living room, steadily inhaling the smoke from the joint he had just rolled. That was something he had neglected to acquire in bulk, so this would be one of the last for a while. He needed to calm down, but the loss of his fortune was playing heavily on his mind. He had nearly one hundred million pounds squirrelled away in various bank accounts and currencies across the planet, but that money was pretty much meaningless now. What could you buy when there was no-one selling anything? Even the gold and the emergency cash in his safe was now pretty much useless. He couldn't even eat it. All his power and all his influence were dying with the world outside the walls of his mansion. He hoped he could retain the loyalty of his men, but even that wasn't guaranteed.

Everything he had planned for was falling apart, and now he was in pure survival mode.

He also realised that he had possibly made a very big mistake. Two years prior, Clay had been given the opportunity to buy an island for a modest sum. It was tropical with its own natural water supply and calm, sandy beaches. Whilst it was uninhabited, it wouldn't have taken much to get construction going to build himself a retreat there. At the time, he had laughed off the idea. Reginald Clay didn't need to run and hide from his enemies, only cowards did that. If people wanted to take him down, they knew where he was, and they could come at him man on man. He would look them in the eye and strike them down like he had so many others countless times before. Even if he was arrested, he figured he was rich enough to make that go away with the necessary connections to back that up. This was not to say he was careless when it came to hiding the illegality of his business and his private life. He was anything but. In essence, his own ego had robbed him of what he needed now…true safety. The only secure place on the planet would now be somewhere people weren't.

The island had seemed like a pointless extravagance. If the law had ever come for him, there were plenty of countries where he could live well without fear of extradition, but that all assumed a safe and stable planet. Such a backup plan didn't work so well when the zombie apocalypse was upon you

The other problem with an island like that would be the crippling isolation. He liked to show off his wealth, to mingle with the elite, the film stars and the footballers. At the time, he figured sitting on an island would have left him dead inside, trapped in a false luxury while his soul was starved of the action and the recognition it craved. Isolation would have also made it difficult to feed his growing need, the sexual urgency that had been building in him steadily. It needed frequent venting, which was why he had set up a network to allow for that. That was where Viktor came in, a man with connections with Eastern European people traffickers.

Most of the woman brought over here were forced into prostitution, but with enough money, the odd unfortunate soul would find her way to Clay's mansion. Initially, they would be relieved by the wealth and the opportunity a man like Clay represented. Then the games would start as Clay revealed his true nature, exposing the evil that owned his heart. That network no longer existed so at least future women would be spared the degeneracy Clay loved to inflict.

In his early years, Clay had been married twice, neither marriages lasting more than a few years. As the months passed in each union, Clay had become more demanding sexually as the depravity in him grew and took root. There was only so much his ex-wives could take, any thoughts of going to the police quickly abandoned when it became clear just how influential, powerful and homicidal Clay actually was. This was in the days before women were truly viewed as equals, where men could still rely on frightened silence to get their way and hide their crimes.

Instead of a divorce, it perhaps would have been easier to just remove the women from existence, but that would have been messy. Both women were linked to Clay, having appeared in public with him multiple times and were even sometimes mentioned in the gossip columns. For them to simply disappear wouldn't have been an option, too many questions being asked. Besides, Clay had other plans for them. Clay liked to break people, and he had an army of lawyers to help with that, destroying any chance that either of them would win a substantial divorce settlement. Having left Clay, they had both hoped for so much, some kind of compensation for putting up with a man who was dark to his very core. Such hopes were soon quashed when private investigators presented "evidence" that proved both wives were guilty of infidelity and so much more.

Clay felt he could still almost taste the failure of their lives as one by one allegations were cast about them. Credit card fraud, shoplifting and drug abuse. By the time Clay's organisation was finished with them, Clay came across as the injured party, the devoted husband who had been betrayed by such wicked and conniving harpies. One woman was still serving time for the crimes she had been framed for. Violence was only one way to get rid of your opponents. Sometimes you just used the power of the State for your own nefarious ends.

Clay realised after this that marriage was no longer a viable option. What he really wanted to do to the female flesh he legally couldn't, so he found other ways to experiment with the demon that was growing inside him.

On an isolated island, he would not have a ready supply of gullible and vulnerable women to vent his sexual frustrations on, nor would it have been viable to ship them to him. Only within civilisation could that need be satiated, the frequency of his perversion increasing year on year as his addiction took hold. In truth, his own frailty and inadequacy had trapped him in the UK. The island hadn't been an option for him, and he had outright and foolishly rejected it.

When Lazarus struck, such an escape option would have been ideal.

Here, his safety was not guaranteed. If he'd had his own secluded part of the globe to flee to, with enough warning, he might have just been able to spirit himself away to escape what was unfolding. Now that chance was passed, and he had to make the most of what he had. Very soon the enemy would be at the walls outside. That wasn't the end of his troubles though because another enemy was lurking in his own head. Viktor had seen it, the issue with his own growing madness. The paranoia was building, and the need to hurt someone could only be held off for so long.

He took another hit of the joint, a calmness descending into his thinking. Part of him wanted to go down to Susan's room, right now, and drag her out by the hair. She would kick, she would scream, but she wouldn't stand any chance against Clay. Clay could squeeze the life out of her with one hand. He wouldn't do that though, because as much as he needed her to help suppress the growing urgency in his sexual addiction, he needed her for something else that was perhaps more pressing. He had three vials of what was supposed to be the cure to the madness out on the streets, but he had no real way of knowing if it was safe or if it worked. He would need a test subject for that.

Susan would be that test subject.

He couldn't use one of his men because the men talked and that even included Brian. If the troops under him learnt there was a cure, there was no way of knowing if that would stoke rebellion or not. He couldn't use Viktor, because Clay wasn't stupid. Viktor was his right-hand man, not someone he could afford to lose. But he was also someone who might pose a threat in the future, so no, Viktor wouldn't be getting a dose of XV1 any time soon. He could trust his make-believe butler only so far and KNEW that given the opportunity, Viktor would likely betray him. Every man had such potential in their hearts.

Clay was many things, but stupid wasn't one of them.

That just left Susan. As much as he wanted to fuck her, she was the only viable candidate to test the antiserum. Florence didn't count either because she was the person who would have to administer it and monitor the patient. Plus, Clay found her woefully unattractive. Clay couldn't risk his doctor, and might even gift her the remaining dose after Clay had been shown its safety. No, he would use Susan for his test, even using the chance of salvation as a further bargaining chip to win her initial compliance to his whims. It would all become part of the game he would play with her.

Clay enjoyed the game above all other things.

That was the way he always played it. Win them to your cause by giving them hope and a taste of the luxury they had never had… and then slowly reveal the utter beast that lived within the dark festering pit Clay called his soul. Break their hope, break their will and then break their body until their minds finally snapped. He'd never yet met a woman who could last more than a month before they had to be disposed of. Some even thanked him when he finally snuffed the life out of them. Would Susan be someone to break the record? Clay really hoped she would because there wasn't anything to replace her.

23.08.19
Peak District, UK

Three armoured personnel carriers came to a stop in the deserted country road. They rested there, their engines dying, the brutality they represented an affront to the natural beauty of the land around them. After a minute, the back door of the one in the lead opened, Jessica and Nick stepping out. Jessica felt blessed by the country air which rescued her from the stuffiness the machine had encased her in. The dead body of Brodie had been wrapped in a poncho, and it would only be a matter of time before the decay process became noticeable to the smell receptors in her nose. Fortunately, she had been spared that so far.

If Brodie wasn't buried, she would have something to say about that. The man was a hero in her eyes as he had very likely sacrificed himself to save her life.

The country road they had traversed was wide enough to take the width of the vehicles, but the surrounding hedges would make overtaking or even turning around difficult without the tracked vehicles crushing them. It was thus a good job that there was unlikely to be any traffic along here any time soon.

This was as close to the middle of nowhere as it was possible to get in England, remoteness one of the only remaining defences against the roaming and obstinate undead. These roads saw little in the way of traffic except for the occasional farm vehicle or even a traveller somehow led astray by their satellite navigation system. For now, they were safe due to the definite sparsity of zombies in the local area.

"Your brother picked his spot well," Nick said. A place like this would have been difficult to find as well as limited in availability. His arm throbbed painfully where it had been assaulted by one of Renfield's bullets, but pain was better than being dead. It was dressed, and it would heal, another hole to add to his collection of scars.

"It's even better than it looks," Jessica agreed, suddenly proud of the brother who she sometimes had subtly scoffed at for years prior. There had always been a degree of respect there though, for Tom had been successful in every business he had put his hand to. It was just a shame he chose to eschew the regular way of being, dragging himself away from the normality of the world to live in the *wilderness* as their mother called it. Nobody had really understood why Tom had decided to become a survivalist, and nobody had really been persistent enough to ask. Jessica, in particular, had always been confused by his need to cut himself off from society, to separate himself from human contact and the family that loved him dearly.

She understood the wisdom of it now. With the amazing foresight he seemed to possess, Tom was by far the wisest person she knew. He might not have specifically predicted the zombie menace, but the plans he had made had prepared for it. They had a place that was secure and free of the virus. How long it would stay like that was a question that only time would answer.

Whether this was the end of her journey, Jessica had no idea. Hopefully, she could stay here and be safe, but deep within the recesses of her mind, there was the growing worry that nowhere would be a sanctuary for her. She had seen first-hand how the zombies had overwhelmed a military position away from where the heart of the infection was supposed to have been. Zombies were forever on the move. How long would it be before one or more of them stumbled onto this enclave?

Even in her dreams, evil pursued her.

And then there was the baby growing inside. It didn't show yet, but it was a threat that would relentlessly march on her. There really was only one option that made sense, but how did she go about getting an abortion when the country's medical infrastructure was collapsing? She would need to have a chat with Beckington and Nick about her pregnancy. As it stood, she was certain that bringing another life into this world would be a disaster.

They had stopped the APC's because Jessica had recognised the entrance to the farm Tom Dunn had bought all those years ago. On their flight from Preston, she had been able to salvage the satellite phone Nick had given her, using it to call ahead and tell Tom they were coming. The mobile phone network no longer functioned for civilians, but Tom had foreseen that eventuality as well. It might have been the simple fact that out here, the average mobile phone got little to no coverage, but Tom also owned a phone that worked via the wonders and the mysteries of satellite communication.

When Jessica had told him the plan that had been developed, Tom had been relieved that Jessica was on her way to him, but at the same time had been very concerned by the news that she was bringing people with her. He had built this retreat for him and a select few, not three APC's full of unknowns.

"You're bringing strangers?" he had asked incredulously.

"Strangers to you. These are the people that saved my life more than once."

His objections dried up at that, even more so when she mentioned most of those with her were either SAS or had some kind of military training. Still, she knew how stubborn he could be and knew this wouldn't be the end of his objections. It would be interesting to see how much of a pissing contest Tom felt he would need to engage in to defend his little piece of England. Jessica reckoned she would soon find out.

There was a rustle from the left, and a section of hedge began to move. It was actually the farm gate that Tom had cleverly disguised to blend into the hedgerow. In the failing light, you likely wouldn't have seen it unless you were specifically looking for it. Even then, it would have been a chore to uncover. Jessica herself had only been able to find this location due to the GPS location her brother had given her as well as the subtle marker on the other side of the road. The array of surveillance cameras that had warned Tom of their arrival were also well concealed. As the gate moved further, the dirt track that led to the farm became obvious, as did the visage of Jessica's brother. For a time there, that had been a face she thought she might never see again.

Jessica ran over to him, and he wrapped her in his brotherly arms, the two of them hugging close. Love was in their embrace as well as pain for their shared loss. There was no chance of her passing the infection on, all the occupants of Nick's APC now no longer in their protective gear and Jessica cleared of being some kind of carrier. That was one of the first things Dr Patel had checked once it had become clear that Jessica was immune. She killed the virus in her blood as easily as a sadistic child kills a helpless ant. And once dead, the virus stayed vanquished, never to darken her lymphocytes again.

Nick didn't interrupt, choosing to let them have their reunion. Instead, he walked over to the second APC and banged on the side, safe in the knowledge that the bleach job Beckington had overseen had disinfected the exterior. Like with the first APC, the back door opened and Haggard disembarked along with two SAS soldiers. Nick didn't hear the orders given, but the two SAS ran off down the road, both laden with equipment.

They would ensure the safety of the area.

"Nice location," Haggard said. As with everyone, Haggard had removed the NBC suit he had been forced to wear anytime he went outside. There were no undead here, so the chances of catching the virus were slim. The remoter the area, the fewer chances there were that the virus had made it there. The nuclear, biological and chemical containment suits were pretty durable, but they were uncomfortable to wear. There was also the worry regarding the filters to the gas masks. They only had so many, and in their rush to leave the barracks in Preston, a good proportion of their supplies had been left behind. Fortunately for everyone concerned, the third APC was filled to overflowing with their equipment because the SAS had already been in the process of loading it up with their assorted shit when the zombies had attacked. It just wasn't enough, not when faced with the apocalypse.

As for who made it out of Preston, they had done better than Nick had first feared. With the body of his dead colleague in his arms, Nick had experienced visions of the worst. Haggard had lost five men from his troop, leaving ten to continue the fight. Altogether, there were eighteen of them, Nick counting them off in his mind. Natasha, Jeff, Jessica, Haggard, Whittaker and of course Azrael who had been asleep for most of the journey. Captain Beckington had grabbed a ride on the second APC. Hardly an army though, and far from what was needed to defeat the legions of the undead.

"Jessica," a frail voice almost wept. Nick turned to see an older woman step out from where Jessica's brother had appeared from. When Jessica took the woman in a loving embrace, it was clear who this newcomer was. Judy Dunn, Jessica's mother.

"What do you think?" Nick asked Haggard. "Hold up here for a few days?"

"My standing orders are to look after Jessica and any other immune that were found. I'll stick with that until I hear otherwise. Unless someone comes up with a miracle, it will all be about survival now." Haggard lit himself a cigarette. "Ultimately I think we need to leave the UK, get somewhere more remote." That was a plan that had merit, but before they ever thought about that, a place free of the virus would need to be uncovered. "Last I heard most of the Scottish islands had sealed themselves off. Get to the coast and grab a boat might be our best bet."

"Thanks for getting us out of there," Nick said. If it hadn't been for Haggard and his men, Nick believed they would all be dead now. The undead had come in too hard and too fast. The unpredictability of this new enemy made them difficult to combat.

"We are all in this together. We were going anyway, happy to drag the dead weight with us." Haggard winked at his friend, no insult intended in the words.

Nick pulled Haggard away from anyone who could hear them, noticing in the corner of his eye Azrael who had stepped out of the first APC. The assassin was still in handcuffs, Jeff keeping a close eye on him. Despite the man's most recent reputation, Nick felt there was something about the man that he could trust.

"When the undead attacked at the base, how did they know to hit us there?" Nick asked. There had been no warning of the attack, the bulk of the zombies the army was dealing with supposedly still concentrated around and inside the heart of Manchester.

"I don't know enough about the enemy to formulate an answer."

"Come on Mad Dog, you can do better than that. This is me you're talking to." Haggard took a long inhale as if the smoke that infused his lungs would somehow reveal the answer to him.

"If it were a conventional enemy, it would mean they had done reconnaissance and gathered intel. But everything Central Command has told us so far is that these things are just acting on impulse. They are supposed to be mindless, but in my mind, that isn't the case."

"Yeah, I think we both know that's bullshit," Nick said. "A lot of where we are at is due to us underestimating what we are up against. That felt like a coordinated attack, as if they were after a specific target."

"I noticed that as well. A lot of them seemed to come for us rather than the rest of the base's soldiers. It's why I lost so many men to these fuckers." The cigarette glowed as Haggard sucked the last of the life out of it.

Nick looked at Azrael again. Something about him was important, had been from the start of all this.

"I don't know why, but that man is the key to this."

"The killer?"

"Yes. I didn't get a chance to tell you, but I think the immune are all somehow connected."

"What, you mean they are related?"

"No," Nick said, a wariness coming into his voice. "I'll go through it with you later once we are settled. I'll warn you now though, you won't believe a word of it."

"I'm sure you can convince me," Haggard said with a wry smile. If it came from Nick's lips, Haggard was likely to believe it no matter how crazy the idea sounded. The pair of them stepped back towards the group.

***

"I know you." Azrael turned to the voice that was clearly talking to him. Judy Dunn had detached herself from her daughter and was pointing a finger accusingly at Azrael.

"Please mum, don't," Jessica begged. Judy might have been in her sixties, but she still had fight in her despite her obvious weakness.

"That's the son of a bitch who broke your heart. I recognise him from his photograph." Jessica had never introduced Azrael, then known as Kevin, to any of her family. During their relatively brief courtship, most of their time together had been taken in hotels at weekends snatched here and there. But the passion and the connection had been undeniable. It had been scary even, sweeping Jessica along in a whirlwind of emotions that were sometimes as painful as they were intoxicating.

When Kevin had disappeared, Jessica had kept it all to herself. But when she had learnt of Kevin's apparent death, Jessica had needed the healing counsel of her mother, the heartache too great to bear alone. That had involved showing Judy the photos that Jessica had taken, and which had been the only memories of something that could have been. There were a lot of photographs, Jessica never really getting round to deleting them from her cloud account. Sometimes you just didn't want to let go even when you knew you should.

"You are supposed to be dead." Judy was not one to give up on the defence of those she loved.

"Mum, it's not what you think." Judy took a step towards Azrael who just stood there apparently mystified. "Azrael, I'm sorry, she doesn't know."

"Azrael?" Judy questioned.

"I'll explain it all later, mum," Jessica begged. "Let's walk back to the house."

"No," Judy insisted. "Explain it to me now."

"You are right to be angry," Azrael said before Jessica could answer further. "The man I was...the man I was before what I am now, he was a coward and a manipulator. To many, he was better than what I have become, but in other ways, he was worse." Judy stared at the man gobsmacked by the nonsense he was spewing.

"What the hell are you talking about?"

"The man your daughter loved died. I am what was born from his ashes."

"Enough of this," Jeff suddenly said wearily, grabbing Azrael's arm. Azrael was surprised that there was little in the way of harshness in the gesture. "This man is a prisoner, he's not here to engage in philosophical chats. Come on, mate, back in the APC." Judy watched open mouthed as Azrael let himself be frogmarched out of sight, disappearing into the interior of the vehicle. Inside the APC, Jeff re-connected Azrael's restraints to the bench he was sat on.

"Thank you," Azrael said. There was relief in his voice as if the conversation with Jessica's mother had been traumatic. He didn't like remembering that he had caused Jessica such pain. Well not him, the man he had once been known as. Did it make it worse that Jessica had fallen in love with a lie, a construct of Soviet Russia's psychological science? Could Azrael even be blamed for the actions he had taken in that programmed life?

"Family mate," Jeff said, "best avoided wherever possible."

23.08.19
Preston, UK

Smith had needed to fire his gun three times just to prove that he was deadly
serious. His three subjects needed to understand that he wasn't fucking about
here. The first time was out on the parade ground where Shah had made to bend
down to pick up a discarded L85A2. Smith wasn't prepared to have his
candidates armed just yet, perhaps not ever. The second time was when
Dawson and Cartwright had got into an argument about who was going to get
the antiserum first, the pair close to coming to blows which would have been
very unfortunate for Cartwright. Short tempers, sleep deprivation and
desperation. Smith found that reassuring, an indication that he had chosen the
correct men for this experiment.

When you considered how close to death the three men obviously were,
Smith was amazed any of them had any energy left to still think about fighting.
They would need every ounce of what they had left to survive the next few
hours, and Smith had guided them towards the medical block. He supposed he
could have administered the XV1 right there in the quarantine facility, but the
scientist in him wanted to control and document the procedure. The more
people he saved with the antiserum, the more he could prove it worked.

"*What's the point of all that?*" The Voice had questioned. "*Just inject
them already.*"

"My work is still important," he had answered, trying to persuade himself
more than The Voice. The three infected men had found it a bit odd that Smith
was so eager to talk to himself, but they kept their concerns unvoiced. Smith
wouldn't have cared anyway, the experiment was everything to him now.

In the barrack's medical facility, the three men now lay strapped down to
trolleys, all together in the same room. They had objected to that at first, which
was why Smith had been forced to fire his gun a third time, almost deafening
everyone in the confined space, including himself. Smith had insisted that all
three men strip to their underwear, not out of some unrecognised perversion, but
so he could treat their injuries once they were all tied down. They each had cuts
and gashes that, while not life-threatening, could pose a risk of infection if not
dealt with. There would be little point saving them from Lazarus only for them
to then suffer gangrene or blood poisoning.

Smith had further insisted that Dawson be restrained first by the other two,
eliminating the threat of the strongest amongst them. Shah was next, and then
Cartwright was instructed to strap his legs and one arm to the bed using the
restraint cuffs. Smith had applied the final binding, holding Cartwright's wrist
tight to prevent any funny business. Then he had left the room to the men's
great distress. Had they been tricked? Was this all some mad game? Their
shouts had followed him out of the room, but they had been ignored.

They needn't have worried, Smith just needing to fetch his laptop and the
cameras to record this momentous occasion. He set up two cameras in total as
well as connecting the men up to heart and blood pressure monitors. His
attempts to contact anyone in the outside world to share in the experiment were

for nought, however. He could not get through to anyone at the Atlanta CDC, nor any of the other people who had been involved with observing the previous experiments. Even his own research facility, Porton Down, stayed mysteriously silent to his attempts at contact.

The screen of his laptop was split into four for the video conference call programmed into the computer, three of the panels just useless snow. The three broken channels were Porton Down, the Atlanta CDC and Glasgow University. The live channel was labelled USAMRIID, but nobody there seemed to be answering his Skype call. All he saw was an empty office interior. As far as he could tell, the internet connection was still functioning, so the problem wasn't on his end. Had things really got that bad out there? Unfortunate as this setback was, it wouldn't stop Smith making his own record. Even if they couldn't watch it live, he was recording everything. People could watch it later, assuming there would be anybody left.

"*I still don't get it. It's not like anyone cares anymore,*" The Voice mocked.

"I care," Smith insisted. "That's reason enough." Again he said this out loud, reinforcing the opinion in his guinea pigs that Smith might not have been playing with a full deck. Even as close to death as he was, Shah, in particular, was starting to seriously think he had made a terrible mistake.

With everything prepared and the patients ready, Smith told them something further about the antiserum.

"There's something you need to know," Smith stated to the three men. "You may have noticed I've been speaking to myself."

"*Oh, do shut up,*" The Voice demanded.

"Hard to miss, sir," Shah replied.

"I have a voice in my head. It tells me to do things, but most of the time, I can resist and retain control."

"Oh Jesus," Dawson said, pulling at his bonds. Despite his muscular strength, he was unable to break himself free. "Get me the fuck out of here."

"No," Smith said. "I feel the voice is a side effect of the antiserum, but I'm not sure. After I had administered it, I was bitten by a zombie. It's possible that attack might have something to do with my condition. I'm thinking I might need to recreate that aspect of the experiment."

"*That's a good point,*" The Voice said. "*I heartily recommend this idea.*"

"I have administered XV1 to one other individual, and as far as I'm aware, he didn't experience anywhere near the side effects I suffered. So other parameters need to be evaluated and taken into account."

"Sir," Shah said, "with all due respect can you stop fucking babbling and get this over with." Smith looked at him.

"Yes, you're right. Who wants to go first?"

23.08.19
North London, UK

Sid, they had once called her Sid. There was nothing left of her in the carcass now, just the dead eyes and the yearning for human flesh that drove the Zombie ever onwards. Before, Sid(Z) had led a zombie horde to a hotel, drawn by the faint aroma of an immune human. Only the bones were left of that individual now, and even some of them the zombies had tried to consume. They had stripped the carcass clean, almost fighting to get the slightest morsel. Sid(Z) had broken several teeth trying to eat the immune victim's hand, a shard of finger bone still stuck deep into the base of its tongue.

The flesh of the immune was the tastiest they had ever encountered. For those who could still swallow the meat in their mouths, the food took away the yearning hunger…if only for an hour or two. While the viral mutation that caused this desire for the immune was rare, it was occurring in an increasing number of zombies across the planet. The virus was intent on eliminating the only thing that threatened its existence. Even a single zombie could lead its dead brothers and sisters to the door of someone capable of fighting off the virus.

The virus was adapting and evolving far in excess of what its creators could have imagined. Soon billions of them would be on the hunt for the immune who dwelled within the rapidly dwindling numbers of humanity. The immune, of course, were rare, so when they weren't present, the undead would just have to settle for plain old regular meat. There wouldn't be any complaints from creatures that didn't even have the capacity to think.

Sid(Z) didn't lead the pack now. Instead, it was pulled along in the centre of the zombie mass that filled the streets, spilling into the surrounding houses and businesses. The zombies were degrading, their bodies wracked with injuries that could never heal. The one big thing in their favour was the lack of guns held by the UK population which had mainly been disarmed by politicians who actually feared an armed populace more than they cared about the protection of the innocent. Even the police lacked sufficient firearms to make a difference which left the military as the only real enemy to the undead. This was the same military that had been routed from London, a scene that was playing out across most of the UK. There just weren't enough soldiers to battle the legions of the returned.

At its feet, Sid(Z) sensed something small moving along the ground, the zombie rat one of the hundreds that travelled with the horde. They were possibly the greater threat to mankind, their numbers growing rapidly, their size allowing them to slip past any defences thrown up by the desperate. Rats found it easier to break into the buildings that the meat cowered in, squeezing through thumb-sized holes and making their own where said holes didn't exist. One bite was all it took, no matter how small the mouth, the teeth they possessed able to gnaw through concrete and brick.

If Sid(Z) had any kind of memory, it would have been able to recall the five rats it had crushed beneath its boots, their bodies left broken and twisted miles behind. This hadn't been a deliberate act, just accidental collateral damage in the war to end all wars.

Much of the police uniform covering Sid(Z)'s torso had been ripped away, leaving it just with a soiled t-shirt to cover what had once been deemed an attractive figure. Gone were the days when Sid(Z) would need to fend off unwanted male advances, or ignore the catcalls she got from the criminal elements when she had encountered them on the streets of London. Its body was for pure slaughter now, no longer even close to existing as a sexual being.

It moved, it attacked, and it ate. There was no other reason for Sid(Z) to be. Despite its lack of consciousness, Sid(Z) was more focused in its mission than the humans it chased.

There was a subtle shift in the crowd around it, the zombies ahead moving onto a wider road. The horde had been moving aimlessly for the last few hours, going in an ever-expanding circle, adding more soldiers to the ranks while abandoning those who had become too damaged. Like with the rats, broken human carcasses lay squirming on the pavements and streets, legs and spines smashed. The individual was irrelevant, all that mattered was growing and expanding their reach and their numbers. They went where the humans were, and those that couldn't keep up were left to their own devices, acting almost like a rear-guard to defend the streets the undead had already claimed.

There was a push behind Sid(Z), the crowd suddenly surging forward. Sid(Z) almost fell, which would have likely been the end of it. Behind it were thousands of bodies, all of whom wouldn't have hesitated to crush any fallen zombie beneath an array of boots, shoes and bare feet. With the undead, it truly was survival of the fittest. And yet there was no individuality. They worked together, but only on a primitive level that served the greater good of the group.

Their prey should have run...but where was there to run to? No matter where man tried to hide, the legions of the damned would find them. And when that happened, it was only a matter of time for the last of humanity to fall. On occasion though their prey fought back.

The sound was alien to Sid(Z)'s rotting mind, but it sensed the danger it represented. Ahead in the road, a tank appeared. The FV4034 Challenger 2 main battle tank was perhaps one of the most formidable weapons the British had against the undead. It was impervious to even the strongest zombie, hard composite armour plating over steel that was more than a match for the pliant remnants of human anatomy. The zombies still attacked it though, it was the only thing they knew to do.

There was meat in them there tin cans, so why not try and pry it out.

The tank rode towards the mob which charged back in return. There was no self-regard in their ranks, and dozens of them quickly fell as the heavy treads of the beast crushed them under its 62-tonne mass. Any creature run over was squashed flat, smeared across the road surface, making the way slick for those lucky enough to escape the onslaught. Some were not destroyed in their entirety, the legs merely removed from torsos that flopped around on the ground helplessly.

Even worse, the bullets from the mounted L94A1 chain gun ripped into those undead that massed around the tank, tracer rounds biting into torsos and cutting off limbs. There were thousands of zombies though, more than the tank could ever hope to deal with alone. It wasn't a lone wolf however, a second tank appearing. Together, the two tanks represented an unstoppable force against a foe that, at first glance, had no apparent way to harm them. To those inside the tanks, the only danger posed by the undead would come when the tanks ran out of diesel and ammunition. Then, they would become expensive metal tombs that their crews would either die in or emerge to try one last heroic stand.

They wouldn't be running out of fuel any time soon though, and the L31 HESH high explosive round the second tank fired bit deep into the zombies' numbers, literally obliterating nearly a dozen undead. Still, the zombies attacked the first tank, climbing on board, safe from its guns and its treads. The partner tank freely fired its machine gun at those trying to scale the first beast, the sound of ricochets of no concern to the desperate soldiers trying to wipe out this particular infestation.

The tank had weaknesses, however. One of its vulnerabilities was its ability to see. From where he sat, the tank Commander and the gunner had an array of ways to view the outside world from the panoramic SAGEM VS 580-10 gyro stabilised sight to the commander's eight periscopes, giving three hundred and sixty direct vision. As the zombies climbed atop the tank's turret, all the Commander saw were the clawing faces of the undead, his vision slowly eradicated as the bullets of his counterpart caused congealed blood and decomposing guts to clings to every external surface. It wasn't long before the tank was driving blind and it was forced to halt, despite its impressive bulk. Reversing course, the tank retreated along the path it had instigated, guided over the radio by the Commander of the second tank.

Already the undead were charging at that second tank intent on wreaking the same havoc as they did with the first. Sid(Z) didn't go with them, its attention still on the initial tank. A writer might say it wanted to pluck open these metal contraptions and suck the marrow from the humans inside, whereas, in reality, all Sid(Z) wanted was to end the sorrow that clawed and scraped throughout its entire being. Not just limited to where the stomach was, now every decaying cell screamed with the need for human flesh, the zombies becoming more desperate the older they got.

The virus knew how to defend itself as it had been built to do. Even tanks were clearly no match for it. With no other real option, the two tanks began to disengage, retreating away from the zombies.

23.08.19
Manchester, UK

Already the symptoms had started. She could feel the walls collapsing in on her, the need for any kind of alcohol crawling into every fibre of her being. She had a pounding headache, one that was steadily worsening rather than getting better. This was past the symptoms of the hangover now, full alcohol withdrawal setting in. She was going to suffer, she knew she was.

Maybe she deserved it, though. Susan had no idea where that notion had come from, but there it was, floating heavily in her mind. It was partly the anxiety setting in, but also a belief that had been building ever since her daughter's body was dragged out of the canal. Susan felt she had failed as a parent, hadn't kept the wolf from kidnapping and ruining the one thing she loved above all else. As a failure, deep down, Susan believed she deserved to be punished, but not to this extent. This was too much. Zombies, Clay, having to be rescued by Brian time and again, a man who constantly reminded her of her dead husband. It wasn't just that Brian looked like him, but he was also a glaring example of how weak her husband had been. To commit suicide and abandon Susan like that just when she needed someone, anyone, to be there for her.

She hadn't been worthy of anything. She hadn't been enough to save the life of her daughter, and she hadn't been enough to keep her husband from ending it all. A failure, there was no other word for it. A failure with an addiction to drink, which was a slow way to kill herself. And now even that was being denied to her.

There was nothing in this room to occupy her mind with. All she had were her thoughts, and they were far from friendly to her. In her head, a carnival of self-deprecation had eaten up any form of self-esteem, and it continued unhindered now, her feelings descending towards the pit. The blackness of final surrender was beckoning to her, she could feel its pull. The pain wasn't worth it anymore, the need to vomit like a toothache in her gut. It was there constantly, coming in waves with no apparent relief on the horizon and with no way to cure it. Well, there was one way, but she had no access to that.

She stood from the bed on shaking feet, the warmth in the room not preventing the shivers that were rippling along almost every muscle. This was it, she was at the end, and stepping forward to the mirror above the room's dresser, she picked up an ornate ashtray and smashed the glass, sending her reflection into countless fragments. Most of the broken glass stayed in place, but a single long and lethal shard fell away as if enticing Susan to do what needed to be done.

Susan looked at the fragile, six-inch dagger, knew its edges would be razor sharp. She could do this, should have done it from the very start, her husband showing her the way. It would have saved her so much pain, but she had been too determined to cling on then. Why? Why had she chosen the slow death of imbibement? Susan didn't have the answer to that, and she plucked the mirror's lance between two trembling fingers. One last bath, one last warm, relaxing ride as the blood flowed out of the wounds that would take mere seconds to inflict. She could do this, had to do it because there was no way she could endure any longer. The drink had been the only thing keeping her alive.

The door to her room opened, and Viktor walked in.

"We cannot allow such foolishness," he said. He noticed how Susan gingerly held the glass, witnessed its length. Any minute she could charge him with it as a weapon. Most likely he would be able to disarm her, but what if she got in a lucky strike? Only four inches would protrude if she clutched it, but those four inches might break off within his body, fracturing further inside him.

"Fuck YOU," Susan suddenly screamed. He could see her building up, pent on some form of destruction. He had been forced to intervene because he had seen this before, knew that suicide was minutes away. Viktor had always told Clay that the mirrors needed to be removed from the room and the bathroom adjoining it, but Clay would have none of that.

"I like them to be able to see what they have become" was all Clay would say.

Viktor reached into the inside pocket of his jacket and pulled out a hip flask. It was half full, enough to take away the growing torment that was building within Susan. Slowly and deliberately, he unscrewed the top. He took his time, noting how she watched his actions. Viktor had taken the vodka bottles, but had left the glasses, and, wary of the woman who could turn violent at any moment, he moved over to the table where the glasses were. The Scotch poured out like liquid heaven, Susan's eyes brightening with what she was witnessing. The glass shard dropped from her fingers, her mind almost going into spasm at the relief that was being offered to her.

She still knew she needed to end it all, but did that have to be done now?

Viktor stepped back. He really should have replaced the glass mirrors with something that didn't break, but it wouldn't make any difference. If someone wanted to kill themselves, there was always a way. What was needed was vigilance, and it was fortunate that Viktor had been looking at the surveillance monitor at the time Susan broke the glass. So there it was, the proof that this woman had to be taken at a slower pace. She had just displayed her willingness to spoil the game, he had seen it in her eyes. That was an important piece of the puzzle that was this woman's mind.

"Your ration," Viktor said, indicating the glass. "Please, do not break things." Stepping back, he watched with fascination as Susan rushed over to the glass. Now she was disarmed, he had nothing to fear from her, and stepping past her, he stooped to pick up the weapon she had dropped. Carefully he placed it in his pocket. As for the broken mirror, he detached it from the wall and took it with him when he left, mindful to keep the pieces from falling. Briefly, he stood in the door, watching with mild amusement as Susan sipped at the beverage, perhaps in the hope of making it last.

"I will bring you more later," Viktor said, "if you promise to behave."

"I promise," Susan said. He wasn't sure he believed her, but he would keep a vigilant watch on her. He had almost messed this one up which wouldn't have done him many favours with Clay. Now wasn't the time for Viktor to make any foolish mistakes.

23.08.19
Frederick, USA

Reece woke up groggy, with a headache that would fell a mule. The air around her was bright, too bright in fact, the whole of the ceiling above her one large fluorescent light. She suddenly had the thought that she was some sort of lab experiment under intense scrutiny. The visible surveillance camera just added to that fear.

She would soon learn just how correct that assessment was.

It took a moment for her eyes to get accustomed to the brilliance and it was with alarm that she discovered she was no longer dressed in army fatigues. Instead, she was adorned in what looked like white surgical scrubs, her feet bare, her memory unable to recall how she had even got here. What alarmed her more was the further discovery that she wasn't wearing any undergarments. Reece had no recollection of undressing voluntarily, which meant whatever Carson had obviously drugged her with had allowed someone to strip her of her clothes and her dignity.

Despite the sparsity of her attire, she felt surprisingly warm, and even though the clothing was clinical in nature, it didn't prevent the feeling of violation to grow in her heart. How did she know it was even women who had undressed her? If it wasn't, Reece hoped the bastards had enjoyed the view.

With care, she sat up on the bed she was lying on, noticing the pair of white slippers resting invitingly by where she rested her feet. The bed wasn't particularly comfortable, just a very basic cot that would just about be superior to lying on the floor. To her right was a metal sink and a metal toilet without a lid. There was also a single and uncomfortable looking metal chair. Other than that, her cell (because that was what it was) was empty. The thought to use that chair as a battering ram briefly came into her mind, but she dispelled it quickly. Whoever had put her here wouldn't have left the chair if it had any chance of helping her escape.

In all, the cell she was in measured less than nine square metres. Not exactly luxury accommodation, but just enough to swing a cat if she had been in possession of one.

The other thing that was instantly apparent was that she didn't have any privacy. The floor was tiled, the roof a lit suspended ceiling. Surveillance cameras were in large abundance, one in each of the rooms she could see. There was worse, for all but one of the walls encasing her were transparent. Reece ran her hand over the cold surface of the wall her bed was pushed against. Not glass, so likely some sort of shatterproof Perspex. It also felt too solid, almost like concrete. The walls allowed her to see the other cells that were laid out in two rows separated by a central corridor that had a door at either end of it. From what she could tell, there were twenty cells in all.

It was clear to Reece that she was a prisoner.

In one wall of her containment was a door, and Reece painfully stood so she could examine it. The door itself was made from the same transparent material as the walls, and she thumped it with the meat of her hand. Solid, the seal between the door and the wall clearly airtight, a thin seam of rubber separating the two. The three metal hinges looked out of place, but they told Reece that the door opened inwards. There was even a hatch that she suspected was how she would be fed and Reece found that by pressing on it, the hatch opened towards her. The room contained the basics for her ongoing existence.

What the hell was this? She had never agreed to such confinement.

Reece also wasn't alone. Two of the other cells were occupied, both of her fellow prisoners seemingly sleeping. A woman and a young girl, the latter curled up facing Reece's cell. Seriously? They were willing to hold children here? The kid couldn't have been more than ten years old, and through the long blonde hair, Reece saw a surgical dressing on the side of the child's head.

The child was in the cell next to hers, the woman directly across the corridor. On closer inspection, she noticed the woman's cell had what Reece assumed was an identification marker on the outside.

JW32WDC

Similar markings were visible on Reece's cell, and reading the characters backwards, she got CR28HT. Through the fog of her mind, she was able to deduce what the code meant. CR was Clarisse Reece. 28 was clearly her age and HT? It took her a moment to decipher that one…Houston Texas.

So the person across the way was thirty-two, had the initials JW and likely came from Washington DC. As for the little girl, her initials were EB, aged ten and from LAC, so probably Los Angeles, California. Where the hell were the kid's parents?

One of the doors on the corridor opened. Nobody entered at first, the door just sitting open, almost taunting Reece. *"Wouldn't you like to go through here?"* the door was saying. *"If only you could get out of that reinforced, bulletproof box you are in. Such a shame."*

"Hey!" Reece demanded, banging the palms of her hands onto Perspex. For the first time, she noticed the Venflon that Doctor Lee had placed was still stuck in the vein on the back of her hand. *Where was Lee now* Reece suddenly thought? Hopefully, the doctor had been treated better than the patient.

A person appeared, dressed in an army uniform. Whoever he was, he was clearly complicit in her abduction and enforced incarceration. But then soldiers always were.

"Goddamnit, let me out," Reece persisted. Could the soldier even hear her though? The newcomer ignored her calls. Instead he proceeded to wheel a gurney in with a large, seemingly unconscious man strapped down to it. A second soldier appeared, and together they moved the gurney to the cell across the corridor closest to the door they had entered. Although there was no obvious locking mechanism on the cell doors, the first newcomer waved an access card across part of it, activating an invisible mechanism.

Sci-fi incarceration. Your tax dollars at work.

The door unlocked, opening to allow the gurney to be pushed through into the cell. Reece watched as they unstrapped their patient, placing him on the cot that was clearly too small for him. If Reece had to guess, her fellow prisoner was at least six foot five. It also looked like he could do someone some serious damage if he put his mind to it, his upper body a mass of muscle.

With the man deposited, the soldiers took their gurney and left, the cell door they had opened closing behind them automatically. Reece shouted one last time, but as before she was completely ignored by both soldiers. They wouldn't even acknowledge her presence. Bastards. That would be a word she would use a lot in her mind over the coming days.

Turning back towards her cot, Reece noticed for the first time that the little girl was looking at her. The child had nervous eyes as if she had been witness to the full betrayal that life could unleash upon someone. Hell, perhaps that was exactly what had happened. Why else would she be here?

"Hey," Reece said.

"Hello," the girl said, still lying down. Her voice was muffled by the wall, but Reece could hear her well enough. Reece grabbed the chair and placed it down by the wall so she could effectively sit next to the girl. Reece expected the child to flinch, but she didn't, instead sitting up with her legs crossed. The child looked painfully innocent though, as if she would break into tears at any moment. The young shouldn't be treated to such indignity.

"What's your name, honey?" Reece enquired.

"Elizabeth, but everyone calls me Lizzy." There was a sweetness to the child that was almost painful to witness.

"I'm Clarice." Reece sat down, distressed that a child was in this predicament. How was this even legal? Likely it wasn't, which meant the government no longer cared about individual rights. Were they really willing to tear up the Constitution just to try and defeat Lazarus? Who was she trying to kid, that was exactly what was happening here.

"I saw them bring you in," Lizzy said absently. "You slept a looong time."

"I must have been very tired. How long have you been here?" Reece asked, almost instantly regretting the stupidity of the question. There was no way to tell the passage of time here.

"Too long," Lizzy said sadly. "I was the first one here. I was scared because I don't like to be alone." Lizzy looked down at her hands, the fingers fidgeting with each other. "I'm not alone now, but I'm still scared."

"Have they said anything to you?" Reece asked, the child just looking at her blankly. Reece had always felt awkward around kids, she couldn't explain why. A grown adult she could run rings round when it came to small talk, but kids were different. Out on the streets, it was always Rodriguez who talked to the children they encountered. He was great at it, but then he'd had ample experience being a father. She wanted to ask Lizzy about her injury but felt that now wasn't the time to approach the matter.

Reece had been adamant that she had never wanted children of her own, the very idea just totally alien, even abhorrent to her. It was as if that part of her genetic makeup was absent from birth. She couldn't remember once ever getting broody when confronted by a small gurgling baby, and would often go out of her way to avoid being handed the little bags of poop and wind. And now here she was incarcerated right next to a child with nothing to occupy her time but conversation. Peachy.

A thumb snuck its way into Lizzy's mouth, and she uncrossed her legs so she could hug her knees into her chest. Perhaps Lizzy detected Reece's reticence, but there was more to it than that. Reece had been a cop long enough to spot someone who had clearly been traumatised, and her anger grew at the injustice of it. Reece might not have been fond of kids, but she hated to see them suffering.

"Well at least you're not alone now," Reece promised, trying to smile. It was then that Reece saw that Lizzy also had a Venflon in the back of her hand. She put her palm on the glass with the hope that Lizzy would do the same, but the child ignored the gesture. So much for that attempt to bond. What had the creeps done to the poor child?

One of the doors to the chamber their cells were in opened again and Carson walked in. He was dressed presently in army fatigues, rather than the full combat NBC suit that he had used in Reece's kidnapping. That would be the word she would use now for what had been done to her by these fucks. Although she had never seen his face, Reece knew it was her abductor because of the almost arrogant way he walked and the fact there was a name tag on the breast of his uniform. He walked over to Reece's cell and stood outside, his face a blank canvas. *Maybe*, Reece thought to herself, *I should have kept my insubordination in check around this guy*.

Carson's presence caused Lizzy to cower away even more. Reece thought she heard the child whimper and it was obvious to Reece that Lizzy was in fear of the man.

"You're awake at last," Carson said, almost insultingly.

"Drugging someone against their will tends to have side effects." Reece stood up and squared up to him, not wanting to give the Marine the satisfaction he so likely craved. It was hard to comprehend that her country's military could tolerate people like this. That was the patriot in her talking though. Every army on the planet would have men like Carson because as despicable and detestable as they were, they always served a purpose.

Carson was taller and had the classic V-shaped torso. In better times, he might even have been described as handsome. But all Reece now saw was the vileness within the man's heart. The eyes were cold, just like the dead stares she had seen dozens of times from those who had fallen foul of the law. Reece knew this man was capable of almost anything, and the one thing you never showed to people like that was weakness. Many of them were cowards at heart, but Reece didn't think that applied to Carson. He was someone who would follow orders and get the job done no matter how inhumane he had to act.

"That was done for your own safety. I don't have to explain myself to you." There was no air of defensiveness in his voice.

"Yes, you do. You can't keep people locked up like this. You realise you are breaking like a thousand laws here?"

"It's not me making the decisions. I follow orders just as you will too. And as for the law, Martial Law gives me a certain flexibility."

"I'm not in the army," Reece reminded him.

"I'm a marine, not army." He seemed satisfied that he had managed to score a point against her.

"Yeah so was my father. And he would be ashamed to see you wearing that uniform."

"Your father was in the corps?" Carson sounded surprised. "Well, he should have raised you to respect authority better."

"He raised me just fine. You can hardly expect me to respect someone who goes around terrifying little girls." Carson's gaze drifted off her briefly, the piercing eyes almost trying to penetrate the now cowering Lizzy. He looked back at Reece.

"You can think what you like about me, but things will go a lot smoother for you if you keep quiet and do as you are told. You don't seem to appreciate how vital you are to combatting this virus. That makes you property of the United States government." Carson stepped just that little bit closer to the thick Perspex. "We own you."

"Is that a fact?" Reece felt it, the anger bubbling up inside. She knew she would control it though, locking it away until the time was right. Now probably wasn't the time to go off on one, but the temptation to tell Carson just what she thought of him was strong. "Then why not make me a partner in this instead of locking us all away?"

"We don't have time for shit like that."

Two more soldiers entered the corridor, the same ones who had brought in the facility's new guest moments earlier. Reece felt herself tense, but it wasn't her they were here for. They stepped up to Lizzy's cell and waited for Carson's command.

"Come on Elizabeth, the Professor wants to see you." Carson didn't have a single gram of compassion or warmth in his voice.

"NO!" Lizzy suddenly screamed. The door opened, and the two soldiers forged in. Despite her kicking and screaming, Lizzy was easy to overpower, and they dragged her out into the corridor, the child in pure hysterics now.

"Oh you bastards," Reece shouted. "Get your hands off her." One of the soldiers gave her the briefest of looks, and Reece saw a hint of distress there. But he carried on all the same, reinforcing what Reece had known all along. Normal people were capable of committing the vilest of acts.

"We aren't going to hurt her," Carson said. His face was stone.

"She's just a child," Reece begged.

"No, she's much more than that. She's the first immune we encountered. Much of what we have learnt so far started with her." Carson turned and walked away. "Don't worry Reece," he said as he left, "the Professor will have lots for you to do. I guarantee you won't be bored."

***

It was twenty minutes before Jessy woke up. Her memory was vague about what had happened after her rescue. There was the madness of the helicopter, and then the sudden sharpness in her neck when the relief of rescue was washing over her. Had someone injected her and if so, what the hell for? Her alarm transformed to muted terror as she saw the cell she was in and the confinement it represented.

"Can you hear me?" the woman in the cell opposite her asked. With effort, Jessy resisted the wave of nausea that flowed through her as she sat up, and put a hand up to tell the woman she needed a moment. Jessy had worked most of her adult life for the US government, and she never thought the country she loved would be capable of this, whatever the hell this was. Tentatively Jessy stood up and walked over to the door of her cell.

Everything looked so space-age and sterile.

The woman opposite was sat in a chair and was talking through the hatch of her door. It took Jessy several seconds to figure out how her hatch worked, and she pulled over her own chair so that she could talk without bending over. The only other person she saw here seemed to be dead to the world just as she had most likely been.

"My name's Clarice," the stranger said.

"Jessy. Do you know where we are?"

"I can have a guess. I was told I was being brought to Fort Detrick, so I'm thinking there. I can't explain all this though," Reece said, waving her hands around her.

"Fort Detrick? That's home to the Army's Infectious Disease Research Institute." Reece seemed surprised at Jessy's knowledge.

"What were you, out in the world?"

"Believe it or not, for a very brief moment, I was the White House Chief of Staff to a now dead President." Not just a dead President, but a man who deserved better than what had happened to him.

"Jesus," Reece responded, genuinely shocked. If someone in Jessy's position could end up here, then there really was little hope of anyone getting out any time soon.

"What about you?"

"I'm just a Sherriff's Deputy who was kidnapped from Houston."

"What do they want with us, do you know?"

"I'm going to take a stab and say you are immune like me." Reece saw no denial in Jessy's face, so she continued. "I think we are to be used as lab rats. Poked and prodded so the powers that be can try and cure Lazarus." Reece regretted the words, seeing how they distressed Jessy. "Sorry, that was a shitty thing to say."

"It's okay," Jessy reassured her. But it wasn't okay, not by a long shot. She'd worked her whole life to do what she could to preserve the rights of the country's citizens, and it had all been for nothing.

"I'm guessing everyone that they drag in here will be immune to the virus." The fact that there were only four though, that concerned Reece. The United States had over three hundred million people living in it. The crisis had been going on for several days now. How could there only be four people immune to this nightmare?

"I was bitten, but here I am," Jessy said in agreement. "I thought the soldiers had come to rescue me because of who I was, because of the position I held. Seems like I was right, but for the wrong reason."

"Where were you when they took you?"

"I was in the White House bunker," Jessy said sadly. "I was there when the President-elect died." She'd never even had a chance to say goodbye to the man.

"Who's in charge now?" Despite the various whispers she had heard from the soldiers and her fellow patients, the news of what was happening in the world hadn't really filtered into the confines of the Astrodome.

"The Attorney General was made President. She's probably the worst person for the job."

"That's Jacqueline Fairchild, right?" Jessy nodded. "Wasn't she the one who insisted on having all the statues in Federal buildings with naked breasts covered up?" Fairchild had caused much mirth and outrage when she had gone on a crusade against the statues in Federal buildings that were showing a little bit too much flesh. It had backfired spectacularly against her when the now President had proposed the measure, the late night talk shows getting hours of comedy material out of the woman's puritanical zeal. For almost a week, stand-up comedians only had to say her name to get a laugh. And now that religious fruit bat was in charge of it all. Jessy had no problem with religion, hell she was a lapsed Catholic herself. It was just those select individuals that took things to the extremes that were the problem.

"That's her. My boss had been onto the President before him to get her replaced, but she was a big hit with the conservative right."

"Any idea how any of this is legal?"

"It probably isn't," Jessy said. "At least not under the Constitution. But the country is in a state of emergency, which pretty much means that those in power can do what they like. If Julian..." Jessy suddenly found the words choking in her throat, remembering the man who had almost been a father to her. Reece gave her time to fight back the tears that were threatening. "If Julian was still alive, I hate to say it, but I doubt he would do things any differently."

"Julian Ryan, the Vice President?" Reece confirmed.

"Yeah. Greatest man I ever knew. He would have made a great President. And he was, but for less than a day." Jessy had lost so much in such a short space of time, it was difficult for her to process it all. The last time she had been able to talk to her parents had been a scrambled affair over a bad phone line. Were they safe now? What about the rest of her friends and family?

They were interrupted by the main door to the containment area opening yet again. A single soldier entered, the one in whose face Reece had seen a hint of regret. He had Lizzy draped over one of his shoulders. Jessy was surprised by how hostile, and animated Reece suddenly became.

"What did you do to her?" Reece was on her feet now, palms pressed hard against the cell walls. She had raised her voice enough to be heard, but she wasn't shouting. Not yet, at least.

"Relax," the soldier said, "she's fine." Reaching Lizzy's cell, the soldier opened it and deposited the child onto her cot. There was a gentleness to the action that seemed to calm Reece somewhat. Whatever part the soldier was playing in all this, Jessy didn't think he wanted to see the child harmed. That was reinforced when the soldier used his hand to carefully sweep the hair away from Lizzy's face. "She just fainted is all."

"How can you do this to a child?" Reece continued, the words more resigned than angry now. The soldier almost reluctantly stepped back from Lizzy and exited the cell, the door closing. He had an embarrassed look on his face.

"Marine, what's going on?" Jessy asked the question.

"Sorry, ma'am," the soldier answered. "I'm instructed not to give you any information." He briefly looked up at the nearest cameras to him. It wasn't just the prisoners who were being watched it seemed.

"Can I at least know your name?"

"Private Howell ma'am."

"No Marine," Jessy pressed, "your name." Howell hesitated, as if to consider if he was even allowed to tell anyone who he was.

"Richard," he said.

"Thank you, Richard. I'm Jessy, and this is Clarice."

"I know, I've been briefed as to who you are," Richard said, retreating further down the corridor. "I have to go now, ma'am."

"That's okay. I understand." Howell nodded and turned, leaving them alone with the sleeping child. Before stepping out of sight, Howell turned and said the words that needed to be said. "I'm sorry for all this. I truly am."

When Howell had left, Jessy's face darkened. Whoever was responsible for all this was somehow going to pay.

***

He hadn't signed up for this shit, but there was no denying that drastic situations needed drastic measures. Carson did not object to being seen as the bad guy. It was a small price to pay for getting the mission done, and that was something Carson would always do, or die trying.

From finishing near the top of his class at Annapolis, Carson had worked his way up the ranks through Force Recon and into a joint CIA task force hunting Taliban in Afghanistan. It was there that his total ruthlessness and uncompromising nature became recognised and he found himself co-opted to the darker side of the US intelligence services. He had no life but to serve his country, and when he was told to jump, he would always answer *how fucking high*.

No matter what the job given to him, Carson never wavered and never questioned the orders he was given. It was, therefore, a no brainer that he should be put in charge of overseeing the military aspect of what was secretly known as "Operation Redemption". For once, the military bureaucracy acted quickly and decisively, and Carson found himself in command of a facility that wasn't even supposed to exist. Above ground, he was just another Marine Major, but down here, his word was law when it came to security and operational matters. The only person with greater power was the head of the research team, Professor Schmidt, a woman with an iron will and a heart that was clearly made of the coldest and purest of ice.

Carson found he admired the way she could remove the weakness of human empathy so as to do everything in her power to defeat Lazarus. To Carson, the virus was an enemy of unquestionable danger, and there was only one way to deal with such a foe...total war with no hindrance or deterrent allowed. Yes, he did not like the prospect of civilians being detained like this, especially the kid, but this situation risked being the end of all things. If they didn't defeat Lazarus, then every one of them would be dead. Carson would have sacrificed his entire family if it meant saving the human race and successfully completing his mission for his country. He wasn't just patriotic, he was fanatical.

In fairness, his soul wasn't as stunted and cold as his persona implied. He had learnt long ago that he had to keep a distance from those who might die under his watch so as not to get chewed up inside when those inevitable deaths occurred. With time he became very adept at locking his mind away from the results of the actions he was forced to take. He didn't have to like what he was told to do, he just had to follow orders in the same way he demanded those under him adhered to his commands.

Whilst he strongly suspected that Schmidt was an all-out sociopath, Carson himself didn't have such traits. He still had the ability to feel empathy, but he could also switch that empathy off when it risked getting in the way of the mission. So, in many ways, he was worse than a sociopath, because he acted the way he did by choice, not through some genetic flaw.

The men under his command either feared him or revered him, sometimes both. He was often able to develop an almost cult-like loyalty in the men who served with him. Only men though, he had no time for women being front line soldiers, political correctness be damned. Even when he did encounter a female soldier that could stand toe to toe with the best of them, his own prejudice would always reject her.

The Generals and the intelligence agencies told him what needed doing, and he and his team would invariably get it done. From Cartel bosses to terrorist overlords, prior to Lazarus Carson was sent across the world raining ungodly hell on America's enemies. Now he was in charge of the procurement and the protection of people immune to Lazarus, perhaps his most important mission to date.

Operation Redemption was run out of the secret facility deep beneath Fort Detrick, co-opting research that was already ongoing into ways to kill the most lethal of viruses. Professor Schmidt and her team were more than honoured to be put at the vanguard in the desperate fight against the Lazarus virus. There were other teams across the world researching the hell out of it, but with the breakthroughs made by Colonel Smith, Schmidt and her team were said to be ahead of the game.

One would have thought, given the nature of the virus, that Schmidt would freely share her discoveries with the rest of the planet's nations, but that wasn't how things were being played here. If a cure for Lazarus was found, America had to own it. That had been a decision made at the highest strategic level. If they had the means to end the plague, America could then decide who was saved and who wasn't. So while Schmidt gave the pretence of sharing data with the international scientific community (a community that was dwindling as the contagion spread) much of the secrets her team discovered were never shared. Not even with the British who had been at the forefront of the research at the start of the outbreak. Britain was done anyway, the American satellite images showing most of its major cities now burning and overrun. The American intelligence agencies had known Britain would fall, and they had been proven right. That's what happens when you pare your military down to the bone through spending cuts.

The biggest perceived problem for the research was the lack of immune individuals, which had created a sense of desperation. It had been Schmidt who had asked for Jessica Dunn to be abducted by David Campbell and his men. At the time, Jessica had been the only known immune person on the planet, and it was thus deemed essential that she be on US soil. Unfortunately, that plan had backfired spectacularly. Carson and his men hadn't been ready to travel across the Atlantic to run the op, so the Americans had resorted to the next best thing.

Next best hadn't been good enough. And then they had found Lizzy, and everything changed.

Two days ago
Los Angeles, USA

Elizabeth Wood was roused from her bed by her mother who warned Lizzy that she was going to be late for school and that she had better get her act together or else she would end up walking. The school bus wasn't just going to sit outside the house and wait for her to get her teeth brushed.

"But I don't feel well, mummy," Lizzy had said, her words sniffly, as if she was full of cold.

"Oh you don't feel well, huh?" her mother said suspiciously, not feeling great herself. "Nothing to do with that math test you have today is it?" Sitting on the bed beside her, Lizzy's mother stuck a cool hand to her child's forehead and noticed the definite warmth there. "Looks like you have a fever kiddo," glad that her offspring wasn't lying to her, but also trying to suppress the concern that mothers always feel when the children they love so dearly come down with some mysterious illness. Math tests could be taken another day, the importance was always the safety and the welfare of the child.

To be honest, Lizzy's mother was glad to have a reason to keep her daughter off school. She was concerned by the news she had seen about Thailand on the TV the night before. Then there was the stuff about England on her social media feeds, as well as the news piece she had uncovered on the internet about the deaths at the CDC in Atlanta. Something didn't feel right, and she would be much happier with the apple of her eye in the same house so she could keep a close eye on Lizzy.

If she was truthful, Mrs Wood felt worse now than when she had woken up, her head pounding and a steady ache spreading through her bones. She had probably caught whatever bug Lizzy had given her, not realising that it was, in fact, the other way around. The day before last, Lizzy's mum had gone to Starbucks with her friend, Claire, who had just returned from Hong Kong with her new fiancé. Mrs Wood was desperate to know every detail of how Claire's husband to be had proposed and, holding the offered hand, had gazed in awe at the substantial rock that had been placed on her finger. That one touch was all it took for Claire to pass the virus on. Lizzy's mum then brought it home and gave it to her daughter.

And now they were both sick, but only Lizzy was fortunate enough to be immune.

As the day progressed, Lizzy didn't get any worse, Lazarus completely unable to take hold in her body. But Lizzy's mum deteriorated rapidly, her insulin controlled diabetes making her more susceptible to infection than the average person. Mrs Wood kept most of how she felt to herself as mums do, but by four in the afternoon, she finally succumbed to a disease that was spreading rapidly across a country that was waking up to the terrifying reality of what was hurtling towards them.

"Mum?" Lizzy shouted when she heard the crash from the downstairs kitchen. Worrying that maybe her mother had hurt herself, Lizzy pulled herself out of the warm confines of her bed and slipped her bunny rabbit slippers on. They were her favourite, both warm and cute at the same time, and the floor creaked ever so slightly as Lizzy made her way from her bedroom. With no response to her call of concern, Lizzy apprehensibly crept down the stairs of the suburban house she shared with no siblings and two parents. Her mother had been only able to sire the one child, complications with the birth and a subsequent hysterectomy meaning there would be no more natural births from her. One child was enough anyway, any more had been just unaffordable.

Understandably, Lizzy's mum was therefore protective of her daughter while accepting the child needed to experience the peaks and valleys of life. Lizzy had been lucky enough to avoid living in a protective bubble of her parents making and had already broken an arm and two fingers in her short life. She had also mercifully escaped any kind of bullying from her fellow school children, most likely because Lizzy was so likeable, able to get on with almost anyone.

When she entered the kitchen, Lizzy found her mum unconscious on the floor, several plates shattered from where they had been brought down by the fall. She didn't see the red clump of hair on the corner of the kitchen unit where her mother had smacked her forehead in the tumble, the impact on the floor worsening the already severe injury.

"Mummy?"

Her mother didn't move, the faint rise and fall of the chest painful to watch, the face facing upwards with closed eyes. Lizzy knelt down next to her injured mother and tried to shake her awake. All that did was to cause the head to flop uselessly from side to side slightly.

"It's okay mummy, I'll get help." Lizzy stood and dragged the phone receiver off where it hung on the wall. She had to stretch, the phone barely in reach. Her parents had deemed it unacceptable for such a young child to be given a smartphone, despite Lizzy's persistent insistence. They could envisage no occasion when Lizzy would not be near an adult who could take responsibility for her care. Even when she played outside with her friends, she never ventured far enough away to cause any kind of concern. The days when kids had free rein to wander wherever the whims took them were long over in this household.

"911, what's your emergency?" the calm voice said on the other end of the phone. Lizzy knew what to do because her teacher had told them all the procedures to follow if something bad happened. Plus, she had seen enough cop shows on TV to know that 911 was the number to ring. She loved cop shows and had cried with delight when Eddie and Jamie had got engaged in her favourite program.

"My mummy has fallen and she won't get up," Lizzy said timidly. There were no tears yet, but that was more from the shock than anything. They would come, in floods.

"Okay sweetness," the woman on the phone said. "Can you tell me where you live?" Lizzy told her. "And what's your name?"

"Elizabeth, but people call me Lizzy."

"Okay Lizzy, the ambulance is on its way. I'm going to need you to stay with your mum now, alright?"

"Okay," Lizzy said sniffling.

"Can you tell me if your mum is still breathing?"

"I think so. I need to phone daddy."

"Do you know the number?"

"No, but it's written on the phone." Lizzy read the number out. The chord on the phone stretched enough that she could kneel down by her mother again and Lizzy stroked her mother's hair, careful of the red welt along the hairline. "Mummy, please wake up," she begged the unconscious figure.

"I will have someone call your dad, Lizzy. We will tell him what has happened."

"Thank you." That was when the tears came.

The ambulance and Lizzy's father arrived within thirty seconds of each other, the ambulance first. The paramedics were waiting at the door to be let in when the father roared onto the drive, leaving his Mercedes at an awkward angle.

"Lizzy," Mr Wood shouted as he threw himself from the car, not even bothering to engage the hand brake. The two male paramedics stood aside with their gurney to let him open the door for them, and Mr Wood forged his way through the house.

"Lizzy?" he shouted again.

"Daddy," came the tired, weeping voice, guiding Lizzy's father into the kitchen where he found his daughter cradling his wife's hand. "She won't wake up. Daddy, why won't she wake up?" Mr Wood was about to try and scoop them both up when the paramedics followed him into the room and took charge of the scene. They quickly ascertained that Mrs Wood was still alive, but her pulse was thready and weak, her blood pressure dangerously low. One of the paramedics looked Lizzy in the eyes as he spoke to her.

"Lizzy, my name is Steve, we're going to take good care of your mum, alright?" Lizzy nodded, watching in horrified fascination as the two strangers attached a bizarre looking collar to her mother before transferring her to the gurney they had manoeuvred into the room with them.

"What's wrong with her?" Mr Wood said, his hands trying to calm the hair on Lizzy's head as she clung to him.

"It looks like she fell and banged her head," Steve said. "We will get her to Huntington so the doctors can take care of her." Mrs Wood, now on oxygen and a heart monitor, was lifted up on the gurney with practised efficiency. "You can follow us in."

Steve was just about to apply the restraining straps to get Lizzy's mum secure when the heart rate monitor made a sound that would haunt Lizzy forever. Instead of the steady beeping noise it had been making, it turned into a continuous shrill sound that filled the room with its madness.

"No," Mr Wood barely said.

"Daddy, what does it mean?" He didn't answer. Instead, he picked Lizzy up so she could cling to him. He positioned her so that she couldn't see what was happening, despair not cancelling out the need to protect his only child from the worst of it. A thought hit his mind then, which he was instantly ashamed of, but it persisted nonetheless.

I can't raise a kid alone.

Steve's partner had already unpacked the defibrillator and had applied its pads to the patient's chest, Steve slipping a tube down the throat to allow oxygen to be administered.

"Assessing patient, please stand by," a strange woman's voice said. Lizzy couldn't see, but it was coming from the machine Steve was now holding. She managed to turn her head to see what was happening, but her mother looked weird and frightening with her blouse undone and the strange men standing over her. She didn't want to watch any more of that, so she buried her face into her father's shoulder.

"Do not touch the patient, assessing patient rhythm, please wait. Shock advised. Charging. Stand clear. Delivering shock."

There was a strange noise as Steve began to force air into Mrs Wood's lungs, the two paramedics moving their patient now, one doing chest compressions. The strange woman's voice spoke again, a high pitched noise making Lizzy cringe again as a second shock was delivered.

"Do not touch the patient, assessing patient rhythm, please wait. Shock advised. Charging. Stand clear. Delivering shock."

Mrs Wood moved.

"She moved," Steve said, confused because the monitor on the defibrillator still said their patient's heart wasn't beating. It had been in ventricular fibrillation, but now there was little electrical activity at all. This wasn't some random movement, it seemed coordinated as one of the arms lifted off the gurney.

"Please save my mummy," Lizzy almost screamed, the words muffled by her father's jacket. She could smell him. Where normally he smelt warm and reassuring, now her father seemed weak and afraid. Mr Wood saw his wife move again, the arm reaching up towards the ceiling, and his heart filled with the desperate joy that she might be alright. That joy instantly turned to ash in his mouth when the hand began to claw, clutching Steve's partner by the throat.

"Hey, Mrs Wood," Steve shouted, "calm down." But Lizzy's mum didn't calm down. Instead, the newly resurrected zombie sat up, hand still firmly around the other paramedic's throat.

"Sixty-two forty," Steve said into his shoulder mounted microphone, "we need immediate police assistance at our location." Lizzy felt herself being lowered down to the floor despite her objections.

"Lizzy, your mother needs me," and putting Lizzy down to the ground, Mr Wood went to help restrain the woman he loved who would now never again be able to return that love. He was too late to stop the zombie punching Steve's partner in the face, the hand around the throat releasing. Lurching for Steve, the zombie actually toppled from the trolley, uncoordinated in its new form. Lizzy saw it all.

She saw the zombie leap up to her feet and rip the collar from its neck in a violent, almost self-destructive motion. It tried to take a bite out of Steve's hand, but the airway already present stopped its teeth coming together. Holding Steve's wrist in a vice-like grip that actually broke bone, the zombie ripped the plastic from its mouth and brought the clenched fingers of its victim up to the waiting teeth.

Lizzy saw her father come up behind the zombie and try and hold its arms by grabbing it in a bear hug, only for the zombie to easily cast off its would-be restrainer. She saw her father get thrown across the room with a strength that defied logic, the first paramedic who was trying to push himself off the floor, breaking her father's fall. Still trapped in the zombie's death grip, Steve once again became the focus of the creature's attention, even as he tried to escape. His desperation and disbelief at what had happened wasn't a match for the zombie's strength.

"Mummy, please stop." But the zombie didn't stop, crushing Steve's wrist now, the bone in the forearm actually snapping to protrude through the skin. At that point, Lizzy closed her eyes, desperate to try and salvage any memory of who her mother used to be before it was replaced by these horrific and terrifying images.

Stood in the middle of the kitchen, hands over her eyes, Lizzy heard the three men fail in their attempts to try and combat the zombie that was now so much stronger than them. She heard her father shout out in pain as a chunk was ripped from his neck by teeth that had been veneered by the best dentist in the whole of Pasadena. She heard Steve beg for help a second time into his radio, the sound of sirens reaching her from the street outside, getting closer, but still too far away. Then Steve was silenced as the zombie lifted him off his feet and threw him into a display cabinet that had been filled with the fine cut crystal glasses that Lizzy's parents had been gifted on their wedding day. Dazed and concussed, Steve was unable to help Lizzy's dad who was bleeding out on the kitchen floor, or his partner who had fled out the back door, blind panic making him unable to deal with the reality of what he knew he was seeing.

It was the eyes you see, they told him everything.

The sounds of the sirens were close now, almost right outside the front door which had been left open, the police car so fortunately close in its patrol of the local area. Rescue was so tantalisingly within grasp. Eyes still covered, Lizzy felt a hand brush her hair, the scent of her mother close, as if the badness hadn't actually happened. Dare she look? Dare she reveal to her young and frightened mind the devastation that had occurred in the safety of her own sweet home?

The fingers parted to allow one eye to see the world. Her mother knelt before her, only it wasn't Lizzy's mother anymore. The face was the same, but the eyes were lifeless, the teeth chewing on something that dripped blood from between the lips. Still, the hand caressed Lizzy's hair, perhaps rougher than in the past, but this was still her mother, surely? There was no sign of life in the eyes though, nothing to say this was the woman who had once held a newly born Lizzy in her arms or who had wept with joy at Lizzy's last performance in the school play.

The zombie's lips tried to move as if to say something. But no words came out, and the fingers slowly curled to grip Lizzy's long blonde hair, painful now, dragging Lizzy close, the lips peeling back to reveal teeth coated in gore. One of the teeth was broken, a tiny gateway to the oblivion that mouth promised.

"No mummy, no" Lizzy shrieked, feebly trying to break the grip, knowing for sure that this was no longer her mother. This was death, and it had come for her, and surely that could only be because Lizzy had been bad. This was the thing in the closet, the creature under the bed, the monster of every child's darkest thoughts. It had consumed and taken over her precious mum, devoured her to make this thing right out of hell itself.

Lizzy heard a shout, heard feet running over the wooden floor in the hall that led from the front door to the kitchen. Then the pain in her scalp was swallowed up by a greater agony as teeth bit sharply on her ear. Not enough to break the skin's surface, but enough to hold the flesh as it was pulled and ripped from the side of her head. The suffering took her then, all too much, heartbreak mingling with the torment no child should ever be subjected to. Just before Lizzy passed out, she heard the loud report of the pistol as the policeman shot and killed the seventeenth zombie to manifest in Los Angeles.

Every crisis had a beginning, and already, the undead were on the brink of rising up all across the city. Lazarus had spread hard, and it had spread fast across LA. The city would fall, but by the time that happened, Lizzy would be far, far away.

23.08.19
Preston, UK

All three men had reacted violently to the antiserum, the machines blaring their disapproval at the health of the men's bodies. So violent were the contractions that Dawson had even broken one of his restraints which had required Smith's swift intervention.

Smith remembered the video footage of the first reported outbreak. The recording of the hospital ward hadn't been of the greatest quality, but it had shown how the zombified Peter Dunn had been able to rip the restraints away, allowing him to attack those who had been intent on saving the man's life. That was before they truly knew the dangers of Lazarus, a time when things like rank and honour still mattered.

Smith had managed to get the flailing arm tied off, more to stop Dawson damaging the surrounding equipment than out of any concern that he would hurt himself. He didn't give a toss for any of these men's personal wellbeing. Smith's experimental subjects lay quietly now, the occasional ripple running through their muscles, the smell of vomit and shit strong in the room. That was something he wasn't going to clean up, they could do that themselves when they were eventually freed from their enforced bondage. All three men had regurgitated whatever was left in their stomachs, and Smith had needed to work quickly with the suction apparatus he had to ensure they didn't aspirate the vile brew into their lungs.

When the contortions had ceased, Smith had untied the men so that he could turn each of them over into the recovery position. That way, if they threw up again, there would be less chance of them drowning in their own spew. Smith had, of course, tied them back up again for there was still one further aspect to the experiment that needed completing. In an ideal world, he would have been provided with dozens of test subjects, each being used to eliminate a variable that might impact the effectiveness of XV1. Any ethics and morals he might once have possessed had now been burned from his mind like hapless trees in a forest fire. The men bound up before him were tools, nothing more.

"*So what happens afterwards?*" The Voice suddenly asked.

"What?"

"*Well, say you prove the XV1 works. Then what?*"

"Then I release them." To be fair, Smith realised he hadn't thought about any point past that. Something was driving him, and he still hadn't fully pinpointed his true motivation for why he was even doing all this. When the zombies had attacked the barracks causing him to flee from the scene, he thought at the time that he had been running for his life. Perhaps there was more to it than that.

"Okay you release them, but then what?"

"I don't know." It was the only answer Smith could give.

"You see why you need me around? You don't even realise what you are creating here."

"I don't need you," Smith insisted. "You are an aberration."

"What if I'm not?" insisted The Voice. *"What if all the people you cure split like we have split? How useful will your damned cure be then?"*

"Just shut up," Smith roared, suddenly frightened that his glory might be tarnished.

"Hey, I'm just saying. No need to lose your shit. Just know that I think you are doing the right thing. I have it on good authority."

"What authority?"

"You aren't ready to learn that yet. You are still too belligerent. A good night's sleep will change all that, though."

Smith stood looking at the three unconscious men. He would need to come up with a plan to keep these three onside assuming their bodies accepted the cure he had administered. The whole experiment was hampered by the lack of scientific equipment to check the three men's blood. So, for now, he would need to rely on the clinical manifestation of the disease. If the men lived, then that would be enough for the present.

Smith left the room safe in the knowledge that the IV drips and the machines would keep the patients stable while XV1 hopefully worked its magic. There was something else he needed to find. Just as had happened to Smith, he needed to expose one of the subjects to a further viral load, and he knew exactly where to look.

Outside, a light drizzle was forming, which chilled the air. Smith didn't care, barely even noticed, so focused was he on his task. He had survived Lazarus, a bit of rain wasn't going to do him any harm. Ahead on the ground, the ruined torso of Stephanie(Z) could be seen crawling across the parade ground. That would be more than adequate for what Smith needed.

"You really want to be carrying that around with you?" The Voice had a point. In the early days of his experiments, they had discovered something. Smith remembered back to the first zombies he had ever seen, victims from the initial attack in Wythenshawe Hospital. He had watched as the infected individuals had died and come back, giving Smith and the army scientists important information about how the virus killed. To his knowledge, though, nobody yet knew just how Lazarus was able to defy the laws of nature. They just knew that it did, so long as the base of the brain remained intact. That seemed to be the centre of it. They had even shoved one of the zombies through an MRI scanner, only the reptilian part of the brain showing any kind of activity.

It had been Smith who had ordered one of the original zombies be decapitated. He had expected that to kill the creature, but surprisingly the head had carried on with its animation, the jaw moving to try and get the teeth onto anything human it could chew. That was the fate that now awaited Stephanie(Z). The body was irrelevant to Smith's needs so he would leave it for the crows. All he required was the head, and he went off in search of something to achieve the task. Surely it wouldn't be too hard to find an axe or a saw in an army barracks?

23.08.19
Frederick, USA

It was the first time Reece had seen Jee outside of her hazmat suit. The doctor came in sheepishly as if she was reluctant to converse with the people she was now being forced to experiment on. Jee briefly stopped to look at the still sleeping giant before walking to the other three occupied cells. She was dreading telling Reece what she knew had to be said.

"Jee, thank God," Reece said, standing from her cot. The child was still asleep, Reece and Jessy having briefly run out of things to talk about. Small talk didn't mean much in the early stages of confinement, but it might become everything as the days progressed. Jee briefly nodded a hello to Jessy before turning all her attention to Reece. "Jessy, this is Doctor Jee Lee. She was with me at the Astrodome." Jessy didn't say hello. To her, Jee just represented another one of her captors.

"Before you ask, there is no way I can get you out of here." Reece seemed to deflate slightly. "And I'm sorry for what was done to you in the helicopter. There's no excuse for it."

"I don't blame you," Reece said genuinely. Reece could see the remorse and the resignation in Jee's face. And whilst she was free to walk about, Reece wondered if perhaps Jee was a prisoner here as well. "What do they have you doing?"

"We are discovering things about the virus that we never thought possible. I've been assigned to the team trying to find a way to make a vaccine."

"And how's that going?" Reece asked.

"It isn't really. The virus itself is hard to isolate, and it's already started mutating, changing its structure. It's like it's fighting against us every step of the way."

"Why are we being held like this, Jee?" Reece watched the doctor's eyes.

"There are certain things I'm not allowed to share with you, with any of you," Jee responded with true regret in her words. "As long as I follow the rules, I can be of some help to you."

"Help?" the woman called Jessy asked with derision, Jee turning to look at her.

"If only a little. You need to believe I'm not the enemy here."

"So you can't tell us what you will be doing to us?" Reece figured it didn't really matter, because she would find out soon enough.

"No, but you need to listen to what I'm about to say Clarice, really listen." Jee looked scared now. "The people running this want results and they aren't prepared to put up with anything that might get in the way of that. If you cooperate, if you do what they tell you to when they tell you, it will go easier on you."

"I don't like being pushed around, Jee," Reece warned. "You know that."

"I know, but there are two ways this will be done. And please, remember it's not me saying this. All of this," Jee said, looking up at the surrounding ceiling, "is abhorrent to me. But at the same time, this place is the only game in town when it comes to fighting Lazarus. As bad as it is here, it's the only chance we have as a species." Jee stepped closer to the door to Reece's cell and unlocked it. The door opened, Reece stepping back briefly. Reece had noticed there were no keys involved, so she was bewildered by how the door mechanism worked.

"Major Carson has promised that if you behave, there will be no repeat of what happened in the helicopter. He did that only to show you that he could, that he was willing to take any and all measures." Jee closed her eyes and shook her head sadly. "I know you will hate me for saying this, but if you play nice, he will make things easier for you. Resist…"

"Sounds a bit like good cop, bad cop this, Doc," Reece insisted.

"It is what it is. Which is why I'm here. They want your help with their latest experiment."

"They?" Reece reckoned she was about to meet the people really running this place. Carson was clearly just a goon, an attack dog sent on errands.

"Yes, Professor Schmidt and her team."

"This Schmidt should be here telling me this," Reece said stubbornly.

"Clarice, please," Jee begged. "That's exactly what I'm talking about. If you had seen what I've seen…" Jee couldn't get the rest of her warning out.

"Fine. What are we waiting for?" Reece was surprised by the amount of freedom she was suddenly being given, and she stepped out of her cell hesitantly, as if it was all some kind of trick. There was no real freedom, not really. Even free of her cell, with no armed guards visible, there was nowhere she could go without other people's permission.

Jee led the way to the door she herself had entered the room through, said door opening without her input. Was it some automatic mechanism, or was someone controlling things remotely? Most likely the latter, the constant eyes watching her every move. Why the hell had this place even been built?

Jee and Reece stepped into a short corridor with a substantial security door at the other end. This area was obviously designed to be some sort of airlock, and to her right, four hazmat suits hung off hooks. With Reece and her fellow patients all immune to Lazarus, there was no risk of them carrying the virus, so the suits were of little purpose. Lazarus couldn't survive in their bodies, meaning the protective clothing wasn't deemed necessary at this time. Not with this part of the research at least.

The facility Reece found herself in had obviously been built years ago, and Reece suddenly had the impression that she was miles beneath the Earth, most likely trapped here for the rest of her days. This was not the time for optimistic, happy thoughts.

Had anyone been in her cell before her, or was she the first victim to be confined there? She suddenly had an image in her mind of dozens of people forced here against their will so that some mad scientist could infect them with God only knew what.

The thick door opened, and Jee motioned for Reece to follow her. Everything remained well lit, the corridor she now stepped into white and curving around to the right so that Reece couldn't see the end of it. They walked several paces before Jee stopped beside a door without a handle.

"Clarice, you know if there were any way for me to get you out of this I would. You know that, right?" Jee was starting to sound too apologetic, as if she was somehow blaming herself for the predicament Reece found herself in.

"I think I believe that, Jee," Reece said. Reece considered herself a fairly good judge of character, and she saw nothing but honesty and regret in Jee. No, that wasn't technically true, there was sadness there as well. It was clear to Reece that Jee was torn. On the one side she was objecting to the way the immune were being treated, and on the other Jee knew that to help cure Lazarus she had to cooperate. How far would Jee go though, before saving the world no longer became her prime priority? Would her inherent sense of ethics override the need to save the planet? Or would she be swept up by the evil of this place for the supposed greater good?

The door opened almost silently. Inside, everything was blackness.

"When you go in, wait for the lights to come on and then sit in the chair in the middle of the room," Jee instructed. "You are safe in this room, despite what you might see." Jee put a hand on Reece's shoulder, the first time the two had actually touched since Reece had come here. "Clarice, don't give them a reason to hurt you." The words were choked and sent a shiver down Reece's spine. They were also clearly forbidden.

"Doctor Lee," a loud female voice said out of the ether, "please abstain from touching the test subject." Reece didn't recognise the voice, but Jee clearly did. Jee recoiled from Reece as if she was a frightened child chastised by a harsh and authoritarian maiden aunt. Jee took a further step back as if to further distance herself, leaving Reece free to step into the uncertainty the room represented.

It had surprised her how warm the floors felt on her bare feet, despite their cold, clinical appearance. It was obvious to Reece that the facility had underground heating, which meant no expense had been spared here. The lack of windows also reinforcing the notion that she was underground, likely in a place kept secret to the world. A few months back, Rodriguez, her now deceased partner, had been briefly obsessed by the government's many subterranean structures, going down one of the many conspiratorial rabbit holes he tended to venture into. Just because you were in law enforcement, didn't mean you couldn't catch the conspiracy bug. If Reece was underground, then this was clearly an example of the facilities Rodriguez had been talking about, funded by billions in money spirited away from the Pentagon's budget. Now that Reece got to experience what the US government was truly capable of, she began to think that maybe there had been secret agendas and plots within plots all along. As mad as it sounded, maybe Rodriguez had been right with his talk about 9/11 and black helicopters.

Stepping into the room further, Reece was engulfed by the darkness. There was no fear for her, even when the door behind closed, shutting off the last of her light. It took three seconds for the illumination to return, revealing she was in a small square room where the expected chair lay waiting.

"Please don't dawdle, time's a wasting," the authoritarian female voice said all around her. It was almost jovial in nature, but there was malevolence there as well.

"Go fuck yourself," Reece said loudly, but she walked forward anyway, somewhat mindful of the warnings Jee had given her. *Clarice, don't give them a reason to hurt you.*

The room with the chair was small enough that if she spread her hands to her sides, she could touch both lateral walls. Although the walls were opaque, they looked to Reece to be made of the same substance as her cell. Sitting down, she waited for what happened next, the chair hard and unforgiving against her buttocks.

Reece didn't have long to wait. The walls to her left suddenly became transparent, which surprised her, her eyes being drawn. She saw a series of four rooms, each like hers, and each occupied. The difference was that the people in the other rooms were all dressed as soldiers. They didn't look at Reece, clearly their training and their orders specific in what was expected of them. In a sense, they were prisoners just like her, only their prison was the indoctrination that stifled their minds.

There was a sliding noise and a before unseen grille opened in the wall directly ahead of her. The holes in the grille were small but enough to see that there was no light in whatever lay beyond. It was also then that she noticed the faint breeze blowing down onto the back of her neck, and Reece looked up and behind to see the vent in the ceiling that was forcing air down onto her. The fact that none of the other participants in this particular experiment were showing any concern did not allay any of the fears that were rolling around in Reece's head.

"You are safe in this room, despite what you might see."

She thought she heard something from beyond the wall in front of her, like bare feet slapping on the tiled floor. It was still a surprise however, when something slammed hard into the wall, making Reece jump. What the hell were they doing here, and why weren't they telling her anything? How had her country descended to this insanity?

The worst shock came when the wall in front of her suddenly went transparent, Reece leaping out of her chair in response to the horror she witnessed. The thing attacking the wall in front of her was a zombie, completely naked, its torso slamming into the impenetrable Perspex, shoulders now hammering on the outer surface. It would have used its hands, but as was clearly obvious, both its arms had been removed as well as its mandible. There was also a metal collar around its neck with hoops that a chain could easily be attached to. How the hell had they managed to capture and do that to a zombie?

Was it possible that the zombie in front of her wasn't so much captured as made? Surely even Carson wouldn't do that to another human being. She was right, Carson wouldn't, but he wasn't in charge of the experiments here.

"The test subject will retake her seat" the voice around her ordered. Gathering her nerve, Reece did as instructed, but not before noticing the discrete speaker in the top corner of the room.

The five small rooms were next to a much larger room that was about ten metres deep, with two doors at the far end. There was only one zombie, and for some reason, it was trying its best to get into Reece's sanctuary whilst ignoring the four soldiers. As blind as it was, the zombie seemed to be staring right at Reece, and she found she didn't want to look back at it. Instead, she searched the corners of her little room, seeking information that could somehow be useful. She didn't discover anything, although she did find herself wondering just why anyone would have built this setup. Reece didn't have the medical knowledge to know it had been originally built to check the ability of different organisms to infect via airborne spread, the layout significantly altered specifically for this experiment.

Pre-Lazarus, the things that had gone on down here were never revealed to the public or even to most of the government. Even the President was never made fully aware of the experiments in a facility that officially never even existed. Plausible deniability was always the best policy, plus there was always the risk that a newly appointed Commander in Chief might object to what were often bizarre and inhumane medical practices that breached so many international treaties as to almost be laughable.

The soldiers began to sound off one after the other, a rolling wave of words coming from them. Although the zombie briefly stopped when it heard the sounds, it was not distracted from trying to attack Reece. Any second she expected it to break through, but the wall was too sturdy.

In the brightly lit room that held the zombie, three soldiers entered through one of the doors. They were dressed in gas masks and body armour, and as they got closer, Reece saw that the armour had been modified by what looked like masses of duct tape. Would duct tape become the new currency, the ideal material to make any item of clothing bite proof?

All three carried long poles with metal loops on them. The zombie turned to the new presence, but before it could try and attack them, the first loop was expertly slipped over its head and tightened. The other two soldiers similarly used their poles, creating a triad of control over the zombie. Despite its superior strength, the zombie was easily manipulated away from the Perspex towards the door next to the one the soldiers had entered. The soldiers in the rooms like hers were once again silent.

"Please remain seated while the experiment continues," the authoritative voice ordered. Once again, the wall in front of Reece went opaque. To her left, she could still see the soldiers, and she stared at them, hoping to see a glimpse of some humanity there. All she saw was blind, unyielding obedience. She waited for what would happen next, not knowing that another zombie would shortly be released to see if it could sniff her out.

***

After fetching Reece, Jee had retreated to an observation room. There were four other people present, two of whom were in the same position she was…scientists who hadn't been told the full story before being dragged here. When Dr Perry, the head of the CDC, had informed her she was being reassigned to directly help combat Lazarus, he hadn't told her exactly what it would mean for her. Perhaps he hadn't known himself, which was a very real possibility. Standing in the observation room, Jee suddenly wondered what would have happened to her if she had point blank refused to get on that helicopter with Carson. What if she had just resigned her position in disgust? She reckoned that would have been a very big mistake on her part.

Jee had been here less than twelve hours, and she was already shocked by the ethical failings occurring at this facility. She understood that people were desperate, but the people running this research had clearly abandoned any concept of morality long ago. When it came down to it, that all meant the ultimate failing and the responsibility for the blatantly illegal practices here was down to the person in charge, Professor Schmidt.

Unlike Reece, Jee hadn't been forcibly sedated for the journey. Instead, Carson and his men had merely ignored her the whole of the way from Houston, any protest she made falling on deaf ears. The helicopter from the Astrodome had dropped them off at Ellington Airport where Reece was transferred to a stretcher. Jee's hazmat suit was decontaminated, and she was required to replace it with the standard army issue with a filtered gas mask rather than bottle supplied oxygen. She had hated the new suit instantly, not only because of the way it felt but also due to the way it more associated her with the monsters that she had all but been abducted by. That task done, a transport plane had then taken them across the country to the Frederick Municipal Airport. There, Jee hadn't even been able to catch her breath as she was bundled into a Humvee and driven at speed under armed convoy. A whirlwind tour across the country that had taken less than four hours in total.

It soon became clear that Carson was indeed more than just an attack dog. His job was to organise the collection and movement of immune individuals across the country whenever and wherever they were uncovered, three rapid reaction teams under his direct command. He was also in charge of security in the facility that, as far as Jee could determine, didn't even have a name. In a way, Carson was impressive, efficient as he was ruthless. Jee had already learnt to hate him before she even saw the true evil in his heart. The man would reveal so much more about who he was, and none of it would surprise Jee.

The urgency and the speed with which she had been collected and transported was not new to her. When you were combatting virulent and deadly organisms, speed was essential, and there had been many times in the past where she had been forced to drop anything and everything so she could travel half the way across the country. That was all part of her job as a member of the

CDC Global Rapid Response Team, and it had created difficulties in her forming any sort of meaningful relationship.

What concerned her was the way the humanity of everything was being stripped away and her own inability to protect the rights of people who were being crushed beneath the boot of desperation. She understood the importance of getting the job done, but that didn't mean one had to strip the compassion out of it. She may have been one of the best microbial researchers in the country, but she was a doctor first. Jee still believed in the Hippocratic Oath, and it was being broken in every instance here.

Fort Detrick was home to the US Army Medical Research Institute of Infectious Diseases (USAMRIID), the Pentagon's lead laboratory for medical biological defence research. With the CDC's building in Atlanta now compromised by Lazarus, it made sense that this was the place where all the research would be centralised. What Jee didn't realise was just how extensive a facility it was. The buildings on the surface only told part of the story. Much of what occurred there was hidden from prying eyes (as well as, it later turned out, Congressional oversight), all done in the fifteen subterranean floors that must have cost the government a pretty penny.

When she had arrived, Jee had found the facility on lockdown and heavily guarded. Inside the razor wire topped fences, the army had established themselves in force, multiple guard towers having been erected to allow the placement of numerous fifty calibre machine guns covering all the approaches. Jee had been surprised by how much building work was ongoing, army engineers creating a high wall inside the perimeter fence from preformed slabs of concrete. Externally, a deep trench was also being dug, the army doing what they could to secure the military installation. Some of the less essential parts of the base had even been abandoned to make the defendable perimeter as small as possible.

Jee didn't think she'd ever seen so many soldiers in one place. As her ride had slowed on the road to the main gates, Jee had been further astonished to see a row of residential properties that bordered the wire being demolished, army bulldozers levelling the land. As much as she hated to converse with Carson, she had felt compelled to ask what was going on. Surprisingly she got an answer, Carson proud of the steps that were being taken to defend the base.

"We need to create a perimeter killing field so that we can defend against future undead swarms," had been the answer that came out of Carson's mouth. "Our snipers need to be able to deal with anything before it even gets close to the perimeter." Jee had just nodded as if it all made sense to her when, in reality, all she could think was how the army was destroying people's homes. "It's also important to ensure nothing escapes." Carson had added that last bit perhaps as a warning to let Jee know she wouldn't be going anywhere any time soon.

Carson also neglected to tell her what had happened to the people who lived in those homes.

When Jee's transport finally arrived at the front gate, she was introduced to what the soldiers stationed here called *The Gauntlet*, Fort Detrick's defence against an unwanted incursion by Lazarus.

The main gate of Fort Detrick had been turned into an automotive decontamination centre. Special trays filled with disinfectant had been set up to sterilise the tyres and tracks of any vehicles that passed through, while the exterior of said vehicles was sprayed with a fine mist of the same noxious substance. You wouldn't want your windows open while passing through that.

It only got more paranoid from that point. All arrivals were directed to a decontamination centre where everyone was put through a disinfection process that resulted in the thankful removal of the NBC suit that she had been forced to wear. To minimise the risks further, the suit had been sprayed and washed down before removal, the gasmask sparing Jee from much of the smell of the noxious liquid that would have likely burned the skin on contact.

The next stage in the Gauntlet was the removal of all clothing so that her skin could be cleaned. She had technically been alone with her nakedness, only a half dozen surveillance cameras witnessing how nature had intended her to be. The chemical shower was nothing new to her, but her life would have been improved by never experiencing it.

The last weapon to stop Lazarus from entering the facility was the blood test. The scientists at USAMRIID had already perfected an efficient and quick test to check for Lazarus. A simple pinprick and the collected blood would indicate within five minutes if Lazarus was present in an unfortunate individual. The last thing anyone wanted to do was to allow the unexpected arrival of the world's deadliest pathogen into the one place that could likely provide the cure. However, it still wasn't deemed one hundred per cent effective, so a conventional blood test was also done.

The CDC had made that mistake in Atlanta. It wouldn't happen here. Despite all the precautions, no test could be effective in every instance.

Jee had passed the initial field test, waiting naked in a designated room while those nervous minutes slowly ticked by. She tried to ignore the assault to her dignity, knowing that everyone would be treated the same, even Carson. Jee certainly wasn't going to give him any form of satisfaction by showing unease. Fortunately, as he had been behind her in the queue to go through the decontamination process, it was unlikely he had been gawping at her via the watchful and ever-present cameras. Jee didn't think a man like Carson was even interested in sex. He would be too busy getting his rocks off singing the Star Spangled Banner.

From there, she was allowed to dress and was directed to sit in an isolation room whilst the standard blood test results were obtained. With a full medical research facility on site, that part didn't take long.

The gauntlet was a laborious process because one could never be too careful. What they hadn't told Jee was what happened to those who failed the blood test. The room she had waited naked in was airtight. Anyone displaying a positive result to Lazarus would have been sedated by gas and sent to a holding facility outside the base's perimeter. Once immunity to the virus was ruled out, those unlucky individuals were offered painless termination. They would then be added to the growing store of undead that was housed deep in the bowels of the facility.

Jee had survived all that, and now she was here witnessing the bizarre experiments that were being done. All under the instruction of the woman who was running the show. Professor Mia Schmidt. A certified genius and quite likely one of the most sadistic individuals Jee had ever had the misfortune to come across. You could almost see it in the professor's eyes. Carson was here also, the two seeming to complement each other's cruelty admirably.

"Explain to me again what the point of this is," Carson asked Schmidt.

"Simple really. The original experiment was to determine how the undead find their prey. With them being blind, we needed to discover just how powerful the remaining senses are. We soon established they were able to smell and hear, reacting violently to any stimuli that suggested a human presence. But with the first test subject, we found that certain zombies always went for the immune individual, depending on where we had acquired the strain of their virus." Even though she knew this, it still horrified Jee. Schmidt had deliberately infected innocent people with Lazarus. "It is my opinion that the virus is mutating to allow the undead to detect individuals who are resistant to the virus, that they can somehow smell them." Carson nodded his understanding. "This experiment reinforces that belief, which is why it is so important any immune individuals you find get transported here."

Jee didn't agree with that last part, although she kept her counsel to herself. Sticking all those who were deemed to be immune under one roof was just asking for trouble. As the old saying went, never keep all your eggs in one basket.

"We have word on two more, but like with Reece, I might need to fetch them myself," Carson advised. "I've got one team grounded in Arkansas, and another chasing a red herring in Portland. Our military is spread too thin, it's becoming more and more difficult for them to spare the men I need."

"I'm sure you will get me what I need," Schmidt said. Jee didn't know it, but there was a subtle dig at Carson there. It was the Major that had coordinated with the DIA to arrange the team that had botched the abduction of Jessica.

"And I'm sure you will avoid killing any more of the immune." The words hit Jee like a sledgehammer, and she stared at Carson, horrified at the revelation. This was the first she had heard about there being any deaths. In truth, there had been dozens of people killed down here, but only one immune individual. It made no sense to fetch zombies out of the wild when you could just create them in the safety of the laboratory. That was another reason the homes that existed on the edge of the base were no longer needed.

"We learnt from our mistake," Schmidt stated angrily. She briefly caught Jee's eyes, the professor just shrugging callously.

My God, thought Jee, *what have I gotten myself into?*

23.08.19
Preston, UK

Smith was very aware as to how he had changed. The lack of any guilt or remorse was in some ways refreshing, as if he had been freed from a curse that plagued humanity. He didn't care about the morality of what he did anymore and knew he was capable of anything needed to get the job done. The thing that did worry him was the way his mind had fractured. The Voice had been right. If XV1 did that to everyone it was injected to, then its use would be severely diminished.

There was something else driving him on with these experiments, something that he couldn't quite put his finger on. It wasn't a fear of loneliness that spurred him on, but something more visceral than that. He was sure the answer would come with time. Smith also suspected that The Voice knew all the answers to the questions nagging him. Only The Voice wasn't one for sharing what it knew. Not yet.

After striking the head from the zombie's body, Smith hadn't returned to his test subjects straight away. Instead, he had sat on the cold, hard floor of the parade ground and picked the head up with both hands. Although its eyes had been pitch black, Smith had felt mesmerised by them and had gazed into the blackness of the void they represented. There were secrets in there that needed to be discovered.

Smith had become lost in himself, even The Voice being silenced as his own mind drifted into an almost hypnotic trance. The eyes told him so many things, secrets that were mind shattering in their truth, spiralling into a never-ending pit of ultimate understanding. Yet, when he finally managed to pull his gaze off the trap he had been sucked into, Smith had no recollection of what he had been shown. He could sense that revelation he had been given, answers to questions that he didn't even know existed. But sensing wasn't the same as remembering or understanding, and a great sense of loss and betrayal washed over him.

There was no concept of time during all that, and Smith was surprised to see that hours had slipped by. What exactly was he becoming? In the back rooms of his mind, he could swear he heard The Voice chuckling.

"The answer will come, you wait and see. And when it does, it will be the end of you. That's why your mind hides it from you. It knows you can't handle what you need to see."

Returning finally to the room with the three men, Smith put the gyrating head on a metal surgical table. The decision he had to make now was which of his subjects to unleash the virus on further. The choice to him was obvious, Shah being the best candidate. He seemed the more reasonable of the three men, the one least likely to have any existing sociopathy. Shah's survival had been through sheer force of will and determination. Dawson was a thug, someone who likely enjoyed inflicting pain, who had survived partly due to his own physical bulk. Cartwright for his part was a conniving, devious individual who would likely sell his own grandmother if given half a chance.

All three men were still unconscious, so Smith was able to do his work in relative silence. The only sound was the decapitated head's incessant chewing, its hunger now driving it to mangle its own tongue. Even without a body, Stephanie(Z) still felt the burning need. It was in a room with flesh that it would never get to taste, its heightened senses sending it into a maddening frenzy, liquid pouring out of its mouth. The salivary glands were still producing their virally laden brew, and Smith wondered how long it would be until the husk of a head simply dried up.

Clearly, that would not be happening any time soon, the saliva pooling on the metal table. Smith acquired himself a sterile syringe and began to suck up the juice where it poured from the zombie's maw. The liquid was thick and viscous, almost oil-like in texture. It had a pale creaminess to it that did not represent any perceived health benefits. Just a speck of this was enough to infect someone with the virus.

With his sample selected, Smith stepped over to his chosen patient.

He wanted to recreate the conditions as best he could, so instead of injecting the concoction, Smith would apply it directly to an open wound. He didn't even need to create one, Shah already having suffered several injuries on both arms and hands. There was a particularly impressive cut on his right forearm that would adequately do the job. Stripping off the sterile dressing he had previously placed, Smith was satisfied that the wound was still weeping. Shah for his part remained unaware of what was happening to him, dead to the world as he was. At some point that injury would need stitching up, but better to see if the subject actually survived everything that was being done to him. There still wasn't enough data to prove that XV1 was successful in all cases, so there was little point battling with a needle and thread if the soldier was destined to die.

"This is a control test of the XV1 antiserum," Smith said to the cameras and the microphone he had set up. "As has been noticed with the second test subject, further exposure of the virus, post serum delivery, may have unwanted side effects. This test is to determine if the side effects are an aberration or an unfortunate result of the antiserum itself."

"*And who are you going to send these results to?*" The Voice asked. It had recently descended into a perpetually mocking tone which Smith found decidedly irritating.

"I thought I told you to keep quiet?" The words were out before Smith realised his mistake. The microphone was listening to everything, and he really didn't want evidence of his madness to cloud the research he was doing. It wouldn't be good for people watching his research to think he was talking to himself.

"*You aren't the boss of me,*" The Voice insisted. Smith did what he could to quieten the volume of the annoying guest in his mind.

"I am applying the virus harvested from the saliva of one of the zombies that attacked the barracks here," Smith said again for his electronic audience. Donning a pair of gloves, Smith picked up the syringe and drizzled the fluid into the gash in Shah's flesh. To ensure the highest chance of getting it into the bloodstream, Smith massaged the liquid into the laceration with his thumb. Shah murmured something as he did so, but other than that there was barely any reaction.

"*Your experiment is flawed because you fail to understand what is happening here,*" The Voice insisted, resurfacing from the box Smith had hoped he had shoved it down into. As much as he knew he shouldn't be conversing with his own mind like this, Smith suddenly felt compelled to defend the scientific process he was using. He resisted the urge to respond, however. Smith didn't see why he had to explain himself to himself. "*However, this approach is necessary as a lesson in your own stupidity. Will you be doing the same with the other two?*"

"That would defeat the object of the experiment. The other two are my controls."

"*What nonsense you speak. I'll come back when there is more chance of you talking sense.*" That was hardly a threat, thought Smith. With that, The Voice disappeared from Smith's mind.

With the zombie saliva delivered, Smith reapplied the sterile gauze dressing. He wasn't too worried about the risk of secondary infection, even though human bites and human saliva were nasty with the bacterial load that could be delivered. One of the things that they had managed to discover about Lazarus was that it didn't just attack human cells. It suppressed the natural floral bacteria present throughout the human body, which explained why the resurrected bodies were so slow to decompose. The zombie's saliva itself was basically as sterile as urine except for the Lazarus it carried. And if the worst happened, Smith had plenty of antibiotics on hand if need be.

Curiosity suddenly grabbed him, his damaged fingers beginning to ache as if to remind Smith about something he had forgotten. Smith stripped the glove off his hands and examined where the zombie had chewed his fingers off, the two missing digits marked by the professionally applied, if not somewhat soiled surgical dressing. Those dressings clearly needed to be replaced, and he stripped them off, anxious to see what was underneath.

The ache intensified into a brief flash of fire that rippled through his arm, Smith finding it almost intoxicating. That was something new to him, and before removing them completely, Smith squeezed the once sterile gauze back onto the stumps that had once been fingers. The pain fired off again, Smith breathing hard as the agony almost overwhelmed him. Smith had been able to endure pain in the past, but he had never enjoyed it before. That was exactly the right word to use for what he was now experiencing.

"*I wondered how long it would be for you to discover that,*" The Voice almost laughed, back again. Clearly, its threat to stay away had been a lie. The dressing fell to the floor, and Smith looked at what should have been ragged remnants of his ring and middle finger. Being a medical doctor, he knew what the wounds should look like, and this was all wrong. Although there was blood still caked over the damaged ends, there was evidence of healing far in excess of what should be possible. He had no hope that the fingers would grow back, but it was obvious that he didn't need to worry about infection. The flesh there was already knitting together.

Was this another side effect of his experiment? Clearly it was, and he had three injured men in his possession to experiment further on in that regard. Smith didn't think he would be unshackling them any time soon, but it was another reason not to stitch up the gashes many of them were sporting. Perhaps whatever he was doing to them would do the work of repair for him.

"*They aren't going to like that confinement,*" The Voice warned. "*You should release them as soon as they come round.*"

"I'm running this experiment," Smith advised. "I say when it's over." This time he did not voice the words with his mouth.

"*Okay, but don't say I didn't warn you.*"

"Colonel Smith?" For a moment, Smith was confused as to who was speaking to him. The sound seemed to come from all around him and a small tendril of fear formed in his brain. *Am I hearing more voices now?*

"Colonel Smith, can you hear me?" Smith looked around, and his fear evaporated when he saw the face on his laptop monitor. An excited woman was looking back to him from the USAMRIID feed. The backdrop was different from the empty office he remembered. Wherever the woman was, it was well lit, the whiteness of the walls screaming sterility.

"I can hear you," Smith said. The woman was not one of the people he had originally been relaying his research to. "Who are you, please?"

"My name is Professor Schmidt. I have been put in charge of combatting Lazarus here at Fort Detrick. We have been monitoring your broadcasts."

"*She looks nice,*" The Voice said. "*You just need to stick her in leather and give her a whip.*" Schmidt's gaunt face and tied back hair did give her the air of what The Voice was alluding to. She was almost a walking stereotype.

"Are you up to date with my present experiment?" Smith was animated now, the chance to share what he knew bubbling inside him. Strangely though, any pride he should have felt seemed to be absent.

"Why don't you give me the bullet points," Schmidt advised.

"I see. Yes, very well. I have administered the last of the antiserum XV1 to these three infected volunteers in the hope of ascertaining its safety."

"*Volunteers? It's not like you gave them a choice really now is it.*" Smith found it difficult to think with the laughter that suddenly erupted in his head.

"Do you have any reason to think XV1 isn't safe? We have already begun harvesting our own immune patients." Smith was surprised by the use of the word harvesting, but what better word was there? He stared at the screen for a moment, pondering just how much he should tell Schmidt. Was there any reason for him NOT to tell her everything he had so far discovered.

"Yes I do," Smith said with regret. "The first test subject showed no side effects, but he was not infected with Lazarus as I'm sure you know." Nick had failed to tell Smith about his belief that Azrael was naturally immune. "You have the data on when I injected myself, I assume?"

"Yes," came the response. "We have the video and the blood test results Dr Patel did after the antiserum had been administered. It shows that XV1 successfully eradicated the virus from your system." It occurred to Smith at that moment that he had never actually confirmed that himself. With the death of Patel and the outbreak of the undead in the North Manchester General Hospital, he had never had the chance to actually ascertain that the virus was gone from his body.

"*Behold the great scientist,*" The Voice scoffed yet again.

"When I came to, the hospital I was in was under attack from the undead, and I got bitten by a zombie. I'm still around, so it implies XV1 protects against post injection exposure as well."

"What are you not telling me, Colonel?" Schmidt's voice was demanding, the face searching for the deception that Smith was so tempted to employ.

"*I wouldn't tell her if I were you.*"

"Shut up," Smith said angrily.

"I beg your pardon?"

"Sorry Professor, I wasn't talking to you. It's part of why I'm doing these further experiments."

"So you were talking to yourself?" There was no alarm in Schmidt's voice, just brutal scientific curiosity.

"Yes. It is my belief that either the XV1 alone or in combination with further exposure to Lazarus resulted in me suffering a psychotic break." There, he said it. Would the future praise him for his brutal honesty, or reject him for his self-confessed madness?

"I see," Schmidt said sadly. "This is not good news." Schmidt had already been made aware of how desperate the new US President was for some sort of cure. It was unlikely the President would accept a healing concoction that turned people mad...unless it was limited in use to her political opponents. The other problem for Schmidt was that, so far, she had been unable to recreate Smith's experiment.

"There's more," Smith added. "For some reason, I have a limited control over the undead."

"*Maybe you should have told her that bit before you revealed you were a stark raving lunatic.*" Smith found himself agreeing with that. Maybe he should have even videoed some of his interactions with the zombies he had been able to command. Something to add to the list of future tasks.

"Do you have proof of this?" Schmidt enquired. Smith shook his head, only to realise he might actually have a way to show her.

"Give me a second," Smith said. The severed head of Stephanie(Z) was still resting on the table, and he brought it over so Schmidt could see. She didn't recoil from the horrific sight, instead moving closer to her own screen. The zombie's head lay there, chewing.

"Open your mouth wide," Smith said, the zombie head following his command. He repeated several other commands which the decaying head followed.

"Fascinating. That would make a great parlour trick," Schmidt said.

"I have just exposed one of the subjects to further viral load. I think we will know in a few hours what the situation is."

"I need to update our files with this data, so please keep this line open," Schmidt ordered. "I will have someone monitoring your experiments. Good work, Doctor." With that, the face of Schmidt disappeared from view.

"*I think she likes you*," The Voice teased. Smith didn't tell it to shut up. He had told his secret to the world, and the world, so far, hadn't rejected him. He should have felt happy, and yet that emotion too seemed to be strangely lacking. Standing there looking at the computer screen, Smith realised he kind of felt dead inside.

23.08.19
Frederick, USA

Anthony Powell or Big T as his friends called him, was no longer asleep but he hid that knowledge from whoever might have been watching. Trust was a concept he would be abandoning for the foreseeable future. With his immense size, the needle they had stuck in his neck had still worked, it's just that its effects were shortened by his impressive metabolism.

In this place, he was known as AP35BM.

Those who knew Anthony generally liked him for he was amiable, humorous and slow to anger. While not religious, he was generous, giving more than perhaps he should to charity, well aware that he earnt more than most and lived a good and prosperous life. His huge size could have been easily used to intimidate people, but he had an infectious smile and a way of making people feel at ease that quickly made people warm to him. Even though he was an African American, he hadn't experienced much in the way of racism in his life. Growing up in a well to do middle-class family helped with that, the schools he was sent to being progressive and left-leaning. The only lessons in the true evils of racism he experienced were given to him by his grandfather who went out of his way to tell a much younger Anthony about how things used to be, and in some places still were. You had to learn from the lessons history gave you.

At that age, there were still states where a black man was considered inferior to Caucasians, but Anthony had not lived in such a state. At the age of thirty-five, he thought he had life pretty good.

Whilst his parents had both been lawyers fighting for the civil rights most people now enjoyed, Anthony had not followed the example of those who raised him. At the age of fourteen, he had woken up one morning and told his parents that he wanted to be a dentist. He had no idea why he had chosen that profession, but it stuck with him, and he had worked hard to get the grades he needed to make his parents proud. Unlike most teenagers, Anthony never really went through a rebellious stage, instead any anger and pent up testosterone was used up in the gym which was something else he had taken to at a relatively young time in life. Strangely for someone of his physical potential, he never enjoyed playing sports, football, in particular, being of little interest to him. And all the while his parents had never pushed him, preferring to support the road he chose, believing that true happiness could only be achieved by finding your own way in life as well as making your own mistakes.

Well, Anthony wasn't happy now. The bastard behind his eyes was easing gradually, but inside, his normal placid nature was competing with outraged indignation at what had been done to him. It was clear to Big T that his forced incarceration was nothing to do with race, the other prisoners here all white of skin. Still, it was an assault upon his person, those liberties his parents had helped strengthen ripped to shreds right in front of his face. The constitution had been desecrated.

One of the other things that had helped him throughout his life was his innate sense of justice about what was right. He knew when to let things slide, and he knew when someone needed to take a stand. You could do that and still maintain that calm and measured exterior. That calmness hadn't worked when the soldiers had taken him though, the injection delivered before he'd had any chance to react, his size useless when faced with their training and their numbers.

Despite his immunity, Lazarus had given him a hard time, exacerbating the asthma that he had suffered for as long as he could remember. People were often shocked when a person as huge as Big T displayed such frailty, and he had been fortunate that it had been under control for most of his adult life. The medication he took and his ability to handle stress had meant it had been two years since he had experienced any kind of attack. That all changed when he visited the coffee house next to his office, picking up the virus from a barista who was only just starting to show the earliest of symptoms. Simply touching the same cup had been enough, the virus greedy to get into another host body. That one coffee shop had been the primary centre for the viral spread throughout the city of Boston.

Late on the night of the twenty-first, the asthma attack had taken him totally by surprise. He had been feeling under the weather all that day, and with the nationwide Presidential Alert that had forced him to close up his office and head home, there was a worry that his grogginess and general mild flu-like symptoms might be down to the biological attack his country was under. His wife had fussed over him, making him take it easy with subtle jibes about his man flu. She too used that to mask her own fears, of course, the symptoms from her own infection still to manifest.

When the asthma attack hit, the inhaler medication did nothing to alleviate it. Anthony's wife did the only thing that made sense, driving him to the nearest emergency room despite the curfew that had been placed across the city of Boston. With so few cars on the roads, it was inevitable that her dash of mercy had come to the attention of a patrol car that stopped her. Fortunately for Anthony and his wife, the patrol officer could see that their reasons for breaking curfew were legitimate, and he gave them an escort to ensure their safe arrival at the hospital.

Once again, Anthony Powell had experienced the opposite of the narrative that all white cops were racist.

Of the cities in the United States, Boston was only in the very early stages of the Lazarus infection, no undead having risen up there at that time. Many who ran the city even thought it might well be possible that they had escaped the virus. Anthony was thus able to be seen in the Emergency Department, his asthma so severe he had needed to be admitted. With no kids to look after, his wife stayed with him, choosing to sleep in a chair next to Anthony's hospital bed. She fell asleep with tears in her eyes and his hand in hers, so full of worry for the man who had swept her off her feet nearly ten years before.

He had not been aware that his blood had been tested for Lazarus, as demanded by the CDC for all hospital admissions. When the results came back positive, he was moved to a secure isolation room by people who were dressed like they were auditioning for a part on the latest remake of The Andromeda Strain. His sleeping body had missed all the excitement.

Nobody had expected him to last the night, and when the people guarding him advised that he was still alive, the doctors re-examined him in compliance with the CDC directive that instructed medical staff to be on the look-out for anyone that might be immune. Anthony had woken up the next day to find everything had changed. His asthma had been much better, and he was deemed Lazarus free, which should have been a cause for celebration. When he had woken up to be given the good news, it was only to find that his wife wasn't present, soldiers standing in the room with him instead. Because of his size, his left hand was also cuffed to the bed, which made no sense to him.

It was explained to him that it was to stop him from running away. Really, nobody wanted to be the one to have to try and stop him should he suddenly decide the hospital was no longer the place for him. The last he remembered was the pain in his neck. He had no knowledge of what had happened to the woman he loved, the men who took him not even showing the decency to treat him like a human being. The medical staff tending to him had been walking on eggshells, clearly in fear of something out of their apparent control. Anthony knew that apprehension hadn't been down to him, but more likely the soldiers who hid behind their respirators. When it had been deemed safe for him to travel and be discharged, the doctor in charge had protested at the order to inject whatever concoction they had given to him.

So the soldier had done it, ripping the syringe out of the doctor's hand while two more held Anthony down. He was big, but so were they.

Now he was here, in this place. If they expected him to cooperate, they could go and fuck themselves. There was something else people said about Anthony Powell, this time often behind his back. He could be a stubborn son of a bitch when he put his mind to it, and he had never backed down when justice demanded action.

23.08.19
Site R, USA

The briefcase didn't actually look like much, but with it, Jacqueline Fairchild had the power to unleash her country's nuclear arsenal. Being in Site R, she didn't really need it, but it was good to know she had the capability in case there was a need to flee what was supposed to be one of the United States' most secure military installations. Already dozens of missiles were being retasked away from their predetermined targets. If there was objection to her orders, nobody voiced such. Everyone around her seemed loyal, but she was certain there would be some snakes in the grass who would need to be uncovered before their treachery could harm her cause. Had not the Devil himself slithered into Eden to corrupt the mind of Woman? And had Woman not then shared the vileness of this deceit just to try and please a man?

She would have liked to have blamed men for all of this. The Virus, the failure to defeat it early on, the Cold War that started all this. Unfortunately, she had the report in front of her about the woman called Mother, so the male of the species wasn't totally to blame. Although saying that, Fairchild was sure men were responsible for creating a woman as dangerous as Mother, just like they were responsible for most problems in the world. So yeah, she would in fact set the responsibility for this whole mess right at the door of the weaker sex.

Site R, the Raven Rock Mountain Complex consisted of a military installation with a substantial bunker network beneath it. Above ground it hardly looked like anything, a few buildings scattered throughout heavily guarded and fenced off forest. But beneath, the complex could house hundreds, keeping them safe for years at a time.

What wasn't generally known was that a large proportion of the missing trillions that had been *lost* from the Pentagon's budget had been used to create a vast underground network across the continental United States. There were the facilities that the public generally knew about, but there were also truly secret installations that had been kept from the public eye. Complex computer algorithms purged their existence from search engines across the globe, any mention on social media causing accounts to be suspended or closed. Whenever a curious journalist uncovered evidence that such sites existed, bad things always seemed to happen. Sometimes they committed "suicide", other times they were framed for heinous crimes. It was so easy to hack into a computer and place disgusting and illegal images in hidden folders. This way, the secret sites remained secret, many of them connected by a vast array of subterranean tunnels that allowed for a clandestine maglev train network to shuttle people back and forth below the surface of the country. It was amazing what you could build when you basically had unlimited funds.

Until the crisis was over, Fairchild wouldn't need to venture to the surface for anything. She had everything she needed right here. Everyone below ground had been vetted for Lazarus, so it was considered that the virus was only a threat to those on the surface.

That was not the case as would soon become apparent.

Site R was the official emergency operations centre for the United States Military, and it was now Fairchild's new home, all the luxury and opulence she had enjoyed abandoned but not forgotten. The normal trappings of a Presidency were denied her as well, but that was okay, she never had liked the décor of the White House anyway. Too old, too stuffy, built for an era long since passed. Site R was one of the three core *officially known* bunker complexes that were designed to keep the elite safe in the case of a national emergency, part of the continuity of government plan that was developed long ago in the Cold War.

With the Cheyenne and Mount Weather facilities, it made up the backbone of America's chance to survive. Only the military, the elite and those who served the elite would be blessed with a place of safety beneath the deserts, the forests and the wheat fields of the United States.

The leaders of the land of the free didn't actually give a stuff for the population they ruled with their corrupt and duplicitous schemes.

The place was definitely designed by men for men, the lack of a woman's touch glaring in its absence. There wasn't a single scented candle in the place. While Fairchild would have liked to change that, she really didn't have the time. Since arriving here, she hadn't been left alone, a legion of generals and government officials bombarding her with demands for decisions that left her head swimming. Normally she was measured and thoughtful in her deliberations, but the speed with which things were happening was already taking its toll on her. She wouldn't admit it to herself, but she really wasn't up to the task the country required of her…but then no single person was.

Even worse, she hadn't had an opportunity to even pray since arriving here.

At present, she was sat in the core command room. It was not dissimilar to the situation room in the White House, a room with a central conference table that could house over a dozen people. She was alone now except for one other person, her new Head of the Joint Chiefs. Fairchild liked him from the start because it was clear that General Franklin, *Old Fire and Brimstone* himself, did not believe in fucking about. He was a man of action, a man nearly obsessed with getting things done. This was no pen-pushing bureaucrat, this was a veteran who had seen action and had the scars to prove it. A man who believed in the use of decisive and overwhelming force.

They both sat looking at a large TV monitor that Franklin was controlling with a remote. He was showing his new President troop movements and deployments. More important were the computer predictions on the rapid growth of the undead populations. Currently, the TV showed a map of California, which was already close to being overrun. Satellite images from Los Angeles, in particular, were showing a mass exodus of several zombie hordes moving through the city and the surrounding area. One of those concentrations was tens of thousands in number.

"The Chinese taught us that nukes weren't enough to handle the situation. Even with the devastation, Beijing is still teeming with the undead."

"Why do you think that is, General?"

"Partly because many of those either infected or resurrected were underground at the time which protected them from the worst of the nuclear blasts. But on the outer perimeters, the radiation just sped up the demise of those already infected. I'm not inclined to use nuclear weapons except on the most concentrated population centres. Los Angeles might have been salvageable if the people hadn't panicked, but it was a primary hub of the infection due to LAX. The infection hit hard and fast. The State Governor is in custody as per your orders." The California State Governor had been woeful in his response to the crisis, taking too long to deploy the National Guard. "Most of downtown LA has been lost to the undead. I don't see us holding the city, even the state. Chicago looks like it might fall as well, so add that one to the list. There is a chance we might have stabilised New York, but we lost a lot of good men and women, and the infection has spread to New Jersey. It's still too early to tell." The President had hoped New York could be saved, it was a city that meant a lot to her. "We do have two other problems that you may need to make a decision on."

"Which are?" Fairchild demanded. The screen changed to a map of Mexico.

"Firstly, Mexico City is in a bad way. The CIA confirmed that any semblance of law and order has collapsed, and even the cartels can't control the local populous. We have a mass exodus of people coming straight for the border."

"What do you propose?"

"You will allow me to be blunt?" Franklin asked.

"I wouldn't want you to be anything but."

"We need to stop that exodus and send a message that the border is closed. We need to shut all the main highways. If we could spare the troops, I would say put them on the border, but that isn't an option. We need to make those people head south, away from us."

"What would be your desired method?" Fairchild watched the General, saw how his eyes seemed to sparkle. There were some who said that Franklin enjoyed the power he had at his fingertips a little too much.

"You said years ago that the wall should have been built, and if that had been done, we likely wouldn't need to do anything. A wall would have allowed us to concentrate troops at any points of weakness. We don't have that luxury so we will need to infringe on Mexico's Sovereignty. I think the only thing we can do is bomb any concentrated human mass that comes near our border."

"You wouldn't recommend nukes?"

"Only as a last resort. The border is too wide, and it's too big a risk to Texas to use nukes anything but selectively. Plus, we will be bombing a sovereign nation which will mightily piss people off." Texas was one of the states where the infection had occurred that was holding its own so far. Franklin stood up so he could point directly at the map on the screen. "If it comes to it though, I say we use low yield neutron bombs."

"Weren't those all supposed to be decommissioned?"

"Yes Madam President, they were supposed to be. But why deprive our armed forces of such a valuable weapon? We have stockpiles for our bombers." Of course we do, thought Fairchild. "I think in the first instance though, we need to try and create a curtain of denial. We are already doing leaflet drops warning the local population not to approach the border, and that seems to be having some effect. Concentrated A10 strafing runs along the largest highways should get the message across as well as surgical strikes on all bridges, highways and railway lines. Even better, we can deploy nerve agents as area denial weapons. If you allow me, I can cut us off from this mass exodus with minimal loss of life."

"That will really piss off the Mexicans," Fairchild said. She had no desire to use any derogative terms for the Mexican population despite the low regard she had for anyone who wasn't Caucasian. They had a right to life, they just had to be kept away from the border.

"I'm sure it would, but what are they going to do. If they try a military response, we will create air dominance within the first hour. You might not be aware that Mexico doesn't have any fighter aircraft in operation at present. Besides, their government has basically collapsed."

"So we can basically do what we want?"

"Pretty much," said the General. "If you give the word, I can have operations started within the hour."

"Do whatever you think is best to defend the integrity of our border, General," Fairchild said. "What is the second problem?" The General used the remote again. A weather chart came up on the screen, showing Florida and the surrounding Atlantic Ocean. Out at sea, a large weather formation could be seen.

"Hurricane Jezebel," the General stated, "is hurtling through the Gulf of Mexico and has just missed the Western coast of Florida. If it continues as expected, it will rip north through the Gulf and destroy any chance we have of containing the virus where it hits." It was predicted to be a category 5 at landfall and would punch right across to either Texas or Louisiana. What the scientists couldn't predict was its exact point of impact. Houston would see the worst of it. Jacqueline felt that she was sorely tested by her God.

She hadn't seen anything.

23.08.19
Manchester, UK

For the fourth time that day, Viktor paid a visit to Susan. Only this time he brought more than drink with him. Flung over one arm he had a sheer, almost see-through dress that would barely hide Susan's modesty. From his fingers dangled a pair of six-inch heeled stilettoes that Viktor knew Clay would adore.

"Your attire for this evening," Viktor said, resting the garment over the arm of a chair. Stepping back, he noticed Susan's hesitation as she climbed off the bed and held the dress up to the light, Viktor backing away from her.

"I can't wear this," she pleaded, "there's nothing to it. I might as well be naked."

"Naked is your other option," Viktor advised callously. "I will leave you for a moment to decide. When I return, we will be going to see Mr Clay, and the dressing gown stays here." It would have been easier to stand over Susan while she put on the Swarovski crystal cut off gown, but such humiliation was reserved for Clay and Clay alone. He left the room and let Susan make her choice. He did leave her a little liquid courage before doing so, of course.

When Viktor returned, Susan was suitably attired, although she looked deservedly uncomfortable. She had even applied makeup which would please Clay immensely.

"Are you ready, Miss Susan?" Viktor asked, although really it wasn't a question. She nodded timidly and followed him out of the bedroom. Susan expected them to go down to the kitchen like last time, but at the stairs, Viktor went up. He was halfway up the flight of stairs before Viktor realised Susan wasn't with him. Turning, he saw that she was still at the base of the steps, desperation almost seeping out of every pore.

"Please, Mr Clay is not to be kept waiting," Viktor ordered, hiding his own amusement at the situation. He put an edge into his voice that suggested unpleasantness would happen if she didn't comply, but it was clear to him that she was well aware of the bad things that would happen even if she followed his commands to the letter. Maybe that was why she still hesitated. "I can always carry you if you feel you are worthy of such indignity." Susan gave him a look then that surprised him, the fury in her face a pleasure for him to see. *Still some fight left in her*, he thought to himself. Reluctantly, Susan began to ascend the stairs.

Susan wasn't the only one to feel surprised when the pair walked into Clay's bedroom. The room was large, with a gargantuan queen sized bed and C configuration leather sofa sunk into the floor, a sofa that could easily seat twelve people. The room was graced with five large floor to ceiling windows and a sense of style that bordered on functionality. Viktor's surprise centred around the presence of Florence, the drug addicted and emaciated surgeon. She was sat at a table by one of the windows, sipping a cup of coffee. Clay wasn't visible, although the sound of urination from the adjoining bathroom could readily be heard. When he finally appeared, he was still half buckling his trousers, the bathroom he deliberately closed behind him.

At least he was fastening them rather than taking them off, thought Susan.

"Susan, you look radiant. Doesn't she look radiant, Florence?"

"Oh yes, she's a peach," Florence said in response to Clay, a hint of jealousy in her voice perhaps.

"You will have to forgive the good doctor, my dear," Clay said. "Age and drugs have taken their toll on her, although I doubt she ever had a figure as splendid as yours." Clay took a step forward, beckoning Susan to enter the room further. "Thank you Viktor, that will be all for now." Viktor was still revelling in his confusion, so it took the briefest instance for him to register he had been dismissed.

"Yes Mr Clay," he said, walking out of the room backwards, closing the door behind him. Susan was glad to see him go, although she still felt extremely apprehensive about what was about to happen. How could people be like this? How could they be so predatory?

"Do you like the dress, Susan?" Clay asked.

"It's too revealing for my taste," she said. It protected her modesty better than a bikini would, but not by much.

"Nonsense," Clay said, "it brings out your eyes, and it cost me a king's ransom." Susan looked at Florence as if the doctor was able to help her, her eyes almost pleading, but Florence gave her nothing back.

"There is little point looking to the delectable Florence here for assistance. She knows where her bread is buttered, don't you Florence?"

"If you say so," Florence said. Susan was surprised by the tone of the doctor's voice. Everyone she had met seemed to treat Clay with reverence, but Florence seemed to regard him with a combination of mild pity and passing disinterest. She tapped a pen impatiently on a clipboard that rested on the table.

"Florence is an addict like you. Before the world ended, I was the only thing keeping her out of prison. Now, with the streets filled with the blight of the zombie menace, the only person Florence can get her precious heroin from is me. I suspect she resents me for it somewhat, but I find her manner refreshing." Clay stepped up to Susan and whispered into her ear. "It can be so tedious to have everyone treat you with such unwavering reverence, although I will be expecting such from you at all times." A strong hand enveloped the back of Susan's neck, and she was pushed forward with just enough force to propel her to the table where Florence sat, Clay following in her wake. "Please Susan, sit. The doctor is in, and she has some questions for you." Susan sat.

"Coffee?" Florence asked, to which Susan nodded, the empty cup on the table in front of her filling. "Black or cream?"

"Black please," Susan said. Her mind felt numb.

"Like your men, eh," Clay added, erupting into a fit of booming laughter, clearly impressed by how funny he thought he was. Florence shook her head in exasperation.

"Now then Susan, I need to ask you some questions. Don't worry, this won't take long." Susan nodded, wondering where this was all going. She wasn't comfortable in Clay's presence, but it was better that there was another woman here. "Do you have any allergies that you know of?"

"Penicillin," Susan answered.

"Any heart problems? Ever suffered angina?" The questions continued, Susan answering no to most of them. "And you are an alcoholic, yes?" The words stung Susan, her face going red. "Oh, you silly thing, I'm a doctor, you can tell me."

"But he isn't a doctor," Susan said sheepishly pointing at Clay who grinned at once again being at the centre of things.

"Just pretend he isn't there. I do that all the time." Clay whooped with delight at Florence's subtle dig.

"Yes," Susan admitted, "I'm an alcoholic." The truth of what she said weighed heavy on her. It was probably the first time she had actually said those words, much of her problems caused by the denial of how bad her addiction actually was.

"Well admitting such puts your foot on the road to recovery," Florence stated. Susan couldn't tell if she was being genuine or just taking the piss. "Although that doesn't seem to have worked for me."

"So what do you think Florence, do we have ourselves a patient?" Clay asked eagerly.

"Well, apart from likely borderline malnutrition, I think so. I've already checked her bloods, so there are no abnormalities there. So yes." *Hey, I'm right here* thought Susan.

"Susan I asked you to make a decision, one that I know was hard for you," Clay said. He pulled up a chair and sat down next to Susan, too close though, breaking into her personal space, making her feel like she had to back away, but that would just leave her pressed up against the windows. A hip flask appeared as if by magic, and Clay introduced a sizeable portion of its contents into the cup holding Susan's coffee. "And your answer is due now, but before you do I have something that might, shall we say, sweeten the pot."

"I don't..." Susan started, but Clay put one of his thick, calloused fingers to her lips. She was powerless against this man.

"Shush now. Let me finish what I have to say." He nodded to Florence, and the doctor lifted a metal case off the floor and placed it on the table in front of her. With a flick of her thumb, she undid the latches, opening the lid. The case spun on the table revealing the three vials that were inside.

"What's this?" Susan asked.

"Oh nothing much," Clay said, "only the cure to the nasty little virus that's ravaging the planet. Take me up on my offer, and you get one of these doses. What do you say, Susan? Are you up for a bit of fun? I'll only bite if you want me to." Susan looked at Clay, then at Florence. She couldn't understand how the Doctor could just sit there while Clay said these things.

"I'm not..."

"Yes or no answer now, Susan. Clock's ticking, and you will have noticed there are only three samples of this cure. If you turn it down now, you won't get a second chance." Clay grabbed her roughly by the chin, pulling her face in close. Alcohol and cigar smoke hung heavy on his breath. "If you hesitate, you lose. Come on, girl, give me a yes." Susan said the only thing she knew she could say.

"Yes." The word escaped her lips so easily. Clay smiled.

"I knew you would see sense. See Doctor, people always know what's best for them."

"You are a sick man, Clay," Florence stated, standing from the table.

"You know me all too well," Clay said in response to the insult, "but another insult like that and I'll cut your ration in half." Florence's face paled. "Leave us until I call for you. Susan and I need to get acquainted before she gets her medicine." Susan looked into Clay's eyes and saw the hunger there. What the hell had she just agreed to?

When Florence left, the Doctor gave one last look at Susan. The look was pure pity.

23.08.19
Peak District, UK

Tom had shown apprehension at letting so many people onto his property, but realistically, what was there he could have done to prevent it? Begrudgingly he had allowed Nick and the SAS to set up in the various buildings of the farm, but Tom had put his foot down and said that the main farmhouse was for his family only. Nick and Haggard had acquiesced to that demand, but only because the other farm buildings gave them enough shelter.

Right now, the bulk of the SAS were working on improving the farm's perimeter. To the casual human, it was truly impenetrable. The farm was basically a plot of land in the shape of a triangle, two of the sides bordered by a fast flowing river. The third wall was an assortment of barbed wire and bramble hedges. The problem with that was the undead didn't care about their skin being cut to ribbons. If enough of them came, they would press against any barrier and sacrifice their own to get through it, and there were areas that they might be able to push through with enough persistence. So the soldiers worked on strengthening the defences, going so far as to put barricades in the small road that led to the farm in the hope of steering any undead away onto a different path. They still planned to leave at some point, so a route out for the APC's was kept.

A few dozen claymore mines and grenade traps were put at the barrier's weakest locations. Taking the lessons from history, the banks of the river were also set up with flare traps just in case something, or someone, made it across. As fast as the river was, military history had shown never to fully rely on natural barriers. Be it the impassable Alps with Hannibal, or the mangrove swamps for the Japanese invasion of Singapore, man often found a way to penetrate the obstacles created by nature.

The final touch in the defences was to program the three surveillance drones they had to rotate around the property, the heat vision cameras they contained there more for the warning of any human incursion. The soldiers knew that the zombies weren't the only threats here. The drones would work in shifts to allow for their batteries to be regularly recharged. Nobody would be sneaking up on the defenders anytime soon.

As defences went, what they had was pretty solid. The dirt path from the road that led to the heart of the farm was the weakest part of it, and this could easily be covered by snipers and the fifty calibre machine guns the APC's had been blessed with.

While the SAS men did what they were trained for, Nick convened his war council. Nick, Natasha, Jeff, Haggard, Whittaker, Beckington and Jessica all now had a part in what happened next. Azrael was also here, still in handcuffs. Nick had something he wanted to discuss.

There hadn't been much of a chance to formulate an official strategy since their retreat from Preston. The initial priority had been to escape the zombie horde that had attacked the barracks, which they had managed with relative ease. Out on the streets though, they had met their next challenge, the tens of thousands of people clogging the roads as they had fled to wherever they thought was safe. The fleeing humanity had become particularly bad around Rochdale, north of Manchester, as the exodus became very noticeable. Manchester, the country's seventh largest city, was being abandoned by its people as the zombie presence there grew too big for the depleted defenders to hold. From the brief radio snippets Nick had been able to catch, Manchester was lost, which meant the surrounding areas would be quick to follow. This pattern was being repeated across the country.

The three Bulldog APC's had traversed the motorways and dual carriageways with relative ease but had encountered persistent obstacles as they diverted to the smaller roads that led into the Peak District. There were now dozens of crushed civilian vehicles, the owners of which either being unable to move, or more commonly, refusing to move. Nick hadn't liked it, but with the traffic as it was, the cars had been useless to those who owned them anyway. The Bulldog was particularly adept at dealing with such obstructions, as well as going off-road, which became more and more common as they made their journey.

On the table between where they all either stood or sat was the armoured laptop that Natasha used to contact Moros. The bullet it had taken had pretty much destroyed the screen but had fortunately left the rest of the laptop intact.

"The laptop screen is shot boss, but I should still be able to access it. I just need a monitor or a TV." Natasha was glad her news wasn't catastrophic, the single bullet from Renfield's gun having done the damage. It could have been much worse. The laptop was encrypted, designed to log into the secure satellite network that linked MI13 agents to the Moros super-computer. Without it, to get access to Moros, they would need to physically go to Central or District, which meant going to London itself.

London was now the heart of the undead legions in the UK. Not somewhere you wanted to be if you could avoid it.

"I'd rather lose a laptop than have one of my team take a bullet in the back." That was the truth of it. Without the protection the computer had given her, Natasha would likely be dead or crippled now.

"My brother can help with the laptop," Jessica said. "But that wasn't what you wanted to talk to us about, was it?"

"No," Nick admitted. "Before we lost access to it, I asked Moros a question. I was hoping to give it more data, but we didn't get that chance."

"The question being?" Beckington asked. He was surprised to have been included in the meeting despite his rank. As the only doctor they had, however, he was deemed just as essential as any of them. His medical training might be able to help in the discussion.

"Jessica and Whittaker are immune," Nick continued. "Although Azrael was given XV1, we think he was already immune before the antiserum was administered. There is indication Azrael was given a vaccine nearly a year ago, but I think his immunity is actually natural."

"Why do you think that?" Beckington asked.

"Because of his dreams. Your nightmares started about a year ago, right?" Nick asked the manacled assassin.

"Yes," Azrael agreed. "I first noticed them several days after I was asked to inject myself."

"Jessica and Whittaker both experienced the same dreams after being exposed to Lazarus. I think the virus, either whole or deactivated in the form of a vaccine activates something in the human mind."

"That's a bit thin, Nick," Haggard warned.

"Just hear me out. Jessica, Chris, if I get any of this wrong, just correct me okay." Both Jessica and Whittaker nodded. "I've confirmed that these three immune all share the same dream and that they see each other in that dream. This was established before they had met each other. I can see no reason why they would lie to anyone and trust them enough to accept that they at least believe in what they are telling me."

"Go on," Haggard added.

"As mad as it sounds, the virus seems to have given the immune some psychic link which they can only access in the dream state. Dr Patel was also sceptical about this, but Moros determined that there was over an eighty per cent chance that what I am saying is true."

"Eighty per cent?" Haggard said with raised eyebrows.

"Yeah. I've never known a Moros evaluation to be wrong." Haggard nodded his head in acceptance. He hadn't even heard of Moros until the other day so it was hard for him to truly assess the super-computer's powers and he supposed he had to trust Nick in what he said. Nick had already explained to everyone else what Moros was…one of the most powerful quantum computers on the planet. The Official Secrets Act be damned.

"Sounds like telepathy," Beckington added.

"Yes, it does. What do you think about that?" The MI13 way was that everyone had a voice.

"Telepathy used to be considered pseudoscience and still is by some. But I've seen too many cases of soldiers in the field being able to feel when the enemy was close by." Those in the room who had served could all attest to that. "There has also been some recent research that indicates humans do have a very rudimentary form of telepathy."

"It's more than telepathy," Azrael suddenly interrupted. Jeff glowered at him but didn't give any verbal reprimand. He didn't agree with Azrael being in the room, but Jeff was willing to give the man some slack because it was what Nick seemed to want. Azrael had most likely saved Nick's life when Renfield had opened fire, and Nick seemed willing to at least listen to what Azrael had to say.

"How so?" Nick asked.

"The nightmares are more than a dream state," Azrael said. "They are like another reality."

"I think he's right," Jessica added. "I remember the dreams, but for some reason, the brutality in them doesn't stay with me when I wake up. I can feel everything when I'm there, and yet when I wake up, it feels more like I've been watching a movie. I should be dreading sleep, but the more times the nightmare happens, the more I acclimatise to its effects when I eventually wake up."

"And you say you can communicate with each other in the dream state?" Nick continues.

"Yes. And every time we are there, the more people like us we see." Jessica looked at Azrael to see if he agreed with her, and he smiled to say that he did. She had loved that smile once.

"How does this help us, though?" Whittaker asked.

"I don't know yet. That's the only answer I can give you," Nick answered.

"There is also the enigma of your Colonel Smith," Azrael said. "He is more important than any of you seem to realise. He is there with us when we sleep. His presence is a recent thing, but he's there. I can feel him."

"Chasing us," Jessica added.

"Hunting us," Whittaker corrected. He definitely remembered being hunted by the threat of the horsemen.

"Yes, hunting," Azrael agreed. "When I am there, in the desert, I always feel like I am being pursued. I can never really see who it is, I just know that they are there and that they are coming. As much as the pain makes me want to stop walking, I know if I do that, those following will catch me."

"And you think Smith is somehow involved?" Nick asked.

"Very recently, yes." The certainty in that word made Nick believe. "I can feel him there now. His essence seems to be in the very wind I breathe."

If this was all true, thought Nick, *then how the hell did they use this information?*

"When did Smith inject himself with the remnants of my blood?" Jessica suddenly asked, Nick providing the answer. "And when did you first notice him Azrael?" Right there was the possible answer as to why Smith had suddenly become such a threat.

XVl.

If that was the reason behind all this, then Jessica's blood wasn't the answer to Lazarus after all.

23.08.19
Emmitsburg, USA

Father Steven Shepherd was aptly named for the role he had chosen in life, that of Catholic Priest. All he had ever wanted since the age of twelve was to be given his own church so that he could bring the word of God to the masses. The thought consumed him, becoming an overriding passion that drove him through good times and bad. Ultimately, the church had finally blessed him, placing him in charge of one of the top Catholic pilgrimage destinations in the United States.

Shepherd had also recently been witness to a miracle in his life, a sign from God that had warped the grief that flowed through his heart. That miracle was his own immunity, the dressing he wore on his arm easily concealed by those who would question what had happened to him. For those who had seen it, the simple explanation that he had burned himself while cooking his sister her lunch had been enough to placate their curiosity.

Everyone seemed to admire the way he so selfishly looked after his sibling whilst also attending to the never-ending needs of his flock.

THE FALL

Seven years ago, his sister had broken her spine in a car crash caused by another reckless driver. Although she had survived, she had been left with most of her body paralysed. To add to her misery, she was then quickly abandoned by a husband who couldn't face a life looking after a virtual quadriplegic, despite the payout the insurance had brought. With no other close living relatives, Shepherd had insisted that his sister come and live with him in the sleepy town of Emmitsburg. Despite only having just over two thousand inhabitants, the close proximity of it to a host of government and military facilities meant that there was ample medical care available to help in the attempted rehabilitation of his sister. And now there was a growing supply of soldiers, due most likely to the importance of one of those installations. Site R was a fourteen-minute drive into the forest.

While his sister left friends behind in California where she had once lived, it was sad to say that most of them had chosen to gradually cut their ties with her, they too realising her friendship was something they could no longer continue with. The selfishness of those around her left her with few other choices.

As if to prove the healing nature and the mercy of God's will, his sister had managed to regain some of the motion in her right arm. This occurred in the second year of her move to Emmitsburg, and Shepherd thanked Jesus for his obvious blessing. His sister wasn't religious and resisted all and any of Shepherd's subtle attempts at conversion. He took this all in good humour, safe in the knowledge that there was always time and that God loved a sinner who finally came to his understanding.

One of the problems with being bedridden was boredom, which is where the internet became a blessing to her. And on the seventeenth of August, his sister had ordered some second-hand DVDs off the internet, safe in the knowledge that they would be delivered promptly due to her paying that little bit extra. They had arrived on the twenty-first, the hapless delivery guy unaware of the death he had just dropped off to a house of the lord. Although the exterior of the packaging was perfectly safe, the contents weren't. The previous owner who had packed them had not been concerned by his temperature and the sweat that kept erupting across his body. He also didn't care when, packing the DVDs into the box, he sneezed all over the interior. The virus, designed to be hardy, had easily survived the journey and had easily infected Father Shepherd's skin when he had opened the box to see what else his sister had bought.

She purchased a lot of things, much of which were useless to her. But it seemed to give her some sort of pleasure, so Shepherd was able to resist the need to chastise her. It was her money at the end of the day, the insurance more than adequate to pay for whatever it was she wanted to buy, as well as covering her round the clock care. Upon her request, he had opened the package and inserted one of the DVDs into her computer. In the process of doing that, he had transferred the virus onto his skin, and then onto his sister's forehead when he brushed some errant strands of hair aside.

In her weakened state, she succumbed quickly, just as the whole world began its rapid spiral into the abyss. By the time it dawned on him that he really needed to be calling the doctor, the TV had told him that the dead were rising and that an army of the damned was surging across the continental United States.

Shepherd heard the confessions of whoever came calling, including people from the nearby government and military installations. One such man, his heart heavy with the things his government was willing to do, had confessed to Shepherd that anyone found to be infected with Lazarus would be taken away and executed. Seeing his beloved sister display all the characteristics the TV had warned him about, Shepherd made the decision to forsake the miracles of modern medicine and instead decide to rely on the power of prayer. He knew that if paramedics arrived, there would be a strong likelihood that he would never see his sister again.

Prayer didn't stop his sister dying. He was there for that event, his heart broken by the loss to a virus that his own body had so easily rejected. This revelation didn't come to him until after the corpse had come back and bitten him. He had been in another room, two glasses of gin already inside him, when the thump from his sister's bedroom had caused him to investigate. With a body that was mainly paralysed, it had still been able to topple to the ground, dragging itself along with one barely functioning arm.

Something in Shepherd's head had snapped then, not the first person to be driven mad by the events of the apocalypse. As powerful as his faith was, it didn't stop the insanity, which was only worsened when, bending down to try and help his sister, it had taken a chunk out of his arm.

The now undead sister still struggled, but was presently bound down to the bed that reeked of the dead fluids that leaked from the moving corpse.

With his sister dead nearly a day, Shepherd went about his duties as if the world depended on him. In a way, it thought it did, people's immortal souls in jeopardy by the corruption to nature that was plaguing the Earth. When the army came into his church, he was faced with an unknown face, an apologetic soldier who insisted that Shepherd undergo the Lazarus test. It wouldn't have been good for the local priest to be infecting his flock. His immunity allowed him to pass the test.

"Is there anyone else who needs to be tested?" the soldier had asked.

"No," Shepherd had said, the lie surely for the greater good. The soldier made the mistake of taking the priest's word for it. A Catholic himself, the soldier had apologised again to Shepherd for disturbing him.

Now here he was, looking out at the packed pews, the need for prayer great amongst the sinners who were faced with the end of the world. He was glad to see so many members of the nation's military here, all servants of God. It was even more pleasing to see men and women from the military here. Everyone was present for the Holy Communion, but wouldn't they be surprised when they got just that little bit more than that? Why else was Shepherd spared the virus if not to deliver it directly to the hundreds in attendance? None of them would notice that the wine had been contaminated by the blood of his now dead sister.

Over two thousand people were living in the vicinity who needed salvation and sparing from what was to come, and another three thousand occupants seven minutes' drive in Carroll Valley. Rumour had it there the army had stationed nearly five thousand troops nearby as well. All lambs of God, all worthy of his forgiveness and his blessing.

Shepherd would do what he could to help bring an end to the suffering of his flock. This was God's mission, God's cleansing of the planet. Who was he to go against the will of God?

23.08.19
Leeds, UK

Night was upon him now, the living room lit by three candles. Prudence would state that it was better to sit in the dark than announce to the world that someone was inside, but with the shutters down, it was unlikely the candle glow could be seen from outside. Besides, the scum of the area already knew where he lived, their jungle telegraph undoubtedly telling tales of the madman with the shotgun. There was no sound of them, the only noise the gentle hum of the wind-up radio he was powering up.

One of two things would happen now. Either he would be left alone, or his house would be attacked. It all depended on the psychology of those engaged in the earlier altercation. He had killed the group's leader and had shown no mercy in that regard. Would they deem him to be someone to avoid at all costs, or would the gang stalking the surrounding houses see him as a threat that had to be eliminated?

Whatever they chose, Andy was as ready as he could be although his body still felt tired despite having been unconscious most of the day. If they were to come, it would likely be at night. The back fence was difficult to traverse, thick foliage making access troublesome. That was one of the reasons why he had chosen this house, the garden of Iain's house the same. To get at him then, they would need to do a frontal assault, which meant getting past the locked gate. Even if they did manage to get over the fences at the back, they would have a nasty surprise waiting for them. He had laid down dozens of wooden panels with long nails driven through them that could easily penetrate the sole of a shoe, or perhaps a knee cap if someone scaling the fence landed poorly.

Why hadn't his neighbours stood up for themselves though? This was something that was irritating him. He knew that some had young children to protect, but together the dwellers of his cul-de-sac outmanned the thugs who could only promise violence and blackmail. A show of combined force by them might have been enough to fend off the vermin that were trying to acquire easy pickings, although that might have necessitated the now dead GT to brandish his pistol. Either way, by their own cowardice, his neighbours had doomed themselves. One by one, they would either run out of provisions or have those provisions taken off them by force.

Andy had been enough to defend them all, but he wouldn't do that again, not unless it was directly in his best interests. With no law and order evident, it was clear that they were in a survival of the fittest scenario. Andy intended to be one of the last men standing, but he knew he could make no plans for what came next. His future was in the wind.

There was little in the way of good news. Although his power was out, by looking out of his bedroom window, Andy could see that streets in the distance were still with electricity. So it was a local issue, most likely a failure in a transformer. In the days before the crisis that would have been fixed in a matter of hours, but with the zombie hordes free to roam, there would be no repair. This was it for him now, the taps finally running dry.

The central heating was out as well, which wasn't a problem at present. But the winter months were approaching and the days would run cold. How many people would survive only to freeze to death? He had no means to burn wood apart from perhaps the leaf burner in the garden, and even if he did, he had little or no wood to burn. There were trees about, but he wasn't any kind of lumberjack. Any wood he scavenged would last days at best, the furniture in his house mostly chrome, glass and metal. For warmth, he would need to rely on clothing, and he, fortunately, had some thermals and a thick coat.

His camping stove with its three gas canisters would last a week at most. Fortunately, most of the food he had picked on his last-minute supermarket dash could be eaten straight from the can. He had deliberately avoided stuff that needed cooking or mixing with water. Corned beef and SPAM were a diet that would likely give him constipation, but it would keep him alive.

His position was better than most, even though it was far from ideal. That wasn't his only concern, however. Andy had seen how easy it had been for him to kill a man. How much further would he descend into violence? If his stocks of food started to get depleted, would it be him threatening to break into other people's houses? Would he become the scum he detested so much? Human desperation could demand despicable acts in the name of survival. How long would it be before Andy was willing to kill the innocent for a can of beans? The thought troubled him because, as much as he said to himself there was no way it could happen, there was a part, deep within, that knew that it would.

"I reckon that's enough," he said quietly, his arm tired from pumping the wind-up radio. Switching it on, Andy slowly crept through the dials, mostly static dominating the airwaves. Some channels teased him with broken words, but it was only Radio 4 that gave any resemblance to normality.

"...three to four days. That is the average quarantine time for those who are infected by the primary version of the virus. To remind our listeners, it is more contagious than measles and can be contacted by mere touch or breathing in the exhaled air of the infected." Andy listened in the hope of hearing something new. "Secondary infection, from direct contact with the undead, can result in death within the hour. For those contaminated by an encounter with the undead, either through bites or bodily fluids, it is imperative that they are isolated. There are still some areas of the country that have active teams that will come out and deal with your infected problem, but most major cities are now becoming no go areas for the police and the military." Andy had thought this was just a public information broadcast, but it turned out it was actually an interview.

"We will be broadcasting a list of cities to avoid, after this program," the radio show's host said. "Please continue, Professor Sullivan." What was he a professor of though? thought Andy.

"Thank you. Some people who are bitten die quickly, within minutes if their injury is severe enough. While zombies will kill, they are more likely to inflict a none lethal wound and move on. We don't really understand how they choose their victims or why they sometimes go into a feeding frenzy which can see a human being stripped to the bone in minutes."

"I'm not sure our listeners need to hear such gruesome..." the host tried to say.

"Don't be fucking ridiculous," Sullivan stated. "The people need to know what they are up against. They need to lock themselves away to avoid infection. The only way we can win this is to starve the zombies of their recruits in the hope that the natural decay process of the human body will somehow decimate their ranks. The military has been shown to be completely ineffective against the threat."

"Do you have any evidence that this natural decay is likely to happen?" the host asked. It sounded like he was almost begging, a Hail Mary in the hope that the Professor had some news that wasn't so cataclysmic.

"I see no evidence for such. What we have seen, in fact, is that zombies don't seem to decay like a normal corpse. While I am sure they will degrade to the extent they can no longer walk, I don't know the timescale of that."

"Is there anything our listeners need to know?" the host asked.

"Yes, when an infected individual dies, you must destroy the base of the brain. Remember the body will be contagious, and any unprotected contact risks passing on the virus. A knife into the back of the skull might be enough. You need to act quickly though because, whilst some zombies can take hours before they resurrect, most return from death within minutes, sometimes even seconds. The next best thing is to lock the body in a sturdy room, but do remember the undead are much stronger than your average human being. We have had reports of them easily smashing their way through PVC and wooden doors. A sturdy external fire door will most likely keep them at bay."

"Thank you, Professor."

There was a moment's silence, only for an automated voice to begin reading out a list of towns and cities that had so far fallen to the undead. It was a long list, but there was one thing Andy noticed. The city of Leeds wasn't on it.

23.08.19
Frederick, USA

Even for those who survived the Holocaust, the surname Schmidt didn't really mean anything despite the atrocities of one individual who held that name. Most people had heard of Josef Mengele, the psychotic and deranged SS officer and physician from the Auschwitz death camps, but for most of the American population, the name Schmidt would hardly register in the world of mass murderers. This despite the fact that the outrages perpetrated by Hermann Schmidt, Mia Schmidt's grandfather, vastly surpassed those of the Angel of Death.

The main difference was the nature of the research undertaken. Whereas Mengele's experiments were purely to fuel his own insane inner cravings, Hermann Schmidt researched the lethality of various pathogens with the hope that they could be utilised against the enemies of the Third Reich. Despite such research fortunately not being used on the various battlefronts of World War Two, Hermann Schmidt's discoveries would become a useful tool for those who employed him after the war's end.

He should have been hung with the rest at Nuremberg. Instead, he escaped the justice of the hangman's noose due to the scientific prowess he was able to present.

When Berlin fell to the might of the Soviet Army, Schmidt fled west, surrendering to exhausted allied troops. Despite the horrors that his research represented, he quickly became a person of interest to the US Joint Intelligence Objectives Agency under what became known as Operation Paperclip. Schmidt, who had personally killed hundreds of Jews and Poles in his search for the secrets of weaponised microbiology, was thus not punished, but rather he was rewarded for the outrages he had committed. He was secretly moved to America, where he was allowed and encouraged to continue his research. "The Plague Doctor," as he came to be known, didn't even bother to change his name.

More than seventy years later, Mia Schmidt was following in her grandfather's great and noble work. Hermann's son, who was born in the United States, grew up to be a mild-mannered accountant, completely oblivious to the atrocities done in the family name. Thus the madness skipped a generation.

The sadism that Hermann was renowned for developed slowly in Mia, bubbling away under the seemingly placid woman's surface. There was little sign of it during her childhood or early university days, the field of virology almost a natural calling to her. Even during the arduous years when she was achieving her PhD, the true nature of the genetics she had inherited failed to thoroughly manifest. It was only when she was approached by the darker side of the US military that the true demon inside her flourished. Could Mia continue the good work her grandfather had been instrumental in?

In her fifties now, Mia Schmidt was a true piece of work. She cared only for the results of her experiments, willing to go to any lengths to find the answers to the questions that plagued her waking mind. Her goal was not to create biological weapons of mass destruction but to find cures for them having so far perfected vaccines for some of humanity's deadliest killers. Whilst what she did might have been vital to the safety of mankind, the way she went about it was reprehensible.

The USA had long since abandoned the creation of diseases such as Anthrax and Smallpox, instead concentrating their efforts on the remedies that would save troops on the battlefield and protect the staff of politicians opening mail that could so easily be filled with the deadliest of white powder. Much of this research was done legitimately, by scientists of renown and moral character (many of whom had been killed by Gabriel in his Gaia-led purge). Some, however, was done in black sites, like that deep beneath the surface of Fort Detrick, by people like Mia who stayed out of the public sphere. The men, for it was always men, who authorised such experiments believed that nothing should be off limits if it could only lead to the eradication of the plagues that scourged humanity. Mia was in full agreement with that philosophy, and she quickly abandoned the ethical notions that often hindered her previous research.

This was why Mia Schmidt was recruited, and as she was steadily allowed more and more freedom for her research, she began to warp into a creature that would make her grandfather proud. Some would say such a mind was needed to combat a virus like Lazarus, but that would only be if she were to show some signs of success.

"24-year-old male test subject with no notable medical abnormalities. The Los Angeles strain of Lazarus, H4N2G7-LAXZ1-32, was administered to a one-centimetre square patch of skin on the sole of the left foot," Schmidt said into the microphone hanging from the ceiling. She was fully clad in the most protective of hazmat suits, the subject strapped to the metal table in front of her exhausted from his attempts to break the bonds that held him. Not even the strongest of zombies could escape that confinement, so his attempts were merely an escapade in futility. The *civilised* thing would have been to sedate the subject, but Schmidt didn't want anything interfering with the virus' progression. This was science and science demanded sacrifice and the purest of data. Naturally, it was others who were the ones who had to undergo the sacrifice.

"Viral contamination occurred fifty minutes ago. Clinical indications show that it has penetrated even the thickest of skin, the infection moving through the bloodstream as well as the lymphatic system. Note how the visible indications of the infection are relatively quick to appear on the whole of the skin's surface displaying the full systemic nature of the disease." Schmidt raised her right hand and made a gesture with her fingers. By her head, a tiny hovering drone moved closer to her subject's feet, its small video cameras relaying everything in high definition to those watching the demonstration. It moved slowly along the man's body, levitating above the surface, recording everything. The black tendrils that marked the viral progression were obvious for everyone to see, already past the groin onto the lower abdomen. Blooms of the tendrils were also just starting to break out across the rest of the body.

"It is clear that the strains of Lazarus passed on by the undead are faster acting than the initial Thailand strain that initiated the outbreak. It would thus appear that Lazarus can change its nature to suit the requirements of its spread, mutating rapidly and often. H4N2G7-BXZ1-1 was clearly manufactured to go unnoticed whilst still being highly contagious. Its four-day incubation period was ideal to allow those infected to move throughout the general population, spreading the contagion. Zombie delivered strains have clearly mutated to provide rapid onset, essential for a disease spread by bites. Previous research has already confirmed that the saliva of the undead increases the potency of the viral load delivered."

The drone hovered by the victim's head now, waiting for further instruction.

"There is no way this virus developed naturally. Whoever designed it has my admiration." Schmidt really did mean that. She was in awe at what had been created, a pathogen more lethal than anything Mother Nature had ever managed to produce. The ultimate adversary for her to try and defeat.

"The subject's temperature is already starting to reach dangerous levels, and respiratory distress is evident. The Los Angeles strain has clearly mutated to be much more lethal than the initial outbreaks. I anticipate death and zombie conversion within the next twenty minutes with this subject, which concurs with previous tests on skin induced infection. Scanning electron microscopy has shown that the virus burrows through the epidermis where it breaches into the dermis allowing it access to the skin's blood vessels. This starts the infective process, and the human body has no natural defences to it. Even the slightest exposure to the virus is a death sentence to those not lucky enough to be immune." The drone moved closer to the subject's face, the eyes wide with terror.

"Still no facial signs except for slight erythema of the skin which matches the raised body temperature." Schmidt ran a gloved finger across the man's skin, the moisture there evident. "Perspiration has increased, most likely as a means to increase the infectivity of the host." Schmidt moved up the steel table and put a calming hand on her subject's shoulder. "Try and relax," she said coldly, "it will all be over soon."

In the corner of the room, the noise from a heart rate monitor spiked. The heart rate was now at a hundred and twenty beats per minute and rising. The blood pressure was also rising to dangerous levels. Schmidt bent over the man's face and carefully withdrew the gag from between his teeth. With his head firmly strapped down, there was no chance he could try and bite her in some last act of defiance. Several others had tried that prior to him, all had failed.

"Tell me what you feel?"

"Please," the man begged, "it hurts."

"Where does it hurt?" Schmidt insisted.

"Everywhere. Just give me something for the pain."

"No," Schmidt said, almost dismissively. "That would interfere with the experiment. You should be thankful; you are about to witness something wonderful." Schmidt was referring to the euphoria that often came at the end of the disease. She had discovered that aspect of Lazarus by accident. Opinion was divided as to why the brain often flooded with opiates and endorphins when death was imminent, Schmidt's own theory was that it was a protective mechanism for the virus, to stop the condemned taking some last drastic measure that would prevent them resurrecting.

At night, on the rare occasions she was drifting off towards sleep, Mia would find herself wondering if Lazarus represented some kind of intelligence. She found the idea fascinating.

"Thankful? You sick fucking bitch." Spittle flew from the man's mouth, landing on the protective shield that covered Schmidt's face. The aerosol created by this man would have killed any unprotected individual in the room.

"You will see, and we will be there with you when you experience it. Won't be long now." Schmidt pulled the man's lower left eyelid down despite the man's objections.

Jee watched in horror at the way Schmidt was almost taunting the patient. No, patient was totally the wrong word to use. Victim fit the role much better. Sitting with three other researchers, she moved her eyes from the computer monitor that was displaying the sick experiment and looked at her fellow scientists. Two of them seemed wrapped in total fascination with what they were witnessing. The other merely looked bored as if he had seen this a thousand times before.

Jee had met people like this before, some on the spectrum of Asperger's and Autism, savants who struggled to interact with the social norms society required. Whilst they were often valuable for the genius they could bring to the table, they were best left working under strict supervision to ensure they didn't slip into the realms of unethical practice. Was Jee the only one who could see how wrong this all was? Could it really be that she was the only voice of reason in this entire facility, and if so, why had the powers that be felt she was right for this role?

"Subject's eyes have become bloodshot," Schmidt reported over the microphone. "I expect uveitis and haemorrhage within minutes." This was not the first such display Jee had endured. For some reason, Schmidt insisted on doing all the examinations herself. She said it was because she didn't trust anyone else with the data that needed collecting, but Jee suspected it was because she got some sort of sick pleasure from the torment she inflicted.

"Do you think blindness will ensue?" one of Jee's colleagues asked.

"Yes," Schmidt's voice replied. The Professor sounded strangely satisfied.

Jee pushed the chair back from her monitor and stood, hands physically shaking.

"Are you okay Dr Lee?" a voice asked, but Jee ignored it despite the genuine concern expressed there. She felt the bile rising in her throat, and she left the monitoring room as gracefully as she could. The door opened automatically enabling access to a narrow, well-lit corridor. Out of sight of the others, desperation suddenly propelled her, a hand now planted firmly over her retching mouth. She could just hold it back, the door to the restroom close enough that she was able to push her way in without soiling the corridor floor. Her head was over the toilet bowl before her stomach unleashed itself. There was very little for her to vomit, her appetite all but destroyed by the stress of what she was being asked to do.

She was being eaten up inside.

For several minutes Jee stayed in that position, resting her cheek on the toilet seat, tears streaming from her eyes at the futility of her life now. She found it difficult to breathe, the panic that had finally erupted in her completely out of her control. How could she carry on with this? How could she be a part of what was being done here? This wasn't science, it was barbarism. What would be the response of Schmidt and Carson if they learnt of her body's revolt to what she had witnessed? Jee had seen what these people were capable of.

If she couldn't get control of herself, would they just discard her and send her away back out into the world. Or would they just use her as another test subject?

Jee knew she had to get herself together here, she couldn't allow herself to go to pieces like this. There was a need for her to get back to her monitor, but she doubted she would be able to stand just yet, so she stayed where she was, trying her best to control her breathing. Jee knew she would need help to get her through this, but there was nobody here that could offer that help. The only person she could even think about talking to about the predicament she found herself in was locked in a cell. Reece really wasn't someone she could burden with her troubles. There was another problem there as well. Sooner or later, no matter how often Jee voiced her rejection of what was being done here, Reece and the others would eventually see Jee as part of the problem just by mere association.

Whilst the research Schmidt was doing had created great strides in the understanding of the virus, how could anyone think the cost paid was justified? Jee knew then and there that she only had one choice now if she was going to be able to look herself in the mirror. Somehow, she had to try and make things right.

Further analyses of Lazarus plague telepathic effects based on existing eye witness accounts.

Data request ordered by Colonel Nicholas Carter, Acting Head MI13

Data analyses indicates a very real possibility that immune individuals have a telepathic link, the mechanism for which is unknown.

No data is available on the speculation that said telepathy is planet wide.

The reports of individual "Colonel Wilson Smith" indicate a similar link caused by the effects of the antiserum designated XV1. If proof of such can be obtained, it then can be extrapolated that others who have XV1 administered may also experience unwanted side effects. Statistical probability would thus advise avoiding the use of XV1 in all but the most life-threatening situations.

A search of the relevant scientific literature allows this computer to form a hypothesis that, whilst possessing a low probability of viability, there is a theoretical chance that the virus, codename Lazarus, can unlock parts of the human brain that are not understood by medical science. This would explain why the dead are able to resurrect and why those who can fight off the infection share a joint reality in what will from now on be referred to as "The Dream World". Extrapolating with the present understanding of quantum theory indicates that "The Dream World" may be some form of parallel dimension. Further data would be needed to confirm the existence of such.

Unable to state whether the designers of the virus, codename Lazarus, knew of these side effects. Speculation states that this scenario is unlikely.

Analysis ends.

24.08.19
Preston, UK

Smith slept, but his mind did not rest. There was no parallel voice here, no chattering annoyance to critique his every action. The other night when he had slept after escaping the horrors of the hospital, The Voice, still seething from the way Smith had treated it, had denied Smith his right to be where he was supposed to be. The Voice relented now and allowed Smith the insight that had so far been denied to him. Here, in the desert of the damned, he and The Voice were finally one.

Deep down, he felt that this was not the first time he had been here, but he had only a vague memory of the place. Part of him had been here before, fractured and incomplete, it had been enough for Azrael to smell Smith on the wind, to detect the predator that was soon to begin the hunt. In essence, a place had been held here for Smith since Azrael had been the first to come here. Smith now claimed that place.

This was where Smith rightly belonged. The oppressive heat bore down on him, but it brought Smith only comfort where others would have suffered torment. His threadbare robes billowed with the wind, threatening to flake away due to a fragility that was mere illusion. This attire of the damned was more than adequate for his needs.

Held between his thighs, the decaying beast stirred slightly, as if to remind Smith that he had a task to fulfil. It was a mission of such supreme importance that it hurt just to think of it. Down there in the valley of brimstone, the innocent fled from him and his kind. Despite the distance from him, it was imperative that none of them escape.

Why exactly, he didn't know, but the need to end them was burnt into him.

To his right and left the vaporous shapes of those like him tried hard to resist the hurricane winds. Still not formed, his brothers in this fight would join him soon enough. Whereas up until now, those chasing the innocent had been nothing but phantoms, their solidity was finally coming to this hell. And with that solidity, they would finally be able to do what the virus demanded.

The knowledge of who he really was came fleetingly, snatched images of his other life. The memories were selective, mainly centring around the regret he suffered for not killing the woman called Jessica Dunn. What was her name in this realm? And which one was she of those distant shapes that were barely discernible? Somewhere down there, her mind suffered in its perdition, the desire to end the torment overridden by the fear for those who followed. Smith knew full well that was how they felt, somehow knew that the innocent were aware of his presence here. The very scent of the air told him this, as if the smoke that swirled through his nostrils carried words and treaties explaining the fear of those whose only choice was to flee.

He had no idea how long he had been aloft this ravaged and necrotic horse, the concept of time slipping from his understanding. It felt right to be riding it though, the beast never objecting to his presence upon its back, its black mane soiled with dirt, holes visible in the skin upon which Smith sat. It shook its head, once again urging Smith to continue the chase he had no memory of ever starting as if Smith was merely a passenger rather than the master of the animal. The flesh he wore here was emaciated, as if hunger had been the only thing he had ever known, the bones of his knuckles almost visible. There was no discomfort in his belly though, food was not something he would ever require. The only sustenance he would ever consume here were souls.

Somehow it felt like this desert and this pursuit had been here forever, and Smith had simply been slotted in to play a piece of some nightmarish chess game.

"After," he said, the horse almost orgasmic as it moved forwards, dust rising up from the fetid ground as its hooves churned up the broken earth. He could not see the faces of those who he pursued, but he would catch up to them in time. And when he did, Smith knew he would descend unimaginable horrors upon those who were foolish enough to believe there was some kind of escape from this place. The innocents headed to the bleeding mountains, a destination that they could never reach in a thousand millennia.

Jessica wasn't the only one he sought. Smith could almost taste his prey, the flavour of Azrael thick on his tongue.

"I had you in my hands," Smith said to the wind, "and I didn't understand." In truth, he was being hard on himself. There had been an occasion when Azrael had been at his mercy, but that had been before the change, before the dawning of The Voice and his entry into this new Eden. He could have killed Jessica though, had even planned to despite not understanding the importance of her death. His failure lay heavy on him.

It was no catastrophic loss, or so he believed. Smith would find her here easier than he would in the world outside. And with her would be the others, the immune scattered across the globe far from his physical reach but so close to his psychic self. He and his forming kind would hunt them down so that they could rip and tear. Their deaths would be over in seconds, and yet they would be forced to endure it for all eternity.

Smith smiled, knowing he would cherish every second of their defilement. The chase was on, and it would only end one way.

***

Shah had briefly come out of unconsciousness, confusion his only friend for the fleeting moment he was awake. Unlike with Smith, the further exposure to Lazarus post antiserum hadn't resulted in a bleed in his brain, so his consciousness didn't fracture. Awake, he was still the same person he had always been, but as his eyes closed again and sleep came, that was when the change became evident.

At first, he was alone in the desert. There was heat, but to him, it bathed him in its comforting warmth. The ground under his feet was cushioned by the thick and heavy boots he wore, the design like nothing he had ever seen. He was no longer virtually naked. Instead, white robes hung from him, their edges caressing the breeze that brought him the smell of where he needed to go.

Shah didn't walk, because he knew he had no need to. With knowledge he had no idea he possessed, he simply waited for the white stallion to find him. It was a magnificent beast, large and muscular, its skin flawless, despite the dirt that swirled in the air around him. He watched as the horse approached, no hesitation or fear in the animal, the two of them joined by something beyond the understanding of a mere man. There was no saddle or bridle, but Shah had no need of such. Mounting the horse easily, Shah found no objection on the part of the animal. If anything, it seemed pleased, and Shah found himself wondering how such a fantastic and noble creature could survive in an environment as harsh as this.

The same could be said for Shah though, and by whatever magic or power commanded the physical laws of this place, he knew they were both right for this place. He and the horse had always belonged. Sitting comfortably and stable on the horse's back, he had no need to hold onto the mane, nor did he need to grip the beast's flanks with his thighs. Shah just seemed to stay there naturally, balanced as if the animal was a part of his own flesh.

The horse moved forward, it knew where to go.

It was mere moments before Shah saw the other horsemen. One second the horizon had been clear, the next there they were. All but one of those who he approached were ghosts of who they were meant to be, and as the horse drew nearer, he saw one solid face looked back at him. Smith. No longer his superior, but not an equal either. They could never be equal because they were too different. Shah saw it all, the horse Smith rode a reflection of his broken and diseased mind. Here, in this place, Smith was corrupted by greed and self-gratification, the horse under him skeletal, rotting in places. Even the robes Smith wore were threadbare, dirty and soiled by the sins he sweated out.

Yet they were to join together in the battle to come.

The stallion stopped next to Smith's tattered animal, the two horses greeting each other briefly. Shah did not say anything, for nothing had to be said. Everything that needed to be done was already known to them both. Out there, beyond their sight, were those that deserved to experience the true nature of hell on Earth. Neither Shah or Smith understood why they knew or believed this, just that it was the only way for things to be. To Shah, the killing of the immune was a sacred duty, handed down to him by his ancestors. There could be no denying that, and the untold agony he was required to inflict, the mind ripping torment that was within his power to unleash was merely the righteous way this world had to be.

It was as important to him as breathing.

There was only one thing that surprised Shah, though. Together they should have been four, and although there were only two disassociated figures representing where Dawson and Cartwright would likely be soon, there was evidence of another. Stronger than them, greater than them, the other would dwarf the power the likes of Shah and Smith held.

When the fifth arrived, things would really get interesting. Then the hunt would begin, and there would be no escape for those who ventured here in the dream state.

24.08.19
Peak District, UK

Azrael woke up to a quietness that denied the cacophony of the desert he had once again endured. A year ago in the desert he had been almost alone amongst those who had surrounded him, their shapes vague due to the distance they held from him, their presence in the desert not yet activated by exposure to Lazarus. Now those who could fight the virus were being awakened into the dream state. Only when they returned to the realm of slumber did they now coalesce into a physical form. Then they were vulnerable, forced to risk the devastation of the desert by their own physical need to sleep. Those there with him would come closer, as if Azrael was some sort of beacon of salvation. One by one, the minds stirred by Lazarus awoke in the nightmare that this desert represented.

And everyone was in danger from the horsemen who followed.

His skin was moist as usual, his body never acclimatising to the constant exposure to that hell he had been suffering for over a year now. The sleeping bag he had been given felt stifling, and he slipped his legs from it, his escape made easy by his never having engaged the zip. Fully clothed except for shoes, he found the restraints he had been placed in annoying and unnecessary. Despite what he had been guilty of in the past, those who held him now needed to appreciate his true worth and the value he could bring. Azrael wasn't a threat to them anymore.

Deep in the forefront of his thoughts, a plan was forming. He knew that he could end all of this if only he were given the chance. Only one man had the power to let all this happen.

The storage room he found himself in was dark around him, ideal conditions to conceal the killer that he once had been. Azrael had not been given the luxury of a bed or the chance for solitude, this room was chosen because it had only one door with barred windows. Once again in his dreams, he had seen the face of the defiler, the horseman now made whole. There was no understanding as to why Smith was the devil in his mind, but Azrael didn't need to know the why. It was enough to know that the deranged Colonel pursued him in a world where Azrael had no power. Sooner or later, the horsemen would come in force, and there would be nothing anyone could do to fight the demons they had become.

Not in the desert at least. Here, in the real world, that was where Azrael had a chance to fight his ultimate battle. This was where Azrael held his strength, as if his training as an assassin had been nothing but a red herring. It was becoming clear that his true calling was perhaps in bringing an end to Smith and his kind.

"You should be sleeping," Jeff said from the darkness. He had volunteered to watch over the prisoner, not trusting the handcuffs that bound Azrael's wrists and ankles. A light came on next to where Jeff was sitting, the lamp filling the surroundings with a depressed glow. Azrael saw the pistol his watcher was holding across his lap. He didn't fear it, death was meaningless to him.

"Sleep is a luxury I no longer have," Azrael answered.

"Nightmares?"

"Worse than nightmares," said Azrael, "the end of everything."

"Why don't you talk like normal folk?" Jeff admonished. He was torn about what to do with Azrael. Nick was certain the assassin was somehow vital to defeating Lazarus, but he hadn't been able to explain why to Jeff. While Jeff was willing to give Nick the respect he deserved, he was still split in his own mind as to whether this assassin shouldn't just be put down. They gave mad dogs that mercy didn't they?

A bullet between the eyes often did wonders for solving problems such as this.

"I need to talk to Colonel Carter," Azrael insisted. There was almost desperation in his words and an almost infectious need. "I think I understand it. I think I understand it all."

"What exactly is there to understand? It's the end of the world mate. Game, set and match."

"No," Azrael argued, "it's so much more than that."

"Well, Nick's outside. Have at it." Jeff threw a set of keys at him which Azrael used to unlock his ankles. "Leave the wrists though." Azrael paused briefly as if weighing up the injustice of it all. Accepting what had been said, he threw the keys back to Jeff and dragged himself from the floor, his body stiff from the hard ground. He hesitated, though. There was always the chance that Nick would say no. What then?

"Go on," Jeff said, "before I change my mind."

Night hit him as he stepped outside, the coolness of the air refreshing. In the past he would have longed for his pit, the foul stench he had created for himself wrapping him in its loving embrace. That idea seemed strangely alien to him now, the experience of being outside somehow revitalising to him. It was clear to Azrael that he was changing, the murderer created by Mother slowly dying to be replaced by something else.

The storage room led out into a greenhouse which was long past its use by date. Several of the glass panes were shattered, the racks where plants once grew now devoid of anything but dust and dirt. This was the building furthest from the main house, Tom insisting that he, Jessica and her reunited family be given some kind of privacy, at least for the first night. Nick had felt there was still a place for common decency, the rules that he lived by still important. He had allowed Tom his indulgence.

Nick was sat on a stool in the door to the greenhouse, the occasional glow illuminating his face as he sucked on a cigarette that he had blagged off Haggard. It was a luxury he had denied himself for nearly ten years. He didn't really have to worry about lung cancer anymore, not in the new Britain.

Nick realised that in his hands was something that would shortly become very rare. With the rise of the undead, there would be no industry left and no international shipping to restore the depleted stocks of nicotine that millions of people depended on. Even worse were the millions in the west that depended on a host of psychiatric medication to help them function. Most would cope with the withdrawal if they actually survived long enough for it to happen, but some would fall apart. The protection of a population, many of whom were psychologically unstable at the best of times was a logistical nightmare.

In the dim light cast by the moon and from the doorway to the storeroom, Azrael found himself a stool similar to the one Nick occupied and pulled it over to where his captor sat. He ignored how the handcuffs chafed his wrists, mere irritations of no concern to him.

"Did you ever get any satisfaction, killing all those people?" Nick asked.

"Yes," Azrael said honestly. "Killing was one of the greatest pleasures."

"Was?"

"I no longer believe as I did. You helped me with that."

"You will forgive me if I maintain a healthy air of scepticism where you are concerned," Nick warned.

"That might be a problem because you need to trust me now." Nick looked at him, an exhale of smoke briefly concealing his features.

"I don't think I need to do anything."

"You are mistaken." Azrael held up his wrists, the handcuffs glinting slightly as moonlight caught the polished chrome. "These are no longer necessary."

"I'm surprised you still have them on. I suspect a man of your skill could have defeated them easily." Nick was never one to rely on handcuffs or manacles, even the ones manufactured specifically for MI13. Almost any lock could be defeated if you had the training and the tools. Much better to rely on armed guards and physical barriers.

"Yes, but that would have sowed distrust."

"Show me anyway," Nick insisted. Azrael's eyes blazed at him, and Nick watched as the killer reached for his left ear. With pressure from the base of it, Azrael pushed upwards, revealing the slightly curved thin carbon fibre rod that had been embedded in the cartilage of the helix. Its presence wouldn't be detected by metal detectors or x-rays. Without even flinching, Azrael pulled the rod from the top of his ear, hardly any blood escaping from the wound. Nick suspected that no anaesthetic had been used when that pick had originally been placed. Azrael was one tough son of a bitch. It occurred to Nick that the man almost seemed to like the pain.

The handcuffs lasted thirty seconds, and they fell to the floor with a satisfying clunk.

"There aren't many people who can handle pain as you do," Nick said with a hint of admiration.

"I feel the pain, but Mother taught me how to lock it away. Pain is useful when it can be controlled."

"Help me understand what to do with you mate," Nick enquired. It took men and effort to keep Azrael under guard and to what end? He would never face a trial, the families of his victims would never be there to scream for justice. There were far greater problems with the world than what Azrael was guilty of.

"You need to let me go," Azrael advised.

"That's a big ask."

"I told you I saw Smith in my nightmares. Did you believe me?"

"I believe you believe it. And I believe you share some kind of link to Jessica and Whittaker."

"And the others." Before he had woken up, Azrael had been unable to count the number of lost souls he could see. It was into the thousands, phantoms from bodies scattered all across the globe. The number might get higher, but all the time there was the threat of the undead killing the immune in the real world. Azrael had seen what he suspected to be the end result of that. Scattered throughout the wasteland had been the statues, the bodies burnt through like charcoal. Just a touch would crumble them to ashes. Immune people who had been killed in the real world.

"What others?"

"Over a thousand of them. All like me, all like Jessica." That sparked Nick's interest, and he turned his body full on to Azrael. Jeff stepped out of the storeroom, clearly having overheard everything that had been said. He had also come to believe in the psychic link some of the immune seemed to share, despite what logic screamed at him. "And there are more every time I go into that dream place," Azrael continued. The virus was revealing those who were immune and unlocking a part of the mind lost to mankind. But with the psychic link came the threat of the horseman. The immune weren't safe anywhere it seemed.

"So why should we let you go?" Jeff asked. Azrael looked at him with an intensity Jeff had only ever seen in the eyes of those who had been in the heat of battle.

"So I can kill your Colonel Smith."

***

Jessica couldn't sleep, which was probably for the best, all considering.

Azrael had come to say goodbye to her, to thank her for the way she had volunteered to help him remember who he was. Jessica had been surprised Nick had agreed to let Azrael go, but she somehow felt that the decision was the right one to make. After several days, Jessica still couldn't get used to calling him Azrael, the face associated with a man she had known as Kevin. It wasn't Kevin though, wasn't even close. The face was the same, maybe a little older, but the person inside was not the man she had loved. There was no similarity whatsoever, no spark of the life she had been drawn to. Azrael was just a solemn, confused clone of the man she had adored, and any hate she held had dried up and disappeared in the first razor sharp desert breeze that had hit her boiling skin. The same went for the affection she had felt. To her, Azrael was just a stranger wearing a mask. There was a connection still there, but only through what they shared in their dreams.

Affection no longer existed, and Jessica felt strangely free of a weight she hadn't even consciously realised she was carrying. Even after his betrayal and his fake death, Jessica had continued to love the man.

Jessica did not miss him when he left that dark morning, his departure uncomfortable for him, as if he didn't have the experience or the words to say his goodbyes. At that moment anyone meeting him wouldn't have believed Azrael was capable of the murders he had committed, the social inadequacy he displayed painting a disguise of weakness. In the past, he had used such disguises as a weapon, a means to get close to his victims. Now his awkwardness was genuine, a side effect of a mind that had never really been allowed to live.

With sleep abandoned, Jessica sat in front of a raging fire that her brother had made. The armchair she was in felt comfortable, her body finally allowing itself to relax from the traumas of the last few days. With her adrenaline levels finally settling, she found herself feeling agitated as if she needed to do something. Instead, she fought against that, watching the flames, mesmerising herself with the sounds as the wood crackled from the heat. The wine in her hand helped, two glasses consumed so far, and more to come.

Azrael had left her alone, the other members of her family now all asleep, perhaps lost in their own dreams. She hoped those imaginings were more pleasant than her own, the memories of such still hard to grasp. Like any dream, her recollection faded quickly, despite the horrors she witnessed and experienced. Even the flames before her didn't bring back the recollection of what she had been required to endure. It was enough to experience the place when she was asleep without having to bring it back into the world of the real. If that were to happen, if she was forced by memory to experience that place in her every waking thoughts, Jessica thought there was a very real possibility that she would lose her mind.

Despite how much she had suffered, there was no denying she was luckier than most. Jessica was still alive, as were most of her family. She had soldiers to protect her and a place to hide far away from the zombie hordes that were tearing down the cities and laying waste to civilisation. For the time being at least, she could sit back and rest and dwell in the hope that Azrael could pull off what he was planning.

Azrael had told her he planned to kill Smith. Jessica sensed he was right in his belief that the Colonel needed to die, but she still didn't understand why Smith was there in the desert with them. Hell, she didn't even understand the desert itself. Why had the virus created this spectral realm so many of them ventured to when slumber came?

There was also the question of what would happen if Smith caught her in the desert. Jessica suspected it wouldn't be anything pleasant, but was she safe when she was awake? Could he be stalking her even now? Jessica didn't think she would be falling asleep any time soon, but she knew eventually it would be forced on her by the frailties of her own humanity.

She remembered watching a film once where it was stated that, if you died in your dreams, you died in real life. When it came to the desert, Jessica knew that this was definitely what would happen.

24.08.19
London, UK

Sid(Z) had survived the tanks, the vehicles retreating as they found the onslaught against them too difficult to deal with. Most of the zombies hadn't continued the attack, instead choosing to wander on their ever increasing spiral, pillaging every human dwelling they came across. Nothing was sacred, Churches and Mosques just as much viable targets as living rooms and office blocks.

For whatever reason Sid(Z) had broken off from the main group it had found itself in, the number of zombies around it less than a dozen now. It had also lost a boot at some point, the damage that was already present in its ankle exacerbated. That might have been why it had been left behind, most of those zombies with it damaged and hindered in some way. The zombie next to Sid(Z), naked and yet completely oblivious to its lack of attire, had a large kitchen knife embedded between two of its ribs. It had actually been the victim of a murder, its former boyfriend sent into a panic by the virus that had taken its human form. Not quite understanding just how Lazarus worked, the boyfriend had plunged the knife into the heart of his sleeping girlfriend, thinking that would somehow save his lover from what lay ahead. He couldn't abide the thought of the woman he shared his bed with becoming one of the undead, but all he did was speed up her conversion. Said boyfriend had then had to flee when the zombie came after him. He didn't get very far.

There was no logic as to where Sid(Z) went, its wanderings seemingly aimless. Despite that, the zombies spread the virus effectively, missing few of the streets that made London the huge metropolis it was. Those who had chosen to cower in their residences were soon uncovered, very few homes able to withstand the sustained onslaught of determined zombies. By heading back towards Central London, Sid(Z) and its group avoided the skirmishes that were still occurring on the outskirts of the city and were free to consume and attack whatever they came across. No zombified rats followed them here. They had all scurried away, forming into packs that disappeared into the dark places, stripping the land of creatures whatever the size.

An hour ago, Sid(Z) and its gang of decay had chanced upon survivors out on the street, a rare occurrence with the level of zombie infestation that had swamped the British capital. The battle had been brutal but swift, the men choosing to fight them actually being able to destroy one of the zombies. Unfortunately, baseball bats and hatchets were of little value against a determined zombie, not with their speed and strength. The zombies took them all, adding all but one to their necrotic ranks. Humans should know by now that you had to bring guns to a zombie fight.

If Sid(Z) followed its present path, the journey would take it right into the centre of London where any semblance of government had collapsed. Even now, half the bodies of the British Cabinet were hunting for flesh on the streets that had held so much history. What you were in your former life mattered not once you died. The undead made no distinction between the wealthy and the privileged. The only discrimination they showed was for the immune whose very presence had to be removed from the planet. As if almost on cue, Sid(Z) moved its head in such a way as to detect the minutest particles in the air. There was another immune out there, and Sid(Z) found itself drawn to its new target.

Its body was degrading though. Still able to walk, the legs were bloated, the blood that had settled there now weeping out of any and every wound. Soon the skin would rupture, the flesh not able to contain the pressure for much longer. It would walk until it couldn't and then it would crawl. Eventually, the ability for the joints to move would end, and even then it would continue to writhe wherever it ended up. It would not liquefy, though. Instead, it would dry out, the virus intent on keeping the carcass mobile and useful for as long as possible. And of course, the original virus was still out there, still spreading through desperate populations. Any zombie that did start to fall apart would easily be replaced by those created from the airborne precursor.

It would be a long time before the undead ceased to be a threat. But eventually, that day would come. Would there be anything left of humanity to remake civilisation though? Would planet Earth ever be free of the virus?

24.08.19
Peak District, UK

It felt strange to be alone once again. For the last few days, there had always been someone near him or watching him, but now on the quiet country road, he was once again the sole agent of his destiny. He would either succeed or fail, the fates and sheer luck helping to decide that. There was no telling what Azrael was up against, so he might even be driving towards his own death. That didn't matter, death held no power over him. He also knew that if he did nothing, Smith would finally catch him in the desert, and that would be the end of everyone. As dangerous as this journey would be, it was the best chance Azrael had of having any kind of a future.

He believed with all his being that he was in danger from the horrors that stalked him in the nightmare world, but he didn't know why any of this was happening. Azrael was certain he could die there, but he was uncertain as to whether he actually had to be asleep for that to happen. Was there a representation of him there even when he was awake? From his own dreams, he had witnessed the figures around him phasing in and out, sometimes solid, sometimes no more substantial as vapour. The phantom ghosts had always been there from the beginning, only the last few days had any of them acquired any kind of substance. It was clear that the virus was obviously unlocking this forgotten part of the human mind.

Azrael also suspected he had seen what happened to those figures when they died in the real world, the fragile ash forms like a marker to the pending failure of humanity.

None of that was his primary concern now. Driving the Land Rover Tom had lent him, Azrael navigated the winding country lanes to get as close to his destination as he could before he was forced to abandon the vehicle. Ahead of him was a perilous journey with three obvious foes. Firstly, there were the desperate refugees of humanity which would be spreading out in all directions, clogging the highways and bringing the virus wherever they fled. Their own selfishness would bring destruction to the country as a whole, speeding up the dissemination of Lazarus throughout the smaller towns and cities. Within their ranks would also be those who reeked of malevolence, preying on the weak even as the apocalypse fell all around them. Such individuals would be wise to avoid Azrael and stay out of his way.

Secondly, there would be the inevitable undead. Azrael hoped he could avoid them for as long as possible. A single zombie he could probably deal with, especially with the weapons he now possessed. If he encountered a pack of them though, then his time on this planet would likely be at an end.

Around his waist was his killing belt, kept for him by Nick's team and returned to him to his pleasant surprise. There was the addition of a Glock revolver with two hundred rounds of ammunition. On the seat next to him was a C8 carbide, with enough spare magazines to hopefully get the job done. He was loaded for the task at hand, so long as he didn't encounter too many enemies. The challenge with that was his lack of awareness of how the undead were attracted to immune individuals. Any zombie that came even close to him would be drawn to Azrael by his pheromones that floated freely on the breeze.

And then there was the third foe, Smith himself. There were others there involved in the chase, but it was only Smith he could truly detect for sure. Why Smith was coming for him in that nocturnal realm was a mystery to Azrael, but mysteries didn't always need to be solved. All Azrael needed to do was kill Smith, of that he was certain. Only time would tell if that was going to be enough to save those who were immune like him. Perhaps it would be. Then again, if he killed Smith, what was to stop the phantoms that had chased him for over a year continuing in their pursuit?

To Azrael, it was clear that the Lazarus virus had tapped into something primal in the human genetic code that he couldn't understand. He wasn't a scientist, he killed people, that was all he knew. And while he was extremely good at that skill, it gave him no help in determining the truth of what was happening in his own mind. Maybe Smith would know, and Azrael knew he would need to carefully plan the demise of the Colonel. A quick death, or an interrogation to reveal the secrets that might be held.

The road ahead arched right, and he steered the car easily despite the lack of headlights. It wasn't wise to announce yourself on such a dark and starless night, the night vision goggles he wore more than adequate for him to see. Still, he never went above thirty miles an hour, mindful that the closer he got to his destination, the more likely one of the first two threats would manifest. With much of the journey ahead likely to be done on foot, Azrael was well aware this trip could take a day or two, longer if he had to hide out or even retreat.

That was of course if he even made it at all.

24.08.19
Outside Moscow, Russia

Claudia Renton fell asleep due to pure exhaustion. When she awoke to screams, she was introduced to the frightening realities of what Lazarus could do.

The Russian response to the threat posed by the virus might have been tyrannical and devoid of the concept of rights for the individual, but it made sense. Following a logical plan of isolation, anyone who could potentially be a carrier was subject to detention and quarantine. This basically meant that anyone who had travelled to Russia from abroad in a designated time period had all been rounded up and sent to hastily recommissioned detention camps. Not a single person was missed, so effective was the Russian security services' monitoring of foreign individuals.

This was where Claudia found herself, locked away on the outskirts of Moscow, sharing a concrete cell with nine other women. Ten mattresses and a single toilet. At no time were the harsh halogens in the ceiling ever extinguished, so sleep, when it came, was a blissful release.

The fact that she was an American citizen counted for nothing. Her American passport might as well have been a figment of her imagination. There was an argument that being an American had made her situation worse, the old prejudices from the Cold War still alive. Russians were not ones to forget the injustices they perceived they had suffered. They had once been a mighty superpower, and the loss of that status rankled.

Now Claudia was awake, watching a woman she had never spoken to attack the others with such ferocity that it was hard to believe that what she was actually seeing was real. The room she was in had seen its occupants separate into several groups, Claudia on her own in the corner nearest the door. Very few of the other prisoners seemed to speak English, which made communication difficult and just increased her sense of isolation. While she hadn't experienced any overt hostility, Claudia didn't feel any kind of camaraderie with her fellow inmates. She was basically ignored, which was perhaps the best she could hope for in this situation.

Awake now, Claudia retreated as far as she could into the corner of the room, trying to limit the chances of herself becoming a target. One of the women she shared the cell with was already lying ruined on the floor, the blood pouring from a gaping neck wound. Briefly, the attacker turned to look at Claudia, the black soulless eyes gazing deep into her mind. Then the zombie continued its attack, grabbing another older woman by the hair and wrenching her to the floor. Nobody helped, because there was nothing anyone could do except wait and pray that their end would be quick.

There was a tearing sound like Claudia had never heard before, and then something came hurtling at her with such speed that the only reaction she could give was to cover her face with her arms. Crouched down as she was, the severed arm struck her on the knees, the blood quickly soaking into the cheap and threadbare blue boiler suit she had been given. The clothes had been better than the naked state she had arrived in, but as the red spread down her legs, the only thing she wanted to do was to strip the material from her body and scream.

She did the latter, she did that in spades.

The zombie threw its next victim against a wall, the woman rapidly dying from the grievous wounds she was receiving. With hands now coated in precious bodily fluids, the zombie struck another woman across the face, its mouth still chewing on the flesh it had torn from the first victim.

Something in Claudia snapped. Whatever caused it wasn't bravery, but some ingrained sense of self-preservation that realised her life was shortly going to be over. With a roar that came deep from some animal instinct long since forgotten, Claudia exploded from where she crouched, running towards the zombie that seemed not to register her presence. She slipped at the last moment, and instead of impacting into the zombie's back, she fell flailing into the back of the zombie's legs, buckling its knees.

The zombie, still struggling with its balance due to its recent resurrection, toppled forward, its face smashing into one of the concrete walls with a painful sounding crunch. The motion was so violent that the head was snapped back, miraculously snapping the vertebrae in the zombie's neck. Claudia tried to stand up, but her hands slipped on the pool of blood she had landed in. Instead, she rolled away, her skin and the front of her boiler suit now slick with the juice from the zombie's first victim.

None of the other women helped her.

As badly damaged as the zombie was, it managed to pull itself up from where it had fallen, its head held at an obscene angle, the mouth trying to open from where both mandibular condyles had fractured. The monster was still dangerous, and it would have gone on to attack the rest of the women if the door to the cell hadn't suddenly opened, admitting an armed soldier. Time seemed to freeze before the cacophony erupted all around Claudia.

The auto shotgun the soldier held blew the head clean off the zombie and sprayed infected brain tissue and bone over most of the remaining women. Claudia turned and looked at the soldier in disbelief. Why had it taken him so long to intervene? She expected the man to finish them all off, but he just swore in Russian and left the room, locking the door behind him. Claudia had no way of knowing the Russians were not just detaining prisoners here, they were also doing experiments of their own.

So this was what Lazarus did. With one zombie killed and two women close to death, Claudia wondered whether the soldier would return to finish what he started. How long before none of them were left? And would her end come before the virus she was now undoubtedly contaminated with stripped the humanity from her?

24.08.19
Peak District, UK

It wasn't long before Azrael found civilisation again, although he wished he hadn't. Thirty minutes out from the farm, he had been forced to abandon the car. The sparse road network quickly became blocked, his Land Rover not able to go fully cross country like the APC's had done. Azrael had tried, but the vehicle had quickly become stuck. He had at least made it close to the A6, but now found all the roads full of cars and from a distance, he could often see the people who were flooding out of Greater Manchester. This was what he had been afraid of. A mass exodus of humanity.

The big question was where the hell did all these people think they were going? Effective escape on an island like Great Britain could really only be attained by heading towards the coast.

It would have been better for him to have come with backup, but this was a journey he knew he had to take on his own. Nick and Haggard couldn't risk any of their men for a mission whose objectives were dubious at best. Travelling in force right back to where they had already escaped from, to kill an officer in Her Majesty's Armed Forces based on the word of a self-confessed mass murderer was something a man like Nick was never going to agree to. Azrael was actually surprised when the MI13 man had permitted him to go on his own, even more astounded when guns and equipment were thrust at him.

"We have more guns than we need, I'm sure we can spare a few," Haggard had said with a wry smile that had been partially hidden by the blackness of the night.

There was a sense that Azrael had been let loose to give him some sort of fighting chance. He had expected Jeff to also protest, but the former soldier had almost seemed relieved that he had been freed of his guard duty. Jeff had voiced no objections to Nick's plan, which was surprising because Azrael had always had a sense that Jeff would have been more than happy to stick a knife in his guts. And yet it had been Jeff personally who had handed Azrael back his killing belt. Azrael didn't know that there was a cost to him being set free.

It was only right before he was due to leave that Nick had revealed the ulterior motive he had been harbouring. Handing Azrael a piece of paper and a satellite phone, Nick had given him a further task to do.

"Natasha has managed to access Moros again," Nick had said. "Apparently the other night a military courier from Dr Patel's hospital was ambushed. Moros intercepted the communication of the people who did that ambush."

"What is that to me?" Azrael had enquired.

"The courier was carrying three vials of the antiserum Smith injected into you and himself. That piece of paper has the GPS of where we think that antiserum was taken."

"You want me to bring it back?" What good would three vials do?

"That all depends on what you find with Smith. Now that I've got access to Moros again, I've been able to ask it things, to come up with probabilities and ideas about what's going on here. I know you suspect that the XV1 turned Smith into this thing you see in the desert. Personally, I wasn't up for fully believing what you have told me so far, but Moros seems to agree with you."

"What do you need me to do?"

"If you survive your encounter with Smith, I'm asking you to go to those coordinates and find those vials. I've learnt to trust what Moros tells me over the years. If you are right, and if the antiserum created Smith, then whatever remains needs to be destroyed."

"Why don't you just send the army if it's that important?" Azrael had asked.

"What army?" Nick had said sadly. "I can't raise any forces left in that area. And even if I could, it's in the heart of Manchester's undead uprising. So it's all on you mate. With luck, I might be able to call in an airstrike, but we need eyes on the ground for that."

"You do realise I probably won't even make it there, right?"

"You'll make it," Nick said confidently. "A man like you doesn't give up easily."

Would he make it though? Azrael had no hesitation in killing anyone who got in his way, but the undead were a force even he couldn't hope to cope with. That was why he had sacrificed valuable space in the rucksack he now carried for the four rolls of duct tape. He was immune to Lazarus, but not to the teeth that spread it. Once applied strategically, the duct tape would protect against bites, but that still wouldn't save him from the strength of the creatures. Stealth would be his only ally here.

The sounds of voices came to him through the night. The words were a mixture of anger and fear, the interaction between the weak and those who preyed on the vulnerable. Azrael felt a pull, a need to somehow atone for his former sins and right any wrongs that were being committed on this country road. He tried to resist the desire to play saviour for it would only slow him down and put him at increased risk. Whoever it was that found themselves at the mercy of the jackals masquerading as humans, they were on their own. If it wasn't directly his fight, he would be foolish to get involved.

Stepping off the road to avoid whatever it was he heard ahead, he pushed his way through a thin hedge into a field that had been left fallow. The ground was uneven and rough underfoot, Azrael stepping carefully. It would be ridiculous to come this far only to sprain an ankle by placing a foot wrong. Stalking, as if hunting the most timid of prey, Azrael made his way parallel to the road, the sounds of conflict growing ever louder.

Through the hedgerow he could now see some of what was going on, several cars jammed up on the road, their lights illuminating much of what was occurring. The beams burst through the foliage in places, and Azrael moved further into the field so as to carefully avoid stepping into that light.

It looked like three men had a family of four at their mercy. As he crawled past, he witnessed the father of the family beaten to the floor by two of the men who rained kicks down upon his face and head with a fury that only came with chaos and anarchy. Some people, released from the bonds of laws and social expectation would easily descend into an almost animalistic state, driven by pure emotion and desire. Azrael understood that feeling more than most. After all, he was created by Mother to do only one thing. Kill. Every death had been ecstasy to him, how better to ensure an assassin would end the life of anyone demanded of it?

The mother was held by the largest of the three, her sobs and her pleas only enriching the experience for the ruffians who seemed to be relishing the noise of her distress. As for the two children, they sat on the road's asphalt clinging to each other, eyes closed. They were both girls, young enough to hopefully escape the worst of what the men could do, but old enough to understand the horrors that were being perpetrated.

Looking at them again, Azrael knew that these men would not care how old they were. Their frenzy would cause them to engage in horrors that would make the eyes of regular people bleed.

Azrael felt that pull again. Never before had he felt the need to protect the weak, and the sensation confused him. He couldn't risk his mission for this, could he? As atrocious as the situation was, it was being repeated across the planet a thousandfold. His intervention here would make no difference. It was hard to deny that something had changed within him though, he could feel it. Perhaps it had been his talks with Jessica or the frankness of his final conversation with Mother that Nick had allowed. Whatever had caused this shift troubled him because it was going to get in the way of what he needed to do. His focus should be getting to Smith at the exclusion of all other things, but here he was feeling concern, feeling pity for people he didn't even know.

It didn't make any sense. Millions were dying all over the world and yet here he was fighting the urge to intercede in someone else's squabble. He didn't even know what the altercation was about. One of the men stomped on the father's face again, bringing a fresh scream from the mother. The crack of bone ricocheted across the surrounding fields.

Too loud, they were being too loud. That was what finally caused him to intervene, the excuse he needed to end his hesitation. Although it was unlikely, there was always the chance that there were undead in the area and they would be drawn towards the mother's cries. Pulling the C8 CQB Carbine off his shoulder, he knelt as best he could on the broken ground and lined up the first shot, safe in the knowledge that the suppressor the gun was equipped with would deal with much of the noise.

The men were less than forty meters from him...they didn't stand a chance even with the bad lighting. The first man's head exploded as the bullet penetrated just above the left eye. It was a steel core lead round, ideal for penetrating armour and bone. A good percentage of the man's brains departed with the bullet through the back of his skull, ending the threat he posed to the family.

The second man didn't have a chance to even react, the bullet that killed him arriving a second later puncturing two lethal holes through his heart. One entry, one exit. Before he was on the floor, the last of the men was killed by another head shot, allowing the woman to break free of his malevolent clutches. Re-shouldering the weapon, Azrael stood and continued walking through the ruined field. That was as much as he was willing to do to help, and he hoped that the use of those three bullets wouldn't be the ultimate end of him.

Best now to stay off the roads as much as possible, which would slow him down even more, at least until he got closer to the cities. When the fields started to be replaced by concrete, then the real dangers would begin. By his reckoning, he was only a quarter of the way to where he needed to be.

24.08.19
Brazil

Sleep did not come easily to Mother these days, so when it finally did arrive, it was like a blessing. You had to take it when you could, even if that meant falling asleep in the middle of the day, which was why Mother had dropped off on the balcony overlooking the forest below. The insects didn't bother her, the fine netting stopping any invasion by the bloodsucking creatures of the tropics.

It was still daytime, but the sun had already begun its descent beneath the horizon, Mother's skin protected from the burning rays by the awning above her. She sat there, reality slowly coming back to her, a sharp mind trapped in a failing and disease-ridden body. As pleasant as the scenery around her was, her thoughts drifted back to the troubles she had unwittingly caused. This was not what she had wanted to achieve, and it was difficult for her to not regret the part she had played in the world's end.

Mother had objected strongly to the creation of the Lazarus virus, but she never should have let herself be usurped by those useless, power-hungry men. There was a moment, years ago, where she had glimpsed the true character of Father and she had not acted upon that revelation. Instead, she had let him warp and distort her dream, the vast sums of money he promised the organisation a temptation that she really should have resisted.

It would have been so much better for the world if she had simply shot him through the heart. If given such a chance, Mother knew she would not hesitate to do so now. In that fleeting instant, her intuition had told her to kill Father, along with the other two. At the time, she couldn't put her finger on why she had felt that way towards them. It was only later when she was removed from any semblance of power that she realised what her own innate sixth sense had been trying to tell her. If only she had listened to her gut like she had so many times in the past. The opportunity had passed, and now the Earth was on the brink of ruin.

She knew she had to shoulder some of the blame for all this.

Mother wondered how long it would take the infection to reach her here. She had months left to live at best, and she would likely live out her days without seeing a single zombie. It was more than probable that the outside world would be held at bay by the forest for that long. There was a dirt track that wound for several miles through the thick Brazilian Rainforest, so the only efficient way of reaching her retreat was by helicopter, not something a zombie would be wont to use, she figured. She had food, fresh water, and power from the solar array on the roof of the villa, storage batteries keeping the lights on during the night. The world could go to hell, and unless she turned on the TV, she wouldn't even know it.

Mother considered herself to be self-sufficient here as well as safe. She should have known better…she had been wrong about so much recently.

Mother began the painful process of standing, gnashing her teeth to help fend off the pain that bristled through every joint. The burning sensation over her liver burst into life, perhaps upset that it had been forgotten, if only briefly. The opiates helped with that, but it was getting harder and harder to deal with. She was already taking doses that would kill a grown man unaccustomed to the various narcotics she had been prescribed. Why was it her body could acclimatise to the drugs, constantly diminishing their effects, and yet the pain got ever more intense? Truly there could have been no loving God, no intelligent design behind the construction of Homo Sapiens. Not unless that God was a sadist of epic cruelty.

In the safety of her bedroom was her last resort, the heroin that she would only take towards the end of her days when the suffering became truly unbearable. Originally that was also how she had planned to end it all as well, an overdose of bliss to remove her troubles and her unending agony. Several times over the past few days, she had contemplated suicide, but that wasn't to be her path just yet. There was still a point to her being here, although what that was she did not know. She had been betrayed by Father, by Uncle, and by Brother…that duplicity required some form of payment. Mother was not the kind of woman to let pain and her inevitable impending death get in the way of revenge. Not that she now knew the truth.

Standing now, she took an agonised step into the living room, the air conditioning there evaporating the sweat that the heat from outside had created. There was something wrong here though, something out of place. Mother looked around the familiar surroundings and realised too late that it was the smell of the place. Someone was here.

So, finally they had come. Part of her had always expected this, despite the precautions she had taken.

"I'm alone and unarmed if that's what you're worried about."

Several corridors led off from the edge of the room, and a man appeared from one of these. Dressed in full combat gear, armed with an AR15, Mother knew instantly that he was an American. A second man appeared from his hiding place, and Mother prepared herself for death. She hoped that wasn't what they were here for.

"Maria Braun, I assume?" David Campbell said to her.

"I have not been known by that name for a long time." Campbell approached her, the other man watching her closely. Mother was pleased to see they were treating her with a level of respect that her reputation deserved. She was not the helpless old woman her visage suggested. In her life as an agent for the KGB and the East German Stasi, Mother had killed twenty-three people. Most of those had been with bullets at a distance, but four had been close and personal. For one of those kills, she could still remember the sensation as the knife slipped through the pitiful resistance offered by the victim's flesh. There had even been a child amongst that number, a boy in the wrong place at the wrong time who had needed to be silenced to stop Mother's identity being revealed. She had no weapon on her person now and she was not going to resist whatever these men wanted of her. If anything, she was glad they were here. "Why have you come all this way, American? Surely this old woman can be of little threat to your country now?"

"Maria Braun, under Title 18 of the United States Code, section 3181, and under Presidential Executive Order, you are hereby placed under arrest for immediate extradition to the United States of America." Campbell, whose face was obscured by the black ski mask he wore, extracted a pair of handcuffs from his belt.

"You would kidnap and handcuff an old woman?" There was mockery in Mother's voice. There certainly wasn't any fear.

"Alpha team cleared for extraction," the other man said into his radio.

"That's exactly what's going to happen. I'd rather not hurt you in the process. I've been told to bring you back in one piece."

"Do I not get to call my lawyer?" Mother pretended to beg. She couldn't keep up the pretence, and she chuckled to herself. "I'm sorry, I couldn't resist it. Hands in front or behind? I would prefer in front if possible, my arthritis you see."

"There won't be any lawyers where you're going ma'am," Campbell said as he stepped behind her, defying her request. She was surprised by how gently he took her wrists so she offered up no resistance. As bad as her body felt, it could always feel worse with a few broken bones or a sprained joint.

From the open window, the distant sound of a helicopter could be heard.

"I see. Am I allowed to take my medication?"

"A doctor will be assigned to you once you are on US soil. Are you able to walk by yourself, or do you need assistance?" Campbell was surprised by how frail the woman looked, he hadn't been expecting that. You don't envisage the person who helped slaughter the world to be so feeble.

"The illegality of my medication is perhaps more than your doctors would be permitted to allow."

"Afraid I can't help you with that," Campbell stated.

"Then we should go," Mother insisted. "I have things I am sure your superiors want to know."

"Thank you for not resisting," Campbell added genuinely. Arresting an old women was perhaps not the height of his clandestine career. He gave Mother a gentle push forward, and together they headed to the lift that would take them to the villa's roof. There was a helicopter landing pad there to facilitate Mother's easy passage on the rare events she left the villa.

"How did you find me? I thought my Legend was perfect."

"We had files on you from when the Berlin Wall came down. You should never have told Colonel Carter your name." Mother nodded sagely. She had known the elusive organisation MI13 would share her details with the

Americans, and yet she had freely shared so much with them. It was thus only a matter of time for someone to have come for her, although they had acted quicker than she could have expected. Mother would have preferred to end her days here, but perhaps a part of her had deliberately let slip the keys to her identity.

"Perhaps that's exactly why I told him," she said with a wink. They were stopped now, waiting for the lift to arrive. Two more armed men appeared.

"Rest of the house is clear," one of them said to Campbell. "Charges have been set."

"Get a last look at this place, Maria," Campbell said. "It will be the last time you see it."

"You will be needing my journal then," Maria stated. There was no hint of deception in her voice.

"Where is it?"

"In the study. The safe is behind the Rembrandt. Do you want to use your precious explosives, or shall I just give you the code?" She was playing with them now. One last adventure to finish off her days.

"The code," Campbell said, "would be very much appreciated." Mother gave it.

"While you are there," she said mischievously, "you might as well fetch my medicine."

24.08.19
Houston, USA

Rupert Clayton had a plan that he was willing to implement. He had the men, and he had the firepower. He thought he would be able to surprise those who were now oppressing the population of Houston. Overlooking the main entrance to the Astrodome was the 610 freeway, and Rupert would position snipers up there as well as a team with a fifty calibre machine gun. That would help clear his entry into where his wife was being held. He needed to act soon as well, the hurricane was bearing down on them, the winds outside already picking up. In better times, Houston would have been evacuated, but how did you do that and fight the zombie infestation?

His other problem would be the armoured Bradley fighting vehicles he had seen, but he knew a guy who could help with that. A few LAW rockets should do the trick in that regard, and Clayton had already arranged delivery. He might not have had the luxury of air support and tanks, but he had a few other tricks up his sleeve. There were nearly three hundred active members in his militia, and nearly half of them were up for the cause. He even figured the army and the doctors would have no option but to release his wife to his care when faced with those kinds of numbers, so perhaps a firefight could be avoided. Rupert would prefer not to actively engage fellow Americans on US soil, but he was prepared to do what needed doing. He didn't hate the men and women who wore the uniform, but he despised the suits in Washington who told them to defy the rights of the American people.

Unfortunately for him, that same US government had other ideas. For years, the Department of Homeland Security had been using Fusion Centres to collect and analyse all civilian telecommunications and internet traffic. The fusion process was an overarching method of managing the flow of information and intelligence across levels and sectors of government to create raw information for analysis. Rupert thought he was a patriot and thought he was clued up about how to plan his mini-insurrection away from the eyes and ears of the Feds, but to the US government, he was just a terrorist who had come to their attention. His use of citizen's band and ham radio didn't protect him from the listening ears of the deep state. His demise, however, was sealed when his satellite phone rang.

"Hello?"

"Rupert, thank God." The voice on the other end sounded weak, the breath raspy.

"Doreen. Sweet Jesus." The woman he loved was all he had been able to think about since she had been shipped to that damned quarantine facility.

"Rupert, I just wanted... I just needed to say goodbye."

"Goodbye, but..."

"Shut up you old goat and listen." The words themselves were harsh, but the tone wasn't. "It's getting bad here, and I don't know how long I can hide this phone."

"I love you, Doreen," Rupert said, his heart in his throat. "Don't you dare quit on me. I'm coming for you. Those soldier boys will hand you over or so help me, I'll kill every one of them."

"It's too late for that, Rupert," Doreen said. Her voice was pained but calm. "The people here are dying all around me. You need to look after yourself. Save yourself."

"No Doreen," Rupert's voice rose as his desperation grew. "I'll not abandon you. If it's the end, then I want you here. If you are going to die, it will be in my arms."

"But then you will get the virus too." She was in tears now.

"Do you think I care about that? Do you think my life means anything without you? No, I'm coming to get you, Doreen." He expected her to chastise him, to try and persuade him otherwise, but Doreen Clayton didn't.

"I think I've always loved you," Doreen said, "even before I knew you. How did I get to be so lucky?"

"I am the lucky one. My life would be meaningless without you in it. You hang in there Doreen. I'm coming for you. And I'm bringing hell with me."

That was why they came for him. Alerted to what Rupert was planning, a predator drone was already locked onto his location where it hovered, awaiting final confirmation to strike. Prior to Lazarus, the concept of using such a tool for assassination within the boundaries of the continental United States would have been unthinkable. The Constitution and the Bill of Rights didn't count now, all that mattered was maintaining whatever order could be established.

Clayton for his part, was sat in the office in his home. He had no idea the drone was up there, nor did he have any clue that his communications had been so ruthlessly compromised. Clayton also wouldn't be the first victim of such a drone strike. Soldiers and law enforcement were needed to suppress the growing zombie outbreaks across the state and across the country. Men couldn't be spared to storm and seize what was likely a militia compound with armed resistance. Nobody had time for that, so with authorisation, the Hellfire missile released itself and hurtled towards the target.

Looking out of the window as he was, Clayton actually saw the missile, but he had no idea what it was. A second later he had no ideas at all, the building he was in obliterated by the one-hundred-pound warhead. Five people died in the blast, Rupert Clayton being one of them. When the rubble settled, any thought of insurrection had evaporated. Without its charismatic leader, the threat from that particular militia ceased to be of any consequence. Its members scattered, driven by fear and their own self-interest. Doreen never did get to see her husband again, and as Doctor Lee had feared, she was one of the first people in the Astrodome to be euthanised before her death actually occurred. Unlike many others who met a similar fate, Doreen actually requested it when she learnt of her husband's death.

The threat of hurricane Jezebel made those in charge of Houston abandon any pretence of hunting for the immune. Now it was time for scorched Earth, and a rapid retreat before the wind started to rip the city apart.

24.08.19
Jersey City, USA

Gabriel had awoken with a headache that would stop an elephant in its tracks. The pain spread down his neck and along his spine, the skin seemingly tender to the slightest of touches. He was alive though, which showed that he had indeed been vaccinated against the virus.

Even with the vaccination, it was clear that Lazarus had almost taken him. Looking at his watch, he saw that he had been unconscious for over twenty-four hours, such was the toll he had paid in fighting off the contagion. A normal man would have lain there immobilised by the agony, but Gabriel was far from a normal man. He sat up regardless, and let the waves of dizziness take him. This was a ride he would endure until it was over. Gabriel had suffered worse in his time.

Within an hour, his pain had subsided to a manageable level, a dull ache settling into every muscle of his body. His first attempt at re-hydrating himself had been met with rejection, his stomach regurgitating the small volume of water he had tried to consume. It was a good way to try and choke yourself to death and Gabriel wasn't willing to risk such a second time. Lying there in the dirt and his own filth, he resorted to more drastic measures, the saline bag he carried in his backpack the only way to get the necessary fluid into his system. With shaky hands, he had injected himself, squeezing the bag with an energy he didn't possess to get the saline into his bloodstream.

His body began to slowly recover. With more time passed, he could now drink, and he consumed the last of his bottled water hungrily. With his thirst only partially quenched, the hunger pangs struck him, but he didn't dare risk solid food just yet. There was a long road before his body would let him do what it was supposed to do naturally. Death had almost taken him, and he was obviously being punished for his refusal to die. He would live though, that was all that mattered.

Mother had instructed him to endure, hence his flight from New York City. He had survived the tunnels that led under the river, encountering his first undead which he had helped produce. He felt nothing in the way of guilt for the part he had played in the carnage of the Big Apple. Orders were simply there to be followed. How was he to know those orders had been sent by people who had usurped the true leader of his organisation? Gabriel was loyal only to Mother, the other faces of Gaia strangers to him.

He was conflicted, though. While they had betrayed Gabriel, whoever had planned this had obviously felt he was worthy of saving. Why else had Gabriel been sent the vaccine, the one he had injected into himself.

Like Azrael, Gabriel had lived another life. He remembered little of it, only flashes remaining. Whatever it was he had done, he had been successful at it, he knew that much. That all ended when he awoke anew in the room of blood. Just like Azrael. Just like all the others who had come before them. Mother had made them, and so he would do what Mother told him to do. He would live. But he had no idea what to do with that life without the constant direction of his creator.

Living wasn't enough when the urge and the passion to kill still flowed through your veins.

24.08.19
Combs, UK

Azrael had avoided the dual carriageway in favour of a single lane road that was, fortunately, free of traffic. The sky above had cleared of clouds, the half-moon providing enough illumination for him to see where he was going. He preferred not to rely on the night vision goggles too much as he found his eyes became tired.

The small town of Combs lay ahead of him, or at least that was what the road sign had said. It would likely be uninfected at present, but there was a risk that it had been swamped with refugees. The plan was thus to skirt around it, avoiding as much of humanity as possible.

Just to the north of Combs, he would pick up the railway line which to him was going to be the best route to follow. There would be no trains running, and the majority of the people in flight wouldn't have even considered it as a possible escape route. The major advantage of railway lines was the way they cut a path through countryside, hills, towns and cities. With the railway line and the handheld GPS navigator he had with him, he would hopefully make it all the way to Preston. It was his best chance of making it there in one piece. First though, he had to get to the train tracks without taking an unnecessary detour, and that meant getting past Combs.

Azrael smelt the trouble before he saw it. Burning, the acrid stench of plastics and rubber on fire, the distant flicker of flames becoming evident as he carried on down the road. He walked with a quietness most people wouldn't have been capable of, and he slipped off the road before those lying in wait for any unwary travellers spotted him. Through fields yet again, it wasn't long before he saw the burning car that was half blocking the road that led into Combs.

He could hear the muted whispers of those lying in wait, the occasional flash of a cigarette exposing their position. Amateurs, driven to act by the desperation they obviously felt.

It was clear to Azrael that this fire wasn't the result of an accident. The car had been set alight deliberately, positioned in such a way so as to be a flaming barricade at a curve in the road. Any driver foolish enough to approach would slow down, concerned by what they saw. Azrael knew what the end result of that would be, could feel the planning that went into the trap. There would be men and perhaps women concealed, all armed with shotguns and rifles, ready to swarm and overwhelm any vehicle that foolishly ventured down here. The car wouldn't burn forever, its carcass a memory of the plunder from a previous voyager. Azrael knew instantly that the driver of that car had been killed along with the passengers, this sleepy little hamlet turned into a death trap. Unless they came in significant numbers, those who approached here were for the slaughter.

Secluded as it was, the people of Combs had clearly come together to defend their tiny patch of earth with a savagery that defied the normally placid British mentality. There would be only one or two roads leading into the heart of the village, all easily blocked off so that Combs could be defended, for now at least.

Azrael had no intention of righting any perceived wrongs here. He understood the actions these people had taken, respected it even. They would be families and farmers, known to each other, intent on protecting what little they had. They would have agonised about the need to do this, probably needing alcohol to break the resistance their own morality might have thrown at them. Didn't they have the right to defend themselves from the flood that threatened to engulf them? If anything, Azrael agreed with their actions, saluting their determination to fight for some last vestige of the lives they had lived. Any one of the strangers from the outside could be carrying Lazarus. Better to shoot first and ask questions later. It was a simple equation that so many would try and deny.

It wouldn't do them any good in the long run of course. Sooner or later, the undead would find their way here and then Combs would fall.

If Azrael had carried on obliviously down the country road, he would have seen the bodies left to rot in the dirt. He would have been able to clearly picture what had happened. The car would have been stopped, likely with gunfire as a warning and the people told to turn back. But they hadn't, so lethal force was used, disabling the car and causing some of the occupants of the vehicle to flee. There was no quarter then, better to not have frightened, vengeful people running around outside such a closed knit community. It made more strategic sense just to kill them and hope for God's forgiveness when that time came. When you created an enemy, your only option now was total annihilation.

The bodies were left as a warning. *"Do not come here"*, the bodies said without the dead mouths having to speak. If not for Lazarus those carcasses would have been strung up from the trees, hanging over the road to deter further invasion by the city dwellers. But nobody would want to touch the corpses, so at least that middle ages stuff was avoided.

Climbing a fence at the edge of the field, Azrael saw more hints of light, the farmhouse in the distance still evidently supplied with power. A little piece of sanctuary in a world gone mad, guarded by those on the cusp of insanity. Azrael didn't envy them, the undead were hurtling this way, and they would wash over the defenders of Comb as if they weren't even there.

24.08.19
Washington DC, USA

The US military had thrown everything they could to regain control of the city. Most of the buildings housing the US government had been deemed temporarily safe, but Washington DC was far from out of the woods. The main problem wasn't the hundreds of zombies left, it was the thousands waiting to join their ranks. Lazarus had spread throughout the various agencies of government, whole departments no longer functioning. The streets were devoid of civilian traffic, the army doing what they could to get control of the debris-ridden city. There would be no concern about the Debt Ceiling for the foreseeable future.

The new viral field tests were helping, but supply and manufacturing issues were hindering the deployment. It would be days before a comprehensive testing regime could be implemented, the power of the virus to spread through the population going unchecked despite the quarantine and the gas masks the soldiers wore. Even now, vital personnel were stationed at their posts with the virus bubbling away inside them. The war against Lazarus wasn't even close to being won.

The helicopter that delivered Mother to her interrogators did not, therefore, land at DIA headquarters which was presently on lockdown, guarded by a contingent of Marines who were itching to take it to the undead sons of bitches that were threatening their nation. Instead, the helicopter touched down in a deserted field in Piscataway Park near an unobtrusive building whose only real distinguishing features were the double razor wire fences surrounding it. Instead of bringing Mother to the DIA HQ, she had been brought to an off the books interrogation facility that very few people in government knew about. It was far enough away from the carnage in DC to be safe from the zombie presence there whilst allowing access by the interrogators who would come and extract any and all information from Mother's ageing head.

This was not an interrogation for the likes of Campbell. He preferred brute force and blatant torture which would likely be lethal on someone as ill as Mother. Subtler, gentler methods would be needed, especially with the noises of compliance Mother had been making on her extradition flight to the USA. She claimed to be willing and able to tell the US government everything she knew about the organisation she founded.

Campbell found himself believing her. His bosses not so much.

Three floors below ground, Mother sat in a room with no windows and one door. It was well lit, her buttocks salvaged from the metal chair by the cushion she had been provided. The metal table that was bolted to the floor held her hands captive, each wrist individually handcuffed to separate ends of a bar that was welded to the top of the table. Even if she had something to pick the locks, her hands were too far apart and too far from her mouth for her to even try.

She had been forced to abandon her clothes in favour of the orange jumpsuit she now wore. None of this bothered her, the information she had divulged to the agent called Campbell the truth in every regard. Men would come, she knew, to question her further, to try and pick holes in the stories she told. They would be thorough, as she had been in her time. In her earlier years with the East German Stasi, there had been many a hapless citizen who had spilt their guts to her. She had been a master at it, knowing which buttons to push, knowing when to authorise the use of electricity and the rubber hoses. She never did the beatings herself, there were plenty of men willing to prove their worth to the party. Some of them had clearly enjoyed that aspect of their work. At least here, she would be spared such barbarity.

Mother actually felt a professional interest to see what techniques they would employ. She had been an interrogator for five years, and the skills she learnt had gone on to aide in her further roles. You became good at knowing when people were lying to you, a useful skill in a world of deceit and lies.

As it happened, they didn't send men, they sent a single woman. The door opened, and Mother watched Winters step in. Mother saw everything, the confidence in the way she held her body, the resolve of her face, the loneliness that dwelled deep in her heart. This was a capable woman, high up in whatever agency she worked for. Most likely DIA, but you never could tell with the Americans and their love of initialised agencies. Sometimes their agents even worked for multiple agencies, utilising the power struggles that occurred for their own selfish advancement.

Mother wondered if the different groups were still fighting amongst themselves. Of course they were, there would always be petty squabbles based on the perception of authority and jurisdiction. It was a weakness the KGB had learnt to use to their advantage numerous times, as well as a strength that they often found difficult to match. Sometimes you could infiltrate one organisation only for another to expose you. Her KGB boss had sometimes voiced the opinion that the Americans deliberately created organised chaos so nobody could properly infiltrate them.

"Hello dear," Mother said. She noticed that the woman had a thick folder under her arm. Much of that would be fake of course, there was no way they had that much data on her. *Make the subject think you know everything already*, had always been a technique that worked well with her. Back in her Stasi days, Mother had never been too popular with those who liked to leave bruises and welts on the soles of the feet of desperate individuals. Much of the information she had acquired from those she had been asked to question was through the use of words alone. "And which three letter agency do you represent?"

"DIA," Winters said. "I have been informed you have been cooperative so far. I would like to believe that what you have told Agent Campbell is true, but you will forgive me if I start from a fresh slate. I'm not in the habit of believing the utterances of mass murderers."

"Not to worry, you can always bring out the pliers and the bamboo spikes if you need to." Mother had a wry grin on her face, but it was more from the discomfort she was in than anything else. Spasms were shooting up and down her arms. They weren't used to being held out like this for so long, and Mother wondered if this torment was unintentional. It was something she was able to endure without it showing on her face too much.

"I'm glad you have a sense of humour," Winters said.

"It's about all I have left. But you do me a disservice."

"Oh, and how is that?"

"I'm hardly a mass murderer. A few dozen over just as many years hardly makes me Joseph Stalin." Winters shook her head slightly in disagreement, a faint sigh escaping her lips. She opened the file in front of her, her attention engulfed by its contents. Finally, she looked back up.

"Do you deny you created an organisation with the end result of bringing about population control?"

"Not at all dear," Mother answered. She wondered if calling Winters dear bothered the woman? If it did, Winters didn't show it.

"And do you deny you used your contacts in the old Soviet Illegals Programme to recruit and train assassins for your cause?"

"I did so much more than that. I didn't recruit them, I made them."

"Explain that," Winters demanded.

"How much do you know of the Illegals Programme?"

"Pretend I know nothing," Winters answered. Mother nodded her head sagely, sure that Winters knew less than she expected.

"The Soviets learnt they could take children and train them to be obedient, skilled in whatever nefarious arts the KGB felt necessary. With the training in place, they used a combination of chemicals and prolonged psychological torture to fracture and fragment the innocent minds. It made the subjects pliable, able to be manipulated to believe they were other than who they were. They implanted false identities which these sleeper agents adopted as their true identities; it became a reality to them, living lives they believed were real with no memory of their Soviet masters. But deep down, the training and the indoctrination was still there, able to be unleashed with the use of a single phrase."

"And that's how you acquired your assassin…" Winters looked at a page in her folder, "…Azrael."

153

"Such a weak man on the surface, but such strength underneath."

"How many more such assassins did you train?"

"Twelve in all," said Mother. "But most didn't last more than a few years. A side effect of the mind manipulation done by the Soviets was that, once the original mind was unleashed, it began to break apart with psychosis."

"How many are still alive?"

"At the last count, three," Mother said.

"Any in the Continental United States?"

"Of course. His name is Gabriel. I believe he is still alive. Pray you never have cause to meet him. I never trained someone so ruthless, so methodical."

"Did this Azrael ever operate on US soil?"

"Yes," Mother said. "The United States is a big place, too much for my Gabriel alone."

"Tell me about Lazarus," Winter suddenly demanded.

"It was never my idea or a plan I agreed with. Although I was told it wasn't supposed to be released upon an unsuspecting world, I have my doubts about that now."

"You expect me to believe you were not responsible for the Lazarus virus? You ran the organisation."

"No, I didn't. I was usurped, by men. You more than anyone should know how duplicitous and conniving men can be." That got a smile from Winters which Mother noted and stored away in her mind. Two people were being interrogated here.

I wonder if this Ms Winters realises this, thought Mother.

"And who are these men?" Mother gave her their real names, all rich and powerful individuals, but not people the average person on the street would have heard of. With notable exceptions, the truly wealthy always kept their identities out of the gossip rags. Father, Brother and Uncle. If only there had been just three Horsemen of the Apocalypse, that legend would have fit well with them quite nicely.

"And where can I find these men?"

"That I am not sure of. I have some ideas, but I will need my journal to help me remember." Winters stood.

"Agent Campbell tells me you weren't surprised we found you."

"No," Mother said. "I think deep down I've always been expecting it."

24.08.19
Preston, UK

Smith was the first to wake with the dawn. He lay there, his mind briefly his own, no interloper dwelling in his conscious thoughts. The Voice was slow to follow from the desert, maybe lingering in a place where it felt more at home. His memories of the dream were clear and stark, the confusion about what he was here for now revealed. He had not created XV1 to save his own life, but to create the person he had now developed into. It did not concern him in the slightest that he had become a tool, an instrument for the virus he had once so loathed. His thoughts accepted that fact without any kind of hesitation.

He had been so ignorant, but now the smoke had been cleared from his sight. Now he knew why he had developed the compulsion to see Jessica Dunn dead, despite her blood being the one thing that had saved his life. She needed to die because of that very blood, because of her ability to defy the will of Lazarus and her readiness to suffer in her nightmare with the rest of them. There was something more about her though, a danger within her body that he was somehow missing. It wasn't just that she was immune, but the fact that she had the power to change everything.

The child! The creature growing within her. Was that what Smith feared?

Smith cared for only one thing now. Hunting her and those like her in the one place she could never escape. As a soldier, he had been inadequate in the great scheme of things, his feeble achievements amounting to little of any worth. But over there, in that place, he was everything that ever was and ever would be.

It didn't matter to him that his body odour was offensive. Such things were irrelevant now. All that mattered was carrying out the task his damaged mind required of him. To do that, he needed companions in the great hunt to come. He was but one amongst many and as weak as the immune were in the desolation, their numbers were into the thousands. Spread out across the charred and ruined landscape, there was no telling how long the great pursuit would take.

He needed allies, and he knew that he had achieved such having already met the manifestation of Shah over there. The other two would follow in their own time. Shah had looked so noble, so righteous in the visage he portrayed, totally unlike the broken, rotting form that Smith had found himself in. Two wasn't enough. So like he had done with Shah, Smith considered taking the zombie saliva to smear it into the wounds of Dawson and Cartwright, both deep in the sleep that their bodies had demanded. Time was needed for them to recover from the trauma of their near-death experience.

"You realise you don't need to do that, right?" The Voice insisted.

"Are you sure?" Smith queried. Wasn't a further exposure to the virus essential in creating who he was?

"I'm sure. Do it if you must, but it will make no difference. Your beloved antiserum is enough when given to those who were exposed to the virus."

"Why didn't you tell me?" Smith insisted almost angrily.

"Would you have listened? And if you had, would you have gone ahead with the experiment knowing the failure it would represent?"

"No," Smith said truthfully. Still, he went ahead with the viral application. He didn't bother to wear gloves this time for Smith knew the bodies in this world were of little importance. The experiment didn't matter to him now. What he needed was certainty.

Already Dawson and Cartwright were likely shaping into their forms in the desert. There they would all feast on the innocent flesh that fled from them.

Once their hunt was complete, there would be nothing left for them except their own oblivion. Smith found a great comfort in that.

Dawson groaned as Smith pulled the bandage off one of his many contusions, the oily fluid needing to be forced out of the syringe as it had coagulated slightly. The zombie's head seemed to scrutinise it all, the remnants of Stephanie(Z) watching vigil with sightless eyes. As the warmth of Dawson's body and Smith's fingers worked on the saliva, it became runnier, returning to the consistency that made it easily spreadable across the soldier's skin.

The same was done to Cartwright who remained quiet throughout. There was no harshness now in Smith's actions. These were both men who demanded his respect, and he theirs. Smith may have blackmailed them into undergoing the procedure, but that was all noise in the great battle that was unfolding. The war to end all wars. The war to end the scourge that was mankind. Inside their minds, the combination of the virus and XV1 was making them who they were destined to be.

"*So finally you understand,*" The Voice said, now like a long lost friend.

"Yes," Smith replied, now content to be joined by the second in his mind. The Voice no longer sneered at Smith, the words and the tonality indicating nothing but respect and companionship. If not for Smith's mini-stroke, if not for his personality splitting, the true nature of his new self might have come to him sooner. As it was, he had needed to go into the realm of sleep to finally heal and discover what he was so desperate to become.

Just as the immune shared their link in the other place, so those infected who were exposed to XV1 became a brotherhood driven by one desire.

Shah's eyes opened. The former soldier looked at Smith as he would view a beloved brother. Fate had thrown them together in this conflict, and they both now eagerly accepted their part in it all, any objection to what they deemed destined to do having been stripped from their minds by the action of the virus. Shah wanted nothing other than to excel in the coming pursuit and despite him never experiencing the desert before this day, he felt as if the slaughter of the immune was the very purpose he had been born for.

"The restraints are no longer necessary," Shah said matter of factly.

"Of course," Smith said, abandoning Cartwright to unstrap Shah's arms and legs. The smell of stale piss rose from Shah, the briefs he wore now dry from the heat of the fever that had been released by Shah's body. To his nose, the smell was unacceptable, his own sense of self still very much intact. He had always been someone who took pride in his appearance, no doubt his elegant robes in the desert a reflection of his inner belief. His character and his commitment to what he had always believed was still there, it had just been adapted to know another truth. In the last moments of its death throes, Lazarus, reinforced by Smith's intervention, had left Shah with one overriding notion.

The immune must die.

"I need fresh clothes," Shah said. "And a shower." He felt tainted by his own self and that he could not abide.

"Why waste such time with such things?" Smith asked, genuinely confused. The Voice concurred with Smith's viewpoint, but really, who were they to be critical of one of their own?

"Because this," Shah said, indicating his blood and sweat-stained skin, "is not acceptable to me." Who was there alive who could argue with that?

24.08.19
Manchester, UK

Susan woke up in the bed she had been allocated, the air around her stale with her own suffering. She had said yes because it had been the only real choice. As abhorrent as Clay was to her, his fevered clawing of her body had been blissfully brief. Clay's only concern had been his own pleasure, and she could still feel his huge bulk, Clay's sweating flesh pressing against hers.

He'd lasted less than five minutes before he'd rolled off, out of breath. Susan hadn't had to do anything but lie there, Clay not wasting his time with any kind of foreplay. She hadn't even had time to take the dress off, Clay merely pulling it above her waist with his big shovel-like hands. Despite his quickness, it had still seemed like it took an eternity.

"You can leave now," Clay had said, his eyes closed. If she had possessed a weapon then, she told herself she would have ended it all right there. Truthfully though, she would have hesitated, the killing blow unable to be delivered by her own morality. There was no weapon of course, Clay wasn't one to leave himself vulnerable like that. Her own sense of outrage at what she had become had not yet reached true desperation, and she knew that if this was to be the worst of it, then it was something she would survive just as she had endured the other injustices of her life. So long as she had the drink to fall back on.

With him finished, she had stood, shaky on her feet but able to walk unaided. The dress had seemed to flow down her body to cover her vulnerability, and Susan had found herself wondering how many dresses Clay actually had for her. Then there was the why. Why would a man like Clay have what appeared to be a whole wardrobe to dress his truthfully unwilling victims in? Susan was not naïve enough to think that she was the first to experience such demands from Clay. There had been many more before her, that much was obvious. This was a process, a system for Clay to seduce, if that were even the word he would use.

"I was sorry to hear about your daughter," Clay had suddenly said, the words seeming to hang in the air. These weren't words of commiseration, it was his attempt to bring back the memories of what had been done to the centre of her life. A form of torment to add to that already delivered. "Did Brian ever tell you what was done to the pervert who had his way with her?" Susan had shaken her head. She knew that the rapist was still alive, that he had been broken at the hands of Brian.

"Brian had wanted to kill him, but I persuaded him otherwise. Death would be so unacceptably final, a punishment not fitting the crime committed."

Clay's eyes had remained closed, his nakedness stark in the centre of the huge bed. Susan had watched him, horrified as Clay recounted what had been done to the killer of her daughter.

"Brian had beaten him, but such injuries are so random. I offered something much more precise, and you can thank Florence for that. For a day she worked on the rapist's body. Keeping him alive and in agony, removing parts of him that he would never need again." Susan hadn't envisaged Florence being a part of that, but who better to extract justice than someone with her surgical skills. "The cock he used to break open your daughter, Florence spent hours on that before she removed it. Let me tell you, she is not someone you want to get on the wrong side of." Had there been a threat there?

Susan hadn't been able to say anything. Despite what Clay had done to her, there was a strange gratitude in her heart. He had just told her the extent of the true torment suffered by a man she despised with all her heart.

"She ruined most of his limbs. Took his eyelids, his lips. She really went to town." Clay had sat up then and looked at Susan with an intensity that had wiped all doubt about what this man was capable of. "You can thank me tomorrow, bright and early. Now fuck off so I can get some sleep, you pitiful slut." Awake, those words still rang in her ears, cutting into what remained of any self-esteem that still dwelled within her.

She was broken and alone. Brian couldn't help her, nobody could.

Sitting up in her bed, sheets fresh from the night before, she saw the bottle of vodka on the nightstand beside her. It was only half full, but she could ration that. Susan knew that this was purely about survival now. If she got through this, if she survived this mansion and those inside it, she now vowed to change the life she was leading. Despite the despair that should have dwelled within her, Susan had hope, for today she would be given the cure to Lazarus. She didn't ask where Clay had acquired it, didn't question why she was worthy of such a gift. And while she was not adept in spotting the lie in a man's words, somehow she believed what Clay had told her.

An errant thought slipped through her defences before she could cast it out. *What happened to all those women before me?* She didn't have the answer to that, nor could she see into the future that awaited her. She would just need to take each hour, each day as they came. The alcohol would help for now, but how long before the urge to end it all overwhelmed her again? That option still lingered there deep in the recesses of her mind, but it had been pushed back below the threshold of being acted upon.

Susan slipped from the bed and carefully unscrewed the lid from the bottle. There was acid in the back of her throat, a common side effect from excessive consumption, but she could ignore that, had for years. The burn of her forgetting juice would scorch that away as it always did. She took a swig direct from the bottle, the medicine hitting her nerves almost instantly. Holding the bottle tipped, she let the one mouthful settle while using her lips to stop more flowing.

"Ration it," said the wisdom in her head. Taking another mouthful, she returned the bottle to the nightstand, returning the lid, fighting the draw that demanded she consume the whole bottle, something she was more than capable of.

That was when the knock came to her door. It sounded different, almost hesitant to the way Viktor always introduced himself. The door didn't open, forcing Susan to stand to answer it. Wrapping the freshly laundered dressing gown around her like some sort of holy armour, Susan answered the call.

It wasn't Viktor, it was Florence. The surgeon looked at her impatiently.

"Come on, we haven't got all day."

"He wants me now? What time is it?"

"Still morning," Florence answered.

"I'm not dressed," Susan said, almost distressed. The clothes she had worn the night before were absent from her room. She remembered taking the dress off, remembered draping it over a chair so she could be unencumbered in her sorrow. Viktor must have taken it, the man having free rein over this room and most of the house it seemed. Susan wondered why it wasn't Viktor fetching her now.

"No time for that dearie," Florence advised. "Besides, the dressing gown will be fine while you get your medicine." Susan was about to say something more when the sound of gunfire erupted from somewhere outside.

***

Brian was already awake, eating breakfast in the large tent that had been erected on the mansion's front lawn. The mansion itself provided more than adequate kitchen facilities for someone intent on putting on a dinner party, but it wasn't big enough to feed the dozens of men that Clay had under his command. Besides, the kitchen was considered off-limits to all but those who Clay invited. The crime boss understood the need to keep people's bellies full but also insisted that he be given the personal space his position demanded.

Brian didn't mind, the fare being served up was adequate for his needs. It wasn't the luxurious breakfasts Clay had bribed him with the day before, but it was food for a belly that was ravenous. Bulldog was the one slaving in the makeshift kitchen today, the gas camping stoves big enough to feed those who demanded sustenance. The men who could cook, of which there was a surprising number, had already organised a rota that they would follow, ingenuity taking the place of orders from Clay. When the men could do what needed to be done without being told, it made Brian's job a lot easier. That was one of the benefits of recruiting from ex-military.

One's ration of the food that had been collected from the surrounding warehouses was determined by your usefulness to the group, a way to keep the men on their toes and try and deter the freeloaders that were present in every organisation. The threat of violence and expulsion also helped with that. Nobody wanted to be on the other side of the wall. Well rewarded as they had been, and protected as they now were, the men who worked and served at the pleasure of Clay knew they would be foolish to invite his ire.

The sausage on Brian's fork had been sliced in two by Brian's teeth just as the first shot of the day was fired.

"Code Red," someone over by the gate shouted. Brian abandoned the meal instantly, his AR15 within arm's reach. He never went anywhere without a weapon now because he was well aware that the building he had found sanctuary in could be attacked at any time. Code Red meant zombies. Slipping his hand into his pocket, he took out the earplugs and inserted one into each ear.

Things were going to get very loud, very fast.

He was the fourth man to reach the front gate. The others were stood back, firing through the imposing iron railings. There were about a dozen zombies, their deformed bodies being hurled at the impressive barrier. Their attempts were futile. Even with the strength of it though, the gate shook as the full weight of the undead was unleashed against it.

Someone had set up a killing zone on the inside of the gate, marked off by, ironically, police crime scene tape. It was deemed too risky to venture outside the wall now, so the tape was the safe zone. When you shot anything, there was always the risk of splatter. Now, most of that would go backwards out of the body, but there was always the chance of errant spray coming towards you, especially with the type of ammunition being used. Thus the need for the safe zone, which hopefully kept the men away from the risk the virus brought.

Inside the walls, nobody wore clothing to protect them from the virus.

Brian lined up a shot and took half a zombie's head off. Last night, he had spent a good thirty minutes loading bullets, the webbing he now wore resplendent with five full magazines of explosive ammunition. The military veterans here had advised that, with the reported difficulty in killing the undead, the supply of explosive rounds that Clay had in stock should be used only for the defence of the mansion, and only given to select personnel. Brian, being one of Clay's lieutenants was thus blessed with bullets that turned the average head into a gaping chasm.

The man next to Brian lost his cool. He slipped his gun onto full auto, spraying the bodies of the zombies as he roared like some deranged demon. When his gun clicked empty, the man stood panting, his shots having had little or no effect. To *kill* a zombie, there was little point in shooting anything but the head. A large hand descended on the man's shoulder, and he turned in shock to find Brian standing right beside him.

"Slow it down," Brian said, leaning his head in so the man could better hear him. He could tell the foot soldier was running on adrenaline and fright, which was hampering his ability. "Take deep breaths. Body shots don't work on these things. Aim for the head and conserve your ammunition." Wide-eyed, Clay's man looked at Brian and seemed to shake himself out of the killing trance he had descended into.

"You good?" Brian asked, a fresh roar of gunfire causing him to wince slightly.

"Yeah, shit," the minion said. He was one of the younger members of Clay's crew, still relatively unblooded. Brain made a note in his mind to get the guy some time with two or three of the military veterans. Brian had suggested that to Clay nearly two years ago, but Clay surprisingly hadn't deemed it necessary, stating that those who had the training would be used for the work that required those with that training. It was all hands on ship now, they didn't have the luxury of being selective.

Brian stepped away slightly, lined up another shot, the bullet slightly off target, taking out a zombie's neck. It was as good as a headshot, the body being virtually decapitated. More zombies came at the gate, some trying to climb now rather than force their way through which seemed to surprise everyone. None of them got more than waist height off the ground before they were brought down.

Weren't the undead supposed to be mindless killing machines?

"This is no good," Brian said to himself. By the side of the main gate, a watchtower had been erected using boards and scaffolding poles, giving anyone up there a clear view of the other side of the wall. Brian climbed its ladder now, the tower shaking slightly which he found unnerving. It didn't topple though, and Brian joined the man at the top who was there to operate a fifty calibre machine gun.

"There's a lot of them," the man said. He was a veteran from the paratroopers, one of the many Clay had rescued from the destitution of the streets. The former soldier wasn't firing, realising early on that the gate would hold without his intervention. "But we can hold them. If they come in significant numbers though, we might have a problem."

To the front of Clay's mansion was a thin, one lane road and fields that led down to further human habitation. They weren't in a secluded position, a dual carriageway within five minutes' drive, but they were far away from the main bulk of Manchester's population which was likely predominantly zombified. Across the field, dozens of undead now charged at them, drawn to the sound of gunfire, coagulating at a single defensible spot.

"Scary fuckers aren't they," the man with Brian said.

"You sure we can hold them?" Brian asked. The veteran nodded. Looking around, Brian's attention was caught by the balcony outside Clay's bedroom. Clay stood there, watching the battle for his fortress, not in any way helping. Clay rarely engaged directly in criminal operations, and it would have raised his esteem with the men if Clay had come down and helped with the mansion's defence. If Brian could see him, others could too; Clay giving the impression he was some high lord watching from the safety of his castle keep.

That was not going to be good for morale, even under those who seemed to have an unquestioning loyalty towards Clay. It was true that Clay had done the right thing by putting the defence of his mansion into the hands of those who knew what they were doing, but he should at least be getting down and dirty with his men.

The gate was getting crowded now. It was fortunate that it opened inwards, the bodies piling up would have blocked it otherwise. As it was, somebody would ultimately need to deal with the corpses. There were nearly twenty killed, another twenty clamouring over the fallen. If the bodies were left, it would just attract all manner of vermin as well as causing a right stink. Dealing with the downed dead was not something Brian would be volunteering for. No doubt though that he would be tasked with picking those volunteers and a bribe of extra rations would need to be made.

Some people would be allowed the luxury of getting drunk tonight.

Now that he had witnessed them able to climb, Brian was fearful that the undead would scale the walls. Clay was big on security for himself and his assets, so although the wall was made of brick, the external surface had been rendered to make it smooth. There were no gaps or crevices for fingers or toes to find purchase, and any nearby trees had long since been cut down. That had ironically been the cause of the only time the police had ever visited Clay's estate. One of the trees cut down had been under a protection order, some mindless drone at the council causing all manner of fuss over its illegal felling. Clay, through his solicitor, had just claimed ignorance as to why the tree was no longer standing. The council official was still in a coma, the victim of a "random" and brutal home invasion that would never be linked to Clay.

For a human to get across the wall, they would need a ladder or rope, and there would be a ten feet drop from the top, most of the ground on the inside of the wall lined with sharp points that would penetrate any shoe landing on them. The ornate spikes that decorated the wall had been hardened by razor wire, although Brian didn't think there was any point in that. Would a zombie care if its flesh was sliced open?

For now, the ring of surveillance cameras would keep watch for anything that approached the outer wall. There were other towers scattered around the perimeter to help with that as well. At the side of Brian, a computer monitor had been set up to allow the feeds from the external cameras to be wirelessly monitored. As long as the electricity held out, there would be no need to rely on the solar array in the back lawn or the rechargeable batteries that could power the whole house when fully charged. The two large generators Clay had installed were the ultimate backup.

Clay had seemingly thought of everything except the effects his own ego was likely to have on the men. The bulk of them would stay loyal to Clay until close to the end, but Brian knew some were already voicing dissent. Quietly, not to the greater group, but the fractures were there for all to see. Brian had needed to have a quiet word with one or two individuals to just express the wisdom of not flapping their lips too much. Clay had already killed one man for apparent disloyalty, there was nothing that would stop him killing more if he got the idea into his head.

There was a thud from below. Leaning over the edge of the tower, Brian saw a thin zombie hitting the wall with its fists. At first, he didn't understand what the zombie was doing, it couldn't hope to break its way through. But then the zombie briefly lifted itself off the ground before falling back down. Swinging his gun around, Brian shot a round through the top of its head. It had been trying to climb the wall by creating its own holes, likely pulverising the fingers and hands in the process. It wouldn't be able to grip into the holes it constructed, but there was little doubt the next zombie would.

Next to the computer monitor, a walkie talkie was strapped to the scaffolding poles by Velcro. Brian ripped it loose so he could speak into it.

"To the guys manning the towers, watch for zombies on the exterior walls. I've just witnessed one try and climb their way up. If you don't spot them and pick them off, we may have an incursion."

"Thinning out," the veteran next to Brian said. Brian could see what he meant, the zombies running in the fields now mere stragglers, some slower than the others. The first wave had hit against their defences and had been repelled. But there would be more.

How long could they keep this up?

24.08.19
Preston, UK

Dawson looked at a land that made him weep with its beauty. He considered tears alien to him, and yet here they flowed freely, surprised with how unashamed he was with this apparent weakness.

He was already on his horse when he manifested in a place that felt more real to him than the green and unpleasant land he had spent all his life in. From an early age, he had never felt settled, as if somehow he didn't belong to the streets and fields that had denied him so much. Now he knew why. This wasteland had always been his home. What to many would be conceived as a harsh and desecrated landscape, was to him the very essence of perfection. For the first time ever, Dawson felt like he could call a place home.

Here in the desert, he would not be denied that which he desired. To feel the skulls of his enemies slowly giving way as they fractured under his relentless torment, the gauntlets he wore digging deep into the flesh, taking the skeleton just to the breaking point before relenting so that he could repeat the torment a thousand times. A death here would be far from quick, even with the demands that would soon be put on his attention. He was here to kill, to purge the wilderness of those who would oppose the new order. The order of the virus, the way the living world was now supposed to be.

The pale horse took a step forward, careful not to plunge down the ridge that overlooked the huge chasm down below. That was where the immune were, their attempts at flight futile, maybe even reckless. Only some of the distant specks would be his to end for they were only vulnerable when their minds came here with sleep. Awake, the immune existed merely as unfathomable spectres whose amorphous form could escape even the mightiest of his blows. Dawson was happy to wait for them, the killing tools that dangled from the horse's saddle enough to put the fear of God into even the bravest of hearts. The spiked club would be his favourite, he already knew that, its weight and its presence matching his own immense physique. It was so easy to break bones and shatter a victim's spine while keeping those he tormented alive.

So large was he here that he feared for the wellbeing of the beast that carried him, his rage at the immune a mirror reflection for the compassion he had for the horse that bore his astonishing burden. It did not buckle under him, and moved as if unencumbered, perhaps possessing a strength greater than Dawson himself. Things were often not as they seemed in this realm of the forgotten. There was no understanding as to where the horse came from, and quite frankly, he didn't care.

His only weakness was the inability to control how long he slept. Despite the fondness he held for where he found himself, Dawson knew that this was not the real. Sooner or later, the demands of his body would drag him back to the waking realm. There he would be vulnerable, his mind now filled with the strategy of self-protection. Even now, he could feel the stillness coming, the strength of the wind diminishing. Looking at the metal of the armour that covered him, he saw the thinness of it as it began to lose it solidity. In moments he would be gone from here, a wisp of his shape left in his place.

Dawson's eyes opened. Smith was there, looking down on him, any hostility he held towards the Colonel now obsolete. Only he wasn't a Colonel anymore. Rank implied some sort of superiority, and there was none of that amongst brothers.

Dawson was unsurprised to find his restraints removed. From the corner of his eye, he saw Cartwright still sleeping. Was sleep even the right word? They weren't asleep in the desert, their wakefulness complete as they witnessed the desolation around them.

"Brother," Smith said, smiling. All the anger Dawson had held, the resentment to the way the good life had been denied him was gone now. There was no self-pity, not with what he now understood. Everything he had experienced, every fight he had been in, every rejection from relatives who had become fearful of his size and his temper...all had been for one singular purpose. He had been forged into this being that could now be used to remove a scurrilous curse from the face of the Earth.

"Brother?" Dawson answered. "I never thought I would hear those words."

"We await one more," Smith stated, briefly looking at the body of Cartwright.

"No," Dawson said. "There is a fifth. The one who forms and who will shape us." Dawson's words sounded strange to him. His mind felt lucid, free of the oppressive violence that had overshadowed it. His head was clear for the first time since he could remember.

"I have felt it too," Smith agreed. And so had The Voice. Deep inside Smith's mind, The Voice was finally pleased with the way things were turning out. Such a shame that The Voice was soon to be consumed by disappointment.

24.08.19
Allied Maritime Command, Northwood, UK

MARCOM, the central command of all NATO maritime forces had been made the headquarters for all remaining UK military forces, and already it was under siege. The undead had found it, and were hurling themselves at the fences despite the withering machine gun fire that was being rained into them.

The reasons this site was chosen were numerous. It had an advanced communications array, allowing transmission across the planet as well as with the nuclear submarines that had all been put to sea at the start of the crisis. It was surrounded by rings of razor wire topped fences, the inner fence surrounding the entrance to a bunker complex guarded by Gurkhas and blast-proof doors. It would need an army to get inside, and that was exactly what came for it.

It was considered small by American standards, the bunker at Northwood giving those who retreated inside the protection they needed. The normal staff of fifteen now swelled to sixty, mostly consisting of high ranking generals. Despite Northwood being a maritime facility, most of the senior naval personnel were on board ships, having opted to find safety from the zombie hordes at sea.

Normally home to two thousand people, the number of soldiers that had retreated here had tripled that number. It just wasn't enough, though.

The Gurkhas and other military personnel guarding the perimeter did their best to not give an inch, and initially, they held off the attack. Any zombie that managed to scale the outer fence either got snagged on the razor wire on the top or was blown apart by machine guns. The fences however, were not designed for this kind of assault, and on several parts of the perimeter, their integrity began to fail over time. They just weren't high enough or strong enough, the boxes of ammunition the soldiers relied upon quickly becoming depleted. The outer layer of defences soon became breached.

The Gurkhas fought with everything they had, sacrificing themselves in vicious hand to hand combat, using their bayonets and their Kukri to inflict grievous injuries on the undead. But even the acclaimed fighting prowess of the Gurkhas wasn't any sort of match for the stronger and more durable zombies. Once past the outer wire, the defenders quickly became overwhelmed, each soldier who fell being added to the ranks of the damned.

The undead couldn't penetrate the bunker complex however, the people inside already vetted for Lazarus by the newly acquired viral test kits. The virus had initially made significant inroads into the command and control hierarchy, over fifty people of those stationed at Northwood found to be contaminated by the virus. But with the testing, everyone secured below ground was Lazarus free. Protected by thick concrete and an air filtration system that could keep out nuclear fallout, those in the bunker considered themselves to be safe from the zombie menace.

The one thing the zombies could do was to stop anyone leaving. So, trapped inside, what was left of the British Army's General Staff saw the situation they were in. They had food and water, but that wouldn't last forever. And whilst they could communicate with British forces across the country, the actual number of those forces was dwindling, whole regiments becoming fractured and ineffective. Contact with London, Manchester and Birmingham had been lost, the satellite images showing whole herds of undead forming at the centres of those cities.

The use of nuclear weapons was still being considered, although several of the military top brass had already rejected the notion. What was the point?

They could destroy their own cities, but there was no telling how many zombies would survive the blasts. Already huge groups could be seen spreading out into the countryside, and it was considered highly likely that the undead didn't give a damn about nuclear fallout. There were still enough belligerent minds who felt that ordering the submarines to unleash their payloads would somehow help the chaos and death that ruled Britain's streets.

There was still hope, cities like Leeds still reporting in. But how long before they fell as well? Although none of them said it, the surviving generals were generally of the opinion that the fight against the undead on the British mainland had been lost. All they could do now was try and salvage what they could. Raining nukes down would just make the environment more difficult for those defenders left. Nuking Beijing had done nothing to stop the spread of the infection or the undead, several large groupings of zombies, totalling into the millions, already spreading out towards the surrounding cities. Why did anyone think raining atomic fire down British cities would be any different? It was thus deemed a plan of last resort, nobody really believing nuclear fire would do anything to stop the zombie menace.

Desperation would soon change people's minds.

24.08.19
Frederick, USA

Reece looked around at her fellow prisoners and noticed that everyone else was asleep. Her slumber had been fractured, her mind not letting her rest more than an hour at a time, never enough for her to drop into the desert where fear and pain waited. Because of that, she wasn't quite aware of what it meant. To her, it was still just an unpleasant dream. A belief that was about to change.

In the cell next to hers, Lizzy moaned softly, her legs moving as if trying to walk. Somehow, the duvet she had pulled up to her chin stayed in place shrouding her in its comfort. Bad dreams? With what Lizzy had been through, nightmares were hardly unexpected.

The big man hadn't uttered a word to any of his fellow prisoners. When he was awake, he seemed to stare off into space, occasionally sending curious glances around at those he shared his fate with. A big part of that would have been the distance his cell was from everyone else. Being near the detention area's main door, it would be difficult for him to have any kind of conversation without shouting. Good for a few words, but no use for a prolonged chat without going hoarse in the process.

The fact that there were still only four of them here was a worry to Reece. Firstly, it represented just how rare those immune to the virus were. Also, with so few of them, there was more chance for them to each experience the bizarre and disturbing experiments those in charge had in store for those trapped here.

The main door to the cells opened. At first, nobody entered, apprehension welling in the pit of Reece's stomach. Who would come through? Who would be the one to start off the day's entertainment?

"Attention," an electronic voice blasted out from all directions, "all residents are required to awake for mandatory inspection. Attention, all residents…" Residents? What the fuck was the point of this fancy use of words? Couldn't they just be honest with themselves at least? Residents implied some form of cooperation on the part of the immune. Nobody was here voluntarily.

"Clarice!" Lizzy almost screamed. Reece watched as the child leapt from the bed, stark terror engulfing her now that she had suddenly been ripped from sleep. She flung herself around her cell, screaming, the young mind battered into submission by the inability to even escape into the realm of rapid eye movement. What had the child seen in her mind to cause all this?

"Hey, kid," Reece shouted. She moved over to the separating wall, did what she could to try and catch Lizzy's eye but to no initial avail. The girl was manic. "Lizzy, look at me."

"It burns, it burns."

"Lizzy," Reece yelled again. The girl finally looked at her and rushed over to the partition, her hair dishevelled, her breathing panicked.

"Where am I, where am I?" Lizzy was almost chanting now. The mania was seeping out of her, but her eyes still flicked this way and that, as if the child was trying to regain some sense of what had happened.

"It's okay Lizzy, I'm here." From the corner of her eye, Reece could see that Jessy was now awake and watching them. Still, nobody came through the door.

"Clarice, you're here," Lizzy said, almost amazed. She looked suddenly embarrassed, as if she didn't know what was happening.

"Of course I'm here honey. Where else would I be?"

"I wasn't here, though." Lizzy, panting from her exertion, sat back down on her bed, the tears no longer streaming but the mind still bubbling on the edge of mania.

"Where were you?" Reece pulled up the chair so she could be as close to Lizzy as the prison would allow her. Despite her aversion to children, all Reece wanted to do was give the child a reassuring hug. That wasn't possible, so Lizzy resorted to hugging herself, the thin duvet on the bed suddenly grabbed and wrapped around her tiny shoulders.

"It was so hot. It hurt so much." The words hit Reece like a freight train.

"What did you say?"

"The desert. It burned." With a shaking hand, Lizzy pointed at Jessy. "She knows. She was there." Reece looked at Jessy whose pained eyes suggested she shared a secret with Lizzy. Jessy nodded.

"This desert, were you being…were you being chased?" Reece had to ask the question for the dream that Lizzy was recounting seemed far too familiar.

"Oh yes," Lizzy almost squealed. "I'm so frightened." Her head was almost swallowed up as Lizzy retreated further into the cocoon she had created from her bedspread. "Why did my Mummy have to die?" The words cut into Reece like a knife, the heartache the child felt almost infectious in its nature.

"I don't know Lizzy. I really don't."

"Why do bad things happen?" Lizzy asked. She was looking up at Reece now, the eyes imploring, searching. All Reece could do was shake her head.

That had been the worst part of the job. The bloated three-day-old corpses, the vomit and the drug addicts going ballistic in the back of her patrol car she could easily cope with. But children in distress? Man, she had a problem with that which was undoubtedly part of her reticence in having children herself. Reece knew in her heart that having a child would have likely broken her from the endless worry.

"She's telling the truth," Jessy suddenly said. She had lowered the hatch to her door so she could be better heard. "I was there with her."

"I don't understand," Reece implored. How could they both have had the same nightmare as her?

***

Big T could just hear the conversation, and it sent chills down him. He was not one to be afraid easily, but the trauma of the desert lingered with him. The first time was always the worst, and for Big T, it had been the most extreme dream of his life. He had been there in the desolation, fleeing something that was beyond the realms of fear.

He sat on the bed that was too small for him, the images from his rest quickly dissipating. There was sweat on his body, despite the neutral temperature of his cell, and he wondered how he was going to get a shower in this place. Likely he wouldn't, the sink the only means of keeping himself clean. So much of his basic dignity was being denied him.

"Up and at 'em," a voice said as a soldier entered through the open door. The soldier was pushing a cart with folded clothes on it, the same colour that everyone incarcerated was wearing. "It's laundry time." The soldier whose name badge had been removed had a sarcastic sneer to his voice. He stopped outside Big T's cell. "You first big man. Let's be having all that shit off you." As if to amplify the importance of his order, the soldier lifted a pile of clothes up and opened the hatch of the cell door. Because Big T wasn't there to take the clothes from him, the soldier rested them on the shelf the open hatch made. "Pull your finger out there. Or do you want me to come in and strip you?"

"I'd like to see you try," Big T advised. He saw the soldier fingering the Taser on his belt. "You better be careful trying to use that on me. You're going to look awful stupid with it sticking out of your arse."

"Strip, now," the soldier insisted. "Or do you want to stink in your incarceration?" Big T actually considered it. Before he had drifted off to sleep, he had gone through the various ways he could have made his captors lives as difficult as hell for them. Forms of passive and active resistance mulled through his mind. From complete refusal to obey any order issued to depositing his shit out the hatch instead of into the toilet, all were eventually abandoned. As annoying as he knew he could be, any inconvenience he created wouldn't be aimed at the true arbiters of his confinement. As much satisfaction as he might have acquired from taking his frustrations out on the grunts working here, it wouldn't do Big T any favours in the long run. He had to pick his battles because there would be so few he could win.

Big T stood and stripped the clothing off of himself. He felt no shame being naked, this was no different to being in a gym locker room. He worried about the women, though. It wasn't right that they should expose themselves to this knucklehead. On top of the fresh clothes was a plastic bag and Big T forced the sweat-stained items he had been wearing into it.

"Don't I get a shower?"

"No siree Bob. That's a negative on that. There's a towel there. You can wash yourself in the sink." Big T picked up the clean clothes and threw them on his bed.

"I'd like to complain to the management," said Big T. "The facilities are not what I was promised on TripAdvisor."

"Funny," the soldier said. He held his hand out for the bag containing the discarded clothes, and Big T reluctantly handed them to him.

"Is whatever they are paying you worth selling your soul like this?" Big T asked. The soldier rolled his eyes dismissively and pushed his cart over to the other prisoners.

Reece watched the soldier approach. He stopped his cart outside Lizzy's cell and lowered the hatch, which made the child jump in alarm.

"For Christ's sake, I'm not going to hurt you kid." The soldier's voice bristled with frustration.

"You really are an arsehole aren't you?" Reece chided. "Lizzy is scared, why can't you see that?"

"Hey, I'm not here to play nursemaid."

"Then why are you here? There are men and women out there fighting to defend this country, and what are you doing? Fucking laundry." That didn't go down well with the soldier. That barb cut deep.

"Hey bitch, I do my part."

"Yeah. Well make sure you don't mix any colours in with these whites," Reece stated. That actually got a giggle from Lizzy.

"You can shut your goddamn mouth," the soldier ordered, his face red with the growing humiliation. He was barely in his twenties and wasn't used to be spoken to like this, not since joining the army at least. Memories of the times he had been bullied and mocked in high school flitted through his memory.

"Private Jackson, please remember we are on a strict timetable," a booming female voice announced to everyone. It was easy to forget that you were constantly under surveillance, even with the cameras. That clearly applied to those working here too. Reece wondered who the owner of that voice was, having yet to meet the renowned Professor Schmidt. She would like to meet whoever it was, preferably down a dark alley and with her loaded service revolver to hand.

Jackson looked suitably admonished. In fact, as Reece looked at him, she realised there was more to it. The man actually looked scared, the voice clearly the cause of his fear-ridden eyes. Jackson deposited a small pile of clothes through the hatch to Lizzy's cell a little bit too forcefully, causing the items to fall to the floor. Lizzy just sat there staring at them.

"Come on, kid. Don't make me come in there and strip you." The words were completely the wrong thing to say, and they set Lizzy off again, the child bawling at the prospect of being manhandled by this brute. Pleading eyes looked at Reece.

"What the hell is wrong with you?" Reece said, astonished at how idiotic this man was.

"Hey, she just needs to change her clothes is all." There was actual regret in the soldier's voice. Even he seemed to realise he had stepped over the line.

"What, you want her…you want us to strip naked in front of you? Is that how you get your kicks?"

"Fucking pervert," Jessy screamed through the now open hatch of her cell, adding to the condemnation that seemed richly deserved. Reece suddenly felt worried that bad words were being used in front of Lizzy, but how ridiculous was that considering what she had been through? "Do you jerk off to pictures of little kids when you're all alone?" Jackson's face was descending into anger. Reece and Jessy were clearly pushing him too far.

"Clarice, don't let him touch me." It was obvious to Reece that Lizzy was too scared to do anything but be scared. There was no way this could end well with a man like Jackson, a man who was very likely to do something stupid out of pure annoyance. Reece looked up at the camera in her cell. She needed to pull this back from the brink.

"I know you can hear me out there. Look, let me help her. Let me in her cell, and I will help get her dressed, okay."

"That's against protoc…" Jackson insisted before he was interrupted.

"Approved," the ethereal voice around them said. "Private Jackson, please facilitate this." Jackson looked shocked, but at no time did he show any desire to argue with the commanding declaration. With a flurry of his hands, he opened both cell doors, stepping back as if Reece was going to come charging out at him. She didn't, there was no point engaging in that kind of rebellion. As bad as her confinement presently was, things could be a lot worse.

Reece stepped out of her cell and into Lizzy's. For a second the girl just sat looking at her in bewilderment, and then she exploded off the bed, wrapping her arms around Reece's waist.

"Hey, what's all this?"

"I knew you would protect me." Reece hesitated only briefly and then ran her hand over the child's long blonde hair, careful not to touch the surgical dressing. Lizzy almost seemed to sigh at the touch. Bending down, Reece picked Lizzy up, the girl's weight easy for her. Something came to her then, some instinct that she didn't even know she possessed. Lizzy hugged into her, a wet cheek burying into Reece's neck.

"I need a hairbrush, and I need your boss," Reece said to Jackson. The soldier looked at her as if she had just spoken Klingon. "And turn your back for Christ's sake so I can get this child undressed."

"Or do you like looking at naked little girls?" Jessy added, continuing her taunting. Suddenly it was clear that Jackson didn't know what to do with himself, and Reece wondered what would have happened if not for the invisible overseer. She had arrested people like Jackson before, bullies, full of self-hatred and doubt. They could be some of the most dangerous people to arrest. When they blew up, it sometimes needed a forensics team to pick up the pieces.

He didn't turn his back however, going one better. From his pocket, he withdrew a small computer tablet on which he tapped the screen a few times. Suddenly, all the walls around Reece and Lizzy went white, just as had occurred in the experiment the other day. The door to Lizzy's cell closed.

"I'm going to put you down now, Lizzy," Reece said, but the child was reluctant. She hadn't had any kind of loving human contact since she had been abducted from police custody. She was basically starving for any kind of connection.

"No," Lizzy implored.

"Hey, it's okay. And we need to get you dressed so that idiot will go away." Lizzy sniffled, but her arms gave way a bit, and Reece was able to pull the child away from her. Gently, she placed Lizzy on the bed. Clarisse Reece, mother of the Armageddon.

The change of clothes only took about two minutes. Reece had to do most of the work, Lizzy more intent on sucking her thumb than helping out. Lizzy had been very close to going catatonic. If Jackson had been allowed to carry out his threat and strip the child, that might have been it, Lizzy's mind switching off to avoid any more trauma. Sometimes the young came back from that. Sometimes they didn't.

If they all got through this, the risk was that Lizzy would be emotionally damaged by her ordeal. It would all depend on how her little and immature mind processed what was happening here. If the world corrected itself and sanity returned, one thing was for certain. Lizzy would need a lifetime of therapy to counter the way she had been abused by the events of the last few days.

Reece sat down on the bed next to Lizzy and put a protective arm around her. She still felt awkward, as if she didn't really know what to do to help this poor kid. It did make her own predicament seem almost tame by comparison. Reece could handle a lot of what was being thrown at her, so she made a promise to herself, there and then, to do what she could to protect this little human being. Lizzy's only concerns should have been homework and icky boys, not being the victim of some mad experiment. Reece wasn't sure how much she could effectively protect Lizzy, but she would do whatever she could.

"Okay, we're done here," Reece said loudly. She had no doubt that microphones were listening to every word that was said in the cells. The walls stayed white only for another three seconds, and then the limited world around her appeared again. Jackson was no longer there. But Professor Schmidt was, and she opened the hatch, thrusting a hairbrush through.

"CR28HT, so good to finally meet you." The cart was still present, so Reece picked up the bag she had filled with the dirty clothes, passing them through the hatch to Schmidt who had no hesitation in taking the bag off her. It was discarded onto the cart. The hairbrush, Reece threw onto the bed so that she could use it later to help calm the child.

"I have a name, you know."

"Yes, I am aware," Schmidt advised, "but for now you will be known by your designation. It does not pay to get too familiar with one's test subjects. You can thus call me Professor."

"I can think of a few other things to call you. And is that all we are to you, test subjects?"

"Yes," Schmidt answered truthfully. "I have no desire to get to know you as a person. The work we do here requires a certain degree of detachment." It was true. Schmidt believed she had to be able to distance herself from any suffering those who were trapped here were going to endure. She had to be able to take whatever steps were necessary to defeat the virus, and she couldn't let empathy and compassion get in the way of that.

"What about common decency and humanity?"

"Oh, there's no room for that. Not here. Your existence is now only for the purpose of my experiments." Reece looked into the eyes of her jailer and saw nothing but coldness looking back. There was no emotion there. A reptile would have been more expressive. Schmidt made Carson seem like a loving human being by comparison. "The sooner you understand that, the better it will be for everyone."

"You can't expect a ten-year-old to comply with that. She's scared, we all are."

"I have no intention of physically harming any of you," Schmidt said, omitting the words that drifted into her head, *not for the time being at least*. "But the child must learn to behave. We can't have these constant outbursts. They are very disruptive." Lizzy whimpered again, so Reece sat down next to her where the child quickly clung to her.

"Disruptive," Jessy shouted from behind her. "Try being locked in one of these cages." Schmidt turned her head wearily.

"Would you rather be on the street above, at the mercy of the undead? Down here, you are safe and fed. There is a whole army ready to protect you."

"This is a world of compensations; and he who would be no slave, must consent to have no slave. Those who deny freedom to others, deserve it not for themselves; and, under a just God, cannot long retain it." The words flowed from Jessy's lips. In her time working for Julian Ryan, she had briefly been one of his finest speechwriters. The person she was quoting was Lincoln.

"All very noble," Schmidt admitted, "but it really doesn't apply here."

"We are Americans," Jessy insisted. "We have rights." Schmidt didn't even honour that statement with an answer. She merely stared at the former civil servant and shook her head at the prisoner's obvious naivety. Schmidt turned back to Reece.

"There are rules here that need to be obeyed. I have allowed you all a certain degree of latitude, to allow you to acclimatise to the situation here. But I will not have any further disorder. You either do as you are asked or I will leave the matter for Major Carson to deal with." In her arms, Reece felt Lizzy shiver at the name. "He is not a brutal man, but he is far less forgiving than I am." Schmidt stepped next to the cart and picked up a neatly pressed pile of clothes. "I trust you have no objection to changing in front of me. I am a doctor, after all."

"That all depends on if you are a lesbian or not," Reece countered. Even as the words left her mouth, she regretted saying them because Schmidt's face darkened.

"This is exactly the kind of disrespect I am talking about. CR28HT, please refrain from that in the future. I won't warn you again."

"Okay," Reece nodded. "Now we know where we stand."

"Indeed we do." Clothes in hand, Schmidt turned and opened the hatch to Jessy's cell and held them through until Jessy took them. She repeated the gesture for Reece. "I suggest you both get changed quickly. I will be sending Jackson back in within the next two minutes. Remember what I said. Resistance and disrespect will be met with unpleasantness."

"I have one condition," Reece advised.

"Really now, you are in no position to make such demands." The exasperation in Schmidt's voice was palpable.

"True, but it will be in your best interest. Move Lizzy's bed in with me. She needs someone to help her through this." Reece let the request hang in the air. "Or do you want her to keep acting up? Because unless you let me help her, that's exactly what will keep happening." Schmidt looked at her for what seemed like forever, as if trying to prise out some evidence of deceit.

"And you promise to ensure the child's compliance?"

"I'm no mother, but I will do what I can. Lizzy has been through too much to be treated just like a lab rat." As if to emphasise this, Reece turned to the child and smoothed the hair down on her blonde head again.

"Agreeable. You surprise me CR28HT, your psychological profile didn't categorise you as the mothering type."

"Believe me," Reece agreed, "I'm surprising myself." She wondered why she was feeling so protective of Lizzy. Was it the sense of justice that she had strived to deliver throughout her working life? She had become a cop to help those unable to help themselves, to protect the vulnerable and to remove bad people, people just like Schmidt, from the street. Was Lizzy a chance for her to somehow regain the identity that she had lost?

Without another word, Schmidt turned and walked down the corridor. As she sailed past Big T's cell, the huge man called out to her.

"Hey Professor," Big T said, stepping up to the wall that separated them

"Yes, AP35BM?"

"I'm going to make you a promise," Big T said. "Sooner or later I'm going to get the opportunity. And when I do, I am going to snap your neck like a twig." He surprised himself with the words, the kind, helpful exterior he normally wore no longer of service down here, deep beneath the surface of the Earth.

"Is that a fact?" Schmidt responded. Reece could have sworn she almost heard the woman laugh. "I can assure you, such an opportunity will not arise. Am I to assume you are going to be uncooperative?"

"No," Big T, "just giving you a heads up as to where your future lies."

"Hmm, appreciate it. Half rations for you though. Let's see how belligerent you are after several days of going hungry." Schmidt expected some sort of reaction from the big man, but he merely shrugged and sat back down on his bed. She would have to have a chat with Major Carson about this one. The Major would have to have a word with them all, tell them exactly what they were risking by being disrespectful and uncooperative. Schmidt exited through the open door that led away from the cells without another word.

Lizzy looked up at Reece with a confused look on her face.

"Thank you, Clarice," she said, "but what's a lesbian?"

Oh God, thought Reece, what have I gotten myself into now?

***

Truth be told, Schmidt was feeling frustrated and pissed off, rare emotions for her. The concern wasn't particularly down to the minor rebellion of her test subjects, as irritating as they were proving to be. It was her inability to replicate the success of Smith's antiserum. From the immune they held, her team had extracted the necessary fluids from the collected blood, only for it to have no effect on Lazarus. She didn't blame her team, never shouted at them or lost her temper, because ultimately the failure was hers. Conversely, when they finally broke the secret to defeating the disease, the success and the glory would rightly belong only to Schmidt. She had looked forward to being seen as the saviour of the planet, and now she had hit a wall that was as formidable an obstacle as any she had ever encountered.

Schmidt didn't have time to deal with the concerns of those she was experimenting on. The likes of Jackson were clearly not acceptable as wardens for the most important people on the planet. She would have a word with Carson and suggest he be reassigned. She was sure a place could be found for him on the front lines fighting the zombie menace.

Twenty infected "*volunteers*" they had injected with antiserum now, and every one of them had continued to deteriorate until death finally took them. There had been no improvement in any of those infected, not even the slightest halt in the rapid progression of the virus. If they couldn't get an antiserum to work, then what hope was there for a vaccine? It didn't matter which strain of the virus they tried the antiserum against, all seemed easily capable of ignoring humanity's attempts at a cure. Attempts to artificially manufacture something had also been completely unsuccessful. Schmidt had experienced difficulties in her work before but never had she been under these kinds of time pressures.

Why had Smith been so apparently successful, and what was she missing?

Secretly, Schmidt was also developing the opinion that a vaccine wasn't possible, but she wasn't prepared to admit defeat just yet. The virus mutated too rapidly, more so than influenza, constantly changing and adapting to make the job of her and the scientists under her virtually impossible. The Europeans had found the same, the research that had been shared showing the same failings. The reported initial success by the Japanese had also come to nothing. Stood now in an observation booth looking in on the latest patient to be injected with their version of XV1, Schmidt gazed on in despair as the machine monitoring the woman's heart rate flatlined. Another zombie to add to the growing pool they were collecting by their failures.

What was different about Smith's version of the anti-serum? She was still waiting on the results of his latest tests and had tried contacting him through the secure video network. Although the video feed was still open, all she saw was whiteness. The sound was also muted, which made no sense to her. Whatever was going on across the Atlantic, she needed to know, and she needed to know now.

Why wasn't that bastard Smith doing what she had told him to do? Glaring at the body that had now started to twitch, Schmidt left the observation booth in disgust. She would try again to get through to Smith. Somehow, she was determined to unravel the secret of how his antiserum worked.

24.08.19
Manchester, UK

The attack by the undead had failed. Now all that was needed was for the mess created to be cleaned up.

Until yesterday, Florence had never had the dubious honour of being in Clay's main bedroom. Initially, she found she was actually surprised that the man had a level of style that was tasteful. That opinion had rapidly changed when she was shown the bathroom.

The bathroom was large and decorative in nature, opulent taps and marble that must have set Clay back thousands of pounds. Whoever had installed the wet room part must have wondered what the hell he was getting himself into, however. In the shower area were an array of metal loops that were embedded in the wall, chains and manacles dangling from them. Florence had no illusion as to what those were for, and once again she thanked her lucky stars that the Gods hadn't graced her with a beautiful face or a fantastic body. This was where Clay finished off those women he finally got tired of, any blood produced easily washed away. The shower stall was strangely too pristine for the depraved purposes it was often used for. The worst of it was that this was Clay's private shower. He would use it every day, the bondage additions a constant and welcome reminder of his own sickness.

Today, the shower area was to be used to restrain Susan while the antiserum was administered. At least, that was the plan.

Florence had brought Susan here thirty minutes ago and had been asked to stand outside so Clay could get whatever pleasures he felt were appropriate for this time of the day. Florence was past caring about anyone but herself, but she still felt a degree of pity for what was being done to Brian's sister in law. It was voluntary only in the sense that Susan really didn't have any choice but to acquiesce to Clay's pathetic fumblings.

"Ready for you now, Doc," Clay said, opening the bedroom door for her. He had his trousers on at least, but he was still buttoning his shirt up over his immense belly. The partial state of his undress was clearly meant to send Florence some sort of message, but Florence didn't care to even try and decipher it. Her eyes stayed on Clay's victim as she entered the room, Susan sat hugging herself on the edge of the bed. She had her dressing gown on, at least she had been allowed to keep that.

"You know, once I administer the drug, you will need to…abstain from any unnecessary contact with Susan," Florence said. She didn't think Clay would listen to her, but something in Florence's drug-addled mind felt the need to give some respite to Susan. Florence suddenly felt she had to try. They were all victims here when it came to dealing with Clay.

"Why?" Clay asked incredulously. It was clear he hadn't even considered such a prospect. Florence got close to Clay, closer than she actually felt happy being, but it was necessary so she could whisper in Clay's ear. It amused her that this actually seemed to make Clay uncomfortable. To this day, she didn't understand why Clay let her speak to him the way she often did.

"I don't know what is in those vials. You were told it is a cure for the virus, but what if it IS the virus?" Clay's eyes went wide. Shit, was there even a chance of that? The idea to test the antiserum hadn't been Clay's who had been all ready to shoot that shit up into his veins. It was Florence who had advised caution, for she was one of the few people Clay had told about his secret acquisition. Florence stepped away. "Are we still going ahead?"

"Yes," Clay said decisively, "but not in here. Susan, I need you to go into the bathroom." Susan stood warily. She was forced to lead the way, Clay pushing insistently from behind, his hands wandering over her backside. Stepping past her, he opened the door to the bathroom and stepped inside, beckoning Susan to follow.

This was where Susan and Florence got to see the bathroom for the first time. Where they got to see the hoops in the large walk-in shower, the manacles dangling from them. *Christ*, thought Florence, *the rumours were true.*

It was too much for Susan, the place looked like it had been transported right out of a torturer's dungeon. Something inside her snapped. Out of Clay's reach, she retreated backwards, shaking her head in defiance.

"Don't you back away from me, bitch," Clay snarled.

"No more," she screamed and suddenly bolted which took both Clay and Florence by surprise, Clay having considered her to now be broken and compliant. Susan was halfway across the bedroom before Clay could even respond. He made to give chase, but he was slow and lumbering while Susan, even in bare feet, was unnervingly quick and nimble. Florence just stepped to the side and let everything unfold.

"Get back here you fucking slag," Clay roared which only spurred more panic in Susan. By the time he reached his bedroom door, Susan was already at the end of the corridor.

Susan took the stairs two at a time, pain already forming in limbs that hadn't been used for such exertion in years. She reached the first floor and descended the next flight, the sound of pursuit seemingly all around her. At the ground floor, Viktor appeared from the main kitchen, but he was too far away to intercept her, and like Florence, he didn't even try. Susan made straight for the front door, its heavy weight opening easily under her desperate demands.

It's so green out here, was the first thought that hit her as she threw herself down the mansion's front steps and onto the gravel driveway. Ten metres ahead of her lay the main gate, and with pure mania in control now, she hurtled headlong at it, almost oblivious to the stones that dug into the souls of her feet.

"Fucking stop the bitch," a shout came from behind her, but Susan barely heard it. Her entire focus was on the gate, the men milling around strangely suspended and frozen in time. She didn't even see Brian as he came out of the breakfast tent to see what all the commotion was about.

Hands tried to grab her, but Susan managed to sidestep their owner, almost slipping on a wet patch of grass. The gate was partially open, you see, and she knew it was her only chance at escape. There were two men on the other side moving bodies away from the previous slaughter. If she could get through and past them, then she would be free.

In her terror, she didn't see the blue police tape, and it merely snapped as she went through it, pulling taught only briefly. The two men ahead of her turned in her direction, dropping the body they were carrying, their gloved hands caked with gore. They seemed to be signalling at her to stay back, but she powered on at them regardless. Nobody had expected someone to try and flee from the compound, so nobody had been ready for it. Most of Clay's men just looked on with mild interest, some with amusement. Brian looked on in horror.

Susan hit the gate, the slime there coming off in her hands. She tried to push herself through, but her feet landed in something cold and wet, the pavement she now stood on slick beneath her feet. Those feet suddenly betrayed her, Susan's balance going, her hands too moist to gain a purchase on the iron bars. Susan fell, her feet and lower legs coated in the guts and the brains of slaughtered zombies. When she landed with a bone-crushing thump, she felt the fluids beneath her quickly soak through the dressing gown. She tried to turn over, to push herself off the ground, hands now managing to grab her, the two men who had been on clean-up duty helping her off the floor.

They wore protection against the virus. Susan didn't. Despite their attempts, she slipped from their grasp and fell to the floor again. Susan ended up on her belly, a decapitated head looking at her with black eyes. It was finally all too much, and her mind deserted her, no longer able to withstand what the world was willing to offer. Susan fainted, the scream that needed to come out dying in her throat.

The virus soaked itself into her body, greedily intent on making her one of its own.

24.08.19
Preston, UK

Cartwright was the last to appear in the wasteland. He found himself sat cross-legged with a self-awareness he had never before possessed. All his life he had been in it for himself, and now he saw the foolishness and the idiocy such selfishness represented. Finally, he had a purpose worth killing for.

For once the hurricane winds didn't blow, the air around him still, thick with the promise of the coming slaughter. The robes he wore were red, his wiry frame resplendent in his almost regal attire. Much of his vision was blocked by the mask he wore, and as his hands explored it, Cartwright found the mask couldn't be removed, as if it was a part of him. Strangely, this did not concern him. If anything, it elated him. He had always tried to hide his true nature from those he met, his pernicious character toxic to those who always seemed to uncover it. Here he could remain hidden and reap the vengeance on those the virus had been denied making its own. Their bodies rejected the gift of Lazarus, so the virus rejected them, an organism acting to protect itself by a mechanism unknown to mankind.

Standing, dust fell from his legs, leaving his garments unsoiled. The cloth writhed around him, seemingly alive, hugging his limbs as if to hide every part of his form. The muscles he possessed here felt powerful, his abilities endless. He knew he could run for miles without getting tired, his energy boundless, and his determination in the pursuit never wavering. He wouldn't have to run, of course, for he had been provided with transport that was much more efficient.

The horse with the dark scarlet skin had been standing behind him all along. It nuzzled him with its hot snout as if expressing a need for urgency and speed. The beast loved him, that much was evident. Cartwright would not be rushed however, there was time enough for what needed to be done. Where the horse came from, he had no idea. He was equally mystified as to why he was here, but he didn't question it just as he didn't question the need to kill the immune. Their death was required, he knew that just as he knew the sun would rise in the morning. The Earth's sun that was, here in the desert, the red suns never set.

Carefully he mounted the horse, the thick blanket on its back reassuringly comfortable to him. From the mist, ghostly riders came, indistinct but present. Cartwright couldn't see their faces, but he knew who they were, had been created afresh by one of them. That act had been forced upon him, but now he felt nothing but thanks for Smith, for showing him the light and the way.

The names of soldiers did not gel in his mind here though, for his companions in chaos were to be known by other names.

The White.

The Pale rider.

The man on Black.

And himself, the Red Waste.

Cartwright also saw a hint of the fifth that would come amongst them, the strongest of them, their leader if such a thing could exist here. But he sensed something more, a danger he was supposed to be aware of. The immune in the vast valley below were of no threat to any of the horsemen. Despite that, something perilous was out there. Whatever it was, the horsemen would find it and deal with it the way they dealt with all things.

When Cartwright opened his eyes, the other three were staring at him, gathered around expectantly.

"Now we are four," Smith said. There was nothing more natural than being together like this. "Now we wait for the fifth to come." *The best of us*, The Voice added. The Voice, dispossessed as it was, had the power to come and go from the desert as it pleased.

"Did you sense it?" Cartwright asked. The others looked at him, confused. "There is something more, something for us to fear."

"Bullshit," Shah ejected, "WE are the things to fear." Showered, he was dressed now in a pressed dress uniform that he had found hanging in a closet, resplendent in tassels and ribbons he had never earned. It was the wrong rank and regiment, but it fit him well enough, the boots a little tight. Much better than what he had awoken in; the look, one of elegance that reflected who he was inside. As if sensing a tragedy to his style, Shah flicked a fragment of almost invisible fluff off his arm, the white gloves pristine and unblemished.

"No," Smith said, "I sensed it too. A force coming for us. A threat that we all must face willingly."

"Then we will face it together," Dawson insisted, "as brothers."

"Indeed we shall," Smith agreed. The Voice would tell him when the fifth of them was ready. When that time came, they would sleep and gather in the desert together. And then the hunt would begin, the final assault on the last defence humankind had against the virus.

"*Isn't there something you have forgotten?*" The Voice asked Smith cryptically. He searched his memory, unsure what The Voice referred to. "*The video feed.*" Of course. Smith turned from his brothers without an explanation and walked over to the laptop. Schmidt's face could be seen there, the video on his end turned to face a blank wall. He could have just shut the feed down, but Smith felt strangely compelled to finish the communications he had started. He moved the camera so it was facing him, Schmidt now able to see his face. Dawson, Shah and Cartwright crowded in behind him, curious as to who this person was.

"Who is she?" Shah asked.

"An American. She thinks she can cure Lazarus."

"Hahaha," Dawson roared, "such stupidity."

"Hey," Schmidt said, clearly annoyed, "I'm right here guys."

"What do you want Schmidt?" Smith asked, the contempt dripping from his words. Now that he understood everything, there was no longer a need for him to prove his worth to other scientists. His need for significance had just been a trick instilled by his virally fractured brain so that he could finish off the experiment and make his brotherhood whole. If only he had been to the desert sooner, so much wasted time could have been spared.

"We haven't been able to replicate your experiments." She looked at the four healthy men visible on her computer screen. It didn't make sense unless Smith was trying to pull some elaborate con job. But what would be the point of that?

"That is not my concern. Do not try and pass on the blame for your own failings."

"Hey buddy, it's your research we are using." There was something very different with Smith. When she had spoken to him before, he had seemed distracted, excessively self-conscious of what he was trying to do. Now all doubt seemed to be absent from him.

"Then you are obviously using it wrong. These fine men behind me are a testament to the effectiveness of my research. All infected by Lazarus and all cured by my hand, only to become something so much greater. But don't feel bad professor, the challenges you face won't matter for much longer." Smith was supremely confident of that statement. When they finally began the hunt, they would eradicate any and all of the immune that had escaped the clawing, gouging hands of the undead. He personally planned to take Jessica's head between his hands before ending her existence in the vilest way imaginable.

"What the hell are you talking about?" Schmidt demanded.

"What I mean, my dear Professor, is that your time on this planet will shortly be over. Your failure isn't in your inability to replicate my research. It is in your inability to understand the true nature of the virus. It completes us as a species. Those immune individuals you think you have locked away safe from the world, they will be dealt with soon enough." With a smile that almost dripped with venom, Smith withdrew his revolver and shot a hole right through the computer monitor. It was clear to him that Schmidt could never understand the complexities of why the desert existed or how the antiserum made from Jessica's blood could create him and his kind. Smith knew he owed Jessica an unpayable debt of gratitude, but that wouldn't stop him gouging her eyes out with his thumbs when he finally found her.

24.08.19
Frederick, USA

Jee was going through everything the British had sent to them at the start of Smith's research. Annoyingly, most of Smith's notes had been made by hand on paper, so she was looking at digital scans. Whoever Smith was, he seemed to write in spider scrawl. Then there were the patient records of Jessica Dunn, the Accident and Emergency admission forms as well as her records from the North Manchester General Hospital.

It was then that she noticed that one of the files hadn't been scanned properly, the bottom of the form missing. Jee enlarged the image on her computer, tried to decipher what the question had been. As she couldn't make it out, she moved to a process of elimination. Jessica had answered negative to all the usual questions about heart disease, high blood pressure and the like. But what was the one question you always asked a woman?

Are you pregnant?

No, it couldn't be that easy. She went through Smith's notes again, page after page of logs and observations. Time and again, Jee found sections that were almost decipherable, and even blowing the words and sentences up seemed not to help. But there was something there, mentioned several times, that might have been the words *"patient is pregnant."*

Could that be it though? Was that why the antiserum from Jessica Dunn seemed to work when Schmidt's versions seemed to fail. If so it was likely a hormonal issue, human chorionic gonadotropin the most likely culprit. She didn't see how that could be the case, wasn't aware of the accidental brilliance behind the construction of the virus and the random mutations and almost god-like coincidence that had lined up everything to create the situation they were now in.

Jee stood from her desk, one of the other researchers giving her a suspicious glance.

"Where is Professor Schmidt now?" Jee demanded.

"In her office, I think," the other researcher said, and Jee stormed out, curious eyes following her.

When Jee knocked on the Professor's door, there was no response. It was only when she knocked a second time that an exasperated voice shouted "What?" Jee entered apprehensively.

"Professor," Jee started, trying to ignore the thunderous eyes that were looking at her and the shattered laptop that had clearly been thrown across the room. "Professor, I need to ask Colonel Smith a question. Are you still in contact with him?"

"You can forget about Smith," Schmidt said angrily, "we will be having no more contact with him."

"Oh," was all Jee could say.

"Why? What is so important?"

"Oh, nothing major. I just wanted some clarity on the notes he provided." Something suddenly told Jee that telling Schmidt about Jessica possibly being pregnant would be a bad mistake. Men don't get pregnant, and neither do pre-pubescent little girls.

"Then if you don't mind, I would like to be left in peace if that's not too much trouble." This was the first time Jee had seen Schmidt angry. In fact, it was the first time she had seen the Professor display any kind of real emotion.

"Yes, sorry," Jee said, closing the door behind her. Maybe she should have told Schmidt, but that wasn't a decision she could rush into.

24.08.19
New Mills, UK

The railway line had been a good choice, but with daylight now broken, he could see he wasn't going to be able to escape conflict completely. With the level of danger increasing, Azrael had stopped to give himself extra protection. The duct tape he carried had been fashioned into primitive armour. It would be useless against bullets and knives, but against teeth, it would be formidable. The tape was now wrapped loosely around his forearms and hands to give the gloves on the latter some extra protection. The same went for his thighs, where it was designed to protect the meat there without restricting his movements. Finally, it held the lobes and the top of his ear against his head to stop them being gripped, while still allowing him to hear. The neck was also given a degree of protection. It was irritating, and by Christ, he looked ridiculous, but survival was the only thing that counted here.

New Mills Railway Station loomed ahead of him. Not a grand affair, two dilapidated platforms that had once allowed the depressed locals to be ferried to the dizzying vastness of Manchester. Now, no commuters were venturing to meaningless jobs, the need for travel and commerce overridden by a thirst to survive.

For a brief moment, Azrael could almost believe that, despite the structures around him that proved otherwise, humanity had never existed.

Just past the station platforms, a road bridge crossed the tracks, a single figure stood there, looking down at Azrael. He knew instantly that the creature was far from alive, the way it stood all the evidence he needed. There were no other zombies that he could see, and he slipped the gun from his back, kneeling to line up a shot. The magnified view of the fiend appeared in his scope, half the face charred and blackened by fire, teeth shattered in a mouth that promised so much violence. Before he could fire however, the zombie suddenly leapt from the bridge, landing awkwardly on the tracks, stumbling onto its side as it hit the ground. It righted itself with difficulty and came at Azrael, but it was clear it was damaged in some way, the speed restricted by a leg that seemed to hang back uselessly.

Azrael took his time in lining up the shot, one bullet all he needed to use. The part of the brain that created the beast was destroyed by the projectile that entered through its open and fractured mouth. As the zombie fell, two more appeared where it had once stood, also jumping from the bridge. They seemed to land in unison, almost synchronised and barely paused before running at him. Had they heard the suppressed shots, or were they somehow being drawn to Azrael? Azrael took them out as efficiently as he had dispatched the first zombie, his accuracy a reflection of the hundreds of hours Mother had put him through on the shooting range during his training.

"Better to waste a bullet here than waste your life in the field," she had often said. No matter how accurate his shooting had been, Mother had always seemed able to beat him.

The air around him was suddenly silent, even the breeze holding its breath. Nothing further came to the lip of the bridge, and Azrael stood, happy that he could at least now proceed.

The short tunnel wasn't long enough to be dark, the rail tracks curving around to the left as they led away. Azrael continued to follow them, safe that much of the borders would offer some sort of barrier to undead and human alike. There were always fences to keep the foolish away from the certain death of being decapitated by a high-speed train. People were often too foolish to avoid even the simplest of hazards. It wouldn't be much protection though for the fences were likely to be incomplete in parts, damaged in others. There was also the truth that any wall or fence could be climbed if someone or something had the determination.

The road bridge was soon behind him, and Azrael figured he was once again safe for the time being. Nature seemed to be intent on giving him omens, however. In the distance, thunder clouds could be seen, their distant rumble a portent on the downpour that might soon come. On an electrical box at the side of the track, a single black raven sat, watching Azrael's approach intently. It was a normal bird, free from the disease ravaging the country, but its presence could be considered a warning, its croaking call echoing through the surrounding foliage. *Go back*, it advised, *there is nothing for you here.* A carrion bird, the raven had often been associated with the dead and with lost souls. Fitting then that it should be here to witness Azrael's epic journey.

Azrael suddenly found himself fascinated by the bird, as if it was here to bring some sort of revelation. Did it have a message for him? Could it connect him to the ghosts of the people killed by Lazarus? More bizarrely, Azrael suddenly had the notion the bird could connect him to the memories and the actions of his lost self, the person he was before the Russian KGB had turned him into the monster he now was. Somewhere in his mind was the rememberings of a child that had been stripped away by chemicals and trauma.

The raven was clearly not in any mood to share, and it took off flying the way Azrael had come. If he had turned and walked back fifty paces, he would have seen the bird land on one of the dead he had shot. He was already aware that the creatures of the land were just as vulnerable to Lazarus as humans, Corporal Whittaker sharing that information with them all. Whittaker had seen evidence of this in the battle for Hounslow, a battle the soldiers had too easily lost.

He was walking parallel with the A6 road now, so his vigilance was heightened, human structures on his left occasionally visible. As a second road bridge came into view, Azrael knew that the new sound that met his ears was the noise of running feet. From ahead of him, he witnessed a bloodstained woman thundering madly towards him, her left arm clutched in her right hand. Despite the distance, it was clear that she was human and she came towards Azrael as if she were a moth drawn to a flame. At that moment, there was no evidence of pursuit, but the undead would be close behind.

"Don't come any closer," Azrael ordered, the woman slowing as she came near him.

"You have to help me," she begged. "I think I lost them, but they were right behind me."

"Have you been bitten?" Azrael asked. The woman looked behind her, panic owning her eyes. When her gaze came back to Azrael, the look on her face told him the answer to the question.

"Please, it's not bad," she said, holding her arm out as if to prove it to him. "You're a soldier, help me."

"I'm not a soldier," Azrael said, the donated military fatigues he wore clearly giving the woman the wrong impression.

"But…" the woman said, stepping closer. Azrael raised his gun, the threat he promised clear.

"Don't come any closer, I said. I'm serious about that." The coldness and the lack of emotion in Azrael's voice spoke volumes about what he was capable of. "When were you bitten?"

"What?"

"The bite, how long ago did you receive it? And how many of the undead were there?"

"There were about thirty of them, and they attacked a whole group of us about ten minutes ago." That wasn't good.

"Was this on the A6?"

"Yes. Why aren't you helping me?"

"You've been bitten. The only thing I can do is spare you from what you are about to become. One shot and I can end it all for you." At no time did Azrael even consider that she was immune. They had bitten her and let her escape so she could spread the virus further when she eventually died and came back.

"You bastard," she roared. Too loud, Azrael said to himself, and he shot her through the head without even a second thought. It would seem Azrael hadn't changed that much. He still had the ability to murder someone in cold blood, even though such an act was tainted by the mercy it represented.

As suppressed as his weapon was, the sound was still stark in the surrounding scenery. He stood on alert for a minute, waiting for what might be the inevitable onslaught. It never came, and Azrael once again resumed his trek.

24.08.19
Leeds, UK

Andy was woken by the sound of voices out in the cul-de-sac. Most of the first-floor windows were now covered with the plywood he'd had in the garage, although parts of the upper windows were left un-boarded so he could see out at the front and back of his property. Dragging himself from his bed, he looked down from his front window, and his heart lifted.

Soldiers. About damned time. If he was honest, the protective clothing they wore worried him.

They were going house to house, the leader of the four soldiers speaking to whoever answered the door. They didn't seem threatening, and although they were armed, the guns were kept pointed at the ground rather than the people. Even so, Andy was surprised by how eager his neighbours were in their trust of these new arrivals, their belief in the system still strong. The army had come to rescue them, what could possibly be bad about that? As the soldiers moved to the next property, Andy noticed those neighbours already visited began leaving their homes to gather into small groups.

When they came towards Iain's property, Andy decided he would go downstairs and see what this was all about. It looked like his neighbourhood was finally under some sort of military protection, and Andy reckoned that was for the best for most of the people who lived near him. They couldn't survive by relying on themselves.

Could this even be the start of an evacuation? Andy wasn't convinced that would be the right option for him. So far, he was safe here, despite the actions he had been forced to take. People meant problems, as had already been proven twice now. With no-one around him, the dynamics would change in his favour. On the one part, he would be less likely to be assaulted by the zombie menace because surely they went where the people were. And on the other, the empty houses around him would soon become meaningless to any scavengers. Although he would be isolated, it was highly likely the risk-reward of attacking his house would plummet to the extent that he would be left completely alone. That was all dependent on an evacuation of course, which he really didn't see happening. There were half a million people in Leeds, where the hell could they be evacuated to?

When he left the house, he didn't take his shotgun. It was no match for the weapons these men carried, and would only risk him being seen as a threat.

"He won't answer," Andy shouted as he approached his property's front gate, the soldiers by Iain's front door drawn to his voice. In the cul-de-sac, people were still gathering in groups, waiting for whatever the soldiers had in store for them. From where Andy stood, he observed the soldiers as they looked over at him. "The occupant of that house is dead," Andy continued. Retreating back down the steps of Iain's house, the four soldiers came over to Andy's gate, three of them holding back slightly. The one in the lead was carrying a clipboard with sheets of paper that fluttered slightly as the breeze took them.

"Andrew Tate?" the lead soldier asked. Clearly, the soldiers were using electoral rolls to ensure they got to everyone.

"Please call me Andy. What's going on here, guys?"

"We are testing the population for the virus. Those found to be carrying it will be taken away for treatment." *Treatment*? Andy said to himself. *I thought there wasn't a cure?* "We also have a distribution centre set up close by with food and water."

"I have all that," Andy said, "inside there." Andy pointed back to his house.

"Quite the fortress," the lead soldier said. Looking at the NBC suit the soldier wore, Andy could see the man was a Captain.

"Thank you."

"But it's not enough to keep you safe," the Captain advised.

"I'm sure I can be the judge of that."

"Will you willingly agree to undergo the test?" the Captain asked. Concern blossomed in Andy's head. He had been exposed to the virus, he knew he had. If he wasn't free of it, what would happen to him?

"I think I'm fine. I can look after myself, and I'm showing no symptoms of the virus." Andy expected an argument, to be told that the test was mandatory. Instead, the Captain merely nodded and turned his head to look at the corpse lying in the middle of the cul-de-sac, the body of the man Andy had shot.

"I'm told that was your handiwork."

"His group were threatening people. Action needed to be taken to remove that threat." Andy knew now he had been right not to bring out the shotgun, but perhaps he should have at least brought the pistol. Standing here, he was defenceless. With a gun shoved down the back of his trousers, he would at least have had options, not that he would feel comfortable about shooting at soldiers. After all, soldiers had a tendency to shoot back.

The Captain indicated he was in agreement with Andy's actions.

"Your neighbours back that up. They also said you defended them against the occupant of that house," the Captain said, specifying Iain's house. "Am I to assume you killed him too?"

"Yes," Andy stated. He wasn't proud of his actions, but neither was he ashamed. "Although at the time, he was undead so I really didn't have much choice about that." He decided not to mention the part about the zombie salivating all over him.

"I assume a search of the property would confirm that?"

"Probably," Andy said, "although my shotgun did make a mess of it. Is this test mandatory?"

"Yes," said the Captain, "and advisable."

"Good to know. And if I refuse?"

"Why would you refuse?" The Captain seemed genuinely astonished.

"Don't get me wrong, it's not that I don't trust you personally, but the radio has been awash with the news that there is no cure for this."

"The situation has changed." The lie seemed to slip from the Captain's lips too easily, but Andy knew it for the falsehood that it was. There could be no cure for this, not after such a short space of time. "Will you volunteer for the test?" the Captain asked again, more insistent this time. One of the soldiers had broken away from the group and was now stood outside Iain's front door. With red spray paint, the soldier marked the door with a large X and several digits that Andy had no clue how to decipher.

"It depends what's involved." Andy could tell the Captain was getting exasperated with him. How far could he push this before they just pointed guns at his face? He suspected that would be a last resort for these soldiers because that was likely to cause the other residents here to panic. The neighbours had seen enough threats to their peaceful lives over the last few days. If the soldiers started in on that tactic, then any hope that they had managed to retain would probably just evaporate into despair.

"Simple pinprick finger test. The tests were airdropped by NATO last night. We need to clear the herd of anyone who might have the virus."

"Clear the herd?"

"Sorry, figure of speech. It was how our company CO described it to us. So do we have your cooperation?" Two of the other soldiers stepped closer to their Captain, their guns raising just a fraction. Andy knew he clearly had no choice and perhaps it would have been wiser to stay inside. Would they have forced their way in, or simply gone on to the next house if Andy had ignored their persistent banging?

If he didn't do what these men said, he knew there was a strong chance they would just shoot him, panic be damned. He couldn't fight back, and he couldn't run. Clearly, he was left with only one option. Stepping fully up to the gate, he extended his left arm out to the Captain.

"Corporal," the Captain ordered. The now indicated Corporal let his gun swing on its strap as he stepped forward. The gloved hands made it difficult for him, but he extracted a testing unit from one of the larger pockets on his military webbing. Watching it being unwrapped, Andy reckoned it looked similar to a pregnancy test. That was exactly what the outer shell had been designed for, the factory where it had been built taken over by NATO to allow fast production of what the Americans had managed to perfect. That factory was now one of the most heavily guarded facilities on the European mainland.

The Corporal did the test, placing it in a self-sealing plastic bag. Andy sucked the blood from his finger, the coppery taste lingering in his mouth, which had suddenly become dry. Fear of exposure?

"We will have the results in five minutes. Please stay here until we can give you the all clear," the Captain said. Andy wondered how many people had refused the test? And how many would fail it?

It was the longest five minutes of Andy's life. He watched, almost mesmerised as the rest of his neighbours were tested, some eager, others reluctant. Most were lucky, but the elderly couple whose house Iain had attacked the other day weren't. They were moved further away from the rest of their neighbours, another red X painted on their house. The X clearly meant *danger, stay out*, the interior obviously bristling with infection.

The elderly couple looked shocked, betrayed even. They got a combination of looks from their fellow neighbours, ranging from pity to outright hostility. There was no community spirit left now, just selfish self-preservation. Andy wasn't surprised at their reactions, he had always known that people lived behind a mask that they rarely let drop. It was only when the shit was flying that you got to see the true nature of someone's character, and Andy found himself looking in disgust at the faces of some of those who had often given him a friendly wave.

Humanity, at its core, was a vicious animal that was kept in check by the artificially created rules society had laid down. It was thus perhaps fitting that order was now being maintained by the soldiers, the ultimate personification of the power the state could bring to bear. Fear of the gun and the fear of Lazarus were now mankind's guiding light.

When the Captain walked up to where Andy was standing, Andy felt himself holding his breath.

"You are all clear," the Captain said. "We have a food distribution point set up if you are interested." Andy suddenly felt the need to tell the Captain everything, but he managed to hold his little secret inside.

"I'm good thanks. Keep the food for those who weren't better prepared." Andy looked at the elderly couple once again. "What happens to them now?"

"A unit will be here to collect them. They are in the early stages of the infection, better to remove them from others before they risk spreading what they are carrying. We can't allow them to be free, not with the safe zone we are trying to create." The Captain reached into a pocket and withdrew a fluorescent green Tyvek wristband. "Can I have your wrist please, Andy?" Andy complied, the band secured. It couldn't be removed without cutting it off, and that would be a big mistake. "Never remove that please," the Captain added.

"How safe is Leeds?" Andy asked.

"We were lucky," the Captain said. "We managed to get the initial outbreaks under control. You can thank my commanding officer for that. He acted quickly right at the start of it all by shutting down all rail and road traffic to and from the city, despite the protestations of the civilians supposedly running things. From what we've seen, the virus hasn't penetrated here like with Manchester and London."

"How long have we got?" Leeds itself might be relatively free of the virus, but the surroundings wouldn't be.

"I don't know," the Captain responded truthfully. "It's only a matter of time, though. We lost contact with Sheffield." Joined by the country's main motorway, the undead could easily use that artery to head north. Sheffield had been hit early on due to a group of Chinese students who had contracted the virus in Hong Kong.

"What are you doing about the gangs, like the ones that attacked us earlier?"

"You shouldn't see any more of that. It's zero tolerance now. Anyone actively resisting the authority of the military and the police will be either arrested for execution or shot on sight."

"Seriously?" Andy asked. He was really glad he hadn't come out of his house with his shotgun now. His eyes were drawn to the people milling around. Only some of them had a green armband like him. At least four-fifths, including the children and the frailer looking women, had orange bands. The elderly couple had red.

"Why the different coloured bands, Captain?" Andy could pretty much guess what red meant.

"How good are you with that shotgun of yours?" the Captain suddenly asked.

"Pretty good as it happens."

"Good, because we are going to need people like you to help defend the city. That's what the green means. It gives you certain privileges, but we also expect something from you in return." The Captain reached out and put a gloved hand on Andy's shoulder. "Consider yourself conscripted."

***

His mates called him Vinny, his mother called him Vincent. Right now, the soldiers screaming at him and called him anything but his name.

He'd had no choice but to accept the blood test, the soldiers moving door to door on the council estate. Some of the lads he had hung around with had tried to run, he'd seen their flight across the courtyard three floors below, but the soldiers had been expecting that. There were only so many ways in and out of the estate, the concrete structures designed as if to easily trap those living inside. One warning shot was all it took for his mates to fall to the dirt in surrender.

There could have been a firefight here, the criminal element who lurked in some of the apartments most definitely armed. Word had it that some of them had already fled though, so when the soldiers came, nobody offered them any kind of real resistance. It wouldn't be like that everywhere, many people fated to die before the zombies even made it here.

Stood out on the communal balcony that joined up all the apartments on his floor, Vinny watched the soldiers as they stood next to him, waiting for the results to process. He was terrified, having felt ill for over a day now. When the TV was working, he had been glued to it, easy for someone with no gainful employment. Then the channels had gradually dwindled, as had the internet. By this morning, all that remained was a single and ominous radio channel that filled everyone who listened to it with growing dread.

The rest of the balcony was cleared of people, except for the woman further along, closer to the stairs. She was sitting with her back against a wall, sobbing, her wrists and ankles restrained by zip ties, a clear victim of the mandatory blood test. Soldiers would knock on the door and then insist everyone came outside before searching the apartment. Then they would test you and stand guard until the test result was in. They looked terrifying in their protective gear, the guns they carried pointed at people without fear of any recrimination. The soldiers clearly had a job to do, under orders to clear the city of any cases of the infected.

There was a sudden gunshot from the floor above, Vinny jumping at the sound. Was that another warning? No, somebody had tried to run, not content to let strangers test them. Non-compliance was an instant death sentence now. Even more shocking than the noise, a body suddenly appeared as if it fell from the floor above. Easier to toss the dead over the balcony than to carry them down the staircase.

One of the soldiers spoke to him, it wasn't good news.

"Vincent McGrath, under the power given to me by His Majesty Charles the Third, and under authority of the interim government, you are to be detained under Part three, subsection one hundred and twenty-nine of the two thousand and eight Health and Social Care Act." The words had been memorised, said so many times already. Vinny made to back away, but hands grabbed him, a foot kicked into the back of his leg, sending him to the floor. Because he struggled, he felt a weight descend as a knee was placed on him. He couldn't breathe, which just made him panic even more.

"Please," he begged, but these were hardened men. Their orders were clear, segregate the infected for the protection of yourselves and your own families. If you can't detain, then lethal force is authorised.

His hands were pulled behind his back, sharpness suddenly cutting into them. The zip tie bit down, perhaps tighter than it needed to be. The same happened for his ankles, and he was left lying on his side, the knee finally relenting. Thank God his girlfriend hadn't been here to see this. Vinny knew what she was like, she would have either gone hysterical or totally belligerent. Neither would have ended well with these men. What he didn't understand was why they even tried to keep up the pretence that this was all somehow lawful.

"Stay down there and don't cause us any fucking trouble," a soldier said harshly. They clearly weren't enjoying their duty, and Vinny expected a kick in the ribs at any moment. That kick fortunately never came, but it was a small mercy for what was coming.

Later, when all the apartments were cleared, the soldiers came back for him. He was dragged to his feet, the ties at his ankles released. There were two other prisoners with them, and together they all moved as a group, collecting the woman who now stank of piss. Nobody could blame her for that, Vinny was close to losing control of his own bowels. He suspected the soldiers wouldn't care. As a group, the infected individuals were marched towards the concrete staircase, nervous curtains twitching as those who had been fortunate watched on. Nobody intervened because really, nobody could. In an unarmed population like the UK, standing up to those who enforced the new order could only result in a quick and merciless death. Even though he wished someone would come to his aid, Vinny knew that if he had been passed as clear, there would be no way he would have stuck his neck out to help those less fortunate.

They made it to the ground floor without incident. It would have been more efficient for those infected with Lazarus to have been executed on the spot, but even a disarmed and cowardly populace would likely have risen up if witness to that. Better then to transport everyone for processing.

"What will happen to us?" somebody asked.

"No talking," came the response. Their only ray of hope was the knowledge that they were being taken away for treatment. Not even the most callous of men was going to tell those they collected that there was no treatment, that this was just a ruse to ensure some form of orderly compliance. Why make your job harder?

24.08.19
Manchester, UK

Brian had watched it all. He had watched Susan faint at the gate. Had watched the two men pick her up, but then stand there impotently, not knowing what to do with her. He had watched Viktor exit the mansion's front door, only for Florence to come barging past him to berate the two members of the clean-up crew.

"Don't just stand there like fucking lemons," she had shouted. "Take her to the decontamination tent." Brian had wandered over to Florence, standing next to her as she stood stoically with her arms crossed. He had never seen the doctor so angry before.

"What the fuck just happened?" Brian asked. Florence had spun around on him with hostility.

"What the hell were you thinking bringing Susan here? Don't you know what Clay is?" Brian had suspected something, had guessed there was an ulterior motive in Clay inviting Susan to find sanctuary at his mansion and had considered it a small price for Susan to pay for her safety. But he had never envisioned this, and if she was honest with herself, neither had Florence. She had known it wasn't fair to blame Brian.

"I thought she would be safe, safer at least than out there on the street. Florence, what happened?"

"Clay happened," she said. "He went too far again." Brian thought that any concern for Susan had long since died. He thought he was rid of her, stripped of any need to be responsible for her welfare. Maybe that was another reason why he had brought her here, to finally be rid of the monkey that was riding on his back. But seeing her like this, carried away from where she had fallen into a pile of zombie guts, Brian realised he had been fooling himself. Florence could sense that he was intent on going over to her, so she grabbed his arm in an attempt to restrain that action. Her slender fingers hardly made it halfway around the circumference of his bulging forearm, but her grip had the desired effect.

"Let me deal with this," Florence said. "At least it looks like Clay has his test subject now. What better way to test his antiserum than by administering it to an individual who just fell down in a pile of zombie gore." The last bit was said in a whisper so that nobody else could hear.

"So the bastard does have a cure." The word bastard slipped out, the first time Brian had ever used it to describe Clay. Florence pressed a finger against his lips.

"Hush now. We can't let the gang hear about this."

From the corner of his eye, Brian felt somebody looking at him, and he turned to see Viktor smiling. The supposed butler kept that gaze for several seconds before breaking eye contact and returning through the door of the mansion.

Brian stormed towards the house, the other men gathered around watching him leave. The intensity of Brian's movement drew their gaze, and they all sensed that whatever was happening here was far from over. None of them said anything, but many of them sensed that lines were being drawn in the sand, that boundaries were about to be tested.

Through the front door now and Viktor was nowhere to be seen. Brian stormed to the stairs which he took two at a time despite his slightly arthritic knees. The second flight beckoned, and he took those, barely out of breath by the time he reached the top. He was in the danger area now, rarely was it allowed for someone to venture to the upper floor without first being summoned. This was Clay's domain, and you infringed upon it at your peril. As if to display that, Viktor appeared from a side door, his menacing presence merely an obstacle that Brian knew he could most likely plough through if need be. The Ukrainian was dangerous, but then so was Brian.

"I need to talk to Clay," Brian demanded.

"That's Mr Clay to you," Viktor said dismissively.

"Shut your mouth you Cossack cunt," Brian warned through gritted teeth. "I'm talking to Clay." Surprisingly Viktor stood aside and pointed at Clay's bedroom.

"Then please, be my guest." Brian walked past him, wary of the risk of being felled from behind. But Viktor didn't follow, he merely stood watching, that wretched half smile adorning his face. The thought occurred to Brian that perhaps Clay was somehow innocent here, that Susan had just overreacted. So he would need to avoid going in all guns blazing. The fury that could so easily build in Brian was restrained, and he managed to push it further below the surface. Outside Clay's bedroom, Brian stopped and paused. There was a very real chance that his life hinged on how he handled this moment.

Taking a deep breath, Brian knocked on the door.

"Come in Brian," Clay's voice said. Brian did as he was told, not entirely sure how Clay knew it was him, although the video camera that guarded the door might have something to do with that.

"Mr Clay," Brian said as he stepped in. He was still angry, but he was hoping it didn't show.

"I must be getting senile in my old age," Clay said, "I don't remember calling for you."

"Not at all Mr Clay, I'm just concerned about Susan."

"And you should be, she clearly isn't of sound mind. I offered her the chance to have the cure, and that was the thanks I got?" There it was, the defining moment. How he answered that question could determine whether he was breathing twelve hours from now.

"You offered her the cure?" Brian barely noticed that the door to the bathroom was closed. If he had been of a mind to investigate further, he would have found that the door was also locked.

"I did." Clay stepped up to Brian. "I hold you responsible for this."

"She's been through too much, Mr Clay. I'm sure she just got scared."

"That's not what I want to hear Brian. *I'm sorry for bringing a nutjob into your home Mr Clay* is what I want to hear you say." Brian could feel his jaw tensing, the old fire there. So this was how it was. Years of his devotion destroyed in an instant. Clay seemed to have forgotten it was his idea to bring Susan here.

"What exactly did you do to her?" Brian demanded.

"What did you say?" Clay sounded utterly incredulous.

"I asked you what you did to her. I need to understand why she reacted like she did."

"You need to consider your next words very carefully, Brian," Clay said with menace. The two men looked at each other, and Brian knew that he had to back down and turn this around.

"I'm just trying to understand why she would act like that. I've never known Susan to be so volatile."

"Volatile is not the word I would use Brian. Fucking crazy is the phrase that more adequately springs to mind. I gave her everything. Food, shelter, even a chance at the cure. And all I asked in return was a little female gratitude. You know what I mean?"

"Thank you, Mr Clay. Now I understand." Brian actually seemed to physically relax.

"Understand?"

"It must have been the other night."

"What the hell are you talking about?" Clay demanded.

"If you remember, I told you she was almost gang-raped. Your amorous advances must have triggered something in her." Amorous advances, where the fuck did he drag that from?

"So you're a psychologist now?" Clay sneered.

"No, Mr Clay. It just seems to be the only explanation." Clay seemed to accept that, the crime boss wandering over to the middle window of his bedroom. He looked out, the decontamination tent hidden from his sight.

"Such a shame, though. She could have had a chance."

"She still can, can't she? Florence said…"

"Don't be absurd," Clay said harshly. "She's obviously infected. And Florence doesn't know shit."

"What better way to test it though," Brain insisted. "The cure I mean." He knew he was pushing, probably too much. If he had any sense, he would have just apologised profusely and slithered out of the room on his belly.

"Of course I've considered that," Clay blustered. He hadn't actually. In the heat of the events, all Clay could concentrate on was the loss of the one thing he could fuck. "But if I give her the cure now, I won't be able to keep it a secret. Better to let her just turn."

"I think most of the men know about the cure already," Brian lied. It was the one card he could think to play.

"That's absurd," Clay demanded.

"They are becoming restless, Mr Clay. The attack on the gate has made a lot of them nervous. Watching Susan run from the house like that has got them talking. I've heard some of them whispering, the secret of your cure isn't a secret anymore."

"Nonsense, unless you told them."

"It wasn't me, Mr Clay. Besides, you never told me what was in that case I acquired for you. Look me in the eyes and tell me if I'm lying." Clay did just that, not realising the actual lie had already slipped past his defences. "But I've heard the men speculating. Now that you've confirmed everything, it's clear some of them seem to know more than they should."

"Then who?" Clay insisted.

"I will try and find out for you. But if you use the cure on Susan, and it works, then that might buy you some time with them. It might also encourage the morale of the men with the knowledge that you have their safety locked away in your safe. They won't know how many doses you have."

"But they will all want it."

"Not if we tell them it only works post exposure, like rabies shots or something. They would believe that," Brian insisted. "We've shown we can defend against the undead. The only threat to the lie is if the walls get overrun, and then none of it will matter anyway."

"Hmm," Clay said, suddenly mulling over the thought that he might face an armed rebellion. As paranoid as he was becoming, that risk hadn't even occurred to him. Clay had always considered that betrayal would come from an individual, maybe two, not the whole group. His warped mind began to play over a scenario that was unthinkable a moment ago. Also, who was the rotten apple in the barrel? If not Brian, there were only two other people who knew about the XV1...well three if you counted Susan, but she wouldn't have been able to tell anyone.

"Okay, you can fuck off now, Brian."

"Yes, Mr Clay." Brian left the way he entered, surviving for another day. Viktor was still where Brian had left him, a certain degree of surprise adorning the Ukrainian's face. As Brian walked by his adversary, he stopped. Looking straight ahead, Brian spoke to the man.

"I'm on to your little game," Brian said.

"Really? I'm thrilled to hear it. And what great crimes am I guilty of?" Finally, Brian turned his head and looked at Viktor. Brian's face was dark, devoid of all humour.

"I've been watching you carefully, and I know what your plan is. Clay might not see it yet, but I do. I'd watch myself if I were you."

"Funny, I was about to say the same thing." Brian didn't say anything else. Instead, he stalked off, Viktor's eyes burning into the back of his head. When Brian was out of sight, Viktor chuckled to himself. "Never reveal your hand so early on in the game my friend," Viktor advised the empty corridor. Good, now Viktor knew what measures had to be taken regarding Brian.

Another of Clay's pawns that would need to be removed.

24.08.19
Jersey City, USA

Gabriel was surprised when his pager went off. In the side pocket of his belt, he felt the vibration, plucking it out with effort so that he could gaze with suspicion at the tiny screen. He had taken it with him more out of habit than an actual belief someone would contact him. Mother had told him her version about how he had been kept in the dark, and he had never expected the organisation that once owned him to contact him again. How could he trust what the operatives of Gaia now told him?

"You have electronic mail."

Gaia never spoke to its operatives over the mobile phone network. Instructions were usually relayed by the encrypted landline phones they used, or via courier. However, on the rare occasion when urgent information had to be transmitted to someone like Gabriel when they were in the field, the silenced pager was utilised. This in itself did not give information, just to state that they should check the email address only Gaia had access to. No emails were ever sent of course, just saved as a draft file in the encrypted email account which was hosted by an array of clandestine servers that even the NSA would have been unable to find and crack.

Standing in the deserted street, he let his attention drift from the pager as he reattached it to his belt. He would check the emails when he was good and ready. There might not have been anyone around him, but he had no confidence that this area was safe. In the distance, gunfire was a constant feature, and there was evidence of a rushed evacuation of this neighbourhood. This wasn't a safe place for him to loiter.

The air was harsh and cool, his body still recovering from its successful fight against Lazarus. How close had he come to death? Very was probably the answer to that.

He moved down the centre of the street, discarded vehicles and the evidence of people's lives scattered everywhere. Every building he passed was marked in some way with orange spray paint. Gabriel was acquainted with what those markings generally meant, an indication that the house or business was empty. There was a large orange X that separated the information into four sections, each informative snippet placed by one of the V's that made up the X. At the top was the date and time that structure was abandoned, which for this street was yesterday night. The bottom section contained the number of live, dead and zombified victims that were found in the structure. As he walked past, Gabriel saw very few indications of dead bodies, but on several properties, he saw the tell-tale number by the letter Z.

The left side of the X had the military unit identifier to show who had cleared the building. And finally, on the right, there was an indication of any other hazards present. All the properties with a number by the Z had NE in large capital letters. NE, No Entry. Don't go in because the virus was likely coating every surface, probably still floating in the dust and the very air.

The markings were for military, law enforcement as well as being useful for future scavengers that might find themselves passing through this area. It had been done systematically, methodically with the precision only the military was able to produce, the evacuation going street by street. Today, rescue wasn't the only thing the military seemed to be efficient at.

At the end of the road, there was a park off to his left, the once lush grass somewhere children might have played, and lovers might have lain during the summer months. There would be none of that anymore, the park now put to another, more shocking use. In the centre, there were ten piles of charred bodies, probably two hundred in total, limbs all intertwined with each other to form bizarre scorched sculptures that only the Devil would have appreciated. Here were all the dead, the victims of Lazarus and bullets. The mounds no longer smouldered, but the conflagrations had clearly been complete, the flesh reduced almost to charcoal. It was unlikely Lazarus could have survived that, and even the rats that scurried out in the open seemed to show only disinterest for the deceased pyres.

Humanity was fighting back the only way it knew how. In doing so, it was starting to strip itself of its own compassion. There would be no burials or ceremony led cremations for the relatives of these bodies to mourn over. The corpses would be dealt with so that there was no chance any of the dead could rise again.

Gabriel didn't stop walking, his destination generally northwards. Best to get away from populated areas, to do what he could to follow Mother's last command. To live, to get through this. The virus was now no threat to him, but the creatures that carried it were. As far as he was concerned, the safest place for him would be the forest. He had the tools and the skills to survive out there for years, although there was no telling if the zombie hordes that were gathering would eventually leave the cities to try and strip the land of everything living. Gabriel had seen first-hand how the virus could be passed to rats as well as humans. It was no jump for his imagination to conclude that the other creatures of the planet could fall victim to it as well. That was why he was walking with exaggerated vigilance. Even a stray cat could be a threat to him now.

He wasn't sure, but he thought he saw some remnants of dog in the mounds of bodies. Gabriel didn't feel compelled to get close enough to confirm that.

Soon, the park was out of sight, his travel quick across the abandoned ground. As he travelled, he saw the same orange spray tags on further buildings, more bodies dealt with in the way that was clearly now standard operating procedure. Gabriel wondered what was being used to set the mounds aflame?. Did the military have the time to build elaborate pyres from wood, or did they just use gasoline and the body's own inherent flammability? Whatever was being done, it was clearly effective.

The distant gunfire was louder now and definitely seemed to be coming from ahead of him. Not close enough that he needed to be immediately concerned, but he knew that it would be wise to hold up and wait to see how the conflicts around him escalated. Just up ahead, a convenience store had been left with its doors open. As he got closer, Gabriel saw from the orange markings that the building had been deemed body and zombie free, with twelve survivors rescued. It was of a sturdy construction, which was likely one of the reasons people had retreated there when the crisis around them had escalated. It would also be a source of food and water.

An opportune time to top up his supplies and check the email account.

The door closed easily, the reinforced glass of the windows spider webbed and fractured in parts. There were also clear bullet holes, Gabriel counting them. Seven in all, fired into the building most likely. The scene around him told him a little about what had occurred here, and stepping inside, he saw the shell casing of people that had fired back. The fact that the windows were mainly intact told Gabriel that the shots had been aimed at those trying to gain entry via the door. The blood he stepped over confirmed that.

If he had to guess, Gabriel would have said that people had holed up here, only for their position to have been attacked. The defence, he deduced, had been successful.

There were plenty of supplies still left here. Most stores like this were already likely stripped clean, so the defence had probably been by the owners who had decided to defend their business against looters. Admirable, thought Gabriel, who found the use of force one of the only honourable things about humanity. Good for him also because he was able to restock on the supplies he had already used. Water, food, all to help his flight into the wilderness. It didn't take long to fill up the spaces in his backpack which now felt reassuringly heavy.

Now was as good a time as any to read the email he had been sent. His phone was a Thuraya X5 touch satellite phone, able to connect to the internet and he used it to open the email account Gaia used. There the message sat in draft format, and he opened it expectantly.

"*Gabriel.*

You have done well, my Son. You have helped bring forth a plan that has been years in the making. Your part is done, however. We urge you to leave New York, to seek refuge wherever it may be found. We release you from your burden.

Father."

The betrayers were the ones who formulated the message. Could he listen to another word of their deception? He replied to the email with his own draft, breaking protocol. His message contained four simple words.

"*You lied to me.*"

There was no way of telling how quickly he would get a response, but whoever had sent his message was clearly monitoring the account. His response came within minutes.

"*This is true, and we are sorry.*

We acted out of haste, driven by circumstances that we had not expected. The release of the virus was out of our control, but once it was out there, we felt there was only one road we could take, that of total commitment. We failed you, Gabriel, on so many levels, just as we failed Mother who perhaps rightly rejected our plans from the start. We hope that in some way you can forgive us.

We are flawed, but the world that is being created is the essence of what Mother always dreamed. The plan was for men like you to be at the forefront of the new world, which was why you were provided with the vaccine. If things had occurred as we had foreseen, you would be here with us now.

You will forever be in my thoughts.
Father."

Gabriel read the words several times. They could have been just words, written to try and placate him. But why, what would have been the point of that? It would have been so much easier to just abandon him. Why go to such efforts, and why give him the vaccine in the first place? Did those who Mother claimed betrayed him actually care after all? Without Mother's guidance, how could he know?

Gabriel's mind span with the implications of it all. He deleted the draft email and switched the phone off. The bleeper he dropped to the floor so he could crush it beneath the heel of his boot. It was foolish to have brought it with him. It would have been so much easier to remain ignorant to the thoughts of those in power. Now he was conflicted, confused about who to trust.

Did it even matter? There was nothing for him to do but survive.

The noise of gunfire erupted again, mere blocks away this time. Was the army fighting the undead or the population as he had seen in New York? Either was a possibility at this stage. Gabriel may have been socially isolated from the world, but he could see the nuances that flowed through civil society, could see humans for the self-destructive species they were. There would be some who saw the military as a threat to them and would violently oppose the only force that could end the zombie menace. The one good thing about the apocalypse was that the inept would be the least likely to survive, stripping the gene pool of their ability to reproduce.

Outside, Gabriel heard a vehicle approaching, and he stepped behind one of the shelves so that he couldn't be seen from the street. An army Humvee pulled up outside, and three soldiers got out. Through gaps in the shelved food, Gabriel watched as they surrounded the vehicle, a man up top manning the fifty calibre machine gun. Slipping further into the store, Gabriel headed towards the back, away from the men with guns. As skilled as he was, he wasn't foolish enough to risk facing that kind of enemy. Behind him, the front door opened.

"Someone has been here," Gabriel heard a man say.

"Hello," another called. "National Guard. We are here to take you to the evacuation point."

Could he trust them? Probably not, not unless he had to. He would slip away like the ghost he was and do his best to stay off their radar. Gabriel didn't need their help, his skills superior to all of them combined.

24.08.19
Site R, USA

Her security detail tried to persuade the President not to look, but Fairchild felt she needed to know the truth of what she was facing. The video monitors relayed the feed from around the base's upper perimeter, dozens of zombies scaling the fences.

"How can there be so many?" Fairchild asked. They weren't near any major population centres, and the army was supposed to have tested the surrounding towns.

"The outbreak started in Emmitsburg," one of the secret service said. He didn't like his President, had even requested a transfer from her detail when Fairchild had still been the Attorney General. Now he was glad that transfer had been denied. He was safe down here, safer than he would be anywhere else.

"Well, what are the army going to do about it?" Fairchild demanded. She couldn't have zombies overrunning the upper facility. As yet they hadn't scaled the fences, but it was only a matter of time. The limited number of personnel above ground had retreated into the bunker complex. They would be able to do nothing against the zombie menace, their numbers too few. Better to save them and let the undead bash their heads uselessly against reinforced concrete.

"That's part of the problem," General Franklin advised. The General pointed to one of the monitors, the two zombies that were tearing their fingers against the reinforced fence clearly in army uniform. "The men we had garrisoned at Carroll Valley are engaged in street to street fighting. We aren't sure how the infection spread so fast, but there is a theory."

"What is it?" Fairchild demanded.

"You won't like it, Madam President." She looked at the General, one of the few men she actually had respect for.

"Tell me anyway."

"We think the infection was done deliberately, by a local priest during a religious service." Fairchild looked at him, gobsmacked. That didn't make any sense. Why would one of God's chosen deliberately spread the virus?

"I see. What do we do about this?" Fairchild pointed a bony and arthritic finger at the screen.

"Nothing," General Franklin advised. "There is no way they can get in. With luck, they will just get bored and move on." Do the undead get bored? "At the worst, we can always evacuate via the tunnels."

"Very good, General," Fairchild said. She was loath to abandon this place, at least until Washington DC was reclaimed. Fairchild turned to the head of her Secret Service detail and stuck out her hand for him to shake. "I owe you an apology," Fairchild said. The man seemed genuinely surprised.

"There's no need for that, Madam President." He accepted the handshake anyway.

"Still, the apology is warranted."

"Very good, Ma'am." There had been an instant where Fairchild had insisted that she go to Emmitsburg so as to take one last pilgrimage to that holy place, hopefully with the view of taking holy communion. The Secret Service had made it clear that this was a foolish and unnecessary risk. Fairchild had insisted, but had eventually backed down when she had seen how adamant those who were there to protect her had been. If she hadn't listened, likely she too would be infected by Lazarus now.

Whatever his great plan was, her God was playing a very strange game here.

24.08.19
Manchester, UK

When Susan came to, she found herself in the decontamination tent, strapped to a trolley. The air was surprisingly warm, and her skin still stung from the chemical shower she had been dragged through. The dressing gown was gone, instead being replaced by surgical scrubs. Florence was there, gowned and gloved up and wearing a respirator.

Susan tried to sit up, but it was then that she noticed she was tied down. Whoever had done it had really gone to town. She could move her head to look around her, but that was basically it where her limbs were concerned. The strength of the undead had been witnessed, and nobody was prepared to take any chances.

"Try and relax," Florence's distorted voice stated.

"What happened?" Susan begged.

"You panicked. Quite frankly, I'm surprised you didn't lose it sooner."

"Why am I tied down?" The desperation in her voice filled the tent with the scope of her sorrow.

"You are infected, Susan. There is no way you could have avoided it." When Susan had run from the house barefoot, the gravel had opened up small cuts on the soles of her feet. Although Lazarus could have made it through her skin anyway, the lacerations just made infection a certainty. Already the signs of the infection were spreading up her legs. Florence marvelled at how much quicker the infection took hold in those who were infected in this manner rather than the initial virus that had spread quietly across the planet.

"Let me go," Susan begged.

"Not a chance," Florence responded unsympathetically. Keeping Susan tied up was for everyone's safety.

"Please, just let me go. I'll walk out of the front gate and never come back."

"Susan, your only chance now is to stay here. Why don't you see that?"

"Where's Brian?" Susan suddenly asked.

"I have no idea where he is. What I do know is that he isn't here." As she was talking, Florence took a vial from her pocket and placed it on the table next to the trolley Susan was restrained to.

"What's that?" Susan asked nervously.

"Apparently it's the cure. Clay is even more eager for me to give it to you now." Brian's conversation with Clay had clearly had the desired effect.

"I don't want to be your guinea pig."

"I know, and I know you would probably rather die than endure any more of this. Viktor mentioned he had to intervene to stop you from killing yourself." Sadness filled Florence's voice. "You are getting this injection, and it is my clinical opinion that we shouldn't wait any longer." What would Clay do though if the injection could be shown to cure Susan? A horrible thought suddenly occurred to Florence. How would Clay ensure the woman of her desires was safe to fuck again?

"You crazy bitch, what is wrong with you?"

"That is a very good question, Susan," Florence answered as if pondering some great philosophical dilemma. "There's a lot wrong with me, has been for a while. I think that's why I'm able to put up with Clay and his merry band. As much as I hate being a party to this, I seem to belong with him." Florence looked up at the ceiling and sighed heavily. "This really isn't how I planned my life to turn out if I'm honest."

"You think I care about that. Help me, you are supposed to be a doctor."

"Yes, so I've heard. The truth is, while I retain the skill, I stopped being a doctor long ago. I now only go through the motions."

"So you do Clay's bidding just to keep your veins packed with your precious heroin?"

"Exactly, Susan," Florence said almost pleased that someone finally seemed to get it. "Although I generally prefer to smoke it."

"You can beat it though, Florence," Susan said in regards to the doctor's addiction.

"Oh, I know I can. Known it for years actually."

"Why not come off it then, break your dependence on that madman?"

"Susan, you wouldn't understand."

"I'm a fucking alcoholic, of course I understand." There, she had said it again. Her mind had finally decided it was time to reject the addiction she had been trapped into.

"Do you like who you have become, Susan?" The question took her off guard. Nobody had ever asked that of Susan before. "Because my addiction frees me. It frees me from the constraints of so-called civil society. It frees me from the expectations someone in my position is supposed to abide by. I can still function at my job while being able to reject the bullshit that comes with it, safe in the knowledge that Clay will protect me. Can your alcohol do that for you, Susan?" Florence looked deep into Susan's eyes and saw that the woman had no answer to that. "No, it can't. You use your alcohol as a slow form of suicide because you are too much of a coward to outright kill yourself."

"Fuck you," Susan glowered through gritted teeth. The words hurt, the truth often does. Picking up a syringe, Florence loaded it with the contents of the vial.

"Heroin takes the pain of my failures away and still allows me to carry on. Plus, it feels damned good when I take it." Florence was basically stating that she had sold herself.

"Don't come near me with that, please."

"Even though it could be your salvation?" Florence expressed the air from the syringe, its contents now ready to inject.

"Salvation for what though? You saw that bathroom. You know what Clay will do to me. Please, just let me die." The words flowed from her lips. She had already been intent on killing herself once but had been prevented. Now she begged for the mercy that the virus could ultimately bring her.

Florence looked at her patient, saw the pleading and the resignation in the eyes. It would be so easy to help her now. She could pull back the syringe plunger, fill it with air and inject that into Susan. The cameras watching her here wouldn't see that, and when Susan died, the claim could simply be made that the cure wasn't any such thing. Florence almost did just that, because Susan was right. Even if Clay never went near her again, saving Susan only condemned her.

That was murder, though, and as twisted as Florence was, she couldn't bring herself to do it. And inaction wasn't an option, because she knew that Clay and Viktor would be watching everything she did. It wouldn't even surprise her if he or Viktor were somehow listening to every word that was being spoken in here too. As much as she sympathised with Susan's plight, Florence had to think of herself first. Both of them were in a hopeless position.

"Actually, I really think we've waited long enough." Just in their brief conversation, the tendrils had started to appear all across Susan's neck. "Just so you know, I have no idea what this will do to you or what it even is. I just wanted you to know that." Susan tried in vain to back away from the advancing needle.

"Why would you tell me that?"

"I thought it best to be truthful... you know, one addict to another."

24.08.19
Newark, USA

John had been sent to collect several of the immune over the last few days, his team dispatched across the country, often with short notice being given between assignments. He and his men were tired, sleep snatched on transport planes and helicopters. Even with ample rations, they were hungry from the lack of a decent meal. They hadn't even been that successful most of the time either, Big T the last patient they had been able to acquire.

With Carson himself collecting Reece from Houston, John's team had been the only other one to bring back any of the immune, but four wasn't anywhere near enough for what the Professor was planning, apparently. John had hoped this trip would be different than those he had been engaged with recently, but fifteen minutes out of Newark Liberty International Airport, they had lost contact with the aid station south of Newark Museum that had reportedly found an immune individual. Now with boots on the ground at the site, he looked at the bodies and ruined tents with the all too familiar dismay. It was clear that he had been sent on another wasted trip. Above them, a Predator drone was overlooking the area, had been for the last ten minutes since its deployment. The remaining troops that had been left at the airport had told him they were preparing to bug out. Manhattan Island had been lost, most of the bridges from it already blown. That was only slowing the undead down though.

"Alpha team to control. Get a message to Major Carson, tell him the package is unlikely to be delivered."

"Roger Alpha team. Please advise on your situation?"

"Nothing here but the dead and the dying so far." John was livid. It was clear that there hadn't been enough troops stationed in this part of Newark. There were four Humvees and an M1133 medical evacuation unit (MEV) indicating a platoon of national guard at best. If the commanding officer who allowed this was still alive, he would wish he wasn't when the Major learnt of this utter incompetence. The word had come from the highest echelons of the military. The immune were of the highest priority.

Of the vehicles, three of the Humvees had been overturned, and the MEV had crashed into a building, its front end seemingly stuck in the hole it had created.

"Spread out, look for survivors," John said to the men with him. His ten-man team didn't even blink before moving stealthily through the small camp, the evidence of slaughter all around them. Intact bodies were few and far between, many of those who had defended here already dead and resurrected, now wandering the streets. To his left, there was a suppressed shot as a crawling, ruined zombie was finally put out of whatever misery it might be suffering. A second shot rang out, John just able to hear the croaking, pitiful voice that had said "Please no". His men knew who to try and save and who to euthanise. Any apparently dead body they encountered that could potentially get up again was made safe by a bullet to the brain. Four shots were fired in total.

"This is Carson." The voice came over John's headset, imposing its will on the situation. "What happened, John?"

"Locals fucked it up, Major. The aid camp has been overwhelmed. The immune individual, if he existed, was left with minimum protection."

"Fuck. Do I have to do everything myself?"

"I know what you mean," John said. This had been an all too familiar scenario that last day or two. The immune kept being found, but when John and his team got there, the undead had time and again stepped in to kill everything.

"Sir, got a live one," one of John's men shouted.

"We might have something, I'll get back to you, Major," John said, breaking the connection to Carson. John had respect for the Major, despite the heartless reputation he carried with him. If you had proven your competence, if you had shown you were worthy of the uniform you wore, Carson would always back you to the hilt. If you fucked up, however, the Major would expect you to take complete ownership of any and all mistakes. Fortunately, any errors here weren't on John's part.

John walked over to the MEV. Even as he got closer, he could hear the clanging coming from inside. Clearly, there was a survivor inside, the noise rhythmic and repetitive.

"Hello, can you hear me?" John's Sergeant was asking through the thick metal. As if in response, the back door of the MEV opened, three people emerging. Two were army, one a civilian. Both soldiers had removed their respirators, but they seemed unharmed. Likely the filters had started to clog, making breathing difficult.

"Report, Corporal," John insisted, speaking to the senior of the two soldiers. Surprisingly the Corporal didn't salute, his eyes almost glazed over by the terrors of what he had seen.

"They came out of nowhere," the Corporal said. "We were helping administer medical care to the refugees when a mob of them just washed over us. Nobody stood a chance."

"And yet you are still alive?" It was a question, but there was a hint of accusation in John's voice.

"We were told how important the immune individual was," the Private said defensively. "We did the only thing we could to keep him safe. When the undead hit us, we tried to get away in the MEV." That escape had clearly been ineffective. Closer inspection showed the evidence of crushed and devastated bodies under the MEV.

"This is the immune?" John asked, looking at the civilian who was perhaps in his fifties and did not represent the ideal of physical fitness.

"Hey, I have a name you know," the civilian countered. His name was Gianni, but he never got to tell anyone. He had a thick Brooklyn accent, and he was completely ignored by everyone.

"Yes sir." There was relief in the Corporal's voice as if he could finally see an end to all this.

"How did your vehicle crash?" John's Sergeant asked. John was wondering that himself.

"They jumped all over us. We couldn't see out to drive and just ended up running into a fucking wall. Then the vehicle got stuck, and we were trapped inside with zombies pounding on the outside."

"Scared the shit out of me," Gianni informed John. "I was told I would be protected. This ain't good enough, you hear?"

"Oh, I hear," John replied, clearly unimpressed with the man he had been sent to fetch. "Have you not noticed that good men died here today?"

"Yeah, well, that's what they got paid for," Gianni said defensively. If he wasn't so vital, John reckoned he would have shot him right there and then.

"I'm going to need you to stop talking now, sir," John advised.

"Hey, I don't like your tone," Gianni exclaimed belligerently. "They said I'm important. You're supposed to treat me right."

"Oh, don't worry, you'll get everything that's coming to you," John advised. There was a definite threat in those words. "When did the undead leave, Corporal?" Something was bothering John about all this. Carson had told him about Schmidt's research, about how the undead seemed drawn to the immune. Why had they then left without taking their prize?

"About twenty minutes ago, sir."

"Any idea why they left?"

"No. We knew a team was coming, so we stayed inside the MEV. It was suicide not to."

"Good work, Corporal," John said, meaning it. The two grunts had done what they were supposed to. "We will take charge of the patient now."

"About damned time," Gianni said. "These guys ain't so talkative." John found the man grating. Stepping up, he grabbed Gianni's hand roughly. "Hey, what the hell?" The immune man tried to pull away, but he couldn't match John's vice-like grip.

"Just keep quiet will you," John ordered. From one of the pouches on his belt, he withdrew a blood lancet and rammed it onto a dirty thumb. Gianni winced pathetically. With the blood starting to well up, John extracted a test strip and held it against the red blob until it was all soaked up. John passed the test strip over to one of his men. This was a different test to the one that detected the virus. Schmidt had developed this purely to help confirm immunity. Only the retrieval teams had them because they had yet to be put into mass production. The way things were going, they probably never would.

The big challenge with finding the immune was that they only became apparent when they were exposed to the virus. In the early stages of the outbreak, that would have been by transmission from other infected individuals. But more and more were now finding themselves victims of the undead themselves, and very few could survive that.

"Alpha team, be advised we have a mass of undead heading in your direction. Twelve blocks out and closing from the South." The South? Shit, that was the direction of the airport. "Be advised, Newark International is a no-go. Advise you use secondary evac point at Essex County."

"Roger, control. Make sure something is waiting for us there." John looked at the two soldiers. "You two, keep up, and we get you out of this. Fall back, and you are on your own. We clear?"

"Yes sir," both men said. John then turned to the man from Brooklyn.

"From now on, you do as I say. You do not speak unless I tell you to. You don't even breathe without my express permission. Am I understood?"

"Hey, you don't need to…"

"I said am I understood?" John's voice rose, violence threatened by every word.

"Yeah, yeah, whatever." His team member handed John back the test strip. He stood there looking at it for several seconds. The test was positive.

"Looks like we didn't have a wasted trip."

"Let's get the fuck out of here," the Sergeant insisted.

"What happened to show that you're immune?" John asked. In his ear, he heard the confirmation that the undead were ten blocks away."

"I was bitten, and I didn't get sick." As if to prove it, the man pulled the sleeve of his shirt up to reveal a surgical dressing. Another confirmation to back up the test strip. Gianni didn't mention how he was saved by two cops who had sacrificed their lives while Gianni had just turned and fled.

"Okay, bring him with us." No test kit could be one hundred per cent effective, and if it turned out the guy wasn't immune, then he was in for a nasty surprise. "Back to the vehicles everyone." As a group they moved together, running now, the man they had come for struggling to keep up, his belly and chicken legs designed for anything but speed. They could have gone faster if not for that, and by the time they were back in their Humvee's the undead had closed the distance. They had parked their three vehicles a safe distance away so they could come in as stealthily as possible, John being forewarned about the state of the aid station.

"Be advised the mass of undead are coming at you at speed now. We definitely think you have been detected." The voice in John's ear was not reassuring.

"Roger that," John said. He was the last one to get in the vehicles, and as soon as his door closed, they started moving. The streets they were on weren't blocked, but they were strewn with abandoned vehicles and the litter of humanity. They couldn't go fast for fear of hitting something. Better slow and steady than risk it all.

John was in the second car. He thought the undead were behind him now, but turning the corner a single zombie ran out at them from a side street. It hit the side of the first Humvee a glancing blow, spinning away and leaving a bloody smear on the car's reinforced driver's window. Another came out, charging at them down the centre of the street. There was no way they could dodge it.

"Drive the fucker down," John ordered over his radio, the soldier driving the first Humvee already speeding up. The grille at the front of the vehicle hit the zombie a crushing blow, sending the creature under the wheels. Gianni was in the car with John which annoyed him, because he really didn't want to hear the guys whimpering. The small convoy turned a corner, a bridge up ahead.

John saw them, the undead gathered on top of the bridge they would have to go under.

"What do I do, Captain?" the Driver of the first Humvee asked. Zombies in front of them, zombies behind, what else was there but to go for the lesser of two evils.

"Floor it," John ordered, the driver not hesitating. The cars all accelerated and John seriously thought they were going to make it, but that was only because he hadn't even considered what happened next. As they approached the bridge, the undead began to jump from it. The driver of the first car had no chance but to slam on the brakes, the car fishtailing slightly as the rear wheels threatened to spin the car out of control. With four zombies on the road and getting to their feet, the lead Humvee hit them, just as another zombie landed, smashing into its windscreen, spidering the glass. A sixth zombie landed onto the roof, falling off to the side.

The second Humvee came to a stop, the driver not needing to be told to put it into reverse, the car at the rear already taking action to evade the threat. To his right, John saw the thin alleyway, saw the stream of undead pouring down it, heading right for the lead car.

"Reverse, reverse," John ordered despite the car already moving.

He had asked himself why the undead had left, and the answer was simple. When Gianni had been sealed inside the MEV, his smell had begun to dissipate in the air. Safe within the airtight vehicle, his residual pheromones had drifted off on the breeze so that the undead could no longer tell where he was. They continued to attack the vehicle, but with no other proof that there was any meat present, they had easily become distracted, wandering off in search of other victims. By the time John and his team had reached them, any of the defending soldiers that hadn't been ripped apart had also wandered off, joining the ever-growing horde.

In his side mirror, John saw the sight that told him he probably wasn't going to make it.

Behind the convoy, the mass of undead had arrived, hundreds of them, a tsunami of death that surged along the street in an unstoppable wave. The driver of the first Humvee was trying to turn the vehicle around now, the steering sluggish, one of the tyres bursting from the brutality that had been inflicted on it. The zombies coming down the alley emerged, spreading out, hitting the lead car together, swamping it, enveloping it. John was rocked in his seat by the impact of a lone zombie who was intent on getting to him, the driver losing control and ramming into the Humvee behind him.

A zombie jumped onto the hood of John's car and began punching the windscreen. The glass quickly cracked and gave way, a shredded hand bursting through, clawing for whatever it could grasp. As damaged as the fingers were, they grabbed the driver's respirator, which was pulled roughly from his head. To the side, another zombie was holding a rock it had mysteriously picked up, the glass it was pounding on suddenly shattering into a myriad of pieces. The smell of them hit John just before the actual zombies did.

Somehow the driver got the vehicle back under control. Yanking the steering round, he took the Humvee off the road and onto the pavement, turning in an arc so as to come back the way they had just come. The zombie on the bonnet tumbled off, more coming at the car. The third Humvee had been lost now, almost invisible behind a mass of undead that was surrounding it. John, his driver, Gianni and the Sergeant were all that were left now. Somehow the driver pulled a miracle out of his arse, getting the Humvee onto a side road, accelerating away from a group of zombies that had broken off from the main group to chase.

They were thirty minutes away from their evacuation point, but they might as well have been in another country.

24.08.19
Washington DC, USA

Mother was tired, but still, the interrogation continued. Hours of constant questions, rechecking everything she had said, looking for deception and half-truths. The irony was that everything Mother had told them had been the whole truth, although two simple facts she left to the end.

"You say you objected to the creation of Lazarus?" Winters asked.

"Yes," said Mother. "As I think it has been shown, it was too dangerous, too unpredictable. They had managed to create it, but could not remove its ability to infect virtually every living species on the planet. How could they even think of releasing something so volatile?" Winters' blood turned to ice at those words. *Every living species on the planet.* If that was true, then there could be no containing it. It would burn through the planet unchecked leaving a dead world.

"Where are these men now? Father, Uncle and Brother?"

"I only heard whispers," Mother advised. She lifted the polystyrene cup that had been placed before her, sipping the water to help mellow her parched mouth. She hadn't spoken this much for years, and the lining of her throat felt like it was cut in a thousand places. At least one of her hands had now been freed, her captors now trusting that she would behave herself. The other wrist remained restrained. They didn't trust her that much.

"Why don't you tell me those whispers?"

"They built a bunker, somewhere in the Atlantic. I don't know what island, or what country. But the likelihood is that they will be there now."

"You mentioned there was a chance they developed a vaccine."

"Yes, I believe Gabriel and Azrael received it."

"But not you," stated Winters.

"No. I was clearly not worthy."

"But why would they create a vaccine to an incomplete virus?"

"It is perplexing, isn't it," Mother said with a wry smile. "I have been wondering if the escape of Lazarus was as accidental as I was told."

"You think it could have been done deliberately?" Mother nodded, wincing from the pain of her ravaged body.

"Are you okay?" Winters asked suspiciously. "Can I get you anything?"

"I am overdue for my painkillers. The pain comes in increasing waves. Soon I won't be able to function."

"You will get your meds, but only when I'm satisfied with your answers."

"You know I used to have your job," Mother advised, knowing that this information was likely in her file.

"Stasi interrogator, I know."

"I was very good at what I did." Mother took another sip. "One of the best. Better than you."

"You will forgive us if Lazarus has stopped us using our best people," Winters said sadly. She didn't rise to the insult. "Besides, you are cooperating. There is no need for unpleasantness so long as that continues."

Both of the women were surprised when the door to the interrogation room opened, and Campbell walked in. For the last few hours, he had been overseeing the decryption of Mother's journal, the record of everything she had planned and done since the first days of starting Gaia. He was holding several photographs, and Campbell whispered in Winters' ear, who then stood and followed Campbell out of the room.

Out in the corridor, Campbell held the photographs over to his superior. He kept hold of one.

"As we thought, it has everything in it. Parts of the journal were written in a code based on an old KGB encryption like Mother said. Seems she was telling the truth about that as well. Our computers were able to crack it. We also have pictures and dossiers of the assassins they trained and used. I can confirm their authenticity because one of those is definitely the man called Azrael."

"What are these photographs?"

"We had to re-task a satellite to get them. In part of the journal, there is a record of purchases. Plots of land, buildings, rainforest in Brazil. But also on an island in the Atlantic." Winters brought the photographs up to her face. The first showed the volcanic island, each subsequent photo zoomed in closer. The last showed a street of the only town on the island. Either people slept outside, or there were dead bodies lying in the street.

"Lazarus?"

"Unlikely. The bodies look unmarked. My guess would be a nerve agent, but I might be wrong. Then there is this." Campbell handed her a final photograph. It showed a short runway, with a concrete bunker complex. "I've had the CIA running through their archives. They can't give us a timeline on when this was constructed, and they have no record of who it might belong to."

"And you think this is the secret base Mother has told us about?"

"The coordinates of that island are in her journal, so it fits. Only one way to find out," said Campbell. His eyes gleamed with the chance to further redeem himself.

"If these three men are there, then they might have access to the vaccine."

"If the vaccine exists," Campbell said cautiously.

"As you said, only one way to find out."

"I'll need a team," Campbell said. "Platoon size. Enough to storm that complex."

"What makes you think I'm sending you?" Winters asked.

"Who else is there?"

That right there was logic she couldn't argue with.

24.08.19
Peak District, UK

"I don't understand what you are trying to tell me." Tom looked at his sister as if she was somehow insane. His eyes drifted over to Whittaker who was here to try and help convince Tom about the discoveries that had been made about the virus. It was proving to be hard work.

"I am immune to the virus, okay."

"Okay, I get that," Tom said to his sister, although he seemed sceptical even about that.

"So is Chris here." Whittaker looked at Tom and nodded his agreement with the statement. "After we were infected, after we beat the virus, we began to experience the same dreams."

"You can't expect me to believe this," Tom said. He could be intransigent at times. If something didn't fit into his pattern of the world, it would often take a lot of convincing. Take his belief in conspiracy theories. No matter what counter-argument Jessica or his brother Peter had used in the past to try and contradict the latest whacky concept he had latched onto, Tom could always argue his way out of even the most ridiculous hole that he would keep digging for himself. It was ironic that Tom expected others to believe what he held dearest to his heart whilst often rejecting the beliefs of others.

"When have I ever lied to you?" Jessica asked, clearly getting exasperated.

"Never, and I'm not claiming you are now. But isn't it at least possible that this guy," Tom said, indicating Whittaker dismissively, "is conning you in some way." Tom turned to face Whittaker, unconcerned that he was a soldier. Despite a level of overconfidence on his part, Tom felt he was more than capable of standing up for himself. "Do you do magic tricks as well?"

"I don't have to sit around for this shit," Whittaker said, rising to leave. He wanted to punch Tom, but he knew he would be able to restrain his desire because only one person would be hurt by the action: Jessica. Jessica grabbed his arm and encouraged Whittaker to sit back down.

"Well, I'm going to carry on telling you what we think is happening. You can choose to believe it or not," Jessica persisted. Time to lay it all out.

She told him everything, although much of what she had experienced was still a mystery to her and to those like her. Despite the insane proposition she put forward, the conviction in her voice slowly began to win Tom over. Really, was it any different to the stuff he had once believed himself? Remote Viewing, Astral Projection, shape-shifting, pan-dimensional space lizards? The more he thought about it, the more what she said seemed to fit into his own warped narrative.

"I've got to say, it sounds crazy," Tom said. "But then, five days ago, I would have said that about the undead walking the Earth."

"Exactly," said Jessica. "So do you believe us?"

"Let us just say I am willing to accept the possibility that what you say is true. How does that affect me?" Jessica gave Whittaker a sly look before leaning forward to grab her brother's hand.

"Tom, we need some of your amphetamines."

"What?"

"Come on Tom, I know you have a stash."

"Don't talk...." Tom started to deny what was actually true and caught himself. He had never been able to lie to his sister.

"Mum told me, alright. You didn't actually think she would keep something like that from me, did you?" Years ago, Tom had found he didn't have enough hours in the day and had started abusing first legally and then illegally acquired amphetamines to reduce his need for sleep. He had managed to break the habit he had formed but still felt the need to bomb occasionally. He had been worried about his own addiction and had sought his mother's advice. She hadn't initially felt the need to share the secret with Tom's other siblings because that was just the kind of worried mother she was, keeping her concerns to herself. But when Jessica had arrived at the farm, she had noticed the uncharacteristic behaviour of Tom to the new arrivals. He was too agitated, too anxious, unnaturally aggressive. A *what's up with Tom mum*? had finally allowed Judy Dunn to unload the burden she was carrying.

Tom shook his head in resignation.

"I'm not addicted, okay. I only take them to stay alert," Tom said in his own defence.

"Well, we need them now as well. And I'm not judging you, Tom. You were the one who set all this up, saw this madness coming and made a safe place for us all."

"Why do you need them?" asked Tom.

"Because we need to avoid sleep," Whittaker answered. "While we can't be certain we will be safe from what is coming after us when we are wide awake, it's better than risking the nightmare until we absolutely have to."

"That's why Azrael had to leave, to go after those who are after us in the dreams," Jessica added.

"Yeah, with my bloody Land Rover. I still can't believe you talked me into that."

"I told you, you did that for all of us." She leaned forward, grabbing his hand, her eyes searching for the love in his heart. "So Tom, have you got enough for the pair of us?"

"Oh yes," Tom said with a sudden twinkle in his eye. "Don't you remember? I was preparing for the end of the world."

24.08.19
Newark, USA

Gabriel discovered that he tired quicker than usual, his physiology still a long way from recovering. The fact that he was cold and wet didn't help, the swim across the Hackensack River arduous for him. Just that and walking the miles from the station where he had emerged from the underground had resulted in a tiredness that was alien to him. He'd needed to hide twice from the army, still not trusting that they would mean anything but trouble for him.

The bank he found was of a sturdy stone construction, its windows high and barred, its main door thick and formidable. This was the place for him to rest, the interior empty. It had been ransacked, the front door left open by whoever had been here before him. Who would go out of their way to steal cash when the end of the world was ripping the heart out of everything?

There had been similar signs of such stupidity, shop windows shattered so that mindless cretins could steal TVs and electrical goods that likely now wouldn't even work. More sense was seen by the multiple stores that had been stripped of food and drink. Despite the soldiers trying to keep order, the chaos had already thundered through, destroying all sense of social unity, corrupting the area which most people had now fled from. He had seen a few curtains twitch, window blinds pulled aside, but to find anyone here in this part of Newark would be a rarity.

His available weapons had been increased by a fortuitous find. On his journey here, he had come across a gun shop that had been broken into and all but emptied. Not everything had been stripped from that store, and he had come away with a semi-automatic shotgun, and a shit load of ammunition. It wasn't the gun he wanted, but it was the best that he was likely to find under what

Gabriel considered to be the area's archaic gun laws. What he really wanted was an AA-12 fully automatic combat shotgun. That would make mincemeat out of anything. Still, six loaded rounds were better than nothing. He had seen the limitation in stopping power his Glock represented.

The door to the bank closed easily, and he tried to engage the deadbolt to stop others following. Unfortunately, the locking mechanism had been shattered. It closed, but it wouldn't keep anything out for long, which was a problem. Awake he was formidable, even in his depleted state. Asleep, a child could take him with a sharpened penknife. Still, he was sure this would be the best option for him to find a safe place to sleep if he could get access to the vault.

The daylight filtered through the bank windows causing visible beams to slowly move across the littered floor's surface.

"Hello," Gabriel shouted. His gun ready in case anything decided to run at him. Nothing moved in the darkened unseen places, Gabriel moving further into the bank. "Hello," he demanded again. "If you are hiding and I find you, I will kill you. Come out now, and I will permit you to leave." That was a lie. He would kill anyone and anything he felt threatened him.

There was a dead body lying in the bank's foyer. An open bag lay at its side, wads of notes spilling from it. It was the zombie apocalypse, and somebody had tried to rob a bank? There was a respirator on the dead man's head, and Gabriel stripped it off to look at the face. The dead eyes stared back at him, their secrets forever lost to the world. He didn't need the respirator for his own protection. There was nothing else of any use, any weapons likely taken by the person who had shot the man.

Nothing seemed to hear his promise, and Gabriel made his way to the back of the bank, snaking through offices that had once been home to deals and transactions likely reaching millions of dollars. The rear exits to the bank were all secure, and he ventured further to the first floor on heavy legs, making sure to fully clear the building. The first office he found had a plush leather sofa, and he suddenly found himself yearning for comfort. That was a distraction Gabriel could resist, and he cleared the floor quickly, confirming nobody else was present. Job done, he returned to the first office.

Standing in the doorway, his mind drifted, something else that was rare for him. Normally he was focused with clarity of vision and purpose. The email he had received still grated with him, and a part of him felt lost as to his place in the world. Sooner or later, his need to survive would end, and the other human needs would come rushing to the forefront of his consciousness.

Most of those needs had been met by killing in the name of Gaia, but Gaia wasn't a part of him anymore. He still intended to head North, but something felt out of place with that plan, something he had never felt before. Gabriel found himself suddenly afraid about how he would handle being truly alone. If he had been given the vaccine, didn't that mean that Gaia still needed him on some level?

It was an emotion he was unfamiliar with. It wasn't so much caused by a lack of human contact, but by a lack of definite purpose. Ever since he had been reborn, he had always thought he understood his place in the world. That understanding had now been stripped from him, leaving a well-trained, but barren husk of a man. The skills he possessed were easily transferable to self-preservation and survival, but that wasn't enough for him. He needed something to fight for, and the preservation of his own wellbeing wasn't enough.

Outside, rain began to fall, hard. The windows almost shook with the force that pounded on them, the downpour of no concern to the zombies that were out there. Zombies didn't get cold or need shelter, and the wet wouldn't bring them to hypothermia. They were immune to the ravages of nature, possibly even able to survive the roasting heat of forest fires. Sooner or later, he knew he would have to face them.

Sooner it seemed if the gunfire he heard outside was anything to go by.

***

John's day had descended into a mound of shit that he was not enjoying. He'd needed to shoot the man driving the Humvee, the car having to be abandoned due to all the streets being blocked. Losing his respirator, the driver had clearly ended up getting infected, the signs clear. John didn't consider the act heartless, quite the opposite. The soldier who he been serving with for two years had asked to be put out of his misery.

"Don't let me turn into one of those things." The driver may have been of a lower rank, but as a soldier, he was John's equal. There were just three of them now, himself, his Sergeant and someone who was a complete waste of the air he breathed. To top it off they were all now soaked through by the rain.

"I can't go on no further," Gianni implored. He had been slowing them down ever since they abandoned the SUV due to the roads becoming impassable. If he were lighter, they would have carried him, but as it was, they had to do what they could to help the man keep up. If he hadn't been immune, John would have left him.

John was still being advised of where the undead were, the Predator drone still circling above them. Through Carson, John had been able to call up some air strikes to slow the undead's pursuit down, several streets still burning behind them. They were far from safe, however. The streets here were chaos, impassable by anything but a motorbike…which was probably why there were no motorbikes visible just lying around.

"I need to rest," Gianni insisted. His face was beet red, and John reckoned if they went any further the idiot might end up having a heart attack. The other soldier fired off a shot, a lone zombie falling to the dust twenty metres away. Clearly, the undead were still after them.

"Alpha team to control, any word on that backup?" At least his radio still worked. If he lost his communications, John reckoned he would be done for.

"Please hold, Alpha team. No support units available at this time."

The Sergeant fired again, and John grabbed Gianni and literally pulled him towards the bank on the street corner.

"We can rest in there."

The three of them hit the front door of the bank running. It opened fairly easily, and Gianni stumbled inside, sitting down on the first chair he found. John and his partner closed the door and began moving heavy desks against it. The marble floor of the bank made that relatively easy, although they had to move the furniture a fair distance.

"I don't know if that will hold," the Sergeant said. Clearly, it wouldn't.

"Let's see if there's a back way out." John was about to say something more, but he was interrupted by a stranger's voice.

"Back's all locked up tight," Gabriel said, descending the stairs. He had his hands in the air to show he wasn't a threat. "I'm guessing there are zombies right behind you?" John swivelled to the voice, his AR15 aimed at Gabriel's head. It took John two seconds to assess Gabriel, and he indicated that the stranger could lower his hands.

"Yep," John said, "whole bunch of them right behind. Sorry for bringing them to you."

"I'm sure they would have found me in time. I had planned to sleep in the vault. Perhaps now might be an opportune time to venture there." Gabriel didn't wait for confirmation, he was already making his way there now. At the front, something smashed itself into the bank's main door. The barricade held, but only just. Now inside, the smell of Gianni was already dissipating outside. Unfortunately, the dead were already here. The three men followed Gabriel, still wary of the threat he might pose.

They walked past the cashier's windows, and into a large open plan office area. Further along, a door led down to the basement. The sound of a desk screeching across the floor put a degree of urgency in their strides. Before descending, John sent his GPS coordinates off to the person at the other end of his radio. When they went down there, the reception was likely to get a bit unpredictable.

"Roger, Alpha team. I will try and get an extraction team to your location."

John wouldn't be holding his breath.

24.08.19
Stockport, UK

Trouble kept seeming to find Azrael. One minute he was walking over a railway bridge, the next he was running for his life.

Most of the railway line here was raised above ground and through heavily built-up areas. He could have tried to take a long detour around the more populated regions, but he reckoned, correctly as it turned out, that most parts of the region would be flooded with both panicked people and the ravenous undead. There would be no getting around it, so the only way was through.

Right now, it was the undead who were chasing him, and dropping his backpack, he turned and knelt, allowing him to fire off several shots. His accuracy didn't fail him. The zombies had been passing on the road below the railway bridge, at least thirty of them, and they reacted instantly as soon as they got Azrael's scent. He had been lucky. Had the wind been blowing the other way, they would have detected him much sooner, and likely more would have come for him.

Three zombies fell, but more appeared, clambering up the side of the bridge with a strength and an agility Azrael knew he could never match. What gave the undead their edge was their complete lack of concern for the health of their own bodies, willingly ripping fingernails out and breaking bones just so that they could get their teeth into something particularly juicy. They were also relentless, never even able to consider giving up. The undead wanted the flesh of man, and as an immune, Azrael was the juiciest of them all.

He emptied out a magazine, felling more of the creatures that came at him in their silent fury. With his adrenaline high and his heart pumping, destroying the part of the brain that mattered was a difficult shot to make. Some of his bullets found their mark, only for the zombie to keep on at him. His finger clicked on empty again, and he ripped the magazine out and slammed in a fresh one.

The thing that saved him was the difficulty the undead had at getting to him on the railway line. They could climb the side of the bridge easily, but only at certain points, meaning their heads and bodies appeared into view in threes and fours. It gave him precious seconds, fleeting moments to line up his shots at the zombies that were no more than ten metres away. With three left by his reckoning, the unthinkable happened.

His gun jammed.

The bullet he had expected to come rocketing out of the end of the suppressed barrel got stuck, making his gun less useful than a club. Azrael instantly discarded it, pulling out his pistol, knowing the stopping power would be limited. The three undead charged at him with speed faster than he could run over this gravel-strewn and uneven ground, so he knew his only chance was to stay and fight. As the three hurtled towards him, two more undead scaled the stone of the bridge, the last one being a beast of a former man.

His bullets were true, but his pistol's accuracy and stopping power didn't match the C8 CQB Carbine he had been relying on. It took a full clip to down the first three zombies, and by then the last two were nearly on him. Dropping the gun, he went to his last resort.

His blessed knives, given to him by Mother herself.

The first of the two to get near him had once been a child, and it leapt into the air as it came in reach, aiming itself straight for Azrael's upper body, intent on clinging on to give it a chance to bite at his face. Azrael aimed the sidekick well, stopping the zombie in mid-air, sending it sprawling backwards where it landed harshly, scrabbling on the floor. The larger zombie paid its smaller counterpart no heed, stepping on it, the sound of the child(Z)'s knee dislocating ricocheting around the surroundings. A kick wouldn't stop this beast, clearly the result of someone who had lived for the power he could gain by lifting weights. Whether that was supported by the use of illicit steroids was no concern to Azrael. All that mattered was how big the thing was, and as it stampeded at him, Azrael sidestepped at the last minute, tripping the zombie that still lacked the nuances of fine motor control.

Still, the zombie almost brought him down, clawing fingers mere centimetres from snagging his clothes. The behemoth landed on the tracks face first, and Azrael pounced, forcing both of his knives deep into the back of the zombie's neck. On a human, that would have damaged the spinal cord, and as the thing tried to buck and push itself up off the floor, Azrael struck again, withdrawing and thrusting the right-handed knife into the base of the zombie's neck. That stilled it.

His safety was fleeting though, for the child zombie had already recovered. Despite its damaged leg, it clawed its way onto Azrael's back, the fingers tearing at whatever they could. The teeth tried to bite into his neck, but the duct tape he had wrapped around the collar of his military fatigues acted as an effective barrier against milk teeth that in the child before had already started to loosen. With the thing clinging to him, Azrael aimed his knives and flung his arms behind him, intent on stabbing the zombie in the back. Multiple times he did so, the bastard thing hardly seeming to care.

Already he could feel his hands slick with whatever juices were erupting from the wounds he was inflicting. His knives were special, incorporating knuckle dusters that his fingers laced into, slightly curved blades pointing upwards with the thumbs of his hands. Their design allowed him to open his hands without dropping them, and he did this now, but not before the diminutive zombie tried to take his ear, its teeth finding the flesh on the outer edge. Clearly, the intent was to rip the organ from the side of his head, but the duct tape prevented that. Azrael didn't ignore the pain but just used it to insist his body not fail him.

Reaching behind himself, he grabbed the zombie's neck with both hands. Knowing the injury he risked for himself, he jumped up and backwards, landing on the rail with the zombie cushioning him. Something in the zombie broke and miraculously the hands that held him loosened, allowing Azrael to roll off. Out of reach of his foe, he came to his knees, the zombie bucking and writhing where it lay, the trauma to its structure somehow stopping it from getting back up. Azrael pounced, using the knives again, his gloves soaking through in parts.

Azrael had killed children before, and the image of his own daughters flashed in his mind as if to punish him for his previous betrayal. "It wasn't my fault," Azrael implored, and he stabbed the zombie again, finally ending its squirming. "It wasn't my fault," the words came again, Azrael standing, panting not from the exertion so much but the flashback that seemed to linger in his mind. He didn't even realise he was speaking. The face of the zombie he had just killed could have so easily been the younger of the two girls he had slaughtered in the house of blood. He saw both faces now, remembered them, remembered their names and the way they had laughed.

What was more shameful? Killing his own children, or forgetting that he had any children to kill?

Mother had always known that, like with all the other assassins she created, Azrael's conditioning would start to break eventually. There was always some trigger, some unknown mechanism that would start to unravel the KGB corrupted brains. Of those who were volunteered into the Illegals Programme, Mother hadn't found a way yet to stop them from eventually self-destructing. This was why she kept the number of assassins to a minimum, only triggering their repressed selves and taking charge of them when the ones before them had finally snapped.

Although it briefly threatened to, that unravelling didn't occur to Azrael now. The door to its inevitability opened just that fraction more though. Sitting there, the threats around him finally silenced, he managed to get his breathing back under control. Slowly, the faces in his mind's eye faded, and his concern for what he might have done long ago changed for the realisation that he wasn't as formidable as perhaps he thought he was.

It took him several moments before he was comfortable to stand. From his rucksack, he reloaded the bullets into the magazines he had used and dealt with the double feed that had caused his weapon to jam. Briefly stripped of his gloves, he also used some alcohol swabs to disinfect his damaged ear, the sting breaking through any fog that still dwelled in his head. Minutes later, the rucksack was back on his back, and he was ready to go, his ammunition supply still healthy, but worryingly depleted.

The bodies he gladly left behind, the rail track crossing another rail line via a bridge. He needed to carry on following this track, but behind him, he heard the sound of feet on gravel. A glance behind him told him more zombies were following, a lot more. They were far too numerous for him to deal with now. Was it possible that he had just clipped the edge of a horde, and that his shots, suppressed as they were, were about to bring him a whole world of hurt? Or had they all smelt him, drawn to the delights he represented?

He ran, for there were too many of the undead to even count. To his left, he propelled himself down the railway embankment towards what looked like a huge warehouse. The perimeter palisade fence held no threat for him despite the spikes, and he easily scaled it allowing him access to the side of the huge structure. The undead swarmed after him, leaving the railway line, his smell driving them on.

Azrael knew his options were limited. A warehouse would mean a loading dock and maybe vehicles, but did he have the time to run around the building? Azrael couldn't rely on the vain hope that there was some sort of salvation there waiting for him. There would be no car sat ready with the keys in the ignition. No, he couldn't depend on some slim chances, not with nearly two hundred zombies after him, their vanguard already hitting the fence he had climbed.

It held them for a moment, but only so long as it took them to figure out they too needed to climb.

That was what Azrael did again, climbing up the side of the warehouse by a sturdy drainpipe that led straight to the building's roof. If that drainpipe had given way, if the screws that held it had failed, it would have been the end for him, but he easily made it to the roof.

Down below, the zombies weren't so lucky. They followed his route as if he were leading a trail for them. Instead of scaling as he had one at a time, the zombies fought each other to get at him, several of them ascending together. One man the drainpipe could handle, but not five and with a terrifying wrenching sound the drainpipe came away from the wall. One of the zombies was flung onto the top of the fence where it became impaled on the spikes, its abdomen pierced. It flopped there on its belly, folded over, unable to gain any kind of purchase to push itself off, forever condemned to rot there until its body finally fell apart. The others landed on their brothers and sisters below.

Azrael ran across the roof, knowing that one failed drainpipe wouldn't save him. The metal roof gave away his position, his footfalls too loud, but he soon got sight of the other side of the building, some sort of construction yard below. There were military vehicles there, and he wondered if by some miracle there would be soldiers here also. His hope was dashed just as the stench hit him. He should have paid heed to the sign that warned that the roof was not a safe structure to walk on. Beneath Azrael's feet, the metal of the roof gave way, and he plummeted to the unknown depths below. As he fell, the futility of his fool's errand couldn't have been made clearer.

Azrael was saved dropping to the hard concrete below by the bodies that broke his fall. Even as his heart leapt into his throat as gravity tried to restore some sort of balance to his body, the stench filled his lungs. Then there was the impact, the bodies below him soft enough to save him any serious injury.

He felt himself being swallowed up, the corpses underneath him giving way slightly as the gas that had been building up in them was released by his unexpected weight. A foul wetness seemed to engulf him, his face suddenly covered in a brown slime that soaked through everything he wore. Most of the bodies had already begun to bloat, human beings just being meat at the end of the day, and despite the Lazarus that had once riddled them, they had started to rot regardless. The gas had built up, the skin pulling taught and in some cases, the carcasses had started to liquefy. That was what Azrael fell amongst.

Fortunate for him that the plan to bury these cadavers in a pit had never been carried out. Instead, the whole warehouse had been left as an impressive charnel house, the bullet-ridden souls abandoned to be dealt with by the power of nature.

What Azrael had uncovered was one of the places the military had brought the undead they had *killed* in the earlier days of the outbreak. There were hundreds here, some days into their decomposition. With the bodies piled eight and nine high in places, it was inevitable that some would progress down the path of decay faster than others. Azrael lay there, and even he found it difficult to breathe, surrounded by the all-encompassing perfume of the dead.

He had to move, despite the assault on every sense he had. Trying to get some purchase, he pushed with his feet, only for the surface to almost slide away, briefly causing him to become trapped amongst the corpses. One of his arms slid between bodies under him, the fist punching through something that had become fragile and revolting. Azrael would not be denied though, his perseverance allowing his arms and legs to get some kind of traction to propel his escape. With effort, he was able to climb from on top of the mound, dropping down to a floor that was slick with the accumulated deterioration of the human form.

A zombie appeared, and Azrael struggled to pull his gun from behind his back. A second zombie arrived, then a third and he knew that he didn't have anywhere close to enough bullets for what was needed here. The three zombies circled each other, ignoring the bodies piled around them, moving their heads, forcing air into nostrils that no longer inhaled.

None of the undead came at him, and as the bulk of this horde became visible now, Azrael realised the luck that had befallen him. As disgusting as everything around him was, he backed up as close to the mound behind him as he could. If they were able to detect him, they would have been on him by now. If zombies hunted by smell and sound, then had he just eliminated one of their abilities? Azrael let his gun fall gently to his side, and as quietly as he could, he slipped his fingers into the grips of one of his knives.

One of the zombies broke away and came into the small maze that the dunes of the dead had been fashioned into. It came to hunt for Azrael who was even now turning and reaching up to a particularly bloated corpse that hung slightly above his head. He thrust the knife deep, opening up the distended belly, the liquid pouring out creating a noise which agitated several of the undead, the closest one coming in, its head bobbing to try and find the scent that it craved. Azrael held his breath, both to save him from the aromatic shower he was now enduring and also so those hunting him wouldn't hear him breathing.

His plan seemed to work, and the undead began to move away from the warehouse loading bay, not content to just stand around when there was fresh flesh somewhere out there for the taking. Today, the dead didn't eat their own, which would have been a pretty sight. Azrael watched them leave, his stomach threatening a final betrayal. Azrael managed to keep things together, and he watched with growing relief as his enemy went in search of him elsewhere.

By luck, he had just uncovered a way to avoid detection. Still, he would wait until the horde passed before continuing on with his journey. What it also meant was he definitely had to avoid human contact now, especially anyone armed. He looked and smelt like the undead, and it would be painfully ironic for him to have escaped being killed by zombies only for some nervous and trigger happy soldier to shoot him dead.

Azrael just hoped the rain would hold off because although he wanted one desperately, the last thing he needed now was a shower. He had survived his first major encounter with the undead. Only time would tell if he would survive the next.

Coming Soon....

The Dead

The fourth book in the Lazarus Strain Chronicles

Did you enjoy this book? If so you can make a big difference

Reviewers are the most powerful tool in my arsenal when it comes to getting attention for my books. Much as I'd like to, I don't have the financial muscle of a big New York publisher. I can't take out full-page ads in the newspaper or put posters on the subway.

(Not yet, anyway).

But I do have something much more powerful and effective than that, and it's something that those publishers would kill to get their hands on.

A committed and loyal bunch of readers.

Honest reviews of my books help bring them to the attention of other readers.

If you enjoyed this book, I would be grateful if you could spend just five minutes leaving a review (it can be as short as you like) on the Amazon page.

Thank you very much.

ABOUT THE AUTHOR

Facebook - **https://www.facebook.com/seandevillesnovels/**

Twitter - **https://twitter.com/seandeville666**

Get free chapters to try before you buy, as well as a free book

Building a relationship with my readers is the best thing about writing. I occasionally write blogs and send newsletters with details on new releases, special offers, and occasional free gifts relating to my books.

And if you sign up to my mailing list, I'll send you all this free stuff:

1. Free Chapters to my zombie horror "Cobra Z"
2. Free Chapters to my apocalyptic book "The Defiled."
3. A free copy of my horror book, "The Profane," Book 1 in the Sheol trilogy

You can get these, **for free**, by signing up at **www.seandeville.com**

ALSO BY SEAN DEVILLE

Have you read them all?

In the Necropolis Trilogy

Cobra Z

What if one day you find your world suddenly torn apart? Entranced by your daily routine, you hear the terrifying news that makes your blood run cold. A devastating man-made virus has been unleashed on the world, a virus so lethal that it rapidly turns everyone it infects into rabid, blood-crazed killers. Maniacs so devoid of humanity that their only goal in life is to rip the flesh from your very body, and kill or infect the people you love the most. Would you panic? Would you rush from your desk in a frantic attempt to save your children? Would you hunker down, and hope the infection somehow passes you by, praying to whatever God you think will help? And what if the very people you care for so deeply are the ones clawing at your door, their blood smeared faces screaming for the destruction of your soul? How would you survive in such a world? And would you want to?

Buy it here

UK: https://amzn.to/2xb8b3S

US: https://amzn.to/2NDCbip

The Contained

When the infection struck, 64 million people never stood a chance. It only took a day for the country to collapse, for the five largest cities to be overwhelmed by the onslaught of the viral hordes. Merciless, relentless, they ripped their way through humanity. They were unstoppable, almost biblical. With no way to protect itself against the deliberate act of bioterrorism, a once great nation began to feed upon itself. Violence and chaos reigned, and those who had vowed to protect a once proud nation did the only thing they could…..they fled, leaving millions to their fate. At the end of the first day, a tenth of the population had become infected…..7 million blood-crazed killers whose only purpose in life was the consumption of human flesh. Stranger, friends or loved one, the infected did not discriminate. They did not care, only the burning hunger within them filled their rabid, predatory thoughts. And as the infected surged out of the cities, their numbers grew, those they fed on swelling their ravenous, inhuman ranks. And with every hour that passed, the infection spread, and humanity bled.

Buy it here

UK: **https://amzn.to/2CPYRaQ**

US: **https://amzn.to/2p5Ff90**

Necropolis

As the virus spread across the globe, the world slept on, oblivious to the threat that was about to be unleashed upon it. And as the armies of the Horsemen threaten Europe, a new force joins them in the destruction of humanity.

In Britain, the survivors from the devastated MI6 building flee to the only safe haven left in the now quarantined country - the military stronghold in Cornwall. With their walls, and their tanks and their guns, will the last surviving remnants of the British Armed Forces defeat the slaughter hurtling towards them through the roads and the streets and the fields, or will they be washed away by the devastating force of the Infected?

Who will live, and who will die when the Infected arrive? And what kind of world will be left when the smoke clears? Will humanity prevail, or will they be cast aside by the force of Abrahams insane gift to the world?

So begins the final battle of the Necropolis

Buy it here:

UK: **https://amzn.to/2MrAG2j**

US: **https://amzn.to/2COe0JQ**

CHECK OUT OTHER GREAT ZOMBIE NOVELS

Z BURBIA
by Jake Bible

Whispering Pines is a classic, quiet, private American subdivision on the edge of Asheville, NC, set in the pristine Blue Ridge Mountains. Which is good since the zombie apocalypse has come to Western North Carolina and really put suburban living to the test!

Surrounded by a sea of the undead, the residents of Whispering Pines have adapted their bucolic life of block parties to scavenging parties, common area groundskeeping to immediate area warfare, neighborhood beautification to neighborhood fortification.

But, even in the best of times, suburban living has its ups and downs what with nosy neighbors, a strict Home Owners' Association, and a property management company that believes the words "strict interpretation" are holy words when applied to the HOA covenants. Now with the zombie apocalypse upon them even those innocuous, daily irritations quickly become dramatic struggles for personal identity, family security, and straight up survival.

ZOMBIE RULES
by David Achord

Zach Gunderson's life sucked and then the zombie apocalypse began.

Rick, an aging Vietnam veteran, alcoholic, and prepper, convinces Zach that the apocalypse is on the horizon. The two of them take refuge at a remote farm. As the zombie plague rages, they face a terrifying fight for survival.

They soon learn however that the walking dead are not the only monsters.

CHECK OUT OTHER GREAT ZOMBIE NOVELS

900 MILES
by S. Johnathan Davis

John is a killer, but that wasn't his day job before the Apocalypse.

In a harrowing 900 mile race against time to get to his wife just as the dead begin to rise, John, a business man trapped in New York, soon learns that the zombies are the least of his worries, as he sees first-hand the horror of what man is capable of with no rules, no consequences and death at every turn.

Teaming up with an ex-army pilot named Kyle, they escape New York only to stumble across a man who says that he has the key to a rumored underground stronghold called Avalon..... Will they find safety? Will they make it to Johns wife before it's too late?

Get ready to follow John and Kyle in this fast paced thriller that mixes zombie horror with gladiator style arena action!

WHITE FLAG OF THE DEAD
by Joseph Talluto

Millions died when the Enillo Virus swept the earth. Millions more were lost when the victims of the plague refused to stay dead, instead rising to slaughter and feed on those left alive. For survivors like John Talon and his son Jake, they are faced with a choice: Do they submit to the dead, raising the white flag of surrender? Or do they find the will to fight, to try and hang on to the last shreds or humanity?

CHECK OUT OTHER GREAT ZOMBIE NOVELS

VACCINATION
by Phillip Tomasso

What if the H7N9 vaccination wasn't just a preventative measure against swine flu?
It seemed like the flu came out of nowhere and yet, in no time
at all the government manufactured a vaccination. Were lab
workers diligent, or could the virus itself have been man-made?
Chase McKinney works as a dispatcher at 9-1-1. Taking emergency calls, it becomes immediately obvious that the entire city is
infected with the walking dead. His first goal is to reach and save
his two children.
Could the walls built by the U.S.A. to keep out illegal aliens, and
the fact the Mexican government could not afford to vaccinate
their citizens against the flu, make the southern border the only
plausible destination for safety?

ZOMBIE, INC
by Chris Dougherty

"WELCOME! To Zombie, Inc. The United Five State Republic's
leading manufacturer of zombie defense systems! In business
since 2027, Zombie, Inc. puts YOU first. YOUR safety is our
MAIN GOAL! Our many home defense options - from Ze
Fence® to Ze Popper® to Ze Shed® - fit every need and
every budget. Use Scan Code "TELL ME MORE!" for your
FREE, in-home*, no obligation consultation! *Schedule your
appointment with the confidence that you will NEVER HAVE
TO LEAVE YOUR HOME! It isn't safe out there and we know it
better than most! Our sales staff is FULLY TRAINED to handle
any and all adversarial encounters with the living and the
undead". Twenty-five years after the deadly plague, the United
Five State Republic's most successful company, Zombie, Inc.,
is in trouble. Will a simple case of dwindling supply and lessen-
ing demand be the end of them or will Zombie, Inc. find a way,
however unpalatable, to survive?

www.ingramcontent.com/pod-product-compliance
Lightning Source LLC
Chambersburg PA
CBHW020106180626
46812CB00006B/2494